Advance praise for
The Magic of Deceit

"Gardner pulls you into a well-formed world of races and guilds, magic and intrigue, and a compelling plot of ambition and deceit. A satisfying read from an exciting new voice and series in fantasy fiction."

—Brandon Ying Kit Boey, author of *Karma of the Sun*

"Familiar, yet strikingly original in the best of ways, *The Magic of Deceit* practically bubbles with alchemical energy as Esen and Thorne navigate the cruel schemes of mages and guildmasters. J.G. Gardner's scientific acumen is on full display as he combines magic with the principles of material science to create The Archive, an academic and arcane instutition that feels right at home with the likes of the Roke Island school of Earthsea. Destiny and political machinations bring together the unlikely duo. One, a husband on the hunt for his kidnapped wife; the other, a mage striving to prove his worth to the world and to himself. In a nod to the classic tales of the genre, the two set out on a harrowing adventure of escapes, chases, and even a brief foray into piracy, all while a powerful practitioner of the arcane nips at their heels. Fast paced and carefully wrought, *The Magic of Deceit* will keep readers engaged from first to last."

—Ryan O'Neill, author of *The Darkborn Saga*

The Magic of Deceit

A novel

J. G. Gardner

Copyright © 2024 by Jeffrey G. Gardner

All rights reserved. No part of this book may be reproduced or transmitted in any form or by any means, electronic or mechanical, including photocopy, recording, or any information storage and retrieval system, without prior permission from the publisher (except by reviewers who may quote brief passages).

This is a work of fiction. Names, characters, businesses, places, events, locations and incidents are either the products of the author's imagination or used in a fictitious manner. Any resemblance to actual persons, living or deceased, or actual events is purely coincidental.

First Edition

Library of Congress Control Number: 2024933278

Hardcover ISBN: 978-1-62720-540-5
Paperback ISBN: 978-1-62720-541-2
Ebook ISBN: 978-1-62720-542-9

Design by Claire Marino

Typset with Palatino Linotype

Published by Apprentice House Press

Loyola University Maryland
4501 N. Charles Street, Baltimore, MD 21210
410.617.5265
www.ApprenticeHouse.com
info@ApprenticeHouse.com

For Mom, Dad, and Kevin

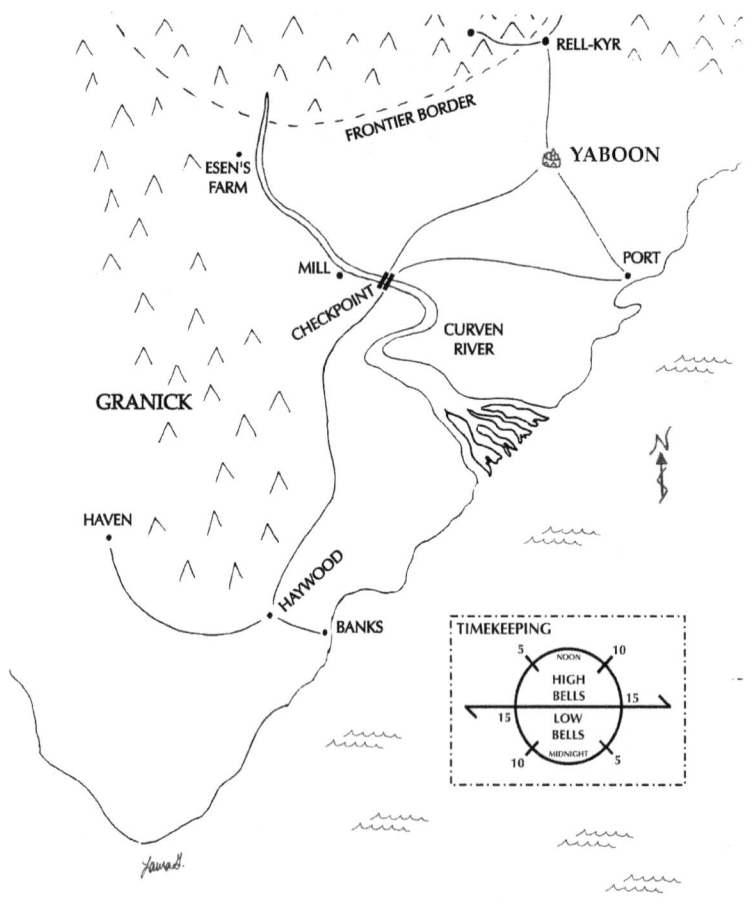

CHAPTER ONE

It was important to show a pleasant demeanor. With that in mind, Reihana maintained a closed-lipped smile as she stepped into the council room on the second floor of the Yaboon Archive. She was one of the last principal agents to arrive and looked for an open chair while hoping that she wouldn't have to sit next to someone wanting to chat.

The large table that occupied much of the room was built from thick timbers, stained darkly, and varnished to a high shine. Around it were three-dozen chairs of similar construction with no ornamentation or cushion. The practical and functional furniture had long been rumored a commentary on the ostentatious finery that was found in the princes' meeting rooms, especially given that Sovereignty emissaries were received here.

Reihana kept her neutral smile but ground her teeth when she saw the closest empty seat was next to Elleora. The thin elderly woman was practically drowning in her voluminous hunter green alchemist robes. Looking up at the late arrival, she croaked, "Oh, Reihana, good to see you. Please have a seat."

"Thank you," Reihana said, barely opening her mouth. "Nice to see you too."

No such luck in having a chance to collect her thoughts before the meeting. Elleora struck up a decisively one-sided conversation about some scandalous rumor she heard suggesting preferential treatment some merchant stalls had gotten in the market square. It was the type of banal prattle that belonged in the dining hall amongst the newest cohort of initiates, not a meeting of the major research group leaders.

"Oh, is that so?" Reihana interjected at one point as she glanced to the opposite end of the table and did her best to appear intrigued with the useless information being shared.

Sitting at the head of the table Tarbeck, councilor of the Yaboon Archive, scanned the meeting attendees with a stern expression. The vertical pupils of the Sehenryu male's feline eyes were thin black slits and the bright white whiskers at the corners of his frown were fanned out in what Reihana knew was an expression of strained patience. The short golden fur on his forearms did little to hide his muscles straining as Tarbeck clenched his fists and rested them on the table.

Next to Tarbeck sat Olaf, which was unexpected. While the councilor from the neighboring province of Granick was a frequent visitor to the Yaboon Archive, it was rare that Olaf took part in general meetings. Something important must have happened that warrented all of the principal agents to be notified.

Eight high bells tolled outside, signaling it was an hour past mid-day. Tarbeck's ears twisted towards the window at the sound. He grabbed a squat onyx cylinder that rested in front of him and rapped it twice on the table. "Let's get started since we have a very full agenda today," he said, projecting his voice to be heard over the rumble of conversation.

Elleora sunk back into her seat, a sour expression on her face, apparently upset she didn't get to finish her story. Reihana ignored her and leaned forward, hoping that whatever news Olaf had to share would be first.

Tarbeck stood up and leveled his piercing gaze around the table before he said, "I'd appreciate that you each give your reports as succinctly as possible. I'd prefer not to have a repeat of last time when this meeting lasted over two hours. Master Ahrmen," the councilor looked down at the man seated to his right, "if you will lead us off."

For the next three quarters of an hour, Reihana half-listened to the progress reports of her fellow principal agents. By and large the reports consisted of the recent achievements by every research group. Some were doing interesting but unimportant work. She heard updates on a mixture of advanced alchemy developments and complex elemental manipulations, with an occasional purely theoretical or historical report. Given the breath and depth of arcane research that the Archive undertook, Reihana found only a narrow subset to be relevant to her.

Whenever the principal agent speaking switched topics to their liaisons with the merchant guilds, then Reihana paid attention in earnest. She took careful mental notes when it was reported what particular enabling technology or service the guild was currently contracting with the Archive on, and any associated problematic negotiations.

Reihana learned that the clothier guild was expecting a volume discount when they ordered production of a wider selection of dyes. The blacksmith guild wanted a new bellows design similar to what was found in the Archive alchemy labs but was unwilling to pay the premium needed for the more exotic resins. The mining guild wanted to re-negotiate the contract for glow sphere technology used in deep mining efforts, specifically to be able to activate them without an Archive agent present. Other reports gave similar updates, and surprisingly there weren't any catastrophic failures or breakdowns in communication with guild representatives, at least none that anyone would admit to amongst all their peers.

When it was Reihana's turn to speak, she sat up a bit straighter in her chair and projected her voice to command everyone's attention. She didn't want anyone daydreaming, because she had an agenda beyond her progress report.

"The advanced resin synthesis group has made incremental,

but significant, progress since my last report," she began. "We've been able to increase both the hardness and durability of our *Quercus*-based resin, and while it still does not match steel we are getting close."

"The gums from *Pinus* are much more versatile and have the added benefit of being abundant in the local forests," came a voice from the back of the room. "Using *Quercus* is nearly as expensive as mineral-based resins, given that we're competing with the cartwright and the shipwright guilds for materials. Wouldn't you agree, Master Reihana?"

Reihana looked at the mage who interrupted her and tried to not show her annoyance. He was someone she didn't recognize, a young human male obviously newly promoted to principal agent. His comment disguised as a question was the type of intellectual posturing that was common at an Archive research seminar, but had no place here.

Keeping her expression calm, she gave him a slow exaggerated nod and replied, "*Pinus* is the substrate more generally used for resins because it has a very low mineral content that facilitates polymerization. If you wanted flexible resins or soft coatings it would be a fine choice, but as we've been hearing thus far today, and specifically for my group's work, we need resins that would be replacements for steel. Only *Quercus* has a high enough mineral content to give that level of strength. And as I'm sure you're well aware, it also has nearly triple the mana absorption over *Pinus*, which makes it the best choice for advanced resins in terms of durability. Wouldn't you agree?"

The young mage's face grew bright red and he slouched in his chair, his gambit to showcase his knowledge and impress those at the table having gone terribly wrong.

"Other questions?" she asked, trying to make her voice sound upbeat while inwardly enjoying the young mage's discomfort. She looked away from him and down the table. When no one spoke up, Reihana nodded in approval and said, "Then, I'll move on. All of our alchemy labs are now fully staffed. It took some time to replace several mages who went on their traveling education. That's a very good thing, because as the liaison to the transport guild, we have received recent word that they are pleased with the new resin-based lacquer for waterproofing carriages and intend to use it on their entire fleet here in the Yaboon province. Pending an inter-province guild meeting, they intend to do the same for all rapid transport carriages."

There were a few murmurs from around the table. To get a guild to place such a large order was impressive, and the contract payment for such work would be very lucrative.

With a small dismissive gesture, Reihana continued, "There have been some minor complaints from drivers about the odor from our new axle lubricant, but I've reassured them that after some use on the open road those vapors will dissipate. That explanation seemed satisfactory to them, but I've arranged to have someone from my group meet with their stable leader here in Yaboon next week for an update."

"Thank you, Master Reihana," Tarbeck said with a nod before shifting his attention to the mage at Reihana's side.

"There's one more thing, if I may, councilor," Reihana interjected.

"What is it?" Tarbeck replied, unmistakable displeasure in his voice. He tugged on the bottom edge of his tight fitting black vest, and the few creases of the garment snapped flat.

Reihana rose from her chair and slowly scanned the table, her expression now severe. "Councilor Tarbeck," she began with a forceful voice, "fellow principal agents, during my meeting with the transport guild, it became known to me that the mercenary guild is still quite keen to engage us in a mutually advantageous relationship."

A few cries of "No!" could be heard over more general

grunts of disapproval.

"Let me finish!" Reihana barked, her face now flushed. "The mercenary guild has overtures of approaching us to develop methods to increase the durability of their edged weapons and to keep them from rusting during storage."

"Reihana, stop this!"

A Venhadar female with tawny hair tied up in a topknot jumped to her feet and slapped both hands on the table. Like all members of her race she was short and thickly built, her powerful arms tensed as she leaned forward over the table.

Reihana steeled herself to clash once again with Master Etaen, who she never seemed to see eye to eye with even on the simplest of matters.

"This is no different than when you proposed the same arrangement with the blacksmith guild some time ago," Etaen accused. "Never mind that you are not the liaison with that guild and grossly overstepped your authority by doing so. Your preoccupation with steering Archive research toward aggressive uses of magic is, to put it mildly, concerning."

"Indeed," Elleora rasped. "It's a very slippery slope towards outright military research, which would wholly be controlled by the Sovereignty prince."

Reihana sighed. "Listen," she began, "That very same research could also support the City Watch, or those patrolling the frontier who are far away from Sovereignty support." She stabbed a finger into the table and said emphatically, "I'm not a warmonger. What I'm talking about is enabling technologies that work towards deterring unnecessary bloodshed, not promoting it. We can no longer think it acceptable for the Archive to be so circumspect in dealing with the guilds or the Sovereignty. As the third pillar of major influence on the continent, we should exert a very persuasive force, a change for good. It is time that we stopped limiting ourselves in how we interact with the guilds and the Sovereignties. We must expand our influence if we wish to continue to grow and thrive."

"We might be one of the pillars as you say," Etaen countered, "but remember how unstable a tripod can be when one of the legs gets broken. I think you forget how tenuous our position is and the very grave cost that was paid to obtain it. You never were much a student of our history."

Reihana stiffened at the insult. She didn't have a ready retort, and for a moment there was an uncomfortable silence in the council room.

"This might be a good time for me to speak," Olaf interrupted, using both hands to help push him up to his feet. "Masters Reihana, Etaen, please." The elderly councilor gestured towards their seats.

Easing back into her chair, Reihana shot a venomous look at Etaen before turning her attention to Olaf.

"Master Reihana's appeal today is rather prescient," the councilor said, "because my news is from one of the prince's emissaries on very similar matters."

Reihana's scowl morphed into an expression of mild surprise at the statement while others shared concerned glances. The tension in the room shifted to an atmosphere of unease as Olaf spoke again.

"I was party to a recent meeting with a Sovereignty emissary who renewed the prince's request that the Archive explore the possibility of military research. Our official reply was the same as always, that we would consider the ramifications of such a partnership, but request more time to confer with all five provincial Archives."

"So we continue with delaying tactics," Reihana said with a scowl. "Just how long do you think a prince is going to wait?"

"Not all of them are fools," Etaen said. "Most have intelligent people advising them, and it is unmistakably understood what backing us into a corner would bring."

"It should make all of us uneasy that our best defense would be the financial shortfalls of the guilds," Reihana answered.

"With their power over commence and communication," Olaf said in a measured tone, "the guilds keep the princes from using military might to force our hand. In exchange, we provide the guilds arcane and alchemical innovation that boosts their profits. In turn the princes get their substantial tax incomes with little disruption. It's a symbiotic relationship."

"Perhaps," Etaen said. "But with an arcane-enhanced military, the princes might become ambitious and desire expanded borders, or even greater taxes from the guilds. In either case, any financial gain for the Archive could never offset the resulting cost in blood."

Next to Reihana, Elleora nodded vigorously and added, "And once the Sovereignty has gotten a taste for it, I have no doubt that the Archive would be the first to be wholly absorbed and controlled directly by the princes. The freedoms we've taken for granted would be gone. It would be little different than the dark times of our past. We must work hard to keep things as they are now. Our disengagement with the Sovereignty has maintained our autonomy."

"But also kept us at arms length from the very people we want to help," Reihana said. "This is just a more generalized argument of what I was saying before. We should be interacting with both the Sovereignties and guilds more, not struggling to keep things static."

"Then we should put additional support into any number of the minor guilds," someone chimed in. "They're the ones who would truly benefit from our alliance and would further buffer us from any overly aggressive overtures from the princes."

"They could never afford it," came an answer. "You may notice all of our innovations for the major guilds come with a high fee."

Localized arguments broke out at the table and a cacophony of passionate declarations filled the room. Tarbeck grabbed the onyx cylinder and pounded it into the table until all voices were quieted down.

Once the room was under control again, Olaf said, "The reason I'm here is to warn you of this renewed entreaty from the prince and to relay it to your guilds contacts. I'm sure they will be displeased with it and will make it known with their Sovereignty agents."

"Very good, councilor," Tarbeck said with a sidelong look at Olaf. Raising his chin up and looking down the table he rumbled, "Now, there will be no further disruptions while the remaining principal agents give their reports. Master Usibal, if you will."

The remaining principal agents gave their reports with extreme brevity, and unsurprisingly there were no questions or discussion from the group. Reihana didn't hear a word of it because she was still livid with how her petition had been discarded. Granted, this was not the best venue, and she was without her most ardent supporters here amongst the principal agents, but she had expected more open-mindedness. With narrowed eyes she looked at the tired and elderly faces of the humans in attendance, and though it was difficult to guess the ages of Venhadar or Sehenryu, their senior standing in the Archive also suggested advanced age. They were the problem, all of them. Too old and comfortable in their set ways. It was time for a change.

"That will be all for this cycle," Tarbeck said as he stood. "Make sure to follow up with your respective groups about councilor Olaf's warning. This adjourns the principal agent meeting."

The Sehenryu smacked the onyx cylinder on the table one

final time and then left it there as he brushed past several mages to lead the exodus from the council room.

Reihana slowly rose from her seat, giving time for anyone who wanted to come and offer an empathetic word, but found that no one was paying her any mind save Olaf. The elderly councilor hung back from the exiting crowd and though engaged in light conversation with a few of the attendees, he would glance at Reihana periodically.

Her interest piqued, she made her way towards the door where Olaf fell in step with her. He remained silent as they walked side by side down a wide hallway that had glass cabinets displaying alchemic synthesis of historical or artistic value along one wall, and the thick doorways that led to the laboratories on the opposite side. There was a slight chlorine odor in the hall where Reihana noticed one of the lab doors ajar. As they approached the top of the stairs that led down to the main level of the Archive, Olaf said quietly, "I would like a word, Master Reihana, if you have the time."

"Certainly, councilor," Reihana said. She turned and walked towards the residential wing, Olaf slightly behind her. As they approached her apartment, she pulled a stubby resin key from her pocket. Unlocking her door, Reihana held it open for Olaf to enter first. The councilor looked up and down the hallway, and satisfied when he found it empty stepped inside.

Reihana wondered why the old man was being so cautious as she entered and closed the door. With no prying eyes or ears, she could finally be blunt. "What is this about, Olaf? You're supposed to be halfway back to the Granick Archive by now."

"There's a problem with your group," he replied, unperturbed by her change in tone.

"Rubbish," Reihana spat. "You heard my report. The transport guild is more than satisfied with my work."

Olaf scoffed and answered, "Not your unimportant resin

group. One of your Paragons has loose lips and is talking too much in taverns. My spies have heard more than a few rumors that I find most distressing."

"My Paragon?" Reihana said in faux shock. "If memory serves, you were the one who had final say in the selection process."

"They are your responsibility. You need to keep them on a shorter leash."

Reihana threw up her hands in frustration. "Then how am I supposed to accomplish anything?" she asked. "I see you're still unwilling to put in even a word of support when it would count. You let me twist in the wind during the principal agent meeting."

Olaf remained silent, but his disapproving expression was more than enough admonishment. She needn't be reminded of who was really in control despite her trying to talk to him on equal terms.

"I'll convene a meeting immediately and you can address this directly," she said, turning her head away.

"Discretion, as always."

"Of course, councilor."

Olaf went to the door, cracked it open, and peered into the hallway. The councilor then walked out of the apartment, not bothering to close the door behind him.

Reihana was able to gently close the door and step back before her anger melted her practiced neutral façade. Her face twisted and she snarled through clenched teeth. It would have been bad enough that her fervent speech at the meeting was met with unyielding resistance, but now to have a problem with their secret project so severe as to call for Olaf's personal intervention was enough to make her blood boil. Alone in her private apartment, she could finally vent her rage.

Storming across the room, she yanked down a thick tapestry

next to a large window that faced one of the many gardens surrounding the Archive. Throwing the wall hanging onto the seat of a richly upholstered chair, Reihana looked at the section of wall now exposed. At shoulder height there was an odd rippling of the stone in a large circle with the center blackened and littered with shallow thumbnail sized pockmarks.

Blowing a fast breath through her nose, Reihana raised her hand and extended her first two fingers. She pushed mana into them and touched the top of the circle, her command of the arcane elements forcing the stone to become pliant. Tracing the circle, Reihana watched it swell slightly and protrude out as the weight from the wall bore down on the structural weakness. She knew the thick walls of the Archive were not in danger, but she did want to have vibrations deadened for her next activity.

Reihana tightened her right hand into a fist near her chest and hovered her left hand over it. Feeling the arcane energy flowing through her body, she pulled some of it to the surface and coated her fist in a transluscent amber film of mana. Then with a grunt, she savagely punched the wall.

CHAPTER TWO

It was a simple meal, but Esen served it with the pride of someone who had a hand in its preparation from pasture to plate. On a polished wooden slab rested a whole chicken that had been boiled in salt water. Next to the poultry sat a bowl full of stewed carrots, green onions, and potatoes. The steam from the vegetables rose up and mingled with smoke from the cooking fire before threading up and out the vent in the ceiling. A small box of salt was near a pair of clay mugs that were filled from the nearby river. Metal cutlery was still a luxury, so the meal would have to be eaten with the wooden skewers he had whittled and seating would be no fancier than the blanketed floor of the yurt.

After arranging the food, Esen sat on his heels and looked up at Claire who had been quietly watching him. She stood next to one of the roof support poles near the cooking fire while shadows danced across her fair skin and got lost in the crinkles at the corners of her green eyes as she smiled. She tucked a lock of chestnut hair behind her ears and then smoothed the front of her simple grey dress before she knelt down.

"You look happy, Esen," she said reaching out to touch his hand. The paleness of her skin contrasted starkly to his, even in the yellow firelight.

"Today was a good day, Claire," Esen answered. Looking down at the food he added, "I hope you're hungry."

"Of course," she said. Her smile widened a bit, but Esen noticed a slight furrow in her brow.

"What's wrong?" he asked.

"Nothing," Claire said too quickly. After a moment under Esen's probing gaze she admitted, "I was thinking about the market."

"You're homesick again," Esen said, trying not to make it sound like an accusation.

"It's not what you think," Claire replied as she absently played with the belt cinched around her waist. "It's just that I'm feeling a little lonely. The total freedom out here on the frontier is nice, but I sometimes miss being around people."

Esen squeezed her hand. "We've already been here two crop cycles," he said. "One more and we'll have been here a year. In two more years we won't be sharecroppers anymore. We'll be homesteaders."

"They'll be taxes then," Claire reminded him.

"The Sovereignty will want our money, yes," Esen said. "But they won't be taking food from us anymore. And more importantly, it means we'll be selling crops and going back to the city again. We'll be the owners of our own farm, Claire. Our own farm." He emphasized the last words.

"I know," she said softly. "On the southern continent you would have gotten nothing from your family and never been anything more than a laborer or bandit."

Esen was about to protest, but Claire gently pressed a finger to his lips and said, "The past is the past, and you are right to be looking forward to our future." Taking her finger away Claire said, "Now let's give thanks before your magnificent meal gets cold."

Esen gave a small sigh, but bowed his head.

Claire's voice became fuller as she spoke, "Blessed are the trinity of the Small House, the mother, the father, and the child. We thank the mother for providing us with fertile lands and fair weather on which we grew this food. We thank the father for the strength to labor honestly and protect what is ours. We thank the child for showing us there can be joy in everything we do. Through your teachings and divine grace we have learned how to live well. And so it shall be."

"So it shall be," Esen echoed.

When Esen opened his eyes he saw that Claire was still bowed in a silent prayer. She had taken out a simple necklace from underneath her dress and held it tightly. Esen's hand drifted up to the matching jewelry around his neck. Dangling from the hempen cord was a holy symbol. Three thin iron bars were welded perpendicular to another iron support. The center bar was about half the length of those flanking it. Representing the trinity of mother, child, and father, there was a small loop on top of the center bar where the cord was threaded.

"Someday," Esen began and watched Claire open her eyes to look at him. "We'll be able to replace these for rings. Proper silver rings."

"What for?" Claire asked.

"To make it official," Esen said. "Our wedding."

"In the eyes of the trinity, it's already official," Claire replied.

"And out here on the frontier that can be enough," Esen protested. "But it's important to me you have something more."

"No more talk of such things, my dear husband," Claire said. Her tone was gentle, but chastising all the same. "The food smells wonderful, and I'm hungry."

"Of course," Esen answered with a faint smile. He retrieved his mug from the mat and took a sip of water. With a grimace after swallowing he said, "The water has that copper taste again."

Claire took her own cup and drank. "It's not bad," she said. "Besides, copper is a blessing from the trinity. Why do you think the wells in the city are lined with it?"

"Extravagant excess of the provincial princes?" Esen said

playfully. He dug his fingers into the chicken and stripped off a large piece of breast meat. Passing it to Claire he said, "The people here on the northern continent might call them Sovereign nations, but it's still the same precarious tripod of military might, economic power, and magical innovation in all of them. It's only a matter of time before one leg collapses and the wars start."

Claire wrinkled her nose at his sermonizing and answered her own question. "Copper keeps the water from spoiling. I'm surprised you hadn't gotten used to it when we were still in the city."

"Well water is for citizens," Esen said. "A foreigner without anyone to vouch for him isn't looked upon too kindly by the City Watch."

Claire's reply was interrupted by the sound of something metallic falling outside of the yurt followed by a loud grunt. "What was that?" she asked in alarm as she looked towards the door.

"Sounded too big to be a raccoon," Esen said as he stood up and dusted off his black canvas trousers. He went to the door, pulled on his well-worn leather boots, and donned a felt jacket dyed a dark red over his nearly threadbare shirt. He ran a hand through thick black hair and looked back at Claire. "Maybe a boar caught the scent of the meal and wanted to invite itself inside. I'll go check," he said.

"Make sure the chicken coop is secure," Claire replied as Esen lit a lantern with a sliver of bark taken from the cooking fire. "There might be another coyote out there."

Esen opened the yurt's door and felt cool night air rush past. From behind him the cooking fire pushed a long shadow out the door and onto the packed dirt path that led to his fields. The remnants of twilight were quickly receding and bright stars in hues of blue and yellow populated a cloudless sky.

"I'll be right back," Esen said as he held up the lantern. He looked over his shoulder at Claire and said, "Please eat. I won't be long, but the food is hot now."

Esen exited the yurt and carefully closed the unpainted wooden door. He took a few steps away and turned around to inspect the dirty white canvas exterior. The ropes circling the yurt and keeping the canvas fastened to lattice walls looked secure, but Esen frowned slightly when he noticed a long slit of light seeping through the normally opaque material at a seam. "Hold together just one more crop cycle," he pleaded softly to the dwelling.

He walked around the yurt searching for the source of the noise when he came upon a pair of shovels on the ground that had been resting against the yurt that afternoon. Esen picked up one and placed it upright against his home. He took up the other one and used it as an impromptu walking stick as he marched toward the chicken coop.

They had converted their covered wagon into the chicken coop once the yurt had been raised and they didn't need to use it for their own shelter any longer. He found that the long gate on the back of the wagon was secure and the ramp undisturbed against a tall wheel. He bent over and passed his light across the narrow gaps along the flanks of the wagon and could see an occasional jostling of feathers inside.

The only livestock they possessed aside from the oxen that had pulled the cart, Claire had especially taken to caring for the chickens. She had an expression of pure joy on her face the first time she held a baby chick in the palm of her hand, and the memory now made Esen smile. Over the past two crop cycles they had raised a sizable flock that provided them with eggs regularly and a boiled chicken dinner occasionally. While some of their crop yields were variable, the vitality and strength of his flock was a point of pride for Esen.

"You're all fine. Sleep well," he whispered.

Straightening, Esen looked up at the sky. After a bit of searching he found the three compass stars that glowed with a blue tint against the quickly darkening backdrop. While he and Claire had used them successfully to navigate the last stretch of their journey to the frontier, Esen still got an eerie feeling whenever he looked too long at the night sky. These were not the stars he grew up with in the south.

Pushing aside the brief moment of unease, Esen took a deep breath and filled his nose with the smell of green earth. While the continental interior was mostly mountainous, there were numerous small valley prairies with pockets of forest criss-crossed by shallow rivers. He scanned the horizon that had taken the dark blue hues of post-twilight and felt gratified that his hard work left him knowing the lay of the land for a league in any direction. He had carved something out for himself here, his adopted home, but he knew he still had much work left to do to protect what he had fought so hard to earn. Despite the slow march of progress by the Sovereignties, the frontier often pushed back violently to remind sharecroppers and home-steaders just how alone they were on the edge of civilization.

Claire's scream cut through the night, and upon hearing it Esen's body first tensed in fear before springing into action. He sprinted back to the yurt, the lantern flinging light as it flailed in his hand. Coming around to the front of the yurt he saw that the door was open and two large figures were pulling a third smaller one outside. Both were dressed in the blue and cream livery of the Granick Sovereignty military. Esen's lantern didn't cast enough light to show if the men wore armor under their tabards, but he could plainly see short swords on their belts.

"There he is," one of the men grunted as Esen skidded to a stop in front of them. "They said you were a big fuck, and so you are."

"Esen!" Claire cried as she unsuccessfully tried to break free from the soldier's grip.

"What's going on here?" Esen shouted as he froze in place, stunned by the shocking scene before him.

"He looks confused," one of them said. "Look at how hard he's squinting his eyes trying to figure this whole thing out."

A voice from behind the men barked out, "He's not squinting, you dullard. He's a foreigner. Get out of my way."

The two soldiers kept a tight grip on Claire as they shuffled to the side to reveal another man standing in the doorway. His features were hidden until he stepped outside and into the glow of Esen's lantern. This third man was smaller than the soldiers but had a more commanding presence. He didn't wear a soldier's garb, but instead the robes of an Archive mage.

"The epicanthic folds you're describing are native to the peoples of the southern continent," the robed man said.

"You're hurting me!" Claire wailed.

The robed man turned slightly in her direction and said, "All this unpleasantness will be over shortly, dear Claire. Your father's ship is waiting for us in Port."

"That bastard is no father of mine!" Claire spat angrily. She lurched forward at the robed man and said, "He can sit and rot on top of that pile of money he loves so much."

"You're not taking her anywhere," Esen said, finally finding his voice. He hefted the shovel he still held and commanded, "Let her go now."

The robed man breathed an exaggerated sigh and then called out in an irritated tone, "Now would be a fine time to act, Irik."

Esen tensed and readied himself for an attack from one of the soldiers who held Claire. When something slammed into the hollow of his knee Esen yelled in pain and surprise as he crashed to the ground. Though he managed to keep hold of the lantern, its light was extinguished when it bounced off the ground, shattering the glass panels and spilling oil. Before he could push himself back up a boot stomped down between his shoulder blades and smashed his chest into the dirt. Whoever was on top of him leaned hard and Esen felt the air being squeezed from his lungs. Gasping, he inhaled a mouthful of dust and retched.

The unknown assailant stepped off Esen's back, allowing him to push himself up onto his hands and knees. Breathing brought an agonizing pain to his left side. Looking over his shoulder he could only see a large shadow in the vague shape of a man. The shadow reached to his hip and pulled a sword free.

"No swords, Irik. We can't have any indication of a murder here," the Archive mage said quickly.

"Who will find him, Karnoff?" the shadow grunted, clearly not happy with the command. "Sovereignty sharecropper collection agents will think it was just another frontier farm raided by B'nisct."

One of the soldiers holding Claire spat on the ground and snarled, "Damn those savages! B'nisct fighters were scouting the northern farms near the capital and killed my cousin about a year back. I'd just as soon send every last pikeman the prince has to go wipe them out."

"Even so," the Archive mage answered. "The nomadic tribes of the continent's interior are not our concern. More immediately, I don't kill peasants who pose no threat. We've got what we came for. Leave him to keep scratching the dirt here on the edge of civilization."

Esen feebly reached out a hand towards the Archive mage. He tried to utter a cry to Claire, but only the most animal of groans came out.

"Early to bed, foreigner," Esen heard in his ear before being roughly grabbed by his hair.

The last thing he remembered was his head being violently pulled back and then smashed into the dirt. Then blackness darker and quieter than the frontier night enveloped him.

CHAPTER THREE

The Yaboon Archive was situated on the western side of the city. The architects made sure it was not the largest structure, lest they draw the ire of the Sovereignty prince, but it was generally agreed upon that the two-story building was impressive. Manicured gardens with tall hedge walls surrounded the Archive and gave a burst of green to a neighborhood populated by dwellings and shops hued in grey. Large floor-to-ceiling windows made from clear resin broke up the otherwise drab walls of brown brick. The mid-morning sunlight streamed through the east-facing windows and onto those who passed along the outer hallways, including a pair of men who walked with purpose away from the atrium on the ground floor.

"For someone just going to a research group meeting, you look far too eager," Donier said trying to keep pace with his taller companion. "There's no award for showing up first."

Thorne shortened his stride and looked over at Donier. He reached out and pretended to pick a speck of lint off of his friend's shoulder and said, "There's no risk of that given how long it took for you to pick out your clothes before we went to breakfast. There's no award for being the best dressed mage."

Donier straightened the front of his green alchemist robes cut in the latest fashion and replied, "Well, there should be. Appearances matter, Thorne."

"Perhaps," the mage replied. He glanced down at his outfit. Grey canvas pants were tucked into black leather boots. Under a lightweight jacket dyed blue Thorne wore a sleeveless white linen shirt. It was dress more suitable for a member of the mercenary guild than an Archive mage. "In any event, it's hard to be eager for anything that Reihana is in charge of, including my research group," he said, not hiding his distaste.

"That smacks of jealousy's sourness, my friend," Donier said. "Reihana is going to be on the council one day."

"That's why I don't like her," Thorne countered. "At least one reason. Her ascension seems pre-ordained."

"She's a powerful, knowledgeable, and well-liked mage here at this Archive," Donier said as if those alone were sufficient reasons, but then added, "And she seems genuinely concerned about other mages' welfare. I've heard her vision for the Archive, one where we have greater visibility in the world and actually work with the guilds and the prince, not just co-exist with them. It's compelling."

At an intersection of hallways both men stopped as a group of apprentice mages came around the corner. The three young women were dressed in matching navy alchemist robes and each held a leather-bound notebook.

"Oh, hello Master Thorne, Master Donier," one said in surprise.

"Will the two of you be able to attend the seminar today?" another apprentice asked with a hint of excitement. "Master Usibal will be reviewing his latest research."

Donier glanced at Thorne and then forced out a little laugh. "I'm sorry, but I'm going to be stuck in an apiary management meeting this afternoon, so I'll have to pass."

"What about you, Master Thorne?" she asked hopefully.

"I'm also busy," Thorne answered.

"Would you like for me to take some notes for you?" the apprentice asked. "It wouldn't be any trouble."

"No," was the mage's terse reply.

"Oh," the apprentice said leaning back on her heels. "I'm sorry to have bothered you then."

Thorne took a few steps past the retreating apprentices before he noticed that Donier was not with him. The mage turned around and found his friend was still watching the three women hurry away.

"Well that won't help things any," Donier said when Thorne returned to his side.

"What do you mean?" the mage asked.

"You have a reputation," Donier said.

"For what?" Thorne answered with an edge in his voice.

"For being difficult to talk to," Donier said. "And you know it. I suspect that you actually work to cultivate it."

"Not true," Thorne said sounding more defensive than he wanted. "I just prefer to keep my own counsel."

"Does that counsel advise taking the contrarian position of disliking Reihana for rather nebulous reasons?" Donier asked rhetorically.

Thorne turned away from Donier and looked out the tall window so his scowl was hidden.

"I guess the masses don't know her like I do," the mage said distantly.

"Right, your research group. What is it you actually do?" Donier asked trying to follow the mage's gaze.

"Advanced resin synthesis," Thorne answered too quickly.

"There it is," Donier said. "The pat answer. You're not fooling anyone. When are you ever in your lab? Whatever it is you're working on, the council will find out about it eventually and then we'll see where the chips fall."

"I suppose so," Thorne replied.

"Fine, keep your secrets," Donier said taking a step back from his friend. "I suppose then I'll leave you to your no doubt stimulating, if not contentious, conversations with Reihana and the rest of your merry band." With a less mocking tone he added, "I'll save you a dinner seat for when you're done."

Thorne turned to face Donier and gave him a genuine smile. "I appreciate it," the mage said. He watched Donier retreat down the hall with a thoughtful but slightly sad expression. Shaking the momentary bad feeling, Thorne stepped away from the window and quickly walked down one of the narrow hallways that branched off from the main outer corridor. The mage still wanted to be just early enough to the meeting that it was noticed.

• • •

Thorne pushed open the door to the small windowless conference room and found that he was not the first to arrive. At the front of the room opposite the doorway Reihana and councilor Olaf turned in unison at the intrusion.

Both were dressed in navy alchemist robes, but that was where the similarities ended. Reihana was a short heavyset human woman about the same age as Thorne. She tried to hide her irritation at the interruption by tucking a stay lock of short black hair behind her ear, but her tightly clenched jaw and hard, albeit brief, look at Thorne betrayed her true feelings. In contrast, Olaf was a thin elderly man with a wispy crown of white hair and skin covered in age spots. The councilman raised a hand limply in disinterested greeting and then turned back to Reihana. The pair now continued their conversation in tones just above a whisper.

"You're blocking the door, Thorne."

The mage turned around and saw a short Sehenryu female standing behind him dressed in tan canvas trousers and a white linen vest. Nearly luminous green eyes with vertical pupils stared at up him with an appraising expression that was common amongst the feline race. Long white whiskers sprung from her upper cheeks and eyebrows, which contrasted with the short grey fur that covered her face and body.

"Sorry, Mirtans," Thorne mumbled as he stepped to the side to let the smaller mage through.

The Sehenryu's ears on the top of her head rotated slightly backwards as she walked past and said, "Just grab a seat in the back like you normally do. The twins are on their way."

Thorne did as he was told and sat down on one of the wooden stools that lined the back wall. There was a large black table in the center of the room with matching high-backed chairs, and the mage watched Mirtans pull one out and sit with her back to the door. Reihana acknowledged the new arrival with only the slightest of glances and Olaf ignored Mirtans entirely.

After he sat down on the stool, Thorne noticed a meek-looking scribe hiding behind Olaf. Trying very hard to be unobtrusive, the young woman stood a few steps away from the councilor and occasionally scribbled something in a small leather-bound notebook.

The windowless room was illuminated with harsh white light from a number of glow globes affixed high along each wall. The bare white plaster of the room gave it a cold sterile feeling, as the only decorations on the walls were the scuffs caused by chairs scraping them.

The sound of heavy footfalls at the door made Thorne turn and he watched the final two meeting attendees arrive. Skevald and Torstein were Venhadar twins, and they both sauntered into the conference room as if they didn't have a care in the world. Both males had short blocky physiques that were typical of their race, with blue eyes deeply set into pale weathered faces and unruly blonde hair that was turning white at the temples. While the long black robes they wore were the traditional garb of an Archive mage, their heavy footsteps suggested boots favored by mercenaries and soldiers. Neither of them acknowledged Thorne as they walked past and sat down a few seats away from Mirtans at the table.

After adjusting his robes and wiggling into his seat, Skevald peered around the back of his chair. "You're welcome to sit at the adults' table, Thorne," he said more loudly than he needed.

"I'm content where I am."

"Leave him there," Torstein said, glancing backward. "He likes playing the part of the pariah. Must remind him of his family."

The private conversation between Olaf and Reihana ended and both turned deliberately towards the table to address those assembled. "Let's get started," Reihana said in a commanding tone. "Thorne, the door please."

"Where are the other two?" Mirtans asked.

"Karnoff and Ghent are out on assignment, but should be back in time to report at the next scheduled meeting," Reihana answered. Seeing the mage had not moved she asked again, "Thorne, the door."

Thorne slid off the stool and with a flip of his wrist swung the door closed. Returning to his stool he saw that Olaf was glowering at the twins.

Without preamble the councilor said, "I'm concerned that you've been less than discreet with your activities, and I'm here to remind all of you that membership in the Paragon program is at the discretion of the council."

"You're not going to kick us out," Torstein said boldly. "And don't think the threat of binding our magic is going to scare us. All it would take is for a note to be passed to some court retainer, and oops! The prince now knows about the secret program in the Archive to develop combat magic."

"Are you threatening me?" Olaf asked menacingly.

"Let me be very clear about this, Torstein," Reihana said.

"You get drunk in a tavern again and start talking about program assignments and you'll wish that the council only took your magic away."

"Is all the cloak and dagger secrecy really necessary?" Skevald asked, trying to defuse the tension. "How long do you really think we can keep the program a secret?"

"It's been nearly two years now," Olaf said. "And we've made incredible progress. What was at first just a set of theories to manipulate and transmute primal matter and energy for combat use has evolved into the training of the first cohort of fighting mages, you Paragons. During that time, you have been able to keep your activities concealed not only from the rest of the Archive, but also the guilds and Sovereignty. The development of combat magic is dangerous to both the prince and the guild system. It would be immediately taken by the Sovereignty military or used as an excuse by the guilds to cripple the technology development and commerce work the Archive is known for by the general populace."

"The stakes are very high, Torstein," Reihana said. "You'd do well to remember your privileged position here. You have access to books, reagents, and equipment that nearly all other mages do not. If I hear any more rumors of fighting mages from my agents then you will suffer the consequences. Until the council is ready to reveal you to the wider world, Paragons do not exist."

"Then you've set us up to fail," Skevald said, not hiding his frustration. "Rumors will soon run rampant anyway as we complete more assignments." The Venhadar counted on his thick fingers as he said, "Defend a frontier farm from a B'nisct swarm, protect a guild ship from pirates, mediate a dispute between villages fighting over contested farmland, and those are just the ones I've done. How long did you expect our good deeds to remain secret?" When Reihana's eyebrows jumped up in shock, Skevald added, "Oh, was the work we did supposed to stay secret even amongst ourselves?"

"The less you know about what each of you is doing, the more plausible deniability you have about the program," Reihana said.

"While Reihana is the principal agent for this group, executive oversight responsibility is mine alone," Olaf said. "Only she and I know the totality of the work you have done, and that is how it will remain until a time comes when we can safely reveal that the program exists and the tangibly good works it has completed across the continent. Until then, keep your exploits to yourself. Is that clear?"

The councilor looked at each person before him and stared until he was acknowledged. Olaf looked at Thorne last and waited as the mage returned his gaze and offered a single nod. Satisfied, Olaf turned to Reihana and said, "You may continue this meeting without me as we discussed." With one last pointed look at Torstein, Olaf strode out of the room leaving his scribe to stay behind and record the remaining proceedings. The timid woman took a position behind Reihana and waited with her stylus poised in her notebook.

"I'll keep things brief today," Reihana said after Olaf had left the room. "The sole agenda item is to get a progress report from each of you on your establishment of independent spy networks across the continent. Mirtans, go ahead."

"I've got spies in Port and Granick and a contact in Morbound," the Sehenryu said.

"Is that all?" Skevald said, clearly not impressed. "Tor and I have got spies in every coastal city in Yaboon."

"What about outside the province?" Reihana asked.

"Or outside a tavern full of drunk mariners," Mirtans nettled.

"We're getting there," Skevald answered with a pointed

look at the Sehenryu. Pivoting his annoyance towards Reihana he added, "You only let us out of the cage so often, so progress has been slow."

"Is that so?" Reihana asked rhetorically. "I think you're not applying yourself as well as you could be." Looking to the back of the room she said, "Thorne, you've been conspicuously quiet. What has been your progress?"

"I don't have many spies, but do have several contacts in every city named so far," Thorne said. "And about as many again in the Granick and Savamont provinces, though mostly in non-coastal cities."

"Let me guess," Torstein said. "Cities all along the major merchant transport lines, right?" The Venhadar gave a dismissive gesture towards Thorne while looking at Reihana. "He's just using his family contacts."

"Contacts can be unreliable," Reihana said. "We need spies that are loyal to you, not money, and I want each of you to have at least four in as many cities established in the next six months. The mercenary guild may have picked up a new crew or two recently. It would do us well to make an inquiry there to see if we can make some contacts in whatever city they came from."

"Not a chance," Skevald groaned. "Those thick-headed fools won't do us any favors. They won't lift a finger to help anyone without a signed contract."

"Even so, I want someone to try," Reihana said.

"Thorne volunteers," Torstein said looking back at the mage. "Bottom rung of the ladder, and all."

"What makes him the bottom rung?" Mirtans asked.

"He's the only made mage here," Torstein answered.

"What of it?" Mirtans said annoyed. "He survived the training, so he's a Paragon like the rest of us."

"No need to defend your plaything," Torstein said. "I'm just stating the simple truth that born mages are more powerful then those who had their mind unlocked to magic."

"He'd give you a run for your money," Mirtans said. "Switching partners means you'd actually have to train and not spend all your time in a tavern."

Torstein glanced back at Thorne with a look of derision. Thorne stared him in the eyes but said nothing. Torstein then scoffed and returned his attention back to Reihana.

"We would all do well to accelerate our training," Reihana said. "Both in theory and practice. As Skevald said, I don't let you out of the cage much, but when I do I expect that you will act in accordance with our namesake." Looking to the back of the room she said, "Thorne, since I didn't hear any protest, I'm tasking you to reach out to the mercenary guild. Sooner is better than later."

"Understood," the mage said.

"That's all I have for you today," Reihana said while scanning the group with a critical eye.

Torstein shoved himself back in his chair and stood up. With Skevald a step behind, the two Venhadar stomped out of the room but not before the twins both gave Thorne a look of contempt as they strode past.

Thorne slowly got off of his stool as Reihana and Olaf's scribe approached him. Without breaking stride, the Paragon principal agent gave him an unsmiling single nod of acknowledgement and was out the door with the scribe scrambling to keep pace before Thorne could respond.

Mirtans loitered near her seat until they were alone before she casually walked up to him. "Still in the mood to train?" she asked.

"You already know the answer to that," Thorne said. "Sehenryu empathy isn't something you can turn off."

"I was just trying to be polite," Mirtans replied. "Let's go collect Garret and be on our way."

CHAPTER FOUR

Thorne and Mirtans found the Archive constable waiting for them in the atrium. Garret was a human male of average height but had a muscular build that age did little to diminish. Pulled back in a short ponytail, his straight thin hair was the color of silver with a neatly trimmed beard and mustache to match. The natural state of Garret's tanned face seemed to be a frown, but there was surprising warmth in his slate grey eyes. His dress was much like that of a guild mercenary, however the white sash worn around his middle clearly identified him as one of the Archive's security personnel. A long resin knife was sheathed on one hip and a short metal rod was tucked into the sash.

"Since you two did a number on the last set, I got you new lumber," Garret said to them when they were close enough. The constable gave a gentle kick to the bag at his feet that resulted in a dull clunking sound.

Reaching down to retrieve the bag Thorne said, "Much appreciated. Let's get going. We're wasting daylight."

Falling in step behind the mages as they walked out of the Archive, Garret said more to himself than anyone else, "Let's see how eager you are after I've put you though your paces."

They exited the Archive and walked through the short tunnel that opened into a beautifully manicured garden with neatly trimmed hedges. They passed a pair of apprentice mages who were tending one of the flowerbeds, and Mirtans gave them a friendly wave. The Sehenryu's mood had brightened considerably once they had left the conference room. Turning onto the avenue that would take them to the main city gate, the trio walked in silence until they reached an intersection of streets that abutted the city's eastern market. Thorne saw Mirtans' whiskers flare out and her eyes widen as she took in a deep breath.

"Do you smell that?" she asked no one in particular.

Thorne breathed in deeply through his nose, but couldn't detect anything. "No," he replied, "What is it?"

"Spiced chicken," Mirtans replied with a wide smile. "Just wait here a minute."

Before either Thorne or Garret could stop her, the Sehenryu took off into the market.

"Should we go after her?" Garret asked as Mirtans disappeared into the crowd.

"We'd waste more time trying to find her now," Thorne said with a shake of his head. "It's better just to wait here."

From the center of the city a chorus of sonorous tones reverberated loudly to indicate the afternoon hour from a carillon. Garret crossed his arms over his chest. "You mages aren't much for keeping a schedule," he said. "We were supposed to be out of the city by thirteen high bells."

Given the circumstances, Thorne couldn't argue with the Archive constable. He threw the equipment bag over his shoulder and watched the throng jostle one another attempting to find the best food or drink from the stalls.

After a short while Mirtans pushed her way out of the crowd. She held something in each hand and had a satisfied expression while she walked back to them.

"Someone was cooking savory chicken pastries and it reminded me of home," she said after rejoining them. Taking a large bite from the pie in her hand she quickly shoved the second one in Garret's direction.

"Here, Garret, my treat," she said.

"Much obliged," he said, tentatively taking the pastry.

"Where's mine?" Thorne asked.

"You're not hungry," Mirtans said matter-of-factly. Jamming the last of her snack in her mouth, Mirtans briefly closed her eyes and relished it before swallowing. "I'm ready now, thanks for indulging me."

"There was little choice," the mage said sulking. "I hope that food doesn't sit too heavy in your belly because I don't want that to be an excuse when I beat you today."

The Sehenryu huffed a little laugh and replied, "You'll hear no excuses from me."

Walking with purpose for fifteen minutes once they left the Yaboon main gate, the trio was silent until they came to a large wooded area that was the closest of the prince's provincial hunting grounds. The forest floor was carpeted with broad leaves from the tall oaks and maples that towered over them. It had rained recently and the ground was soft under their feet. They walked into the woods until they could no longer see the footpath that had brought them into the forest.

"This should be fine," Garret said as he looked around the sun-dappled ground. "Looks level enough for you lot to run around in for a while."

The mage opened the bag he carried and pulled out his makeshift training weapon. It was a board as wide as his fist and twice as long as his forearm. At the midpoint a thick resin semicircle was attached and acted as a handle. At one end a pair of leather straps formed a miniature belt, while the other end tapered to a rounded point. Grabbing the handle and resting the board along his forearm, Thorne used his left hand to secure the leather strap around his right arm near the elbow.

While he adjusted the board over his wrist to a more

comfortable position, Mirtans retrieved a similar looking mock weapon from the bag and also secured it to her arm. Once they were both armed, Thorne and Mirtans turned to face Garret.

"We'll continue working on an aggressive defense. Thorne, you'll start out as the attacker. Mirtans, I want to see a strong parry and fast transition to a counter strike. Get into position."

Thorne took a few steps back from Mirtans and turned to face the Sehenryu. He extended his left hand palm out and brought his weapon hand back as if he was going to throw a punch. The mage gripped the resin handle of his unconventional wooden sword tightly.

"Let's not be too eager here on drills, Thorne," Mirtans said with mocking smile. "You'll wear yourself out before the real fun starts."

"Save your love talk for the end," Garret barked. "Thorne, advance and execute a basic strike, strike, thrust sequence. Mirtans, defend with a double parry and counter strike. Begin!"

• • •

Nearly an hour later, Thorne was sweating and breathing hard. Garret had been a taskmaster and the wooden training weapon belted to his arm was now heavily dented and splintered in a few places. Flipping the buckle, the mage wriggled his arm free of the strap and let the board fall to the forest floor. Thorne rotated his wrist to unstiffen it while he rubbed where the leather strap had dug into his skin.

He glanced over at Mirtans and saw that she had also freed herself of her training sword. The Sehenryu did not seem to be nearly as winded as he was, but was gently prodding her arm where she had suffered a particularly hard blow. She looked over to Garret and said, "How do you think we would have fared in your regiment now that we've been properly trained?"

"You say that like your training is complete," Garret said with an expression of disapproval. "Back when I was a pikeman in the Sovereignty military, you'd get flogged if you didn't train every day. I know it's not the same with you since this has to be done in secret, but you're still a long way from what I'd call battlefield ready."

"That's why it's time to make things a little more real before we end for the day," Thorne said.

"I don't know why you insist on saving the most dangerous stuff for last," the Archive constable answered with a shake of his head. Garret retreated a safe distance and leaned against a wide tree with his thick arms crossed over his chest. "Magic is beyond my ken, so I'm just going to step aside and watch so I have something to report to Master Reihana. Try not to kill one another."

"No promises," Mirtans said flashing Thorne a sly grin.

The mage grunted and lifted his right forearm in front of his chest. He hovered his left hand over his bent elbow and took a deep cleansing breath to quiet his mind. It was in that focused state when he felt it, the magical power surging through his body, mana. His arms tingled with a sensation that was similar to the pins and needles of paresthesia but without the associated clumsiness. In fact, the feeling had the opposite effect and the mage perceived the slightest movements acutely and with a precision beyond what he could normally.

The mage felt the mana in his arm and carefully pulled it out to coat his skin in a transparent ocher film. Running his hand down his forearm, Thorne encased it in a shell of mana and then pulled the arcane energy past his clenched fist until he had formed a faintly luninescent blade. Dropping his left hand to his side, Thorne rotated his right forearm and inspected the weapon he had forged, which the Paragons called a mana knife.

With the summoning of his weapon complete, Thorne felt

an emotional rush of euphoria that was more potent than any narcotic. It was the dangerously addictive side effect of manipulating his arcane and life energies. He knew that waiting for him was the inevitable crash, one of the many prices paid for wielding magic, but right now he felt invincible.

He looked up and saw that Mirtans was waiting for him with her own mana knife ready. Once eye contact was made, the Sehenryu darted towards Thorne with her energy blade leading. While each of them had not put an edge to their mana knives, the hard energy would still hurt plenty if a blow connected. Thorne quickly parried Mirtans' strike and stepped to the side as the Sehenryu rushed past.

Mirtans spun around to face the mage with her mana knife in a defensive position. When she saw that Thorne wasn't going to attack, she lowered her arcane weapon slightly and said, "At least you didn't take Torstein's bait this time when he made that comment about your family or being a made mage."

"Torstein still thinks it's my family that got me in the program," Thorne said with a biting tone. "If his spy network was worth a damn he'd know that the Archive doesn't exploit any familial contacts with the merchant guilds." He drew back his arm in preparation to strike and took a measured step towards the Sehenryu.

"As it would be with the family outcast," Mirtans answered. She began to slowly circle around Thorne and added, "But I know that's not what really cuts deep. Despite the armor of aloofness you try to encase yourself in, I know that even now as a Master you feel shame for being a made mage."

Thorne's body tensed and he stopped his advance. He turned to track Mirtans' movement and replied, "I feel shame for a great many things." He reached out with his mana knife and pointed at her. "But not for what I am."

"You don't fool me. I know how much it matters to you.

How much it drives everything you do," she said. Mirtans stopped moving and stood straight, though her weapon was still at the ready.

"Then you are the only Sehenryu to make mention of it," Thorne said, no longer trying to deny the accusation. "Or at least the only one intrusive enough to scan me so thoroughly."

"I don't need my empathy for this," Mirtans said. "Just watching how hard you work to design a new elemental manipulation, or complete a complex alchemy, or train here with me, and it's obvious to anyone watching even casually that you're desperate to be seen as competent."

"Distinction in all forms of magic, isn't that the Paragon creed?" Thorne asked rhetorically.

"Perhaps," Mirtans said, "but I would be lying if I said that the others share your earnestness in trying to live up to that ideal."

"As born mages they don't have to," the mage said bitterly. He energized his left hand with mana and thrust it forward, pushing a column of wind towards Mirtans. The gust hit her just before Thorne rushed forward with a powerful overhead strike

Mirtans deftly blocked the blow and stepped in with her off hand and grabbed Thorne's wrist.

Thorne used his height as leverage and tried to lean over her and drive the Sehenryu to her knees, but was surprised when she used both arms to push back and away to hold her ground.

"An air manipulation to put me off balance might have been a clever tactic before," she grunted. "But I've grown wise to your tricks."

Mirtans snapped her arms down and arced them around to free her mana knife.

Just before the blades unlocked Thorne jumped back only to lunge forward and try to skewer her on the tip of his weapon.

Mirtans parried the strike aside and was quick enough to counter with the flat of her mana knife against Thorne's ribs. The Sehenryu's arcane weapon hit him hard and knocked the wind from his lungs. Despite her small size, Mirtans was deceptively strong.

With a gasp, Thorne backpedalled while Mirtans assumed an attack stance but did not pursue him. The mage reflexively held his aching ribs and positioned his mana knife in front of his chest like a shield. "If I can't fall back on raw talent like the twins, then all I have to work with are my tricks," he said with some effort.

"Do you really think that being clever would change Torstein's mind?" Mirtans asked.

"Perhaps," Thorne said, though his voice was unsure. "But I know for certain that I need to do something to impress Reihana. It's obvious she sees me as the weak link in the program. My assignments have been throw-away, especially now that I know what Skevald has done."

"What have you done?" Mirtans asked stalking towards Thorne again.

"Just like today," Thorne said. "Courier to the guilds or an agent of the prince. She's argued that I'm laying important groundwork that will build the support we'll need when the program finally goes public, but that's just an excuse to keep a close eye on me. She doesn't trust made mages." He paused and then added, "I need something that matters. An assignment where there are real consequences if it isn't done well."

"You'll get your chance," Mirtans said. "You just need to be patient. There's no shame in being the last to get an assignment outside of the city."

"How do you know I'm last?" Thorne asked surprised.

Mirtans' feline features did little to hide her guilty expression. "Just a guess," she said lamely.

Thorne's face flushed in anger and the muscles in his neck strained as his teeth ground together. He had been marginalized by Reihana and harassed by Torstein for some time, but had been able to keep his composure in all Paragon dealings. But Mirtans was his friend and her patronizing tone made him furious.

With a bestial roar Thorne discarded any duelist's subtlety and rushed towards Mirtans. A series of savage strikes drove Mirtans back onto her heels, though she was able to deflect them all.

The small Sehenryu spun on her heel and used the momentum to drive an open palm into Thorne's hip, jerking him off balance. Using the opening, she sliced dangerously close to the mage's neck.

"Easy there you two," Garret called out in a concerned voice that neither of them heard.

Despite Thorne's size advantage over Mirtans, the mage could not overpower her. She always twisted out of the way just in time or interrupted his assault with a deft strike of her own. The mage was rapidly fatiguing, but Mirtans appeared fresh and relaxed. Breaking away from Mirtans, Thorne glared at her and seethed. "Why are you toying with me?"

"You need the practice," the Sehenryu said. "You've got the heart of a fighter, but ferocity will only go so far. You need to build endurance for maintaining your mana knife for longer encounters."

"So now you're going to lecture me?" Thorne asked sarcastically. "We're both Paragons, you said so yourself. What are you going to teach me that I can't learn on my own?"

Mirtans' expression hardened. "Perhaps some humility," she answered. In a rapid movement the Sehenryu whipped her mana knife over her off hand and summoned a second arcane blade. The Sehenryu loosed a violent hiss and dashed towards

Thorne, her twin mana knives slicing the air as she pumped her arms.

Thorne dropped to a crouch and pressed his off hand into the forest floor. The mage realized too late that he had stretched himself too thin as he pushed his mana into the ground and felt his arcane blade dissolve. Lacking the strength to manipulate the earth and keep his mana knife summoned, Thorne pushed what mana he had left into the ground with a strained yell. Now connected with the patch of earth in front of him, Thorne pulled open a chasm under Mirtans' feet.

The Sehenryu lurched forward as her lead foot lost purchase with solid ground. Without breaking stride Mirtans stabbed the empty space in front of her and a narrow column of wind pushed a large rock up from the chasm. She stepped on the makeshift platform and leapt into the air. As if pulled by invisible cords, Mirtans rose over the chasm, ascending to a great height before launching herself downwards toward Throne.

Exhausted both mentally and physically, the mage could do nothing but watch as Mirtans crashed on top of him. The Sehenryu's backside crushed down on Thorne's chest as she leaned over, poised one mana knife over his throat, and raised the other to strike.

"That's enough!" Garret barked harshly as he ran towards them. "Reihana wants you tempered, not broken. Training is over for today."

Mirtans rocked back on her haunches and lowered her mana knives. She sat there a long moment watching him.

"How did you switch from a wind to gravity manipulation so quickly?" Thorne strained to ask. "Your movement in the air was uncannily precise."

Mirtans grunted as she climbed off Thorne and stood over him, both mana knives hanging stiffly at her sides. The Sehenryu's hands convulsed as her conjured weapons and associated gauntlets evaporated, the manifest arcane energy quickly reabsorbed back into her system. She took a step back and grimaced as her hands continued to spasm.

Thorne struggled to one knee and then stood. Looking to Mirtans, he saw the flash of panic in her feline eyes as she gazed down at her limp arms. The mage took a step towards Mirtans and asked quietly, "Is it a bad one?"

"I can't feel them, my hands," she said just above a whisper. "I'm watching them move, but I can't feel them."

Thorne reached out and gently touched her shoulder. "You'll regain control of them soon," he said trying to sound reassuring. He stole a quick glance back at Garret who was watching them both closely. "But let's get you checked out at the infirmary all the same when we get back."

・・・

The infirmary staff took Mirtans in and tersely ushered Thorne and Garret away so an assessment of the Sehenryu's condition could be made without distraction. The pair stood awkwardly in the hallway for a moment before Garret excused himself. Thorne watched him retreat down the hallway back towards the atrium when the mana crash finally hit.

It started with a tingling feeling in the back of his head that traveled down his spine and out to his extremities. The tingling became a painful soreness akin to the cramps of overexertion. Next every muscle in his body contracted forcing Thorne to lean on the wall for support. His head thumped against the wall and starbursts filled his vision, even after squeezing his eyes closed. He stifled an involuntary groan as his body tried to squeeze his insides out. The mage's mouth went dry and he broke out into an oily sweat. Trying to take a steadying breath, Thorne did his best to endure the near debilitating consequences of expending a large amount of mana.

"Are you alright?"

Thorne slowly peeled his head off the wall to look behind him and saw an elderly Venhadar female with a yellow sash around her waist, which identified her as infirmary staff.

"Just admiring the wall," Thorne croaked as he turned around.

The medic scowled as she looked him over. "Mana crash?" she guessed.

Thorne shook his head, which made the hallway spin and his stomach flip. "No, just having a rough day," he replied with a thick tongue.

"Look, I know how proud and stubborn mages can be," she said putting her hands on her hips. "Now I can give you something here, or I can go get the principal physician and he can order you to bed rest."

"In that case, a muscle relaxant would be welcome," Thorne answered.

"Wait here," she commanded turning back to the infirmary.

"No risk of me running, I assure you," Thorne said weakly as another wave of cramps tried to compact his body into a fetal position.

A few minutes later the medic returned holding a small square of waxed paper in her palm. In the center was a small mound of a tan gritty substance that looked like sand. Holding it out to Thorne she said, "Careful, it's very bitter."

Thorne took the paper and dumped the powder onto his dry tongue, grimacing as he swallowed. The terrible flavor of the coarse powder stayed in his mouth and distracted him from his mana crash as he tried running his tongue around his teeth to wipe away the foul taste.

"Thank you," Thorne rasped as he handed her back the empty paper. "I appreciate your ministrations. Even more so if you kept this out of the infirmary logs."

"Why?" she asked.

The mage took a tentative step forward and found that his sense of balance was returning though he still felt weak. The truth that he didn't want his concerning lack of arcane stamina getting back to Reihana wasn't an option, so he lied, "This was just from a little overexertion in my laboratory. I'm synthesizing something for a special someone. If she ever found out that I got sick making it, well that would ruin the gift for her."

The Venhadar's expression softened a little. "Lucky girl. I'll let it go this time, but if I catch you hunched over against a wall again, I'll carry you myself to be admitted to the infirmary."

"Understood," Thorne said with genuine relief. With a little wave goodbye, the mage slowly made his way back towards the Archive's dormitory wing. As he walked he felt his muscles loosen and his gait become less jerky. The world slowly righted and he didn't feel as off-balance, but his fatigue wasn't going to lessen until he ate something.

Only the most senior personnel at a given Archive had single apartments, so most mages, even those like Thorne who had attained the rank of Master, made due with communal accommodations similar to military barracks only more comfortable. He pushed open the door quickly enough to hear the sharp intake of breath made from someone who had been crying. Thorne looked down the line of four beds and saw a young human male dressed in a dark red alchemist robe sitting on one. He looked at Thorne with an expression that was a mixture of surprise and hurt.

"What's wrong, Alix?" Thorne asked as he walked towards the apprentice mage doing his best to maintain a composed façade.

"Nothing, Master Thorne," Alix said as he quickly rubbed a hand over his eyes. "It's just been a long day."

"For you and me both," the mage said after sitting on the bed next to the young man. Thorne's body obeyed his commands under protest, but at least now that he was sitting, he didn't feel as exhausted.

"It was supposed to be a simple alchemic resin synthesis," Alix said, either not hearing or ignoring Thorne's comment. "But I must have incorrectly weighed one of the components because it took way too much mana to crystalize. I knew something was wrong, but you how it is when you're riding the high, right?" The apprentice looked at Thorne searching for some sort of confirmation.

"Sure Alix, I remember what that was like," Thorne said. His memory flashed back to his training with Mirtans just an hour before. He didn't want to admit to the apprentice that a Master still reveled in the high that using magic brought.

"When it was done, it just looked so brittle," Alix continued as he looked up at the ceiling. "Nothing like the rest of the class, and," the apprentice's voice caught a hitch before he could continue. He swallowed hard and then managed to get out, "And Master Kent dropped it on the floor in front of everyone! Shattered it into a million pieces. He said I lacked focus and would be the last in my cohort to achieve Master, and certainly the last of the made mages."

Alix's face scrunched up in an ultimately futile attempt to not cry. As a few more tears escaped and ran down his face, he said, "That's the worst part. I thought once I achieved the rank of apprentice no one would care anymore who was born into magic and who was made aware of it. I guess that was stupid naiveté on my part."

"Listen Alix," Thorne said in a comforting tone, "Made mages can be just as gifted as those born into magic, but we need to work harder than them to be distinguished." The mage leaned over and tried to look Alix in the eye, but the young man continued to stare upward.

"Do you really believe that?" Alix asked. The apprentice looked as fragile as the resin he had synthesized earlier.

Thorne was about to reply when he heard a shout followed by the sound of several people running down the dormitory hall. The mage gingerly got up off the bed and opened the door. He saw two people with yellow sashes dash around the corner towards the main thoroughfare of the Archive. The mage turned his head down the other direction and saw that a Venhadar female had also watched the commotion. "What's going on?" Thorne called out to her.

"Something happened at the infirmary," she answered. "They're pulling in extra staff because whoever is there isn't looking very good."

"Mirtans," Thorne whispered as his stomach cramped again, but this time not from his mana crash.

CHAPTER FIVE

Thorne pushed open the infirmary doors and scanned the receiving area for medical staff. He had been hopeful that the Venhadar that helped him before would still be around, but no such luck.

The infirmary was a large high-ceiling room with white fabric dividers blocking off areas and creating lanes for foot traffic. There were a few treatment bays visible from where Thorne was standing, but they were empty and their cots unoccupied. The waning evening daylight that fell through a bank of skylights and tall windows in the back wall was overpowered by rows of bright white glow globes arranged high along the walls. Coupled with a vaguely chlorine smell, the entire space felt cavernous, sterile, and unwelcome.

"Stop him from thrashing!"

A stern voice beyond the labyrinth of fabric dividers cut through the heavy silence. Instinctively, Thorne walked toward the sound and heard a different voice answer frantically, "Let me go, I have to find an Archive mage named Karnoff! He took Claire!"

"He's delirious. Bring me a sedative now!" the stern voice commanded behind a divider to the mage's left side.

Surprised to hear a name he recognized, Thorne pulled back the white cloth partition and found three infirmary staff, a Sehenryu female and two human males, who were restraining a disheveled man on a cot that was too small for his large frame.

The Sehenryu held what looked like a long black sewing needle between her index and middle fingers. Made of alchemy resin, the hollow needle was the preferred method of administering medicines that were not ingested or applied topically.

The uncooperative patient began to weaken as the anesthetic took affect and the two male medics pushed the man's arms to his side and held them down. The Sehenryu rested two short fingers on the man's neck and nodded her head as she counted his heartbeats and breaths. Satisfied, she gently placed the resin needle on a small table next to the bed and turned to Thorne. "What are you doing here?" she demanded.

Taken slightly aback by such directness and still not feeling well, Thorne stammered, "Um, I'm looking for Mirtans."

"Who is that?" the Sehenryu physician snapped.

"She was brought here earlier," Thorne answered with a weak gesture back to the reception area. "She had a bad mana crash and her hands went numb."

The Sehenryu looked at one of the medics and ordered, "Take him to bay seven." Looking back at Thorne she said, "You should have waited in the reception area. I don't need these distractions."

"Sorry," Thorne said quietly as he was ushered away by the medic.

Suddenly the man on the cot tried to sit up and uttered in a pleading voice, "Karnoff, please help me find him. He took Claire." With little resistance, the remaining medic pushed him back down to the cot. Staring up at the now dark skylights the man kept repeating his last sentence, each time in a weaker voice until he was just mouthing the words.

The principal physician said to the medic, "Give me another needle. He's bigger and stronger than most here, so a single one won't keep him down for long it seems."

"This way, please," the medic guiding Thorne said in a tone

that suggested the invitation was compulsory.

"What happened?" Thorne asked as he was led out of the treatment bay.

"It's hard to say," the man replied. "Someone found him collapsed outside in the front courtyard. By the time he was brought here, he had come to, but was ranting about having to find someone named Claire. He kept saying he needed to find an Archive mage that came to his frontier farm and took her."

"Kidnapping?" Thorne said confused. "Out on the frontier? That doesn't make any sense."

The medic raised his arms in a gesture of concession and said, "Someone worked him over pretty good. He's got a couple cracked ribs, a broken nose, and likely a concussion. That's all from a very preliminary diagnosis. Now that he's sedated, we'll be able to determine just how hurt he really is, but seeing how he just shrugged off that first needle he might not get much rest tonight."

The medic led Thorne to an area of the infirmary where several of the bays were occupied by resting patients. Finding Mirtans fast asleep, he noticed her fingers flex a few times, but they weren't the jerky involuntary movements that he had seen in the forest.

"Don't stay too long," the medic said quietly. "You'll be doing her the most good by letting her sleep here."

Watching over his friend, Thorne didn't notice the infirmary staff leave him. The medic was right, of course, but he felt that just by putting forth the effort to be there, even if he wasn't actively helping, was better than nothing. Mirtans had made a comment about it once to him, that he wasn't very good at being patient and would rather vibrate agitatedly than try to relax when a problem was out of his hands.

The mage wondered how many times this exact scenario had played out in the infirmary, a silent vigil kept over a friend who had crashed hard. "You might be stuck here for a couple days," the mage said more to himself than the Sehenryu. "But at least you're not in as bad a shape as that frontier farmer. Poor sod won't have anyone but infirmary staff to check on him later."

Suddenly struck with a thought that overrode his need to watch over Mirtans, Thorne left the infirmary.

• • •

As expected, Reihana was not in the cafeteria like most other mages at this hour, but instead in her laboratory. She was peering over the hunched shoulders of an apprentice, a Venhadar male with short black hair and beard, as they both watched a round bottom flask filled with an orange fluid gently boil above an alcohol lamp.

Without looking at Thorne as he entered, Reihana held up an open palm and commanded, "Don't move. An extra body in here is going to change the air temperature just enough that we'll have to observe this reaction even more carefully."

After studying the reaction vessel heat for several minutes and then watching Reihana and the apprentice stare at the flask, Thorne began to get restless. He realized that the feeling was a good thing because it meant the muscle relaxant was taking effect and the other symptoms of his mana crash were abating. Not wanting to agitate her, Thorne stood quietly and examined the contents of Reihana's alchemy laboratory while he waited.

The haphazard collection of reagents lining the shelves surprised the mage. He had expected Reihana to be as fastidious as other alchemists in their workspace. A large table in the center of the room had a black stone top and showed the wear of many years of rough use. Despite the glow globes on the walls being charged to full illumination, the dark paneling on the walls and grey tile floor made the room feel small and cramped, especially since the large window opposite where he stood was closed and shuttered.

"Ah," the apprentice breathed out audibly as the orange fluid took on a pearlescent sheen.

"Do it now," Reihana said quietly, but clearly excited.

The apprentice pulled the alcohol lamp away from the flask and blew out the flame. His hand hovered over the mouth of the flask and his arm stiffened as he manipulated the air within, pulling it out to create a vacuum. Quickly stopping up the flask once all of the gas was evacuated, the apprentice looked at Reihana with a hopeful expression.

"That should do it," Reihana said with a small satisfied smile. "The solution should be stable for a couple of hours. More than enough time to add the mineralizer." Looking over to Thorne, her brow furrowed for an instant but quickly smoothed out when she asked, "Can I help you?"

"I need to talk to you," the mage answered. In a lower voice he added, "It's urgent."

"We should step outside," Reihana said. "I don't want our talking to be a distraction here." She gestured toward the door and followed Thorne into the hallway. Her composed tone changed the instant she had crossed the laboratory threshold and was out of earshot of her apprentice. "What is so important that you felt the need to interrupt an important synthesis?" she asked him, clearly irritated.

"This is something for our group," Thorne said using the agreed upon name for discussing Paragon matters where a keen ear might eavesdrop on the conversation. "A foreigner was just brought in from the frontier nearly beaten to death and delirious."

"This is hardly something for the group, Thorne," she said not hiding her annoyance. "Assaults on the citizenry are the domain of the Sovereignty military when outside of the city."

"He said he was looking for an Archive mage named Karnoff," Thorne argued, emphasizing the name. "That Karnoff took someone named Claire. I don't know what the relationship amongst the three of them are, but this farmer staggered here from the frontier after being beaten to a pulp."

"That's ridiculous," Reihana replied. "Karnoff is nowhere near the frontier."

"Are you sure?"

Reihana simultaneously pursed her lips and furrowed her brow. Thorne had seen the gesture before when the principal agent didn't like what she was hearing, but wanted to take a moment to think before responding. "What are you asking, Thorne?" she finally said.

The mage took in a breath and held it a moment. He had to be careful here and appeal to Reihana's logic and desire to make the Paragon program succeed. Any hint of eagerness on his part would instantly ruin his chances of success. "Let me go," Thorne tried to say evenly. "No one would want this as an assignment anyway, investigating a frontier kidnapping."

"You already have an assignment," Reihana said with a shake of her head.

"I can do both," the mage replied. "It won't take long to confer with the mercenary guild."

"Volunteering for an assignment of your own design sounds like an attempt to do some work similar to the others," Reihana replied. She put her hands on his hips and added, "Don't be jealous of what Skevald has done. You'll get your chance."

"When?" Thorne shot back, his composed pretense now gone. "If you never give me an assignment that has some risk involved, I'll never be able to prove myself."

"Prove yourself?" Reihana scoffed, her tone now one of rebuke. "Despite the petty games that some of you play when you think I'm not watching, the work we do is part of something much bigger than any of us. You need to remember why you were asked to participate."

Thorne crossed his arms and hardened his expression. "I joined," he caught himself before he uttered the word Paragon, "the group because I thought it would be a way to fight for those who couldn't themselves. Right now there is a man from the southern continent trying to scrape together a living on the frontier and an Archive mage, someone we may know, might have done something terrible. Helping people like him is the reason our group should exist."

"All of this could be in his head," Reihana said with a dismissive wave of her hand. When Thorne remained silent she added, "But I will acknowledge that it also might be true."

She sighed and looked past Thorne as another alchemist left her lab a few doors down the hall. The human female had the slouched posture of someone very fatigued. As she shuffled down the corridor away from them Reihana focused back on Thorne and said, "This is what I will do. When the infirmary deems this unfortunate fellow is well enough, I will speak to him and try to get his version of what happened. If, and only if, I decide that his story has merit, then I will discuss it with you. Until then, I want you to focus on your current assignment. You should also take this time to review your notes and perhaps spend some time in your lab. I don't think you'll get much training in the short term with Mirtans also in the infirmary."

"You already know?" Thorne asked as he rocked back on his heels in surprise.

Reihana nodded and answered, "Garret came here once you returned. You're not the only one who doesn't seem to think interrupting me when I am working in the lab is a concern."

The door to Reihana's lab opened and her apprentice peeked his head out. "Master Reihana," he said deferentially,

"I've weighed out the mineralizer and prepped the mold. Are we going to continue or pause for dinner?"

"Let's keep going," Reihana said, her voice once more pleasant and light. "You've been doing very well and I want to capitalize on our momentum. We should be finished before the cafeteria closes," she turned and looked at Thorne, "as long we are done here, Thorne?"

"Yes," the mage said stiffly. "Thank you for your time." He watched Reihana and her apprentice retreat back into the lab and didn't move for a few minutes after the door closed. Standing alone in the hallway Thorne had the unsatisfied feeling that came with an argument only half won. When his stomach growled, the mage realized that hunger was also part of the problem. He turned and made his way down to the Archive cafeteria.

• • •

True to his word, Donier had saved him a place at one of the long communal tables where Archive residents ate their meals. The cafeteria was located at the west end of the Archive and was one of the largest interior spaces in the building. The walls were painted with murals of tranquil nature scenes that seemed to have a life of their own as the glow globes affixed to the wall changed colors to reflect the movement of the sun over the course of a day. The only windows were along the back wall of the open kitchen, and those were small and functioned for ventilation more than for light. The din of countless conversations and cutlery clashing against plates and bowls could be heard from well outside the hall.

"Just the man I wanted to see," Donier said with a wide smile as Thorne sat on the bench holding his steaming clay bowl of food. "You can lay this matter to rest. What say you on the matter of councilor Tarbeck's rumored proposal to significantly increase our service rates with the mining guild?"

"I don't know of it," Thorne replied truthfully as he looked down at his meal after setting it on the table.

"See, I told you," Donier said in a self-satisfied manner looking around to those seated nearby. "Thorne's so consumed with the work of his exclusive research group that he has little time to add grist for the rumor mill."

"The only thing I'm interested in at the moment is how the food tastes," Thorne said still looking down at his meal. He picked up a copper spoon, but hesitated to eat despite his hunger.

"I wouldn't know," said Marcus, one of Thorne and Donier's contemporaries who sat across the table. "Donier says the stew is too salty and the bread could easily be mistaken for a used bath sponge. Alas for me, it all tastes like paper."

"And have you eaten much paper recently, dear Marcus, to know the difference?" chuckled a portly mage in russet robes who Thorne did not recognize. "Even so, you've paid a steep price for your magic. Lucky are us who haven't had the Iron Bane claim our palates yet."

"Give it time," Donier said sourly. He rapped a knuckle on the table and added, "The Iron Bane will eventually get us all."

A nervous-looking Sehenryu apprentice sitting on the other side of Donier timidly asked, "But it's still worth it, right? Using our mana to power alchemical manipulations, to learn about the very nature of the universe, we're doing important work." She looked around as if searching for some type of confirmation that she had made the correct choice with her path in life.

"Of course we are," Marcus said reassuringly. "But someone young like you shouldn't worry about such things as the Iron Bane yet. Don't let us scare you with our gallows humor. We'd gladly do it all over again. Magic is a special thing, and if it were easy and risk-free, then alchemists and mages would be a lot more common. It takes a certain type of person to want to be here."

The conversation continued, but Thorne tuned it out and finally took a first bite of his dinner. Archive food was nutritious, but mages excelled at using herbs and extracts in alchemy, not necessarily in food. Thorne agreed with Donier's assessment of the meal. It was much too salty.

As he ate, Thorne's ruminations shifted to his conversation with Reihana about the foreigner in the infirmary. He replayed the exchange in his mind and tried to find something in her words or mannerisms that betrayed what she was really thinking, but came up with nothing. The mage wondered if approaching her was a mistake, and would be penalized with more tedious and unimportant courier work. A part of him argued that with Mirtans in the infirmary he might have the opportunity to take her assignments, but almost instantly he felt guilty for such a selfish thought.

Finishing his meal, Thorne set his spoon down and looked over to watch Donier's animated storytelling. Detached from the discussion, the mage resolved to go visit Mirtans later to see if she was awake and wanted anything while the cafeteria was still serving food. For now he was content to listen to his friend play the role of raconteur.

CHAPTER SIX

"With luck, Wynn, we'll have no more interruptions and we can complete this synthesis tonight," Reihana said to her Venhadar apprentice.

She tried to push the troublesome conversation with Thorne to the back of her mind as she stepped back into her laboratory and took a critical look at the orange liquid in the flask. It had taken on a cloudiness the color of pearl, and despite not being agitated appeared to be languidly eddying. Next to the flask rested a small mound of black granules on a square of waxed paper, along with a copper spatula. A short distance down the bench Wynn had put the alcohol lamp and a bronze mold with a matching set of tongs.

Reihana glanced over at the Venhadar as he ran a hand over his short black beard, which she had seen him do countless times before when he was nervous. "We should be all set once you get a bucket of water," she said.

"Oh, right," Wynn said quickly, betraying his embarrassment.

As her apprentice went to the small hand pump attached to the laboratory workbench and began working the handle to draw up water into a large glass basin, Reihana had a few moments to consider Thorne's unwelcome petition. She had wondered how long she'd be able to keep him in the city as an errand boy, but she was still unconvinced he could be trusted with something more important to the Paragon program. Not only was he a made mage, but he also didn't share her views on Archive politics. Though they had rarely spoken of them directly, Thorne's opinions were irritatingly more akin to the calcified old guard, the dead weight of the Archive who hadn't had an original idea in decades. He was increasingly going to be a problem.

The thunk of a full basin hitting the workbench jolted Reihana from her contemplation. Wynn had brought back the required water bath and was now looking intently at the flask on the ring stand. There was a light sheen of perspiration on his brow, though Reihana doubted it was from the effort it took to draw up the water.

"All right," she said, giving him a reassuring smile, "As we agreed before, you control the solvent temperature to just below a boil and then I'll add the mineralizer."

"Are you sure? You'd have a much easier time with the heat management."

"You need the practice," Reihana admonished, still smiling.

"Yes, Master Reihana," the Venhadar said, subdued. "I just don't want to mess this up. These materials are all really expensive."

"The resin we're making will be significantly more valuable," she countered. "But not more than the experience you'll gain. Remember, it's the mages here that are the real treasures, not just the things we make."

Wynn smiled weakly and nodded. He took up a position directly in front of the ring stand and held out his hands such that each palm was close but not touching the sides of the flask. With a deep breath, his arms tensed and a small field of yellow light filled the gap between his palms and the flask. The swirling liquid began to agitate more aggressively as it was heated.

Reihana carefully watched the flask while Wynn worked, occasionally glancing at her apprentice's face. His mouth was clamped shut and his nostrils flared as he took deep breaths, straining to control his arcane energy and its transfer to the flask.

As the first vapors rose up from the orange liquid, she picked up the spatula with a sure hand. After pressing her index finger on the wax paper to keep it from moving, Reihana took a small scoop of the black sandy substance. She unstopped the flask and dumped it in. For a moment the solution cleared before becoming cloudy again.

"Keep the heat up, Wynn," Reihana said, intently watching the flask. "The mineralizer absorbs a lot of energy. We can't have the resin solidify prematurely."

Wynn grunted an affirmative while she took up another scoop of mineralizer. This time when she added it, she noticed her apprentices hands quiver slightly as he tried to adjust his energy transfer. She was pleased to see that the solution stayed a cloudy pearlescent mixture.

She took up one final scoop of mineralizer and then with her off hand grabbed the mold. While keeping the spatula level over the flask, she pushed some of her mana into the mold, transferring thermal energy into the bronze. Heating the mold was necessary to keep it from cracking after the molten resin was cast. With precise movements Reihana added the last amount of mineralizer. It disappeared into the cloudy solution and for a moment things appeared stable before the liquid suddenly changed to an iridescent blue-black.

"Kill the heat," Reihana commanded.

The glow from Wynn's hands dissipated as he pulled them away, and let out a relieved sigh. He took a step back and grabbed the bronze tongs from the workbench. Carefully grabbing the flask, he poured the contents into the mold that Reihana had set back on the workbench.

Reihana could feel a wave of heat pass over her face while

Wynn worked, and only after her apprentice set the empty flask back on the stand did she take a step closer to the mold.

"Now the fun part," she said with a grin. "Remember water first, then the mold."

"Right," Wynn acknowledged as he grabbed the basin and slid it next to the mold. He then plunged his left hand into the water and kept it there as he held up his right hand and pushed mana into it. After his fingers and palm were coated in a pale white film, he reached down and grabbed the extremely hot mold.

A flash of light raced from the hand holding the mold, up Wynn's arm, across his chest, and then down his other arm into the water. With an angry hiss the water instantly boiled to steam and leapt up into the air. After the energy transfer, Wynn let go of the mold and made a sound that was a mixture of groan and sigh before stepping back from the bench.

Picking up the now cool mold, Reihana knocked it against the edge of the workbench once before flipping it over. After the resin ingot flopped into her waiting palm she hefted it a few times. It was much heavier than it appeared. She then took out a glow sphere from her pocket and charged it with a small amount of mana. The clear marble absorbed the arcane energy and radiated a clean white light. Holding the ingot in front of the glow sphere, she carefully inspected the resin.

"Very nice work, Wynn," she said approvingly. Looking over and seeing him hold his head with one hand she asked, "You crashing?"

Wynn shook his head and replied, "Just a headache. I'll be fine." With his free hand he gestured toward the resin and said, "Who's that going to again?"

"Farm guild. They want only one of these for now, but when they see how much better the resin plow is compared to a steel one, they'll gladly pay for more."

"I suppose it's a good thing that we're forging the plow here ourselves," Wynn said. "If the blacksmith guild ever got ahold of one of these resin ingots, they'd probably try to turn it into a couple of swords and charge a small forturne for them."

"Their forges don't have the temperature control needed to work this," Reihana replied. "All they know is one level of hot. They'd have to hire an experienced mage to heat the ingot for forging, and I just came from a principal agent meeting that reported back that they are still too stingy to want to pay for our services, no matter the benefits to them in the long run."

They studied the resin ingot a bit longer until the tolling of two low bells filtered in from the window. Looking towards the sound, Reihana offered the ingot to Wynn and asked, "Can I leave this here with you? I'd prefer to stay and help tidy up, but I'm supposed to have a meeting in the records library now with a guild liaison."

"Sure," her apprentice said as he took the resin. "Don't worry about things here."

Reihana gave a warm smile to Wynn and passed him their shared work before leaving the alchemy laboratory. Once in the hallway she quickened her pace, descended the stairs, and entered the atrium. Standing next to the large lectern near the back of the cavernous room was the major domo, a female Sehenryu, and an unfamiliar human male. When the stranger saw Reihana he said something to the major domo, who gave a single nod of her head and gestured toward Reihana with a white furred hand.

The stranger intercepted her in the middle of the atrium. His expression was unkind when he said, "You're late. I was told you'd be here at two low bells."

Reihana swallowed a sharp reply and instead downcast her eyes. No matter that it was mere minutes past the tolling, now was not the time to engage in a scuffle for dominance with a guild representative. He needed to be moved out of the atrium and dealt with in private.

"Of course you are right, my apologies," she said quietly. "I have arranged a comfortable place for our discussion. If you will follow me please," she paused and looked up, waiting for the stranger to introduce himself.

The stranger scowled, but then said, "Quinten. I am Geridan's representative here in Yaboon."

With the surly guild agent a step behind, Reihana walked down a wide corridor that led into the interior of the Archive. The glow spheres that lined the walls lit the hall with a soft bluish-white light. There were thick tapestries along both walls that were there for both decoration and to dampen the sound of footfalls from the tiled floor. Neither Reihana nor the guild agent looked at the scenes of ancient wars, dragon myths, or alchemic laboratories embroidered on the wall hangings, but instead both kept their eyes looking down the hall.

She was becoming accustomed to the iciness of their silence when they arrived at the records library. Stopping at a set of thick double doors, Reihana turned to Quinten and said, "I've arranged for us to conduct our business here."

"I'm sure Geridan will appreciate your discretion in this sensitive matter," he said stiffly.

Pulling the rightmost door open, Reihana led Quinten into the small library and was instantly assailed by the odors of oiled leather and dusty documents. The records library had none of the grandeur of the alchemic library on the second floor or the large main library near the atrium. Much like the history library near the residential wing, this space was utilitarian and infrequently accessed except by those with specialized interests. More often than not, scribes, scholars, and the occasional apprentice used it to study, write correspondence, or hold a private meeting.

An elderly human man looked up from a small square desk situated in the corner furthest from the door. When he saw Reihana and Quinten, he gave a small closed mouth smile. With effort he rose from his seat and slowly shuffled towards them. As she waited, Reihana ran her fingers along the spines of a few thick ledgers that were on a shelf at chest level near the door. All of the Archive's public dealings with the major guilds were here, along with those of the various minor guilds thought to be of enough import to record. In due time, the transcription of the meeting she was in earlier that day would eventually make its way here, along with every report, agreement, and contract she had drafted as a guild liaison.

"I shooed away a couple of apprentices a short while ago who wanted to take your table," the librarian said as way of greeting when he stopped in front of Reihana.

"Thank you," she said. "This shouldn't take very long."

"No need to rush. If it wasn't for those two youngsters and you, I probably would have sat all alone again here today."

"I'll make an effort to visit more regularly," Reihana answered.

The librarian made sound somewhere between a hum and a grunt, seemingly pleased with Reihana's reassurances. She watched the librarian unhurriedly return to his seat and thought back to when he had become one of her spies a number of years ago. Thankfully he was one that served her out of loyalty and not blackmail so her occasional neglect wasn't penalized. The assistance and kindness she gave him so long ago didn't seem like much at the time, and he had more than paid it back over the years, but given his advanced age Reihana supposed he must feel some type of familial fondness for her.

"If we may move things along," Quinten said impatiently.

"For certain," Reihana said, her deferential manner from the atrium now gone. She walked over to a short rectangular table with a high-backed chair on either end that was situated near one of the bookshelf-lined walls. She pulled hers out and sat down. Not waiting for the guild agent to get comfortable, she demanded, "What's this all about?"

Quinten gave her an appraising look before he replied, "Geridan is anxious for an update."

"You are the second messenger he's sent about this matter in as many weeks. Impatience is a surprising trait for a guild master."

"Perhaps," Quinten replied before he stabbed an index finger on the table. "But I am to make clear now that your deal is in jeopardy. Geridan will rescind his offer to bring Archive business to the guild masters' meeting if his daughter is not returned to him within the month."

Reihana frowned and leaned back in her chair. She crossed her arms over her chest and replied in a cold tone, "The frontier is far away."

"Well," Quinten said leaning over the table and giving her an unfriendly smile. "You promised Geridan that your Paragons were elite Archive agents, capable of getting fast results by working outside the normal confines of Archive diplomacy and favor trading. Could you have oversold their capabilities?"

She worked to keep her anger in check, nettled by the questioning of a smug go-between. Thinking quickly, she found a weak point and attacked it. "How much would Geridan's reputation tarnish once it was known that his daughter's arranged marriage was foiled by an elopement to a foreigner?"

"She didn't elope. Claire was kidnapped!" the guild agent barked.

Reihana didn't know if Quinten's quick anger was from personal feelings for the woman or a passionate allegiance to Geridan, but either way, she had scored more than the hit she was seeking. Unfolding her arms and placing both palms on the table she said calmly, "That is your guild's business, and something Paragons hold with the upmost discretion. I think Geridan can appreciate our position as well, given the back door channels that were required to work with us. We are not known to the Sovereignties, or even most other people, and would very much like to keep it that way until we have proven our worth to powerful guilds, such as yours. While Geridan's request will put considerable pressure on us, go and tell him that the task will be complete before the month is out. Of that you have my word."

"Geridan simply wanted reassurance that you were putting your full weight behind Claire's recovery," Quinten said, his emotions back under control. He rose from his chair and looked towards the door. "I have a rapid transport waiting for me at the main gate. I am to return to the Haywood guildhall in Granick immediately."

"I will see you out," Reihana said as she stood.

The return to the atrium was as before, in silence. At the Archive entrance Quinten paused after opening the door. "Trust is hard earned, Master Reihana," he said and pulled the door shut behind him before she could reply.

Reihana looked at the closed door and her expression dropped for a moment. Let him have his last word and feel important. As long as Karnoff brought Claire back to Geridan, she'd be one step closer to getting a toehold into guild matters. Then her real work could begin.

Composing herself again, she turned around just in time to see a scribe near the major domo's lectern turn away quickly and scurry down the hallway that led towards the cafeteria. She had only a brief moment to see the young Venhadar female's face, but Reihana recognized the scribe as being attached to councilor Olaf.

Spying was so common it was rather mundane at the

Archive, and it was well known that Olaf had one of the most expansive networks. While she had suspected that Olaf might have extra eyes watching her, Reihana was suddenly struck with a cold jolt of suspicion. Of course Olaf would be watching her, but not for any of her formal Archive duties. No, he wanted to make sure she kept the Paragon program, his off-the-books project, from being revealed to anyone. She couldn't let him know of her dealings with Geridan, her secret within a secret.

Keeping her expression pleasant, she crossed the atrium on her way back to her apartment. Despite it being well into the dinner hour she was not hungry and instead wanted nothing more than to deal with the problem in the infirmary who could undo all of her carefully laid plans. The foreigner who ran off with Claire not quite a year ago had somehow made his way to the Archive.

Attempting to keep her pace from looking hurried, Reihana entered her private apartment. The wall she had assaulted the day prior was now cool and the tapestry covered the new black smudges and shallow pits underneath. With sure movements, Reihana flipped open a lacquered chest at the foot of her bed and retrieved a nondescript black robe with a deep hood. Fishing around in the chest she found a pair of black leather gloves. After tossing the clothes on the bed, she closed the chest and then looked out the window. She'd have to wait until three low bells, which brought a scheduled staffing change at the infirmary. Until then, she would have to wait alone in her room and curse Karnoff for forcing her to deal with this loose end.

CHAPTER SEVEN

The receiving area of the infirmary was unstaffed when Thorne returned after dinner, which the mage thought very unusual despite it being just past the chiming of three low bells. However, the mage was reassured when he heard someone's footsteps behind one of the curtain partitions off to his right. Not wanting to disturb the quiet atmosphere, and now less uneasy that the infirmary wasn't deserted, Thorne made his way to Mirtans' treatment bay.

Still sleeping soundly, the Sehenryu's face was relaxed save for the occasional twitch of a whiskered eyebrow. Mirtans' hands were resting on top of her sheet and Thorne was relieved to see that the claw-like rigidity and erratic finger movements were gone. Thorne stood at the foot of her cot for a few minutes. The gesture was pointless for her actual recovery, but Thorne thought Mirtans would appreciate it nonetheless if she knew he was there.

Thorne turned to leave when the sound of a metal tray crashing to the ground reverberated through the infirmary. The mage's head jerked towards the clamor as a hoarse voice cried out for help. Without hesitation Thorne hurried toward the sound, clipping the corners of the cloth walls as he navigated the movable infirmary corridors. Unsure of what he would find, the mage lurched to a stop upon discovering the source of the commotion.

In a treatment bay a small figure in a black robe with the

cowl pulled low loomed over the lying foreigner. The pair grappled for control of a large needle held in the robed assailant's gloved hand. Struggling against the foreigner, the assailant tried to drive the needle into the bedridden man's chest.

"What are you doing?" Thorne shouted as he quickened his pace towards them.

The robed figure disengaged and took a moment to look at the mage, but their features were hidden in the shadows of their hood. Before Thorne could take another step forward, the hooded assailant shoved a small pushcart towards him and dashed in the opposite direction to escape.

Easily deflecting the cart, Thorne took off in pursuit. As he passed the confused but otherwise unharmed foreigner, he shouted, "Stay here," over his shoulder. The mage chased the assailant around a corner and along the outer wall of the infirmary where a long series of tall windows were shuttered for the night.

Suddenly the robed assailant stopped and pressed a gloved palm against a nearby window.

Thorne slowed and then stopped several paces from the figure, wary that the assailant might still be hiding a needle in their other hand. "You've got nowhere to run now, my friend," he said icily. "Why don't you take a step away from that window. You won't be able to throw open the shutters before I've tackled you, and I've only got to hold you down long enough for the constabulary to get here."

The hooded figure gave no reply, but kept their hand pressed to the window. A high-pitched buzzing noise came from the window just before it shattered. The myriad shards did not fall, but hung aloft by an arcane power.

Thorne recoiled in shock as he watched the glass fragments slowly rotate in midair as a breeze lazily drifted into the infirmary while the obliterated shutters swung limply outside. "You fiend," Thorne whispered. "You're one of us!"

Behind him, Thorne heard authoritative shouts from Archive security and the pounding of their boots on the tile floor. In seconds they would storm down the corridor and be able to help.

The hooded figure looked past the mage and uttered a low growl before flicking their hand outward. The suspended glass shards flew towards Thorne with frightening speed.

Acting on instinct, Thorne summoned his mana gauntlet, but instead of forging a blade the mage dropped a rigid film of arcane energy perpendicular to his forearm to form a makeshift shield. He crouched down and ducked his head behind his defenses and momentarily lost sight of the hooded assailant as the glass impacted on the conjured barrier and burst into countless fragments with a thunderous crash. Thorne looked up after feeling the last impact and saw that the hooded figure was gone.

"He jumped out the window!" a voice blared behind the mage.

Thorne looked back and saw two white sashed Archive constables running towards him with resin knives drawn. The mage dissolved his mana shield and gauntlet as the two men dashed past him and peered out the destroyed window. After scanning the darkness for a moment they both turned to scrutinize Thorne.

"Who was that?" one of the constables asked as he approached the mage. "It looks like he dropped down into the infirmary gardens."

"I don't know," Thorne replied with a shake of his head. "He tried to attack one of the patients."

"Stay here," the other constable commanded already walking away. "We'll need to hear more about what happened after we've searched the grounds."

"Let me help," Thorne called after him.

"I said stay here," the constable answered. "I don't know what magic you used to stop that glass, but you were lucky. Let Archive security take over now."

Thorne watched the constables run down the corridor until they turned a corner. He then slowly walked to the broken window and peered outside. Directly below the shattered frame and shutters were several neatly trimmed evergreen shrubs. Given the apparent power of the hooded figure, and their familiarity with Archive grounds, Thorne thought there was little chance of a search yielding a suspect.

The mage's whole body shivered as a mana crash, much weaker than before, washed over him. Planting his feet more firmly Thorne took a few deep breaths and was able push back the urge to expel his recently eaten dinner. He closed his eyes tightly and raised his face into the fresh breeze that wafted through the broken window. He was beginning to feel a bit better when a voice from behind startled him.

"I have to find that man."

Thorne whirled around to see the foreigner quite close to him. The big man had draped the sheet from the cot across his shoulders and wrapped it around his bare torso as a crude cloak. His trousers and boots were worn and spotted with the dirt and grime collected from the roads leading to the city. Despite his obvious fatigue, he looked quite strong.

"Who was he?" Thorne asked quietly.

"I don't know," the man replied. "But he knows where to find Claire."

"I was told to stay here," Thorne said. "You should do the same."

"If you won't help me, then I will go by myself."

The big man turned and took a step down the corridor when Thorne quickly called out, "Wait. What's your name?"

The man turned back and replied, "Esen. And you?"

"Call me Thorne."

"Will you help me, Thorne?"

The mage pursed his lips, trying to think quickly. "There will be too many questions if we walk though the Archive with you dressed like that," Thorne said. "Come with me."

The pair got a few strange looks from the yellow-sashed staff at they navigated the cloth-walled corridors of the infirmary. Thorne led Esen to Mirtans' treatment bay.

When they came into view the Sehenryu tried to blink the grogginess from her large eyes. As she sat up she pulled the sheet up over her unclothed chest and tucked it around her armpits. "What's going on?" she croaked.

"Someone tried to attack him," Thorne said pointing at Esen. Abruptly changing the subject the mage asked, "Can I borrow your shirt?"

"What? Why?" Mirtans asked confused.

"We're never going to be let out of the Archive if he's dressed in a sheet," Thorne said.

"We're wasting time," Esen said urgently. "We have to find that assassin!"

Thorne watched Mirtans stare intently at Esen. The mage waited while she used her empathy to scan the foreigner's emotions. After a moment she turned to Thorne and said, "My tunic is on the cart."

The mage found the garment neatly folded on the bottom shelf of the cart near Mirtans' cot. He snatched the garment and shoved it into Esen's hands. "Put this on," he commanded.

Esen tried to comply, but it quickly became clear that the tunic was far too small for his large frame. Grunting in frustration, he tore the material underneath the armholes to create a makeshift tabard. It was unusual dress, but certainly less conspicuous than wearing a sheet or walking around bare-chested.

"OK, now we need a way to sneak past the staff at the

entrance," Thorne said.

"I can help with that," Mirtans said. "Get close to the door. You'll know when to go."

"Thank you," Thorne said with genuine gratitude. "I'll owe you one after this."

The Sehenryu waved the comment away and then silently pointed down the corridor towards the infirmary entrance.

Thorne and Esen walked away from Mirtans' treatment bay and took a circuitous route towards the infirmary entrance. Pausing at an intersection just before the reception area, Thorne peeked around the corner and saw that two infirmary staff, one Venhadar female and one human male, were standing near the door. Thorne pulled back behind the corner and tried to give Esen a reassuring look. "Any minute now," the mage said trying to sound confident.

A moment later they heard a loud metallic crash near the back of the infirmary quickly followed by Mirtans' calling out, "Someone help me! I fell from my cot! My legs don't work!"

Thorne peeked around the corner again just in time to see the medics run from the entrance down the corridor that led to the treatment bays. The mage looked over his shoulder at Esen and nodded before making his way to the door. With Esen close behind, Thorne opened the door and exited the infirmary into the empty outer hallway of the Archive.

The mage didn't realize he had been holding his breath until after he opened the narrow auxiliary exit at the end of the hallway and felt cool air hit his face. With a sigh he tried to relax his shoulders as he scanned the darkness in front of him in an attempt to find the patrolling security forces. "It wouldn't look good for us to be skulking around out here," Thorne said to Esen. "Follow me."

Once it became clear that the mage was leading them away from the Archive, Esen slowed Thorne's quick pace by clamping a strong hand on the mage's shoulder. "Where are we going?" the foreigner asked.

"I need time to think," Thorne answered shrugging himself free of Esen's grip. "That assassin is long gone. We're not going to find him, especially with all of the Archive security alerted and searching the grounds. We're going someplace that I know will be safe for a while and where we won't attract much attention."

Esen thought for a moment and then nodded. "Go," he replied.

• • •

The *Blue Beryl* was a favorite of mages, and being the closest tavern to the Archive it was full with apprentices new to the city who wanted a livelier environment to dine at than the cafeteria where Thorne had eaten earlier. The single story building was packed full of Yaboon society including guildsmen, mercenaries, mages, and even a few of the prince's courtiers, all looking for drinks, camaraderie, and perhaps the chance at a mutually beneficial deal on some shared enterprise.

As they made their way thorough the crowd, the mage heard a few calls of "Master Thorne!" made by apprentices trying to get his attention. Politely raising his hand in greeting, the mage walked by all of them until he found two vacant chairs at adjacent, but occupied, tables near the wall opposite the bar. Finding a small space along the wall, he arranged them so they faced the crowd before sitting down. The foreigner followed suit and was about to say something when a rough-looking Venhadar female wearing wrinkled clothes and a dingy apron stepped up to them.

"What are you drinking?" she demanded with both hands on her wide hips.

"Beer," answered Thorne.

"Water," Esen replied with a sidelong glance at the mage.

"Only paying customers can have seats when we're this busy," the Venhadar said scowling at Esen.

"Then get him a beer too," Thorne said shortly.

"And water," Esen added with equal agitation.

"Do you have any money?" she asked with a disapproving look at Esen's torn tunic.

"We're going to be here a while," Thorne said softening his tone. "Just count our mugs when we're done and we'll square up with you then."

The Venhadar gave them a hard look before she turned and shouldered her way back to the bar.

Thorne glanced over and saw that Esen was staring wide eyed at the scene. He had the look of someone completely overwhelmed and out of his element.

"Don't worry," the mage said. "There's no way that assassin would get another chance at you in here, or even outside. There are just too many people and the City Watch has regular patrols in this area at night."

"It's not that," Esen said still watching the crowd. He was silent for a short while before adding, "This is the most people in one place that I've seen in a long time. I'd forgotten what it feels like being in a tavern. I've been on the frontier for so long now, I'm out of touch with the rest of the world."

"I'll bet," Thorne said absently.

A hole in the crowd opened up and the Venhadar server emerged in front of them holding two clay mugs in one thick fist. She shoved them towards Thorne and said, "The boss told me that you two only get water until you produce some money. If somebody wants your chairs and has coins in their pocket, then you two are standing with the other wastrels here."

"Fair enough," Thorne said as he took the offered mugs and

passed one to Esen.

After the Venhadar was absorbed into the crowd once more, Esen took a drink and winced. "How can you stand the metallic taste of city water?" he asked.

Thorne took a sip from the mug and then rested it in his lap. "Just something you get used to after living in the city for a long time," the mage said. "But that's not important at the moment. Right now I want to hear what happened to you."

Esen recounted the attack on his frontier farm and Claire's kidnapping. He did not remember much of his trek to Yaboon, only recalling periods of light and darkness, which Thorne could only assume was the passing of day and night. The mage was amazed that in such a state Esen was able to walk at all, let alone do it without food, water, or rest. It was for certain a testament to the man's vigor, but also to a considerable will.

"A harrowing story," Thorne said with a shake of his head when Esen has finished. "You're lucky to be alive. Do you have any idea why they would take Claire?"

"I don't know," Esen admitted after he took another small sip of water. "But the Archive mage said they were going to her father's ship."

"Where is it docked?" the mage asked.

Esen shrugged his shoulders and replied, "I can't remember, maybe he didn't say. Claire's father is a guild master in Haywood. Yaboon is the closest big city to my farm, and it has an Archive, so I thought I could get help here. Someone who knows him."

"The soldiers called him Karnoff, correct?"

The foreigner nodded and then said fiercely, "His face is burned into my memory. I'll go anywhere to find him."

Thorne leaned back in his chair and looked at the open raftered ceiling while he mused. "Well, there are a number of small port towns along the coast, so his ship could be anywhere.

But if he was going to use a guild ship, then the only harbor big enough is Port. You should go there and book passage to Banks."

"Why?" Esen asked. "I don't understand."

"Because you're never going to find Claire directly," Thorne said gazing back to Esen. "But Banks is the closest harbor town to Haywood. Traveling by sea is faster than regular land routes, and there are no border checkpoints to worry about if you're on a ship. If you can get to her father before whoever took her, then you might be able to find out exactly what is going on. For all you know, she might have been kidnapped for a ransom. It's not unheard of to have rich guild members extorted that way."

"Is kidnapping a normal Archive machination?" Esen asked with a cocked head.

"No," Thorne said, rankled by the disingenuous accusation. "That doesn't make any sense. Why would an Archive mage be part of a kidnapping? And the part about him employing Sovereignty soldiers is also suspicious. We're not exactly on the best of terms with the prince right now."

Pausing for a moment Thorne was suddenly struck with the thought that maybe their flight from the Archive was a mistake. "Let's return to the Archive," the mage said. "Let me talk to some people there, people who can get you help."

Esen shook his head so violently he sloshed some water out of his cup. "No!" he growled. "An assassin tried to kill me while I lay on a cot there. I have no idea how they found me, but I'm not going back. You said we could board a fast ship at Port, so let's go there. We must get to Claire's father with all speed. That means we leave tonight."

"Hold on there," Thorne said raising up a hand. "Why not wait until morning? Besides, I can't just drop everything and go with you. I have duties to perform at the Archive."

Esen's face quivered in agitation, before settling into a mask of grim resolve. "I can't sit still another moment knowing that Claire is in danger," he said firmly. "If you cannot help me any more, then this is where we part ways." He stood up and drained the water from his mug. Setting the cup on the now vacant chair, Esen turned towards the door.

"Wait!" Thorne exclaimed. The mage's mind raced as he tried to identify and then rank his choices.

Reihana would certainly be as shocked as he was by the attempted assassination, which might be the deciding factor in sanctioning his proposed investigation. Going to see her again tonight seemed like a good decision until he realized that she might send Esen with Torstein, Skevald, or Ghent instead. There was also the issue with the Archive constables seeing his mana gauntlet. They were certainly going to ask him about it, and once that information got back to Reihana or Olaf, there would be no escaping some unpleasant consequences. However, if he could discover the identity of the assassin, or better still, find Claire, things might turn out considerably better.

Thorne realized that he had made his decision back in the infirmary. He stood up and said to Esen, "I'll help you, but we're at a disadvantage if you insist we leave tonight. We have the clothes on our backs and even that is lacking." He gestured to Esen's torn tunic for emphasis and continued, "Let me sneak back to the Archive and quickly get some things. Then we can go."

Esen was about to answer when a young man dressed in alchemist robes excitedly came out of the crowd and stood too close to Thorne. Swinging from his neck was a silver chain with a small medallion that identified him as an apprentice mage of the Yaboon Archive. His eyes were wide with excitement as he exclaimed, "Master Thorne! I thought it was you! What are you doing here? I just came from the Archive and a bunch of constables are looking for you! Something crazy happened in the infirmary tonight, but no one is saying anything."

Thorne swore under his breath. With people actively looking for him at the Archive, there was no way he could return unnoticed. The checklist of items he had wanted to go back and retrieve instantly dropped down to one. The mage looked at the earnest and eager face before him and momentarily felt bad for what he was about to do. Looking the apprentice square in the eye, he asked, "Can you keep a secret?"

The apprentice stammered, "Y-Yes, of course."

"Are you sure?" the mage asked with his gaze locked on the apprentice. "We're talking about something serious, something at the level of a Master." The mage took a step back and critically appraised the young man. "On second thought," he said. "Maybe I should tell someone more senior than an apprentice."

"No!" the man shouted. "I can keep your secret, Master Thorne. What happened in the infirmary?"

"Give me your guilder and any credits you've got," Thorne commanded.

"What's going on?" the apprentice asked, practically vibrating with excitement as he took off the Archive medallion and placed it in Thorne's waiting palm.

After accepting a small leather coin pouch, Thorne leaned in close to the young man and said quietly, "I am part of a delegation that is going to meet with a prominent guild to broker a deal. It's something that will be of great importance to the Archive."

"Which guild?" the apprenticed asked as he leaned forward.

"A major one," Thorne with a look over his shoulder. "Be wary about anyone commenting freely about guild activities at the Archive. We're talking about the balance of power being disrupted across the continent. The council is terrified that we've been compromised."

"Compromised how?" the apprentice asked. "I don't

understand."

Abruptly Thorne looked towards the door and said, "I've stayed here too long. Remember your promise to keep this secret!" Leaving the apprentice, the mage tried to push Esen towards the door, but the burly foreigner didn't budge until deciding himself to move towards the exit.

Parting the crowd easily with his size and strength, Esen led the way out of the *Blue Beryl* and into the quiet street. "What was all that about?" Esen asked once they were outside and walking away. "You didn't really answer any of his questions."

"Misdirection will buy me some time back at the Archive," Thorne said as he looked over his shoulder to make sure they weren't being followed. "And it was a way to get this." He held up the Archive guilder.

"Why is that medallion so important?" Esen asked.

"You'll see in a minute," the mage replied. "Follow me."

The two men walked down a dark side street until it intersected with the main road that led into the city. There regularly spaced lamps cast large spheres of yellow light to push back the night. They did not see anyone out until they approached the main city gate and were stopped by a pair of City Watchmen. The huge timbers of the city gate were lowered and the Watchmen blocked the small door that was built into the gate. As they stopped before the gatekeepers, four long low tolls from the city tower rang out.

"Four low bells," one of the Watchmen mused out loud. "Best be getting home you two. If you're waiting for someone to enter the city, I can tell you that no one has passed through here since before sunset."

"On the contrary," Thorne said with a confidence that he didn't feel. "We're leaving the city tonight, so if you'll open the door, then we'll be on our way."

"What is your business leaving the city at this hour?" the

other Watchman said roughly.

Thorne held up the Archive guilder and said in a flat voice, "Archive business."

The Watchman that questioned Thorne snatched the guilder and examined it. "This is an apprentice medallion," he accused. "You'll get mauled before first light on the open road. Even this close to the city, the prince's road is full of brigands."

"A good thing I have a bodyguard then," Thorne said with a gesture back to Esen.

The first Watchman grunted and said, "Just let them go. No skin off our nose." Looking at Thorne and then Esen he said, "At least you got yourself a big one. What's your destination?"

"Port," Esen said before Thorne could reply.

"Must be in a hurry to get there if you're leaving now," the Watchman said. He turned and pulled a series of thick bolts that held the door shut. As he tugged the door open he said disingenuously, "Godspeed to you, gentlemen."

After Esen and Thorne crossed the threshold the door slammed shut and bolt locks engaged. Standing on the other side of the gate, Thorne realized that they did not have a lantern to light their way. Perhaps that was for the best if the Watchman's warning about bandits had any truth to it. The mage looked up and examined the overcast sky. They would be getting no luminous help from the heavens tonight.

Thorne looked over at Esen and found the foreigner also looking up at the sky. "You ready?" the mage asked.

Esen nodded as he peered down the prince's road. It didn't take long before the path was swallowed up by the darkness. "Let's go," he said without emotion.

With no more words to exchange, Thorne and Esen began a lonely walk though the night.

CHAPTER EIGHT

The sky was streaked with pink and gold as the sun rose the next morning. Overnight the cloudy sky gradually cleared as Thorne and Esen continued their walk towards Port. The adrenaline of their flight from Yaboon had worn off long ago and Thorne was feeling the ill effects of being overtired. Coupled with the recent depletions of his mana, the mage knew he had to be careful not to get sick in his weakened state. It wouldn't take much more than a large meal and full night's rest to recover, but he was unsure when either of those things would happen. Even at their slow pace, they had been walking for nearly twelve hours and Thorne was beginning to reach the limits of his endurance.

Thorne looked over at Esen. The foreigner's face was haggard, but his eyes were clear and focused as he looked up the long shallow rise they currently traversed. Esen's stamina was truly impressive, but Thorne was increasingly worried that the big man would collapse from exhaustion given that he had been increasingly dragging his feet despite the gentleness of the grade on the hill they now climbed. He had only been on an infirmary cot for a few hours, which was woefully inadequate given the ordeal he endured to get here.

"Are you doing alright?" Thorne asked, breaking the silence of the past several hours.

"I'm fine," Esen said. "I'm not familiar with this road. How far along are we towards Port?"

"Walking the prince's road as we have, it takes about thirty hours to get to Port," Thorne said. "We left the city at four low bells, so we're not quite halfway. Now that it's light do you want to stop and rest? We should be coming up on a major crossroads here soon."

"No," Esen said firmly. "Every minute we delay is that much further Claire gets away from me. We need to keep moving."

Thorne wanted to tell Esen that with no food, water, or rest, even if they made it to Port in record time they would be in no state to search for her once they arrived, but he decided to keep his opinion to himself. The foreigner's determination and physical strength had probably seen him through a number of hardships on the frontier, and Esen was unlikely to change his ways for some Archive mage. Even so, Thorne needed to find a way to save Esen from himself soon for both of their sakes.

As the sky continued to brighten they finally crested the hill and Thorne saw what looked like an encampment in the distance. There were two covered wagons with a large ox attached to each. Nearby there were a number of small simple tents, which were little more than tarpaulins supported by a few short poles. The mage did not see any signs of smoke from cooking fires or the shouting of orders and bustle of activity that was the norm of merchant caravans. The atmosphere coming from the camp was considerably more somber.

As he and Esen walked the gradual decsent towards the camp Thorne was able to count about twenty-five people moving between the tents. It seemed to be an equal mix of races and genders, nearly all of them dressed in long formless tan garments that weren't quite robes as the material appeared to be thin. There were very few children in the group as far as Thorne could tell, and as he got closer and heard someone singing the mage understood why.

"Hymns," the mage muttered with a frown. "It's a

pilgrimage."

Esen perked up as he listened to the song. "I know this," he said, his voice tinged with awe. "We need to stop and get a blessing from the shepherd."

"What for?" Thorne asked with a creased brow. In an irritated voice he added, "You didn't want to stop for a rest before, but now it's fine to waste time here?"

Esen didn't answer, but pulled away from Thorne as he trotted down the slope.

The mage kept his relaxed pace and watched a pair of rough-looking men step up to the road when it was clear that Esen intended to enter the camp. Wearing studded leather armor and swords on their hips, the pair of mercenaries stopped Esen just at the edge of the road.

Thorne stepped close to Esen's side and looked at the big man, unsure why he wasn't asking for entry into the camp. After an awkward moment of silence, from behind one of the covered wagons a man with broad shoulders and a round belly emerged. Over a simple tan garment he wore a thick brown cloak and carried a shoulder-height pole. With a full white beard and matching wiry hair, the man's head looked like a cotton ball with grey eyes.

"What can I help you travelers with?" the shepherd said as he stepped up alongside the mercenaries. "It is uncommon for people on the road to stop for the likes of us."

Esen pulled out a small charm from around his neck, which Thorne recognized as a holy symbol of the Small House, one of the more prevalent religions on the continent. "Shepherd," Esen's voice was thick with emotion, "I humbly ask for a blessing. My wife…"

Esen couldn't complete the sentence, as his last reserves of strength finally gave out. He slumped to his knees and teetered for a moment before Thorne reached out and grabbed Esen's shoulder to steady him.

"Take him to my tent," the shepherd said to one of the mercenaries. "I will be there in a moment." As Esen was half guided, half carried into the camp, the shepherd looked back towards a cluster of tents and called out, "Orin, can you come here please?"

A boy of perhaps fourteen or fifteen years left the small group of pilgrims sitting near a tent and trotted up to the shepherd. He had fair hair in need of a cut and blue eyes that looked coolly at Thorne.

"Yes, shepherd," he answered. "You called for me?"

"Orin, can you take our friend here," the shepherd said with a gesture towards the mage, "and converse with him while I tend to the hurts of a lost lamb?"

"I can do that, shepherd," the boy answered.

"There's no need," Thorne said, trying to hide his distaste for the situation. "I'm fine waiting here at the edge of the camp."

"You would refuse a chance to rest comfortably?" the shepherd said surprised. "All are welcome here, regardless of creed."

"Is that so?" Thorne said with a sneer. He pulled the Archive guilder out from under his shirt and let it fall back to his chest in plain view. "I believe our creeds, as you say, are at cross purposes."

The shepherd seemed unfazed and replied, "Not at all. In fact, talking with someone like you is all the more important for Orin to broaden his experiences and learn about the peoples of the continent."

The shepherd turned and walked back into the camp, leaving Thorne and Orin looking at each other, the mage's expression disapproving, the boy's wary.

"So you're my keeper now?" Thorne said crossing his arms on his chest. "Since I'm at your mercy, tell me how we are going to pass the time."

Orin's brow furrowed for a moment as he thought. "Let me show you something gruesome," he said eventually. "Come see our flagellant."

Thorne couldn't tell if Orin was trying to impress or shock him with such a suggestion. Without waiting to see if he was being followed, Orin turned and walked into the camp. With little alternative, Thorne trailed the boy, walking past several tents and small groups of people. The pilgrims in the camp were moving at an unhurried pace, but there seemed to be purpose in their work, whether it was tending to pots of food being cooked over low fires, deconstructing the simple tents in preparation for the day's journey, or singing hymns in quiet but clear voices.

The mage found Orin a short distance from a bare-chested human male sitting on a small keg with two females, one human and one Venhadar, attending him. The man was having a thick white paste applied to the dark skin on his arms, back, and chest. Care was being taken to cover a multitude of raw-looking wounds, and the man was doing his best to keep a serene face, though it was obvious he was in pain.

"There's our flagellant," Orin said, pointing at the man.

The two attendants looked up at Orin and gave chastising looks, but returned to their work when they saw Thorne there with them. Clearly they did not want to say something with the mage present.

"He looks hurt," Thorne replied, not knowing what else to say. He had been brought up in a secular family, and consequently the rituals of the continent's religions were mostly lost on him. However, something about the paste's sheen on the flagellant's skin seemed familiar, and it took him a moment to recognize it.

"No, he's fine. They're putting medicine on him," Orin answered.

The mage watched the attendants work in silence for a bit longer before he turned to Orin and asked, "What happened to him?"

Orin pointed to a flail on the ground near the man's feet. "He whips himself so we don't get hurt on the pilgrimage. He makes sure the trinity keeps us safe."

Thorne looked over his shoulder and scanned the camp. He was able to easily identify a number of hired swords that were milling about the tents or watching the road. "No," he replied, "I'm pretty sure it's the mercenaries that keep you safe."

Orin either did not hear the comment or ignored it and continued, "He whips himself every day, but he never gets sick because of the medicine they put on him. It's very special because it helps him heal faster."

"You might be told that divine influence protects your pilgrimage, but it is the ingenuity of mortals that keep him alive," Thorne said gesturing towards the paste being applied to the flagellant. "That's an Archive-made salve they're putting on him."

"How do you know?" Orin asked with an indignant expression.

"I'm from the Archive," the mage replied.

The boy's expression changed to one of curiosity, and he asked, "Are you a wizard?"

Thorne's expression soured even further. "We don't like that term," he said. "We prefer to be called mages or alchemists."

"What's the difference?" he asked.

"Perhaps to you nothing," Thorne said, "but I think you can at least appreciate that words have power. Wizard is a word that has a lot of history attached to it, not all good."

Orin was quiet for a moment, and Thorne briefly thought he might have made an impression on the boy. "Can I see some magic?" Orin asked.

"No," Thorne answered as he slumped in disappointment. "Why not?"

Thorne's agitation was turning into anger. "Magic is not for entertainment, but to learn about the workings of the world and shaping it for the better."

"The shepherd says that the trinity makes the world better. He tells us stories from the journals about how we can do it too."

"So the various races of the continent actually make the world better, right?" Thorne asked rhetorically. "Not some invisible, yet mysteriously benevolent presence?"

"I don't know," Orin said, his voice sounding unsure. "But I can show you something that proves it. Wait here." He quickly disappeared behind one of the covered wagons.

"Proves what? Well that's what I get for arguing religion with a child," Thorne said looking up at the brightening morning sky.

"The young often see more clearly the truth of things," the flagellant answered from across the open space. "Magic is a divine gift, even if its practitioners do not share such faith."

Thorne's gaze returned to the earth. The attendants had finished applying the salve to the man's body and he now sat alone with his forearms resting his knees. The mage walked up to him and looked down. "The religious, regardless of age, all have the same view of magic. The only way they can justify its existence is by saying magic is a divine gift. Otherwise it lessens the power of whatever gods they worship," Thorne said.

"Is that so?" the flagellant said as he ran a hand over his cropped black hair. "Only the earthly races care about how power is allocated. About who has it and who doesn't. The power of the trinity is without limit, so giving some of their divine light to those who want to work magic is a small thing."

Thorne found his hands were in tight fists. Experiencing

firsthand the calm confidence that bordered on smugness of the pious left the mage infuriated. "Power without limit?" he scoffed. "You've moved beyond magic and into the realm of fantasy. The world has physical rules that must be obeyed, and while mages can bend those rules, they are absolute. The elemental manipulations and alchemistic transformations at the Archive are real and tangible. Your belief in a triad of deities with infinite power? They cannot exist, and if they do, why would they waste their time on us?"

The flagellant chuckled, which only raised Thorne's ire further. "Do you find something funny?" the mage accused.

"Only that you sound more like a zealot than any Small House evangelist, and I doubt you will find any willing to become Archive converts here," the flagellant answered. "The Archive works with the various guilds, principalities, and religions of the continent, and would do well to remember they are just one piece on a very large and complex puzzle."

Thorne felt the flush of shame on his face at his outburst. He should know better than to malign someone of faith, in their own pilgrimage camp no less. "You sound more educated than most on the basic workings of the intricacies that drive modern society," he said, trying to calm down.

"Perhaps, but what I have learned is not important for the time being. During this pilgrimage I have forgotten my past life and even my name. Until we have completed our journey I am only the flagellant, and my duty is to suffer for the good of the group."

"You volunteered?"

"Of course," the flagellant said. "Suffering under duress is torture, but to suffer as a calling, as part of your faith, that is divine. While large, there is a finite amount of suffering in the world. If I can take more of it during the pilgrimage, then that means there is less for others to endure. I would even go so far as to argue that this sacrifice is not so different from the time when your magic first manifested itself. When you realized you were born into magic, did you not feel it was your duty to master it?"

"You are mistaken that I was born with magic," Thorne said. "I chose to have my mind unlocked, so I am what is known as a made mage."

"I see," the flagellant said contemplatively. "Then your conviction is undeniably stronger, fully knowing the sacrifices required to obtain arcane ability. You are much braver than I am."

Thorne was about to ask what the flagellant meant when Orin came back around the covered wagon. He held something tightly in his hand and wore a smug smile. "I have something for you," he told the mage.

"What?"

Orin grabbed Thorne's hand and slapped something into his open palm. Searing pain instantly shot up the mage's arm. Thorne yelled and jerked back his hand, letting the object fall to the ground. He looked at his hand and wished he hadn't. Three thick lines were burned black into his palm. The skin surrounding the burn was bright red and underneath the mage could see his veins were an unnerving ashen color.

Orin gasped when he saw the mage's wound. Bending over he picked up a small metal symbol, three parallel bars very similar to what Esen wore around his neck. The boy looked at the symbol and then to Thorne's hand. His eyes got wide and he said aghast, "You're a demon!"

"Get that away from me," Thorne hissed through clenched teeth as Orin waved the trinity symbol at him. "It's the iron in your ornament, not some holy power, that burned me."

"Orin, step back!" the flagellant said hopping off of the keg. He inserted himself between Thorne and the boy. "Mages are very sensitive to iron because the magic they use reacts badly with it."

"I'll go get the shepherd!" Orin shouted as he took off into the camp before he could be stopped.

Careful to avoid his fresh wounds, the flagellant scrapped up some white paste off his chest and offered it to the mage. "I don't know much about your condition, the Iron Bane, but I do know that you need this more than I do at the moment."

Scooping up the salve from the flagellant's hand, Thorne caught a glimpse of an expensive looking chain and the edge of a guild medallion tucked into the flagellant's waistband. The mage couldn't identify the guild, but it seemed that the flagellant was someone of standing. He gingerly rubbed the salve into the three burned grooves in his palm. At first there was a feeling of cold and shortly thereafter of nothing as the numbing effect of the paste deadened the nerves in his hand. The other chemicals in the salve would help with infection if his skin had been broken, and also with any swelling he would experience with the iron burn. It wasn't the first time he had gotten one, and would probably not be the last, but it was still an extremely painful experience he would have liked to avoid on the open road.

"Thank you," Thorne was able to say once he lost feeling in his injured hand. "I know that salve is in short supply on a pilgrimage."

"I'm happy to be of help," the flagellant said. He looked down at the streaks on his chest and added with a smile, "I'll just need to be careful where I strike with my flail on today's walk."

Orin returned with the shepherd in tow, the former with a panicked expression, the latter with one of genial confusion. "Is everything all right, Master mage?" the shepherd asked once he stopped in front of Thorne. "Orin told me you were hurt."

The mage covered his injury with his good hand and replied, "A small burn, but nothing too concerning." He paused when he noticed that the foreigner was not with them. "Where is Esen?"

The shepherd looked at the flagellant and then at Thorne before he replied, "Come walk with me. The flagellant needs to complete his morning prayers before we leave for the day. Orin, please continue with your duties." He ushered the mage forward towards the road.

Once they were isolated from the other pilgrims, the shepherd bade Thorne to stop. Both men looked back up the hill that returned to Yaboon as the sun rose in the sky. While the shepherd watched the rise, Thorne took the opportunity to more carefully examine his burned hand. Grimacing at the ugly sight, the mage realized he would have to be more careful. If a pilgrim's trinket could injure him, then even a glancing blow from a knife or sword could be fatal. He made a mental note to keep Garret's training and soldier's mantras more in the forefront of his mind while on the open road.

"Esen is exhausted," the shepherd finally said. "He is in need of both physical and mental respite. He is resting in one of our covered wagons that were designed to carry the sick and injured on our pilgrimage. Thankfully those are few in number, so there is ample space for him. I offered to transport him to Port, as that is your destination. It is on our way, but he seemed reluctant and wanted me to ask you."

"Why?" Thorne asked with a creased brow.

"He trusts your judgment," the shepherd answered.

"I can't say the same," Thorne replied. "I met him just last night. We're little more than strangers."

"Even so," the shepherd said. "There must be some reason why you are helping him."

The mage remained silent. It didn't feel right lying to a holy man, but telling the truth wasn't much better. Thorne had told Esen that he would help him find his wife, and he would, but a part of him felt guilty about how Esen was being used as a means to advance his standing in the Paragon program.

As if sensing Thorne's unease, the shepherd said, "Well, I suppose it doesn't matter why. Esen is grateful."

"He said that?" Thorne asked.

"Not in those words," the shepherd admitted, "but he spoke of how you left everything you were doing in the city behind to take him to Port. I can only assume that he's grateful to have an Archive mage as an ally."

From atop the hill in the distance Thorne noticed a small puff of dust. Traveling down the hill it grew in size leaving Thorne to guess a rapid transport was approaching. These vehicles were the fastest means of travel across the continent, and given the extreme rarity of horses, they were the only way to make good time between cities. Typically only high-level guild members or members of the prince's court could afford using them. While walking from Yaboon to Port would take a full thirty-hour day, a rapid transport could manage it in less than half that time.

Watching the dust cloud as it raced down the hill, it dawned on Thorne that they had spent more time in the camp than he had anticipated, but given Esen's state they might actually travel faster with the pilgrims. "Alright," the mage said finally, "we'll travel with you for the day."

"Very good," the shepherd replied. Following Thorne's gaze up the rise to the rapid transport and added, "Someone must be in a hurry. We too should be on our way. Come."

The mage followed the shepherd towards the interior of the camp where the two covered wagons were located. While the shepherd showed Thorne where Esen was resting amongst the other sick and injured pilgrims, the rapid transport thundered past. He felt the vibrations of hooves pounding the ground as a team of four powerful caribou strained against their harnesses while pulling a small lightweight carriage. The driver atop the coach was hunched over and his gloved hands gripped the reins tightly.

After the vehicle had passed and the dust was settling back down on the prince's road, Thorne absently wished that he and Esen could have secured such a way to Port. The din from the charging caribou would have left his ears ringing after the journey, but the mage thought that would have been preferable as the pilgrimage began to sing their morning hymns in full-throated exultation.

CHAPTER NINE

Reihana stepped out of the rapid transport in front of the Port stables, eager to be free from the small carriage. Six high bells had just rung from the carillon nearby. It was mid-morning and she had made good time from the Yaboon Archive despite last night's debacle.

Thorne's appearance at the infirmary was extremely problematic. He had stopped her assassination attempt and put the Archive on high alert. Worse, Thorne had used Paragon techniques that were seen by the constables, which meant that Olaf would have some very hard questions for her when she returned. She had to quickly find and silence the foreigner. After the confrontation in the infirmary, there was never any question in her mind that Thorne had to be killed as well. What he knew about Claire's abduction could destroy everything she had been secretly building up. His family history suggested that he'd never be won over to join her crusade, and being a made mage, Reihana didn't think Thorne would have been of much use anyway. His inclusion in the program was a terrible mistake.

"Give my regards to Ormand," she said looking up at the coachman, referring to the transport guild secretary. It was a letter bearing his signature and seal that allowed her to get a carriage and be out of Yaboon with a quickness that was typically reserved for high-ranking Sovereignty representatives. She was still pleased with herself in the decision to align first with the transport guild. It had made some of her plans easier to execute, especially ones where she needed to travel into the neighboring provinces and return to the Yaboon Archive before her absence became suspicious.

As Reihana walked the short distance to the harbor, she replayed the last several hours in her mind. After hiding her black robe and gloves outside the Archive, she hastily navigated back alleys and side streets to a tavern in a more affluent section of the city where she was known. Trying to appear as though she was casually stopping by for a drink and the company of some non-scholars, Reihana sat in a small booth along the wall and tried to figure out her next move.

Given the foreigner's tenacity, it was most likely he would continue searching for his wife despite the assassination attempt. With Thorne helping, they would go to Port and get passage back to Haywood where Geridan administered the glassblower guild. With no way to know where Claire was at the moment, going back to her father was the most logical move and one Thorne would be smart enough to pursue. However if Thorne and the foreigner got to Geridan before she could find them, a nasty revelation would be waiting for them regarding the guild master. Thinking a bit deeper, her smile faded. Geridan would certainly be unimpressed with her work if Thorne and the foreigner confronted him before Claire was returned.

She had left the tavern without finishing her drink and went straight to the transport guild stables. Cashing in more than a few long held favors, she secured a rapid transport for Port and rode through the night. She had dozed lightly until sunlight bled through the thin curtains inside the carriage. A short time later she was inside the walls of Port, the largest merchant marine city in Yaboon province. It was a safe assumption that she would pass Thorne and the foreigner somewhere along the way given the latter's injuries and that both were traveling on foot. Getting to Port first meant she had a bit of time to cast a wide net to catch them.

The air was saturated with briny sea odors and a tinge of smoke as Reihana walked perpendicular to the broad wooden piers in the harbor. She stopped near one where a pallet of crates was being loaded into a ship that had a mining guild flag drifting in the breeze. There were calls to and from the ship as crew and stevedores jostled each other on the ramp while attending to their respective duties. About halfway out on the pier a man in guild regalia sternly watched the proceedings, a large leather-bound ledger tucked under his thick arm.

Approaching him, Reihana stopped a few steps short behind and waited to be noticed. Her hands were close together at her waist, fingertips lightly touching together in an inverted steeple. She attempted to look relaxed and agreeable while trying to catch the man's eye. When he turned to watch a pair of stevedores pick up a heavy crate, the guild official finally acknowledged her.

"What're you about, eh?" he drawled, giving her an askew look up and down.

"I'm here to warn you about a dangerous criminal, a mage," she answered gravely. "He'll be traveling with a foreigner from the southern continent. Are you the lieutenant of this ship?"

"Yup. And who're you, eh?"

Reihana worked to keep her composure. It seemed this fellow had a rather irksome habit of making every utterance a question. "My name is Iris," she said, using one of the many pseudonyms she adopted when leaving Yaboon unannounced. "I'm an Archive mage tasked with tracking down and capturing one of my brethren who has gone rogue."

"This is a cargo ship, eh? We don't take passengers."

"They're still going to try and barter passage with someone here," Reihana said. "You'll naturally deny them, but I'm asking you to contact the harbormaster if you see them. I need to catch them quickly." She briefly gave a physical description of Thorne and the foreigner.

"Have the City Watch help you, eh?" the lieutenant said when she was finished. He wasn't really paying her much attention anymore at this point, but instead resumed watching the crates being loaded onto the ship. He pulled out the ledger from under his arm, undid the buckle, and flipped to the last page that had notes.

"They're smart enough to evade the City Watch," Reihana said, trying to hard to hide her impatience.

"They won't be getting on my ship, eh? Can't promise if I'll inform the harbormaster, though. Very busy today, eh?"

"Then send one of your crew with a message."

The lieutenant snapped the ledger shut and scowled at Reihana. "You think I'll waste time and effort for this, eh? I've no interest in your mage friend, or you. Neither of you are going to make me any money, so why don't you be on your way, eh?"

Reihana opened her mouth to reply, but then clamped it shut. Arguing with the mariner would be fruitless. He clearly didn't understand the relationship between the Archives and the major guilds, likely because his authority went no further than this ship and he never interacted with senior guild leadership in any meaningful way. She supposed it was to be expected, given that the Archive's work for the major guilds dealt in trade secrets and enabling technologies developed specific to each guild.

"Thank you for your time," she said, her deferential tone evaporated. Quickly turning, she left the pier and looked over to the next ship in the harbor.

Fortunately, her attempt at getting help from a second guild ship representative was met with better results, as did her third. Both had agreed to notify the harbormaster if a mage or a foreigner tried to get onto their respective ships. Reihana felt better that now that it would be much harder for Thorne to escape via the harbor. By now, eight high bells had run out across the harbor indicating it was noon. As the day got hotter the work on the docks would steadily decrease until after the sun had set. There would then be a flurry of activity as ships scheduled to leave on the evening tide were prepped for voyage. She'd return later and approach members of the stevedore guild. It would likely take a bribe to get their help, but given that they'd be constantly walking the docks while loading cargo, someone was sure to spot Thorne.

Reihana returned to where several of the streets from the city converged in front of the harbormaster's office. The heavily varnished single-story building was little more than a large shed with a single window left open to let some light and fresh air inside. She went to it and pulled open the door wondering if she'd have better luck with a Sovereignty official rather than a guild mariner.

Inside, a large dark green curtain hung from the ceiling dividing the single room. In the small area where she stood a long counter separated those who entered from the space in the rear of the building. Behind the counter a young man dressed in a uniform that was too big for him sat and studied a stack of documents. He looked up and raised a hand in silent greeting.

Giving a small smile, Reihana stepped to the counter and said, "Is the harbormaster in? I am Master Iris, an Archive mage."

"Ah," the youth vocalized as he studied her for a moment while tucking a lock of dark hair back behind his ear. Turning his head toward the curtain, he called out, "Harbormaster Jenma, an Archive mage would like to speak with you."

There was a moment of silence before a curt voice replied, "Send her back."

Reihana stepped around the counter past the clerk and slowly pulled back the thick curtain. Along the walls were low shelves full of books, naval navigation equipment, and large rolled-up documents that Reihana surmised were maps. A breeze from the open window shifted the curtain behind Reihana after she let it go.

The harbormaster sitting behind a cheaply constructed desk was a Sehenryu female, the fine fur on her exposed arms a patchwork of black and white. The tailored vest she wore was embroidered with the emblem of the Yaboon Sovereignty. Short whiskers protruding from her cheeks coupled with vibrant green eyes gave her an intensely alert visage.

"What business does the Archive have in Port today?" Jenma asked in a reserved tone.

"I'm trying to find a mage who has gone rogue," Reihana said, doing her best to sound concerned.

"Missing persons are the domain of the City Watch or the mercenary guild."

"You don't understand. This man is dangerous and will try to sneak onto a ship to escape me. I've already discussed the matter with several guild ships and if they see him, they're going to report to you. I need to search elsewhere in the city where he might hide, so can you send a messenger to *The Hornet's Nest* if contacted? If I could entreat your office to help find him, the Archive would reward you handsomely."

Jenma leaned back in her seat. One of her ears twitched on top of her head. "What did he do?" she asked as she reached up to scratch it.

"That's Archive business," Reihana said quickly. Leaning in towards Jenma, she added, "This is not a waste of your time. This is important."

"Is that so?" Jenma asked, lowering her hand and narrowing her eyes.

There was an uncomfortable moment of silence before Reihana realized that Jenma was scanning her. The harbormaster's empathic powers, innate in all Sehenryu, were probing her emotional state. Jenma couldn't read her exact thoughts, but would be able to feel any emotions that might betray duplicitous intent.

Reihana emptied her mind of everything save her need to find Thorne. She inwardly focused on that single thought while outwardly tried to have a patient expression, as if being scanned wasn't a problem. "I understand this is rather uncommon," she said seriously. "But due to its extreme urgency I didn't have time to get a letter of introduction from the Archive, or even collect my guilder."

"I see," Jenma replied thoughtfully.

"So, is there anything you can do?"

"No, I don't think so."

"Oh?" Reihana said, more than a little surprised. "Why not?"

Jenma sat up straight in her chair and answered, "To be blunt, mages can be useful, but you are a strange lot and are to be dealt with only when necessary."

Reihana barked a mirthless laugh and then said, "That's a rather common view of those who deal with the Archive rarely, but I would argue that the major guilds have greatly benefited from working with us."

"If the guild ships have already promised you that your rogue mage won't be granted passage, then the task now falls upon you to apprehend him," Jenma said. "However as a Sovereignty agent, I'm interested only in official business. Do you have any?"

Reihana sensed the warning in Jenma's voice. "I apologize for wasting your time," she said. "You're right that my request would be better fulfilled elsewhere."

Jenma nodded and then returned to reading her ledger, giving Reihana time to make a quick retreat back outside to where the streets met the harbor. Once back in the sunshine, she took a deep breath to shake off the unpleasant feelings from her last conversation.

As she walked up the nearest avenue, she considered which aspect of her spy network to deploy next. It would be a porous net she was laying given the relatively few agents she had in the city, but as Thorne was equally unprepared from his flight from the Archive, Reihana was confident that she could still catch him before he got on a ship. She hastened her pace into the city interior.

· · ·

The Hornet's Nest was the type of tavern that mariners loved, and anyone who wanted peace and quiet hated. At night its windows were wide open for songs, cursing, and general rabble rousing to reverberate out onto what was known by locals as Stagger Street due to the high density of ale houses located there. However during the day, it was a much quieter locale, and as Reihana pushed open the door not long after nine high bells, shortly after most people took their mid-day meal, she found the main room sparsely populated. Three people were spaced out along the bar, each leaning over a bowl or mug and paying little attention to her as she crossed the threshold. The barman was slouching on the back wall and watched her enter with a lazy disinterest. At a table near the cold hearth a Venhadar female and a human woman, both wearing grimy aprons, were sitting close together in quiet conversation, the latter with her long hair pulled up away from her face. Reihana made a straight line for the barmaids. They looked up in her direction, but only one recognized her.

"Reihana," the Venhadar said, standing up and resting her hands on the back of her chair to put some distance between them. The human woman slid out of her seat and quickly retreated behind the bar to watch at a safe distance.

"Brein," Reihana returned evenly. The barmaid had become one her spies before Reihana had learned a hard lesson to hide her identity and was one of the few in the city that knew her real name. "I trust your father is doing well?"

"He's surviving. If he could be treated at your Archive's infirmary I'm sure he'd be doing much better."

"While Crumst disease isn't contagious to humans or Sehenryu, any Venhadar mage would be at great risk if he was brought in for care. You very well know he'd be turned away to protect those at the Archive, which is why I offered to deliver to you the very expensive medicines you need to keep him alive."

"Yes, for a cost. What do you want?"

Reihana tolerated her acid tone because she knew that Brein loved her father more than anything else and would continue to serve as her agent as long as the life preserving medicines kept being supplied periodically to the tavern. Brein would never be her best spy, but she would stay loyal for fear of losing Reihana's lifeline.

"Just information this time. Have the mariners talked about any unusual passengers they've picked up? I'm looking for a mage named Thorne and a foreigner from the south."

"I don't know."

"I need to find him and I can't return to the Archive until I do. How is your current medicine supply?"

"It's very nearly gone, as I'm sure you are well aware."

"Indeed, so I think it best if you help me find him."

Brein glared at her, but said, "I'll talk to the girls. We'll find them for you."

"See that you do. I will return later tonight. Give your father my regards."

Without waiting for a response, Reihana turned and walked out of the tavern. The afternoon daylight was still bright enough that she had to stop and squint as her eyes adjusted. It took a frustratingly long time. The Iron Bane had been cruel enough to attack her vision first.

Through teary eyes, Reihana saw someone standing a short distance from her in the street. While she couldn't yet make out much detail, whoever it was wore the unmistakable travel pack of an Archive apprentice on their traveling education. The person looked around and appeared lost by the way they shuffled in place and turned around repeatedly.

After rubbing her eyes and forcing them into focus, Reihana saw a short man with blonde hair and a matching beard. He was dressed for travel, with the cuffs of his trousers starting to fray and his boots covered in layers of dirt.

"Are you lost, apprentice?" she called out to him.

"Just getting my bearings, thank you," he replied in a friendly though slightly dismissive tone.

"Where are you trying to go?" Reihana tried again to engage him in a conversation.

"Well I just got here, to Port I mean."

Reihana could sense the apprentice's apprehension. The Archive had frequently warned those going on their traveling education about overly friendly strangers. "Be at ease, apprentice," she said. "I am Master Iris from the Yaboon Archive. You're unfamiliar to me, so where is your home Archive?"

"Barnterc," he replied. "Sorry to be so suspicious, but if you're an Archive mage, show me your guilder."

"I don't have mine right now," Reihana said. "But give me one of your glow spheres and I'll prove it. What's your name?"

"Um, call me Ed," he said while slinging his travel pack to the ground. He jammed a hand into one of the outer pockets and pulled out a small globe made from translucent resin.

Taking the sphere from Ed, Reihana hefted it a few times in her hand. The material had less desirable optical properties than those used on the walls of the Archive, but it was much more durable and therefore useful out in the real world. She wrapped her fingers around it and pushed some of her mana into the resin. The charged sphere began to glow brightly white, easily visible even in the afternoon daylight. She then shifted the color to vibrant blue, and then finally to magenta before retrieving her mana and extinguishing the light.

"Satisfied, Ed?" she asked, offering back the glow sphere. "Will that get me a bit of trust?"

Taking back his light, Ed replied, "Yes it will, Master Iris."

"No need for honorifics here, Ed," she said with an understanding grin. "We're not at the Archive. Now, I'm actually very happy to have run into you because I could use your help."

"Really? With what?"

"I'm tracking down one of our mages that went rogue. Nasty business too, running unsanctioned alchemic experiments. Nearly killed someone too and now he's fled. The council put an internal bounty on him."

"It's that bad?"

"Unfortunately so," Reihana continued to lie, "and councilor Tarbeck wants him taken back to the Yaboon Archive so his Awareness can be bound."

Ed took a step backwards as if struck. "Incredible!" he exclaimed. "They'd seal his magic away?"

"He's not going to come back quietly either. The last I heard, he was traveling with a foreigner from the southern continent. This mage, his name is Thorne, looks unremarkable, but the man he's traveling with would be easy to spot."

"And you need my help to find him?"

"Quick study," Reihana said approvingly. "But remember,

Thorne is dangerous. Don't confront him. If you see him or his companion, come back here to *The Hornet's Nest* and talk to a Venhadar barmaid named Brein. She's one of my agents. Understand?"

Ed nodded.

"Now I know you're on your traveling education, so I just need your help for the next day or two. After that you can be on your way to wherever you're traveling next."

"I'll do what I can. I don't want this fellow giving mages a bad name. We've got our work cut out for us as it is now." Ed picked up his pack from the street and hefted it onto his back, then said, "Good hunting, Master Iris."

As the apprentice walked towards the harbor, Reihana nodded and felt a small amount of satisfaction. One more mage aligned with her. Ed might not be immediately useful for her ultimate goal, but the more groundwork she laid now and contacts she collected would only benefit her once she finally moved to exert her will on the Archive and shake the council out of their stagnant ways.

As she turned Reihana noticed that one of the people who was previously sitting at the bar in *The Hornet's Nest* was now loitering near the street corner. The human woman was thin with dark features and a quick manner that suggested a hard life lived on the street. Reihana now questioned the wisdom of her very public discussion of Thorne with Ed. The day prior he had reported that he had spies in Port, and perhaps it was his network that was making him so hard to find.

Her mood once again soured as she spun on her heel and stormed up the street away from the harbor. She had a few guild contacts left to interrogate, and perhaps they could help her get some supplies for a longer search. She was becoming less hopeful that this would be over quickly.

• • •

Reihana returned to the docks once the carillon towers had rung out four low bells. The tide would be going out soon and she wanted to watch if any ships were preparing to set sail. Her search had been fruitless during the day and none of her spies had seen or heard anything about Thorne or the foreigner. They had to be in this city, but where?

The sky was clear and had taken the purplish hue of waning twilight. In the still air Reihana could hear the slow groans of ships rubbing against their moorings. With the day's work done and cargo secured, the taverns would now be packed and the docks nearly empty. Occasionally a mariner left their ship and ambled into the city, or a Sovereignty official would appear to survey cargo for tax assessment before returning to their comfortable offices near the governor's estate. From the streets leading into the city, Reihana could see the glow of street lamps lit by the City Watch. Save for a few lanterns hung from large hooks on the docks, the harbor was only going to grow darker as the night drew on.

Reihana glanced up from where she stood at the pair of huge warehouses a short distance from the docks. As a holding area for whatever goods were being shipped, the cavernous buildings were owned and operated by the stevedore's guild. She craned her neck up to take in all of one two-story building with blue-gray stained walls and thick iron bars protecting the sparse glass windows on each level. The huge gate that opened to the platform leading to the piers was closed and bolted from the inside, with a smaller door just around the corner on the side of the building facing a narrow alleyway.

While deciding where to go next, she heard a shrill whistle from one of the docks, followed by a catcall. Reihana ignored it until she realized it was directed at her. She turned and saw three brawny figures walking toward her. Though it was difficult to make out their features in the rapidly fading dusk, she could see that all three were bare-chested, with nearly matching loose pants and heavy boots. Two of them had long knives sheathed on their belts. As they drew closer, Reihana could smell them, a noxious mix of greasy sweat and seawater.

The apparent leader of the trio looked at his mates, chuckled crudely, and then said, "I was right. This here was the same bitch who was snooping around the docks this morning. What you looking for?"

"I'm looking for a mage and a foreigner," Reihana answered evenly.

"Nah," replied one of them, "I'm thinking you're looking for a good time. We'll give ya one."

Reihana's features darkened slightly, but inwardly she felt some relief. Finally, she had an opportunity to vent the built up aggravations from the day. Making sure to keep her eyes on the three mariners, she slowly backed around the building and down the alleyway. If she kept going the long alleyway would open into the wide streets near the harbor. It was very unlikely that there would be any people around who could help her, but she didn't want or need help. On the contrary, she wanted to make sure that what was about to happen was not witnessed by anyone.

The three mariners came around the corner and spread out to block the way they had come from the harbor. "Where do you think you're off to, darlin'?" one of them said with a leer.

About a third of the way down the alleyway Reihana stopped next to a window on the building to her right. As the mariners stalked towards her, she pulled her right sleeve over her hand and slid it between the iron bars. Wiggling two fingers free, she charged them with a burst of mana and then pressed them on the glass.

A web of cracks raced across the window an instant before the glass shattered. As Reihana yanked her hand back, the sharp shards followed. Manipulating the glass required a combination of techniques, wind and gravity, which was tricky even for many Master mages, but it something she had learned long ago. Intent on unleashing a more effective attack here than the one against Thorne in the Archive infirmary, Reihana sent the glass streaking towards the mariners with deadly force.

One of the mariners was quick enough to hide behind the leader whose bare chest was pierced multiple times by shards of glass. His last breath came out as a sighing grunt as he collapsed to the ground and did not move again. The remaining mariner received several slashes on his legs and crashed to the ground close to his now dead comrade.

"You cunt!" The injured mariner bellowed as he tried to prop himself up. Looking up at his uninjured companion, he yelled, "Cut her down!" before rolling onto his back and clutching his leg.

The uninjured mariner ripped his knife free and positioned himself into a fighter's stance.

His wariness gave Reihana the time needed to summon a mana gauntlet on each arm, with an arcane blade protruding over her right hand. Not waiting for the mariner to attack first, Reihana dashed forward and tried to slap away the mariner's knife with her left hand.

The mariner instinctively slashed and the steel blade bounced off of the arcane energy of Reihana's mana gauntlet.

Seeing an opening, Reihana darted forward and slashed at the mariner with deceptive agility.

The mariner twisted to the side to avoid the strike and ended up with his back against the wall of the warehouse.

Charging mana into her left palm, Reihana thrust a column of wind into the mariner and knocked him hard into the side of the building. With her target momentarily stunned, Reihana drove her mana knife deep into his chest. She wrenched the arcane blade to widen the wound before letting the slain mariner drop to the ground.

As the last living mariner watched while she approached, the fear in his voice was unmistakable. "Who are you?" he gasped.

Reihana had narrowed eyes as she stood over him. "I am your death," she replied.

Once she was done, Reihana stepped out of the alleyway feeling much better and scanned the docks. Port was a large city, but Thorne had to be here somewhere. Looking back at the alleyway she briefly thought about hiding the slain mariners, but decided it wasn't worth the effort. Killings in Port were not uncommon and the docks had a reputation for being very dangerous at night. The City Watch would most likely reason that the grisly scene was the outcome of a dice game that went wrong and ignore the peculiarity of the mariners' wounds. She casually walked toward a ship prepping for departure, the mana rush from the violence just a few minutes prior already gone.

CHAPTER TEN

The sun was setting and the gates of Port were within sight when the pilgrimage stopped to set up camp. As part of their vows of self-reliance, they relinquished the comforts of civilized living and only ventured into populated places to pray at special shrines along their pilgrimage route or to draw water when what they carried was exhausted. Already having adequate water and with Port being a city of economic and not religious importance, the pilgrims seemed content to set up their tents within an arrow's shot of a soft bed and hot food that was better than what came from their communal cauldrons.

Thorne had sullenly nursed his injured hand and rebuffed the occasional attempts at conversation by a few curious pilgrims. As a result he was largely ignored as they walked, which allowed him to listen and watch the various peoples in the caravan. All three races of the continent were represented, short and burly Venhadar, feline Sehenryu, and humans. After listening to smatterings of their conversations and the lyrics of the hymns sung throughout the day, Thorne realized that his belief system couldn't be more different than theirs and consequently dismissed them as simple and dull.

Thorne's feelings for the caravan were universal, save for the flagellant. The mage had watched and still could not fathom why someone would voluntarily whip themselves for hours to appease some imagined deity. The flagellant had stayed in the middle of the procession throughout the day's march, and while his singing was not as loud as those around him, the sound of his flail slapping his bare torso could clearly be heard. The mage had to admit that the sting of the flagellant's words about magic being a divine gift had hurt more than the iron burn, or at least had stayed on his mind longer.

He decided that standing at the edge of the camp looking at the city was not going to make the gates of Port draw any nearer and found himself wading deep into the camp to find Esen. Coming around one of the covered wagons, Thorne discovered the foreigner talking quietly to the flagellant, while two attendants wiped blood off of his back and did their best to make him comfortable.

"How are you feeling?" Thorne asked Esen when he joined them.

"Better," Esen said with a coldness that the mage found strange. "By the grace of the trinity and the generosity of the shepherd, I was able to rest much of the day's travel inside that wagon."

One of the flagellant's attendants retrieved a short barrel and a steaming bowl of soup from the camp and handed the meal to him after the battered man settled onto the impromptu seat. Between sips of soup the flagellant asked Thorne, "And how is your hand? I've heard that iron burns can be crippling if severe enough."

The mage looked down at his palm and slowly flexed his fingers. The blackened veins had returned to their normal color, but the angry red burns in his skin would be there for some time. Thankfully, there was just a familiar soreness and not any concerning pain. It would be weeks until he could hold a stylus comfortably again, but his hand was fully functional.

"I'll be fine," Thorne tried to say casually. "It pales in comparison to what you put yourself through today. Some of those gashes look rather deep."

"Yes," Esen said pointedly, giving Thorne a sour look before his expression softened as he addressed the flagellant. "Thank you for lessening my and Thorne's suffering today. I will pray for your continued strength of will and for the safe passage of the pilgrimage. Where is your next shrine?"

The flagellant gave Esen a grateful though tight-lipped smile and replied, "Your prayers are appreciated. Haven is still many days of travel away, but there we will find some respite inside the city's shrine. That is where we are going next, still walking the prince's road."

Thorne looked in the direction of Port and said to Esen, "If we want to find a ship captain while they are still sober, then we best be on our way. Once on land, mariners do little other than sleep, drink, or brawl." He started walking to the edge of the camp, but felt that Esen was not following. Looking over his shoulder, the mage found that Esen had remained in place, but was giving him a disapproving expression that bordered on anger. Still perplexed by the foreigner's behavior, Thorne called back, "What is it? Have you changed your mind about finding your wife?"

The bluntness of the question seemed to shock the antagonism out of Esen, and he quickly joined the mage and kept pace with him as they walked past the mercenaries stationed at the edge of the camp. Thorne noticed none of the fatigue from the day prior in the foreigner's posture and was impressed and more than a little jealous of Esen's quick recuperation. In Port he knew of a few shops that catered to alchemists and mages, and he would be able to get another small jar of salve that would accelerate his own recovery.

"It'll be dark soon, so the docks will mostly be empty," the mage said absently. "And those hanging out there aren't people we want to tangle with at night. We best find a boarding house and hope to not catch any fleas before morning."

"If you say so," Esen responded shortly.

Thorne stopped and turned to face the foreigner. "Is there something on your mind?" the mage asked with an edge in his voice.

Esen folded his arms across his broad chest and leveled a stern look at the mage. "You've been welcomed into the pilgrimage, but your behavior has been ungrateful," he said. "I am ashamed to be associated with you."

"That's what this is about?" Thorne asked slightly exasperated. He glanced at the open gates of Port before returning to stare down Esen. "Things are about to get a lot less comfortable than traveling in a pilgrim wagon," the mage said. "And I can assure you that none of your overly religious friends would be much help where we're going. Be angry if you must, but soon enough you'll be thankful that someone pragmatic like an Archive mage is your ally now."

"That remains to be seen," Esen said resuming his walk towards the city.

At the entrance to the city a pair of sentries stopped them. They looked like new recruits by their relatively unwrinkled faces and the newness of their City Watch tabards. "State your business," one of the gatekeepers said with a mixture of authority and boredom.

"Transport to Banks," Thorne said quickly before Esen could answer for them. "Archive business," he added holding up the apprentice guilder he had obtained at the *Blue Beryl*.

"Courtesy of which guild?" the Watchman asked.

Thorne felt a jolt of fear as he realized his mistake. The mage had been so fixated on what needed to be done at the harbor he had forgotten what it would take to just get into the city. To be allowed transport on a guild ship usually required a passenger contract, and had an associated fee paid to the guild. This fee was taxed, and therefore guild ship transport was usually arranged far in advance.

"Glassmakers," Esen answered. "Guild master Geridan's daughter Claire is also a passenger. She should have arrived before us."

"That well may be," the sentry said. "Do you have a letter of introduction?"

Thorne said quickly, "Since we started our journey after Claire we rushed, and in our haste forgot the letter."

"Without a letter, we will need to verify this with the ship captain," the sentry said. After taking their names, he pointed Thorne and Esen towards a patch of ground that had been worn bare by a multitude of others who had waited for entry into the city.

Esen continued to act standoffish, which left Thorne to alternate between watching the pilgrimage make camp and stealing glances past the remaining sentry and into the streets of Port. The mage looked up at the battlements above the gate and counted no fewer than a dozen bowmen, with more than a few watching closely.

The sentry Thorne had talked to returned much more quickly than expected, which seemed to be a bad sign. He stepped up to Thorne and Esen and said flatly, "Glassmaker guild ship left here two days ago. They're well south now along the coast."

"Then we'll arrange passage on another guild ship going to Banks," Thorne said with more irritation than was probably prudent given the situation. He held up the Archive medallion again and continued, "We're not some pair of vagabonds looking to stir up trouble on the docks. The Archive would be rather displeased to find that their emissary was turned away by the City Watch."

The sentry shrugged and replied, "Not my concern. I don't answer to the Archive, but the governor here. Unless you want to magic some travel documents into my hand, then you best go back to wherever you got that guilder. The Sovereignties have decided to keep closer tabs on their people these days, so just holding a medallion won't get you into Port, any other major city, or across any border checkpoint without the proper documents."

As the sentry walked back to his post Thorne resisted the urge to open up the ground and entomb him. He blew a strong breath out of his nose and turned to Esen. "Don't worry," he said with a defiant tone. "I'll think of something. We'll be inside the city before two low bells."

"I already have an idea of my own," Esen replied. "Stay here."

"Wait, what are you doing?" the mage called out as Esen trotted slowly back towards the pilgrim caravan. Thorne watched Esen until he disappeared into the distant camp.

"Oh, what the fuck is this?" he muttered as he watched Esen return with the shepherd and a single mercenary escort, the latter carrying a lantern to light their way in the increasing darkness.

"Hello again," the shepherd said when they met. "Esen tells me you're having trouble getting into the city."

"A minor setback," Thorne said. "Esen shouldn't have troubled you. I would have gotten us into Port."

"For certain," the shepherd replied. "But since I'm here, I might as well expedite things."

The three of them approached the sentries at the gate and were again stopped. The shepherd pulled out a sheaf of parchment and carefully undid the white ribbon. "I have here my pilgrimage documents signed by the prince's representative on religious matters," the shepherd said. "I'd be most grateful if you would allow Esen and Thorne here into the city."

"Are they part of the pilgrimage?" the sentry asked, incredulous.

"In a manner of speaking," the shepherd answered. "They have traveled with us for the past day. Esen is a lost lamb of the trinity and Thorne is a potential convert."

Thorne scowled so violently his face hurt at the thought of making any religious vows.

"If they're part of the pilgrimage, then why do they need to enter the city?" the sentry asked.

"As I said, they are new and therefore need some more time to reflect upon their commitment to the journey," the shepherd said calmly. "Should they be moved to do so, and with the blessings of the trinity, I'm sure they will find a ship that will take them to Banks, which would put them on a path to meet again with us as we continue towards Haven."

Despite knowing the truth of the matter, the sentry gave a sigh of defeat. Thorne could see the resignation in his face that there would be no denying the request of a holy man bearing signed documents from a prince. The sentry glared at Thorne and Esen for a long moment before he said, "Be on your way to the harbor. Hopefully your luck continues to hold."

"Safe travels," the shepherd bade Thorne as he left with his escort.

The mage ignored the comment and strode quickly through the city gates with Esen a few steps behind. As his footsteps transitioned from the soft padding on a dirt road to a crunch on stone, Thorne heard the sonorous rolling tones of the city's bell.

Looking up in the general direction of the sound Esen said, "Well, you were right about gaining entry before two low bells. Where do we go from here?"

"I know where we can get a decent place to sleep for cheap," Thorne replied sourly, still agitated at being saved by the shepherd. "With the glassmaker guild ship already gone, there's no use going to the docks tonight. We'll head to the harbor at daybreak before the tide and see if we can barter passage on a ship going south."

"Lead the way," the foreigner said.

• • •

The air had a salty tang as Thorne and Esen surveyed the docks the next morning. After a good night's sleep in a passable bed, the foreigner's mood was much improved. He eagerly followed Thorne to the harbor to broker passage on a guild ship.

"What about that one?" Esen asked, pointing at a modest ship with a crew that was moving with purpose to stow their last pallets of cargo. From the quarterdeck an imposing figure dressed for sea travel watched the men toil with a critical eye. His hair was braided in a single thick plait that hung nearly to the small of his back. A tight-fitting violet shirt was tucked behind a sliver-threaded belt and black trousers. The belt hung low on his left hip as it supported a cutlass scabbard that showed more than a little wear.

"Textile guild, by the look of shirt," Thorne mused. "Maybe mining guild with that silver belt. Either way, both are major Sovereignty guilds so we should have a decent chance of gaining passage. Let's go see if we can get an audience. They look to be getting ready to cast off soon."

As they walked down the pier they were forced to weave a path around stevedores hauling heavy loads. While they approached the ship, the lieutenant left the quarterdeck and Thorne lost track of him as he walked towards the stern of the ship. Once they reached the ship's gangplank and it was clear that they wanted to get onboard a rough looking woman in a sleeveless shirt barked down at them from amidships, "Oy! What're you about?"

Thorne stopped and held up the Archive guilder. "Requesting permission to speak with the captain," he called out. "I'm a representative from the Archive."

"Stay down there and out of the way," the woman commanded. "We're on a tight schedule to load up and ship out." She then disappeared from view.

Esen gave Thorne a skeptical look and said, "That didn't sound very welcoming. Maybe I picked the wrong ship?"

"It'll be fine," Thorne said with a confidence he didn't feel. "Guild ship captains need to put up a tough front otherwise they'd lose the respect of their crew. If we can just get him away from so many eyes on these docks, we'll have more than a decent chance of buying passage."

"Is whatever money you got from that mage in Yaboon going to be enough?" the foreigner asked.

Thorne touched the pouch tied to his belt and felt the source of his lack of confidence. "We'll see," he replied noncommittally.

From amidships the captain appeared and glared down at Esen and Thorne on the dock. He was dressed in fine clothes and had a white sash draped over one shoulder, which was the traditional symbol of a guild ship captain. As he nimbly descended the gangplank to the dock he called out forcefully, "What business does the Archive have with the most distinguished textile guild?"

The query sounded down the pier and nearly every stevedore turned in the direction of the captain. The more experienced workers quickly resumed their labors, but a few stopped to watch the exchange. The captain stomped onto the dock and leveled a critical eye at Thorne and then Esen before he said just as loud as before, "I am Captain Telmachus. What do you want?"

"Only a few minutes of your time," Thorne began as calmly as he could manage. "If we may move from the pier to the harbormaster's office I can explain."

"I scarcely have a minute to spare," Telmachus boomed.

"Can you not see we are in the midst of final preparations? This ship will leave before the next tolling of the high bells. Speak here and now."

"The two of us need passage to Banks," Thorne said, dispensing with any more attempts at subtle discourse. It appeared that Telmachus was a man who would only be dealt with directly. Pulling the Archive guilder from under his shirt and letting it fall out in full view the mage added, "I am an Archive mage and this is my bodyguard. We are prepared to pay our way, and work on the ship if need be."

Telmachus barked a mirthless laugh and said, "Now your large associate might be of use, but an Archive mage? You lot are so soft that the touch of a nail will lay you low!"

Thorne heard a few laughs from dockhands near them, but a sharp look from Telmachus sent them all scrambling back to work. The captain turned back to the mage and said, "I suspect that you can make this worth the effort. The most distinguished textile guild is known for quality, not charity. Therefore, I can assume that as the Archive's representative you are prepared to offer satisfactory compensation?"

"Indeed," Thorne replied with a serious expression. He removed the pouch from his waist, opened it, and carefully poured out a few translucent red disks. "I am prepared to offer sixty Archive credits."

"Credits?" Telmachus cried out in disbelief. The captain then tilted his head back and laughed heartily. After he was done, the captain looked with a mocking sort of mirth at Thorne and said, "What good are those to a mariner? Credits are worthless except in cities that have an Archive, and those are all inland. Unless you've got another bag filled with Sovereignty coins, you've wasted enough of my time, Archive mage."

"The Archive in Savamont is on the coast," Thorne corrected, but he knew it was a moot point. Telmachus had made his position clear, and with so many eyes watching on the pier there was no way Thorne would change the captain's mind.

"What about another ship?" Esen finally spoke up, talking to Thorne just as much as the captain. "There has to be another guild that would help us."

"Good luck to you!" Telmachus said to the foreigner. "Bugger me if you find some fool of a captain that will take your trinkets over cold hard coins. If you're that desperate for a ship to Banks, then you best sit your asses on the pier and wait for a military vessel. I'm sure you could bribe some Sovereignty soldier to sneak you onboard."

Without the courtesy of formally parting, the captain spun on his heel and ascended the gangplank leaving Thorne and Esen standing awkwardly on the pier.

"We need to try another ship," Esen said as he looked around the harbor once they were alone.

"We'll get nowhere talking to a guild captain," Thorne said still watching where Telmachus boarded the ship. "Our best bet right now is to go the harbormaster's office and see if we can find out what the scheduled arrivals are for the next few days. Let's go, I'm getting tired of being gawked at by dockhands."

Thorne stepped off the pier with Esen in tow and had walked a short distance along the stone promenade towards the harbormaster's office when a slim woman with dark features approached him from the side. "Leave the street quickly, Master Thorne," she said in an urgent but hushed tone. "Come with me, please."

"What's going on?" Esen asked as they hastily followed the woman between two large buildings that were used as warehouses and cargo staging areas by the stevedores. Still early in the morning, there was little activity and the trio was able to find privacy behind a stack of wooden pallets.

Thorne ignored the foreigner's question and looked at the

woman with a grim expression. "This goes beyond your usual caution, Merhai," he said. "How did you even know I was here?"

The woman's golden eyes flicked over Thorne's shoulder to make sure they were not being watched before she looked back at Thorne and replied, "Reihana is here."

"What's going on, Thorne?" Esen asked more urgently. "Who's this?"

The mage gave a quick smile at the woman and answered, "Merhai is my agent here in Port. She keeps me informed about any goings-on that might be of interest to the Archive."

"A spy," Esen muttered with obvious distaste.

"Master Thorne," Merhai's voice was soft but urgent, "You need to leave immediately. Reihana arrived by rapid transport yesterday and has been turning over nearly every stone in the city looking for you."

"How did you learn of this?" Esen asked.

"That's Merhai's special talent," Thorne said with a knowing but melancholy grin. "Amongst Archive agents, there are those who work to line their pockets and those whose service can't be bought. An agent who spies on other agents is a tricky undertaking, but something at which Merhai excels." Turning his attention back to her, the mage said, "I'm grateful that you found me first, but there's more to this than simply Reihana looking for me, correct?"

Merhai nodded and replied, "I don't know what you did at the Archive, Master Thorne, but Reihana has vowed she's going to bind your magic once she finds you."

The color drained from the mage's face. He knew that Reihana would be angry when she inevitably found out he absconded with Esen, but to hear that she wanted to impose such a severe punishment made Thorne's blood run cold. With a sinking feeling the mage realized it had probably gotten out that he had summoned a mana shield in the infirmary and Tarbeck, or worse Olaf, were now asking pointed questions at the Archive.

"Laying low isn't really an option, Merhai," Thorne said trying to keep his voice steady. "Esen needs to track a glassmaker guild ship that left here a few days ago. That's why we were at the harbor, but not having much luck."

"Nor will you with any guild captain unless you can pay an outrageous sum in Sovereignty coins," Merhai said. She paused and looked towards the sky for a moment before returning her gaze to Thorne and Esen. "I think I know of someone who can help, but he's not exactly on the up and up."

"We don't have the luxury of being fastidious," Thorne said. "Tell me."

"There is a Venhadar captain named Amos here in Port," Merhai began. "He's not affiliated with any guild, though he transports their cargo on occasion."

"No doubt to help keep the taxes levied on guild ships low," Thorne commented wryly. "A smuggler is unlikely to stay in a major coastal city for long, which benefits us for more than one reason. Where do we find him?"

"Near the stevedore's residential area there are a few narrow alleyways," Merhai said as she turned and pointed in the general direction. "Find the one with a bronze bust at the entrance and go down until you reach a tavern that caters to Venhadar mariners, called *Shorty's*. Amos will be holding court there. He's something of a local folk hero."

"Merhai, you have outdone yourself once again," Thorne said with genuine gratitude. He pulled the pouch from his belt and handed it to her. "I'm certain that Amos won't barter with Archive credits, and you can find a better use for them."

Merhai took the pouch gently, but then held it in a tightly clenched fist at her side. "Be careful, Master Thorne," she said taking a step back. "It would break my heart to see something bad happen to you." With her warning given, she stepped out from behind the pallets, walked around the corner of the warehouse, and disappeared from view.

Thorne's face felt hot for a moment as he watched her leave. Before Esen could make any comment, he gestured in the direction that Merhai had indicated. "Best stay off the main thoroughfares," the mage told the foreigner. "Let's go find this Amos fellow."

CHAPTER ELEVEN

They found the alleyway that Merhai described easily enough. The polished bronze bust, a monument to a stoic-looking mariner of local fame, glittered brightly in the morning sunlight. The alley narrowed as they walked down it, to the point where Thorne was able to reach his arms out and touch the buildings on either side. Most of them looked to be small workshops or homes, but despite few being more than two stories, the alleyway felt claustrophobic.

Their walk was mostly solitary and quiet due to the fact that Thorne and Esen had to travel single file through the narrow street. A couple of times they encountered a local and got a scowling appraisal or a disapproving grunt as they passed.

"We're not welcome here," Esen said after one such meeting.

"Perhaps," Thorne replied as he looked up to see someone quickly retreat from an upper-level window. They were being carefully watched, but so far the mage didn't think they were in danger. "Though I would welcome Mirtans' company right about now," he added softly.

"Who's that?" Esen asked.

"The Sehenryu in the infirmary," Thorne answered, noting that Esen's hearing was surprisingly acute. "Her empathy could put our minds at ease if she were here."

"Is she a friend of yours?" Esen asked.

Thorne opened his mouth to answer, but then snapped it shut. His relationship with Mirtans was complex and not something he wanted to talk about, let alone with someone he just met. "We help each other out," the mage said.

The alleyway opened into a cul-de-sac that felt spacious compared to where they had been. Sunlight hit the open circle of paving stones and both men raised their faces to take in the salty marine breeze that drifted down. Feeling refreshed, Thorne surveyed the buildings around them and then pointed. "Looks like this is the end of the line."

The entrance to *Shorty's* was four feet high, more than enough for a Venhadar to pass through, but any other race on the continent would have to stoop or get on hands and knees to enter. The tavern roof couldn't have been more than six feet tall and looked to be wedged in a wide alleyway between the two adjacent buildings.

"I don't think we'll fit," Esen said as he tilted his head to get a better look.

"I'd wager that's the point," Thorne answered. He suddenly felt exposed standing in the cul-de-sac as he remembered that Reihana was searching for him. "Inside we go," the mage said, a bit of tension sneaking into his voice. "This is likely a Venhadar-exclusive bar, so I'm fairly certain we're not going to get a warm welcome. But if Amos is in there, we have little choice."

Both men approached the door and got down on their knees. Thorne pulled the door open and shuffled inside with Esen trailing behind. It took a few seconds for his eyes to adjust to the darker interior of the tavern after being outside in the bright sunlight. Lanterns lined long walls, but they were sporadically lit and did little to push back the feeling of claustrophobia in the cramped tavern. Along the wall to Thorne's left was a low counter and a row of stools, with the remaining open floor space packed with small round tables where Venhadar mariners were standing and drinking in groups of three or four.

Esen grunted and said softly in Thorne's ear, "This place

reeks of sweat and spilled beer." The foreigner frowned as he slouched to prevent hitting his head on an exposed ceiling beam. "I can't believe this is an actual bar. It looks like something built for children."

The drinkers nearest the bar glanced over in their direction and chuckled at the sight of two grown men shuffling on their knees towards the bar, but they didn't seem particularly surprised. It appeared that while *Shorty's* catered to Venhadar patrons, other races from the continent were not unwelcome.

From behind the bar a jovial-looking Venhadar female with a tight bun of black hair and a broad apron around her middle turned to the new arrivals and called out, "You sure you're in the right place, my lovelies?"

"We're looking for Amos," Esen answered in a clipped tone.

The foreigner's words had an immediate effect, but not in the way that Thorne had hoped. All nearby conversation stopped and the mood of the tavern changed palpably. Thorne felt a nervous sweat start to slick the small of his back when more than a score of grizzled Venhadar mariners stared him down. In such tight quarters, if they were rushed, there would be no way to defend themselves, let alone retreat quickly.

"What do you want with the captain?" a Venhadar male with an open vest asked in a tone that warned the mage to choose his next words carefully.

Thorne raised his hand in a placating gesture, as much to signal to Esen to be quiet as to the Venhadar that they meant no offense. If Amos was their best chance of getting out of Port, then the mage would have to make amends to those who apparently were very loyal to him here. Thorne cursed his previous generosity as he realized now that buying the whole bar a round and toasting the captain would have been a wise maneuver.

"Oy! Let them say their piece," shouted a powerful voice from the shadowy back of the tavern. "I can't imagine that a pair of humans would be fool enough to crawl in here just to start some shit. And even if they were, I'd at least give them credit for courage before I kicked their fucking teeth in. Step aside, mates."

When the barrier of mariners parted, Thorne and Esen shuffled towards the sound of the commanding voice. Thorne heard normal bar chatter and drinking resume behind them, though he still had the uncomfortable feeling of eyes watching him. At the back of they tavern they found a lone Venhadar reclining on a small chair with his legs raised up and heels resting on the only low table in the bar. "You're looking for Amos," he said. "Well here I am."

Captain Amos had the relaxed confidence of a Venhadar who knew he was the master of his domain. His clothes were typical for a mariner, as was the rough skin on his hands from a life at sea. Amos was brawny, even for a Venhadar, and the sky blue shirt he wore did little to hide the tightly corded muscles in his arms, shoulders, and neck. He had dark skin and eyes, with his head shaved save for a wide strip of coarse black hair that ran from his forehead to the back of his neck that ended in a short braid. A modest beard covered his jaw, but it didn't hide the toothy grin he gave Thorne and Esen as they awkwardly approached him.

The mage was unaccustomed to kneeling for so long a time, and sacrificed some dignity when he shifted to a sitting position on the floor. Crossing his legs, Thorne sighed in relief as the pain in his knees lessened. "We need transport to Banks," the mage said without preamble as he looked up at Amos. "It's urgent."

Amos ran his hand over his beard and contemplated Thorne's request a moment before he said, "A ship has limited resources when at sea. How do you propose to make this worth our while?"

"If we had money enough to pay for passage, we could have chartered any of the guild ships in the harbor," Thorne answered. "I was told that alternative arrangements could be made."

The captain barked a quick laugh and said with a smile, "I have a reputation for many things, but charity is not one of them. You need to be bringing something to the table to keep this conversation going."

"You shouldn't have given all that Archive money to your spy," Esen said sourly to Thorne.

"Credits? You're a mage?" Amos asked with raised eyebrows.

"I am," Thorne replied in a guarded tone.

"You have a guilder?" the captain said. "You'd be surprised how many people I've come across who pretend to be mages."

Thorne pulled the medallion out from under his shirt. "I'm from the Yaboon Archive," he said looking the captain square in the eye, daring him to challenge the authenticity of the guilder.

"Well," Amos said, not the least bit threatened, "Now this is a conversation worth my while."

The mage didn't like the shift in Amos' tone in what was apparently an unexpected windfall. "So you can help us?" he asked as he tucked the medallion back under his shirt.

"It just so happens that we're to depart later today," Amos said. "If you agree to lend me a hand on the voyage, then I'm willing to transport you and your friend here to Banks when we're done."

"What do you want us to do?" Esen spoke up.

"Well, I don't have anything specific in mind," Amos replied. "But I reckon things will go all the better with an Archive mage and a strong-looking lad onboard. What do you say, mates?"

With Reihana actively looking for them in Port, the mage knew they needed to leave immediately. He had little choice but to accept Amos' proposal. The mage nodded, but then cautioned, "I'm not sure what you're expecting, but I hope you know the stories they tell about mages being able to influence the weather are all lies. Our control of the arcane elements is very local in nature."

Amos chuckled. "I know that one very well, mate. What should I be calling you two?" Amos stood up after Thorne and Esen introduced themselves. "There are no guild contracts here, just the bond of your word. Do I have yours that you'll be good mates while I conduct my business on the sea? In return I'll transport you to Banks in a timely manner afterwards." The Venhadar captain extended his hand towards Thorne.

After a quick glance towards Esen to see if there were any last minute protests, Thorne grasped Amos' hand and shook it firmly. The captain then offered his hand to Esen, who followed the mage's lead.

"Alright then," Amos said with satisfaction. He looked over Thorne's shoulder and called out loudly, "Dirty Dreebs!"

A peculiar-looking male Venhadar disengaged from one of the standing tables and took a step towards the captain. He was thin to the point of gauntness, which was for certain a rarity amongst the Venhadar race. Moreover, he was not dressed in the colorful clothes favored by mariners, but instead was garbed in navy trousers with a matching shirt that hung loosely on his boney frame. "Yes, captain," he said with a resonant voice that held a surprising amount of power.

"How much beer do you have left in your mug?" Amos asked.

Dirty Dreebs looked down at the cup in his pale-skinned hand. Lifting the mug to his lips, he took two huge gulps from the cup and then answered, "I'm all done, captain." The features of his face were slightly wrinkled, which betrayed that he was a Venhadar of some age, but his green eyes shone vibrantly as he addressed Amos and hinted that despite his outward appearance, he carried an inner fortitude that likely matched that of the stout mariners in the tavern.

Amos gave one quick nod of approval and said, "Good. Take these lads to the *Formica* straight away. Help them get their bearings and make introductions where necessary. I'll be there myself before ten high bells."

Dirty Dreebs nodded and went to the bar. He pointed at the shelves while making eye contact with the barkeep. "For the lads that drew the short straw and are on the beach," he said.

The barkeep smiled at him and replied, "Well, aren't you a darling?" She pulled down a bottle and handed it to Dirty Dreebs. "You give them my best, you hear?"

Dirty Dreebs turned and looked at Thorne and Esen. "You heard the captain. Come with me," he said ambling towards the door.

As they slid on their knees to follow the thin Venhadar out of the tavern Esen said, "That went better than I was expecting."

Thorne's expression darkened as he replied quietly, "We just made a bargain that we'll soon regret. Of that I have little doubt."

• • •

Dirty Dreebs led them through a labyrinth of narrow alleys in the stevedore's residential neighborhood until they reached a city gate that did not appear to get much use given that one of the pair of City Watchmen posted was sitting on the ground taking a nap. The Venhadar approached the one still awake and whispered a few words before shoving something into the sentry's hand. The Watchman nodded lazily and barely gave them a second look as he unbolted the heavy iron-banded door.

As he stepped outside, Thorne saw that they were entering

into a wooded area with the coastline visible through the trees on his left side. There was a dirt path that ran parallel to the shore. "Where does this lead?" he asked Dirty Dreebs as they took up a quick march away from Port.

"This will circle back around the city and empty out onto the prince's highway," the Venhadar answered. "But we won't be on this for very long."

True to his word, after about a half hour of walking Dirty Dreebs stopped and pointed at the sharp turn away from the water ahead of them. "Follow that bend, you'll come round the city," he said before gesturing back towards the coastline. "But it's here where we're leaving the beaten path. The ground's rocky and uneven, so mind your footing."

Thorne and Esen continued to walk in relative silence after entering the underbrush save for the occasional grunt and curse when either one of them stumbled over a branch or hidden root. In contrast, the Venhadar seemed to know exactly where everything was and walked quickly with a sure step. The mage estimated they had walked for nearly an hour with the water always in sight when they finally emerged from the woods onto a broad sandy beach shaped like a crescent moon. On the far side of the cove Thorne saw eight small overturned rowboats and two people doing their best to find shelter under one of them. Dirty Dreebs took the lead walking onto the sand, and they were nearly halfway around the cove when Thorne finally could see the figures were human males dressed in cut off pants and green striped vests that were well on their way to becoming threadbare. As they drew nearer the mariners noticed them and scrambled to put on their boots.

With a smirk on his face, the thin Venhadar held up the bottle taken from *Shorty's* and waved it over his head. The men must have recognized Dirty Dreebs because their movements became less panicked and they eventually came to greet the group a few steps away from the rowboats. Dirty Dreebs handed the bottle over to one of the mariners and said, "Thought you two would be thirsty. Astrid sends her regards."

The mariner holding the bottle pulled the cork out and took a long pull. Exhaling a satisfied sigh, he passed to bottle to his companion and said, "It's appreciated. Who're these two?"

Dirty Dreebs made brief introductions, and then said, "They bartered passage with the captain to Banks. He told me to get them onboard and acclimated." He gestured with a bony hand at one of the overturned rowboats and added, "Captain wanted this done and you back on the beach here before ten high bells, so we best move along quickly."

As the two mariners flipped a rowboat over and prepared for launch, Thorne looked out across the water and scanned for a ship. About halfway between the cove and horizon sat a two-masted vessel unperturbed in the calm waters. The mage thrust his chin in the direction of the ship and asked, "Is that a clipper?"

Dirty Dreebs glanced quickly out to sea and then back to supervise the rowboat preparations. "Of sorts," he answered vaguely. "The *Formica* is a brigantine that's been refitted for our particular type of work."

"Why would you name a ship after an insect?" the mage asked with an askew look at his escort.

Dirty Dreebs gave Thorne a little smile and replied, "Just like the ant it's named after, the captain says the ship is small, but mighty. You'll find many of the crew are Venhadar, but don't worry, you'll fit in just fine after a few days."

With the rowboat in the water and steadied by the mariners, Thorne and Esen clumsily got in and sat on the bench seat in the back. They both emptied their boots of seawater while Dirty Dreebs got onboard and knelt down at the bow, leaving the middle bench for the two mariners to handle the oars. With a few powerful strokes the rowboat cut through the water and glided towards the *Formica*.

The mage noticed that Esen was very quiet and tense once they left the shore. When the wind picked up about halfway to the ship, Thorne saw the foreigner grip the plank they were sitting on so tightly that all of the color blanched from his knuckles. "Are you alright?" Thorne asked quietly.

Frozen in place, Esen glanced at Thorne. "I can't swim well," he murmured. "It's not something I really thought about until now. I was too focused on getting to Claire."

The mage was a decent swimmer, but had his own personal apprehensions about deep water, so he could empathize with Esen. "It's alright," he said. "Just stay away from the ship's outer railing and you'll be fine. Brigantines rarely capsize in the open seas." He tried to sound reassuring, but given that the *Formica* likely hadn't seen a proper port in some time he wondered what kind of shape the vessel would be in once aboard.

Thanks to the mariners' strong backs and a light tailwind, the rowboat made good time and quickly reached the ship. Ascending a simple but sturdy rope ladder Thorne, Esen, and Dirty Dreebs climbed over the gunwale of the *Formica* and stood on the main deck. Dirty Dreebs shouted down to the mariners, who quickly disengaged from the ship and returned to the shore to ensure they were waiting for the captain and not vice versa. As Thorne and Esen surveyed their surroundings a shout from atop the forecastle made them jerk their heads up.

"Bringing me some new hands today, chaplain?" boomed a Sehenryu male. He wore brown trousers with matching boots, but no shirt, and his short leopard-spotted fur nearly glowed in the bright sunshine. The feline features of his face gave him a natural appearance of aggression, which was only enhanced by a thick scar that ran down the left side of his face. His eye had not been spared and was milky white and sightless.

"Not crew, Vechas," Dirty Dreebs answered. "Passengers. The captain struck a bargain with them." He gestured at the mage and continued, "This is Thorne, an Archive mage, and his companion is Esen."

"If they're not able hands, then just make sure they stay out of our way, chaplain," Vechas rumbled before he stepped back to the bow of the ship and out of sight.

"Chaplain?" Thorne made the title a question directed at Dirty Dreebs.

"Are you surprised to find the religious amongst mariners?" the Venhadar's eyes crinkled in mirth as he spoke. "Goes against common knowledge in the Archives?"

"Just thought I'd be free from sermonizing and doctrine for a while," Thorne replied, casting a critical glance at Esen.

The foreigner frowned at the implied insult. His hand touched his chest where the symbol of the trinity was hidden under his shirt, but he otherwise gave no response.

"No need to worry," Dirty Dreebs said. "Things are much more practical on the *Formica*. No regular services and the only songs you'll likely hear come from the taverns, not the temples."

"Then why are you here?" Esen asked as his hand dropped to his side.

"I provide council and guidance when asked for it," Dirty Dreebs answered. "The captain finds that my presence on the ship dampens some of the more aggressive behaviors of the crew at times."

"That didn't really answer my question," Esen replied.

"Not all ministers get to choose their congregation," the chaplain said cryptically. Before Esen could press any further, Dirty Dreebs said, "Follow me. I'll help you get your bearings."

As Dirty Dreebs walked them across the deck of the *Formica* and then through the interior of the ship, he made passing introductions to those they encountered. It was more to let the crew know that Thorne and Esen belonged on the ship at the captain's invitation and were not stowaways. Trying to do his best to keep track of names and faces, Thorne guessed there were about two score of mariners currently onboard. While the crew seemed to be mostly Venhadar with an occasional human or Sehenryu, there were few female mariners aboard.

The Venhadar showed them the cramped crew quarters in the forecastle where they could find a hammock to sleep. After introductions to the cook in the decently stocked galley, Dirty Dreebs led them back to the main deck. Once they were all standing out in the sun again he finished the tour by saying, "I reckon that the captain will have more to say about your duties once he's aboard, so until then I would find some shade here on deck. It'll get hectic once everyone else returns, so you'll want to be visible to him right away."

"Everyone else?" Esen asked. "How many more are coming?"

Dirty Dreebs pointed back to the now distant cove and answered, "There were eight rowboats there. We've got another twenty-five and their gear coming with the captain." He turned back and looked towards the quarterdeck. "Which reminds me that I'll have to leave you lads now. I've got my own duties to attend to before the captain arrives."

Thorne left Esen near the foremast and walked to the starboard gunwale. Resting his hands on the railing, the mage felt the warmth of wood that had been out in the sun all day. It was a comforting sensation, and for the first time since leaving the Archive, Thorne took a truly relaxed breath. What had been at times a frantic and anxious departure from Yaboon took a turn for the worse in Port after learning about Reihana's pursuit and impending wrath. However, now floating on the *Formica*, Thorne felt like he had regained some sense of stability and could now consider how to best find Claire and ponder the identity of the mysterious assassin encountered at the Archive infirmary.

"What makes an Archive mage so desperate that he wants to associate with the likes of us?" rumbled a voice behind Thorne.

The mage turned around and saw Vechas watching him with his arms folded across his chest. The pupil of the Sehenryu's good eye was a thin black bar in the bright sunlight surrounded by a brilliant yellow iris. His unblinking gaze ended Thorne's brief sense of calm.

"We're looking for someone," Thorne replied. Pointing to Esen he said, "His wife was abducted."

Vechas' eye remained fixed on Thorne. "Why not just wait for the ransom demand?"

Not wanting to discuss the details of their plight, Thorne answered vaguely, "Just being proactive, I suppose."

Vechas grunted and continued to stare at him.

The mage realized that he was being scanned by the Sehenryu's empathy. Trying to clear his mind of any betraying emotions he asked, "Do you expect to make good time delivering the cargo? Amos said he'd take us to Banks once that work was done."

The Sehenryu blinked and assumed a relaxed posture with his arms dropping to his sides. Whatever Vechas had learned from probing the mage's emotional state must have convinced him that Thorne wasn't an immediate threat. "Delivering cargo is never the problem," Vechas said. "There's always someone eager to get their hands on guild goods without paying taxes. No, it's always the acquisition of said goods where things get messy. But don't worry, when the time comes to collect, I'm sure the captain will send you below decks until it's over."

"When the time comes for what?" Thorne asked with a rising sense of alarm. "Isn't the cargo already onboard?"

"Nope," Vechas said as he pointed out towards the horizon.

"It's about a day or so in that direction on a slow and unprepared guild ship."

Thorne's eyes widened and his mouth gaped. His shocked expression caused the grim-faced Sehenryu to roar with laughter.

"Captain Amos didn't let slip that little detail did he? What a twisted sense of humor!" Vechas exclaimed. "We'll then, let me formally welcome you onboard the *Formica*, the most profitable corsair ship to stalk the southern coast."

CHAPTER TWELVE

Two days had passed since the *Formica* left the cove near Port and sailed into the open ocean in pursuit of the guild ship. The initial shock and anger that Thorne felt had mostly subsided. Even with his severely limited options in Port, and knowing that Reihana was hunting him, the mage still felt it was underhanded of Amos to mislead them about his true goals.

The Venhadar captain still hadn't discussed what roles he and Esen would play in the raid. Amos had been plenty visible on the ship, but he was a frenzy of action working twice as a hard as any regular mariner, and often times roaring with laughter during his labors. On the first afternoon at sea Thorne had seen him simultaneously steer the ship, fix some snarled rigging, and varnish a section of gunwale. It was obvious that Amos was strong, even for a Venhadar, but that level of activity meant that he had little time to talk to his reluctant passengers. Thorne had tried to approach him a few times to get a explanation, but was gruffly pushed aside by a mariner who told him to stay out of the captain's way.

Eventually Thorne gave up and decided that Amos would talk to him when ready, but with no tasks assigned to them, he and Esen simply tried not to be liability on the ship. Esen spent his time in the forecastle or somewhere below decks, no doubt feeling safer surrounded by four walls where there was no chance he could fall overboard. He had been pleasant to Thorne when they had crossed paths, but Esen had not made much of an effort to be in the mage's company.

Thorne found the open air much more appealing, and the views from the *Formica's* deck were spectacular. He now stood at the rail amidships as the sun touched the horizon and watched the calm waters become a brilliant mix of blue and orange. Despite the tranquil scenery, Thorne was becoming more restless with each passing day. He had made no progress on figuring out the identity of the assassin that tried to kill Esen. More presently, he feared that the guild ship might not have Claire aboard. Despite these uncertainties, the one thing the mage did know was that when the time came, he would have to fight with the corsairs to take the guild ship. He decided that some training might rid him of nervous energy and better prepare him for what was sure to come.

The mage turned from the rail and looked to see who was on deck. Vechas prowled the quarterdeck above him and a few other mariners tended to their duties, but none seemed to notice or care what he was doing. Thorne reasoned that since none of them knew anything of Archive proceedings hiding his Paragon techniques wasn't necessary, especially since he would probably have to use them during the raid. What they saw would hopefully be dismissed as just another tall tale from a mariner looking for an audience at a tavern.

Thorne pulled arcane energy out of his right arm and fashioned a mana knife. He felt acutely alert as the tingling charge of magic raced through his body. Exulting in the high a moment, he reclaimed focus and began executing attack sequences with a level of precision and aggression that would have met Garret's approval.

After a half hour of training, Thorne heard a shout above him.

"Who trained you? Some old cavalier?"

The mage looked up at the quarterdeck and saw Vechas

peering down at him. The Sehenryu's feline features were drawn back in a facsimile of a smile, but his mocking tone left no mistake what he really thought about Thorne's drills.

Thorne let the mana knife drop to his side as he wiped the sweat off his brow with his free hand. His eyes narrowed and his answer was clipped, "What of it?"

Vechas pointed at the mage's mana knife and said, "You might be using some kind of fancy Archive weapon, but those techniques are antiquated Sovereignty military. They might still work on a battlefield in a formation with a score of your mates, but out here they'll get you killed real quick. Those movements are too slow and rigid."

"I've been able to hold my own with them," Thorne said, though he knew it was only half true given his last duel with Mirtans.

The Sehenryu put his hands on the quarterdeck railing and leaned over it. His one good eye grew wide as he called down, "Show me. Let's see if any of the stories I hear about Archive mages are true."

Thorne noticed everyone within earshot had stopped what they were doing and now watched him with keen interest. The mage tried to fool himself into believing it was the implied insult to Garret that made him eager to accept the challenge, but deep down he knew that this was a chance to prove to himself he was a fighter. It was also an opportunity to vent his frustrations from being tricked onto a corsair ship. "The last person to duel me ended up in the Archive infirmary," he said.

This drew hoots from those watching, but Vechas alone laughed loudly. "Then I like my chances since they didn't end up buried," he said before shouting to a nearby mariner, "Yves! Fetch me a blade!"

By the time that Vechas had sauntered down to the main deck he was met by the mariner and given a short saber. "Is it true that iron burns you?" the Sehenryu asked as he squared off with Thorne. "I can't have you so hurt that you're useless to the captain."

The mage swung his mana knife into a defensive position and replied, "Yes, but your blade has to touch bare skin." He widened his stance and stared down Vechas. "And I'd prefer it that you didn't cut my clothes either."

The Sehenryu used his saber to point at Thorne. "Now is not the time to worry about your wardrobe. We fight until first blood is drawn."

Vechas lunged forward and flicked his saber upwards in an attempt to knock Thorne's mana knife aside.

The mage easily deflected the weak thrust and countered with a powerful swipe aimed at Vechas' middle, but it was too slow.

They traded another set of weak strikes meant to probe each other's range and reflexes before Vechas said, "You're a curious one. I would have expected more fear from you. Archive mages aren't known for their courage."

Thorne realized the Sehenryu was using his empathy while fighting, something that could be done only if Vechas was putting forth a minimal offensive effort. A flash of anger hardened the mage's features and he grunted, "You need to get off this boat more."

With his free hand, Thorne reached back while keeping his mana knife pointed at Vechas. Pushing mana into the spaces between his splayed fingers, the mage felt the weight of the air around his hand. Grabbing the air, Thorne threw it at Vechas. As the strong jet of wind buffeted the Sehenryu and momentarily distracted him, Thorne rushed forward and slashed downward with his mana knife.

Vechas blocked the blow and then locked up their blades with his saber's cross guard. Although they were of similar height, the Sehenryu was much stronger than Thorne. As Vechas pushed down on his blade Thorne had to use his off-hand to brace his mana knife to keep the struggle even.

With their faces inches apart, Vechas said, "Now you're in trouble, mage. With both hands tied up on these locked blades you're at a disadvantage."

"How's that?" Thorne asked through clenched teeth as he gained some leverage and pushed back.

"Because now I can do this!" hissed the Sehenryu as he threw a savage punch with his free hand.

Thorne felt the crunch of cartilage in his nose and starbursts of pain filled his vision as he was knocked to the ground. Landing hard on his back, he looked up dazed at the sails and rigging of the *Formica*. With the Sehenryu looming over him, Thorne felt a thick wetness on his upper lip. When he clumsily wiped his nose, the back of his hand was coated crimson.

"First blood," Vechas said as he appraised the mage. "I win."

Thorne groaned and dissolved his mana knife. As the arcane energy reabsorbed back into his arm, he felt a momentary easing of the pain in face, but it quickly returned worse then before. His eyes watered as he lay there trying to regain his wits.

Before the mage knew what was happening, Vechas grabbed his arm and hoisted him up. The Sehenryu held Thorne steady for a moment as the mage got his legs underneath him and a wave of nausea passed. "Learn to use your off-hand in a clash," he growled. "It might save your skin some day."

Vechas let go of Thorne and walked up the steps to the quarterdeck.

Blinking hard until he could see straight again, Thorne turned around and found that Dirty Dreebs stood a few steps away.

"You lasted longer than a good number of us," the Venhadar chaplain said. "And perhaps more importantly, you got a nod of approval from the captain."

"Amos was watching?" Thorne croaked.

"Right up until the end. He sent me to help you get cleaned up and extend an invitation to eat with him tonight. He wants to talk about the raid."

• • •

When Thorne arrived at Amos' cabin, he noted that Esen was already there. The foreigner was sitting on the floor next to a small table in the center of the room. In the rear, the captain sat behind a beautiful mahogany desk. All of the furniture appeared to be made custom for a Venhadar sailor.

Beckoning him in, the captain said, "Please tell me you are not as devout as your companion. Esen has been fine company, but I'm mighty parched and it's bad luck to drink alone on a ship."

Esen made a show of looking at the full cup of wine on the table before he pushed it towards Thorne.

The mage picked it up and raised a toast to Amos, "To your health, captain," he said before taking a sip. The wine tasted sour, but not bad, and he felt a familiar warmth in his belly after a second larger swallow.

Amos snatched up the cup on his desk and drained it in three huge gulps. Behind him, the entire back wall was made of thick glass squares. He struck an impressive figure when back-lit by the waning daylight.

"That wind you blew at Vechas," Amos began after wiping his beard with the back of his hand and refilling his glass with the pitcher on his desk, "could you conjure us a gale to give speed to our advance on the guild ship?"

"No," Thorne answered. "Maybe a group of mages could manipulate enough air to fill a sail, but even then not for very long. Even the most powerful of us can influence the elements and physical forces at only at a proximal level. The stories of mages calling down thunder or hail storms are nothing more than folktales and superstitious lies from the dark past."

"That's what I thought but wanted to make sure," Amos said, sounding disappointed.

A knock on the door had them all turn their heads.

"Come," commanded Amos.

A mariner entered carrying a small covered kettle and some dishes. He set the meal on the low table next to Esen and then stepped back towards the door.

"The crew seems happy tonight with the food," the mariner said.

"Tell Johan he's doing good work, as always," Amos replied.

"You eat the same food as the crew?" Thorne asked after the cook's assistant had left and closed the door.

"I'm a mariner first and captain second," Amos said. "I eat what they do, and I work like they do."

"From what I've seen, you work harder," Esen said.

Amos ignored the complement and said, "Get settled, Thorne, and I'll tell you what to expect during the raid."

After getting a refill for his empty cup, Thorne sat at the small table and sipped, allowing the wine to dull the ache in his nose and sinuses.

Amos opened a desk drawer and pulled out two small leather-bound books. He placed both of them flat on the desk and said, "We'll imagine these books are the *Formica* and the guild ship. Right now our hold is full of empty casks that we'll drag behind the ship once we're in sight of our prey. It'll slow us down, but it won't arouse any suspicions as we draw near."

"What colors will you be running?" Esen asked as he eyed the food that had been set on the table.

"That's one of the things that I thought Thorne here could

comment on," Amos said with a grin. "I'm sure the Archive is privy to the current alliances amongst the guilds. Normally I have to guess because sailing without a flag arouses too much suspicion."

Thorne looked up at the thick timbers that ran across the ceiling as he thought. He was well versed in the current relationships between the major guilds on the continent, but it wasn't because of anything having to do with the Archive. With a frown he said, "The glassblower guild and the brewer guild are on very good terms at the moment, but the latter doesn't do much cross-Sovereignty shipping."

"Not a problem," Amos replied. "I've still got one of their banners."

"With the redesigned crest?" Thorne asked.

"What?" Amos said, his head rocking back in surprise.

"The brewer guild changed how the wheat on their crest is depicted," Thorne said. "Now it's six strands instead of four and wrapped with a hop vine."

Amos creased his brow then dismissed this minor detail with a wave of his hand. He took a pen from his drawer and laid it across the two books. "Can you conjure the proper colored thread and embroider the new crest?" he asked, sounding unhopeful. When Thorne shook his head, the captain nodded like he knew the answer all along and continued, "Then it doesn't matter. It's a minor detail that I doubt anyone will catch. Now, once we get in close we'll launch our heavy ballista loaded with harpoons. When we have a half-dozen or so in the hull of the guild ship, then there's no escaping. At that point we'll draw in our sail so it doesn't catch fire."

"Fire?" Esen asked alarmed.

Amos nodded and replied, "We'll be trading arrows by that point, and theirs will no doubt be ignited." He gestured with his cup towards Thorne and asked, "You wouldn't be able to do anything about that would you?"

The mage shook his head and answered, "Is the cargo really worth the cost of repairs you're going to need?"

"Why are you so reluctant to raid a guild ship, Thorne?" Esen interjected. The foreigner looked at Thorne with a disapproving expression.

"I have my reasons," the mage said with an edge in his voice. After a long paused he added, "Not the least of which is the reputational damage to the Archive if it got back to any of the Sovereignty princes that a mage was in league with corsairs."

"Fuck the Sovereignties!" Amos cursed as he pounded his fist on table, causing the pen to tumble to the floor. "It's the ambivalence of the princes to the guilds' greed that allows ships like the *Formica* to prowl the coasts. They just sit in their crystal spires and maintain enough military might to collect taxes and prevent the borders on the map from shifting. It's the guilds who are really running the continent."

"So you're raiding guild ships to turn around and sell the cargo to other guilds?" Thorne asked rhetorically.

"Not always," Amos said. "Sometimes a guild wants their own ship raided so they can claim a loss on the goods and not have to pay taxes on them. After the loss is claimed we give the cargo back, for a holding fee of course."

Thorne was incensed at the idea and seethed, "No major guild would do such a thing! It goes against the principles of all the major guild charters."

"You've been walled up in an Archive for too long if you're that naïve," Amos said. "Or maybe you got family in a guild and that's your pride talking?"

"Something like that," Thorne said looking away.

"Claire has got to be on that ship if it is the same one that left Port before us," Esen said trying to get the conversation back on track. "That means Karnoff will be aboard as well. He won't have anywhere to run once we have taken command of it."

Now that the debate was two against one, Thorne knew he was beat, but tried one last excuse. "Assuming we can catch them, and that this ship isn't burned to a cinder by flaming arrows, and that we actually draw up side them for a raid, do we have the numbers to secure both ships?"

Amos laughed and replied, "Did you not see the two score that I brought with me? Best freelance mercenaries that money can buy."

"Freelance?" Thorne scoffed. "If they're not guild mercenaries, then they're just highwaymen. I hate everything about this plan."

"It's a long swim back to Port," Amos answered, his smile gone. "We had a deal. I saw you handle yourself well enough against Vechas. Will you fight?"

Thorne was silent for a moment while he weighed his options.

"I will," the mage said finally.

"And you?" the captain leveled his intimidating glare at Esen.

"Yes," the foreigner said with resolve.

Amos relaxed once again. "There's some good mates," he said with a smile. Pointing at the table he added, "Now let's eat, I'm famished!"

• • •

After eating, Thorne and Esen went directly to the forecastle as the air had cooled considerably and thick cloud cover made the sky prematurely dark. Rain was on the way. They both sat on the floor near a bulkhead opposite from where several mariners were dozing in hammocks. There was one small lantern lit near the door, but the soot-coated glass only let a yellow haze of light escape. Thorne leaned against the ship's wall and waited for his eyes to adjust while Esen sat with his legs crossed next to him.

"If I had a glow sphere I could give us a bit more light," Thorne said as he glanced over at the foreigner. When he got a confused look from Esen, the mage added, "It's a small resin ball that mages can charge with mana to make it glow."

"Without the right materials a mage isn't so useful outside of the Archive, I suppose," Esen said. He then coughed so forcefully his body rocked back and forth with the effort.

"You alright?" Thorne asked after one of the mariners nearby grumbled and shifted in his hammock.

"Throat is dry," Esen said hoarsely.

The mage looked near the lantern where a large barrel was lashed to the wall. Resting on the lid was a ladle and several wooden cups. He pointed towards the barrel and said, "There's water right over there, but we'll have to go find whoever keeps track of the rum on the ship."

"No alcohol," Esen croaked with a shake of his head. "Teachings of the trinity forbid it."

Thorne thought back to dinner and the untouched cup of wine next to Esen. The foreigner hadn't drunk anything at all in the captain's quarters and the mage wondered how much of anything Esen had imbibed on the ship.

"You're dehydrated," Thorne accused.

"I tried drinking the water from the barrel by itself, but it made me feel sick," Esen replied, his voice slowly returning to normal. "It happened before when I came from my homeland. I survived."

Thorne creased his brow and said, "The stakes are a bit higher now, don't you think? How are you going to help Claire if you're too sick to stand? Or fight?" He stood up and said in response to Esen's questioning expression, "Just sit tight a minute."

The mage crept to the water barrel and took two of the wooden cups that were set nearby. After filling one to the top, he poured a small amount of water into the other and returned to Esen. He placed the mostly full cup next to the ship's wall to keep it from tipping as he sat. With a firm grip on the nearly empty cup he pressed the palm of his free hand over the top to make a seal.

"What are you doing?" Esen asked as he looked between the full cup on the floor and the one in Thorne's hands.

"Being useful outside of the Archive," Thorne said sarcastically.

The mage pushed mana into the hand covering the cup and felt the air inside respond to the arcane energy. He pushed it down, creating a vacuum at the top of the cup. With his hand now protected, the mage pushed mana into his other hand and rapidly heated the small amount of water in the bottom of the cup. Maintaining a constant flow of mana, Thorne kept the cup hot for several minutes before breaking the seal and releasing the pressurized steam with hiss.

"Now that I've got a clean cup, I can move on to this," the mage said as he exchanged cups.

Having pushed mana back into the hand grasping he cup, Thorne could acutely feel the water inside. Though he didn't have the molecular control that some of the most accomplished mages did, he still could feel the comparatively large particles of grit swirling in the water. More importantly, he could also feel the microbes swimming around, and those were what he was working to remove. He compressed all the contaminants down into a small black button at the bottom of the cup and then carefully poured most of the water into the other steamed cup.

"Drink this," Thorne said offering the cup to Esen. "It's clean now, but it might taste strange. I would need the equipment from my laboratory to distill it pure."

Esen took a tentative sip and then greedily swallowed the water. "More," he demanded giving the cup back to the mage.

"For a price," Thorne said. "I want your story. Why were you out on the frontier with Claire?"

"What's it to you?" Esen said defensively.

"I want to know why an Archive mage took her," Thorne said, refusing to move until Esen gave in with a nod.

As Thorne purified another cup of water, Esen mused, "It has to be her father. I'm sure of it."

"Tell me," Thorne said as he handed over another cup of purified water.

Esen sighed before taking a sip of water. Holding the cup with both hands, he said, "I'm the youngest of five sons. Do you know what that means on the southern continent?"

Thorne shook his head. He knew little about the culture and people from other parts of the world.

Esen continued, "It means that I was locked into a life where I would tend my father's herd, which would eventually become my eldest brother's. My other brothers were content to continue the family tradition of staying together to live and work. This had been done for many generations, but I was different. I saw how some of my uncles chafed under my father. They wanted their own herds and freedom, but they were trapped. The family that kept them fed and sheltered also kept them prisoners."

"Why couldn't they leave? Work for someone else?"

The foreigner looked up at Thorne, searching to see if the mage understood. Before Thorne could say anything, Esen looked down at the cup and said, "A lone man looking for work is an outcast. Other families would never take him because he was ostracized by his own for some terrible offense. To be shunned by your family is the worst of punishments."

Thorne considered Esen and could see the guilt on his face.

To be pushed out by your family must be devastating, but was that what really happened to him? Not wanting to pry too deep into Esen's personal affairs, the mage instead asked, "How did you learn our language?"

"There was a Small House missionary who came to live amongst us. He brought seeds and worked hard in the field, so my father allowed him to stay for several years. From this man I learned the words of the northern continent from songs. He was always singing."

"Why did he stay so long?"

"I don't know, but I'll never forget the day he left. He got up early one morning, collected his few possessions, and then walked away. Not a word of goodbye was said to anyone." Esen chuckled humorlessly, and then continued, "No one seemed to care but me. As I watched him get smaller and smaller, I finally realized that it could be that easy. I could just leave my life behind. That's when I got the idea to come here."

"To the northern continent?"

Esen nodded and replied, "The missionary sometimes spoke about the frontier, places he had been, and farms where he worked. He said by working on someone else's farm you could eventually get your own, and I became obsessed with that idea."

"So you left? That must have been hard."

"No, I was surprised at just how easy it was to do," Esen answered. "But what I wasn't prepared for was what it truly meant to be on your own. Once I got here I quickly learned that no one would hire a foreigner. For weeks I pleaded with every farmer that entered the guildhall while living on the streets, doing whatever it took to survive. It was pure chance, or maybe the providence of the trinity, that I met Claire."

"What was she doing at the farm guildhall?" Thorne asked. It wasn't lost on him that Esen didn't talk about how he had traveled to the northern continent or why he went so far inland to Haywood.

"She was on an errand for her father and witnessed one of my pitiful displays. After I was kicked out again she found me in the street and offered me a deal. If she could get me a writ from the prince to be a sharecropper on the frontier with some equipment and supplies, then I would help smuggle her out of the city."

"Why?" Thorne asked, stunned by Claire's request.

"She hated her father, how he controlled every aspect of her life and how he used her to further his own ambitions within the glassmaker guild. He kept a very watchful eye on his entire family and Claire desperately wanted freedom. When she told me this, I felt a kinship with her, having just escaped a fate not dissimilar."

"How did you make it out of the city?" Thorne asked.

Esen waved away the question as his face soured. "It didn't go exactly as planned, and Claire had to stay with me the entire journey to the frontier. She got the freedom she desperately desired, but was now stuck far from her home. It took some time, but after a crop cycle she grew accustomed to a farm lifestyle."

"How long were you out there together?" Thorne asked.

"Two crop cycles," Esen answered. "And during that time what started as a mutually beneficial and lucky arrangement, turned into true affection, and ultimately love." Esen's face scrunched up as he fought back tears. "When a shepherd came to our frontier farm on a mission, we married. I was not adherent to any religion in my homeland, but Claire was part of the Small House's flock. I happily converted to that faith to wed her. For a very brief time I had everything I ever wanted."

"Then the Archive mage came," Thorne said. "You said his name was Karnoff."

Esen used his thumb to wipe his eyes and replied, "Yes, he came with Sovereignty soldiers." His face grew hard and he said with a quiet intensity, "I'll not stop until I get her back and bring her home."

Thorne did not know what to say, so he remained silent.

After a moment, Esen regained his composure. Reaching into his pocket, he pulled out two octahedral dice. In a clear attempt to change the subject and lighten the mood, he said, "I found these earlier in the corner. Do you know how to plays Sevens?"

"What do the teachings of the trinity have to say about gambling?" Thorne asked skeptically.

"There's no money at stake here," Esen replied as he swirled the dice gently in his palm. "That means it's just a game."

They spent a few quiet minutes taking turns tossing the dice against the ship's wall. Neither of them were very good players. Eventually Esen took the dice and held him in his hand. "What do you think of Amos' plan?" Esen asked.

"If the guild ship is holding a standard company, then Amos has more than enough fighters," Thorne mused. "He's survived this long, so he knows what he's doing. It should be fine."

CHAPTER THIRTEEN

"Raise our colors!" Vechas shouted. Favorable weather had brought them far south along the Yaboon coast. It was mid-morning when the guild ship was spotted, and this set Vechas in motion, yelling orders and making sure lines were tight and the deck cleared. The Sehenryu now stood relatively at ease on the main deck and watched the brewer guild flag hoisted quickly and unfurl fully in the strong tailwind that pushed the ship towards their unsuspecting prey.

At the stern of the ship, Amos kept a sure hand on the rudder wheel and oversaw the scant number of crew still on the deck. The mercenaries and remaining crew were hidden below, but were ready to burst out when called. The corsair wanted to give the impression that the *Formica* was running a small crew when they were within spyglass range.

Thorne and Esen had been given permission to remain topside as long as they stayed out of the way. They both stood at the rail near the forecastle and watched their steady progress towards the guild ship.

"Won't be long now," Vechas said as he approached them. "Even with us dragging those barrels, it'll be maybe an hour before we're within ballista shot. Things are looking good so far, since they're not even running full sail.

"I'm in no rush," Esen said looking down at the belaying pin he carried as a makeshift weapon.

"For all the good you'll do in the fight, you might as well

hide below deck," the Sehenryu said. "You can earn your keep when it's over by moving the cargo between ships."

"No, I told Amos I would fight, so I'm going to fight," Esen answered as he hefted the belaying pin. "With this I should be able to knock someone down so hard they don't get up again."

Vechas grunted, unconvinced, and gestured at Thorne. "What about you? You have any misgivings about killing a man?"

"I'm not as experienced as you, but you saw that I have some combat training," Thorne answered. He would have liked Vechas to teach him more about fighting like a corsair, but the first mate was far too busy. The mock duel was a bit of sport for Vechas, but he had real work to do, and instructing an Archive mage wasn't part of it.

"Training isn't the same as the real thing," Vechas said as he crossed his arms across his chest. "Have you ever been in a real fight? One where your life was on the line?"

The mage thought about lying, but then decided it would be pointless since Vechas' empathy would detect his unease. "No, I haven't," he admitted.

"Well today's your chance to see if that magic blade of yours is worth anything," the Sehenryu replied, then crossed the ship and ascended the quarterdeck steps to join Amos.

The activity on both ships slowly increased as they drew nearer, but for very different reasons. On the guild ship, curious mariners could be seen leaning over the rail in an attempt to get a better look at the *Formica*, occasionally shouting and waving. They seemed to be excited at the unexpected opportunity to meet and talk with other mariners. In contrast, Amos kept his crew very focused on their tasks, while Vechas and a few other mariners discreetly stationed themselves near the loaded ballistae.

Thorne's shoulders felt stiff as he counted the number of

mariners on the guild ship over and over again. He tried to take a deep breath and relax, but his chest felt tight. The mage rubbed the sweat from his palms on his pants, and looked over at Esen. "You seem calm," he said, hoping that saying something out loud would make him less jittery.

Esen didn't acknowledge what Thorne had said, but kept staring at the guild ship like it would disappear if he blinked. "Please, Claire, be on that ship," Esen whispered, staring at the other vessel. "Then we can go home." The foreigner held his belaying pin tightly.

The mage found himself jealous that Esen had something to focus his energy on. Once the actual fighting started, Thorne felt confident he would be able to handle himself, but the waiting was getting to him. He counted again all those he could see on the guild ship's deck.

After an agonizing few minutes, they were within range. From his vantage point on the quarterdeck, Amos bellowed, "Fire the lines! Drop the sail!"

Every mariner on deck shouted the order while the mercenaries of the *Formica* swarmed outside and banged their weapons on the railing to intimidate those on the other ship. The sails of the corsair ship were taken in just as the ballistae fired their heavy harpoons. The projectiles crashed into the guild ship's hull and held fast while the thick ropes attached to them were secured to the *Formica*.

The groaning of the tethered ships was quickly drowned out by shouts and calls to arms from the crew of the guild vessel. They rushed to grab weapons and take in their sails to prevent the mast from breaking as another round of harpoons slammed into their ship. Chaos ensued as they hastily prepared for the imminent assault.

"Pull the lines! Ready the grapnels!" Amos shouted. The corsair captain threw off his shirt and picked up a mace that was resting at his feet. "We fight until we take their white sash!"

The entire crew of the *Formica* raised their weapons and cried out with terrible ferocity, "White sash!"

Winches pulled the heavy lines from the harpoons, and the two ships drew together, with very different reactions from the crews. On the *Formica*, the mercenaries began a rhythmic slapping of their weapons on the railing and grunted loudly in accompaniment. When close enough, several crew members threw grappling hooks that dug into the railing of the guild ship and helped pull the vessels together. On the guild ship, the crew had armed themselves, and lined up shoulder-to-shoulder several steps back from the railing. Stone-faced, they appeared resigned to the inevitable fight to come. The lone voice that carried was from someone trying to bolster their courage, but it wasn't appearing to have an effect.

"Look at this sorry lot!" Vechas called out and then laughed lustily. "You heard the captain! Go get that white sash!"

As the first wave of mercenaries prepared to board the guild ship, its crew yelled out in defiance. In unison, the guild mariners took a single step to the side, revealing a host of archers with arrows nocked and ready. The opening volley felled many of the mercenaries as they attempted to vault over the guild ship's railing. While the archers readied another round of arrows, the guild mariners rushed forward to meet their adversaries at the railing, not intending to give them an inch of ground.

Amos thundered down the quarterdeck steps and roared as he launched himself into the fray. The corsair captain's momentum and strength punched a hole in the guild ship defense, scattering the archers and crew alike. As Amos pushed forward on the guild ship deck, the mercenaries quickly followed and the battle began in earnest.

Thorne watched the unfolding chaos and felt a compulsion to act. Leaving Esen, he summoned his mana knife and scanned the guild ship for archers. Seeing only swordfights, the mage stepped up onto the *Formica* railing and leapt onto the guild ship. Instantly, fighters' screams and the clash of steel surrounded him. It was only then that Thorne realized just how unprepared he was for battle.

The mage frantically swiveled his head around trying to determine if he was going to be attacked, his mana knife tentatively held out defensively.

"Die, you damned pirate!"

Thorne spun around just in time to deflect an overhead slash.

The guild mariner followed up with a lunge in an attempt to run him through.

Thorne quickly stepped sideways and swatted the thrust aside as his training took over. He assumed a practiced combat stance and waited for the next attack.

The guild mariner reached back and attempted another overhead strike, but Thorne dodged just in time. Losing his balance, the sailor lurched forward and thrust his free arm out sideways to keep from falling.

With the mariner's chest unprotected, Thorne found his opening and stabbed his mana blade into the man's torso. He felt the blade slide between a pair of ribs.

The mariner's eyes widened in shock and his final exhalation was a quiet groan as he fell to the deck.

It was over so quickly that Thorne was momentarily at a loss what to do. After his duels with Mirtans, one of them picked the other up before replaying the fight and discussing other possible outcomes. It was an academic exercise, albeit a martial one, and the mage had never really grasped the severity of the stakes before.

Thorne took a step back and looked down at his mana knife. There was no stain, no blood, on the arcane blade. Having never drawn blood with it before, it was a strange sight and he wondered if it was because his weapon had only some of the properties of physical matter. Shifting his gaze to the dead mariner, the mage saw a red pool slowly spread from the body onto the deck. He knew he should feel shocked and horrified at what he'd done, but instead he felt nothing. This absence of remorse bothered him, not the actual killing. A good person should feel bad about taking a life, so why didn't he?

"White sash!" The savage cry from the guild ship quarterdeck stopped all nearby fighting.

From the quarterdeck, Vechas bellowed the words while waving a long strip of fine cloth. At the Sehenryu's feet knelt a man with a demoralized look on his face and his opulent clothes in tatters. With the guild captain's surrender and his symbol of authority in Vechas' hands, the battle was over. The mariner crew across the entire deck disengaged from fighting and threw down their weapons.

Amidst the clatter of discarded weapons, there were also a few cries for quarter. Close to where Thorne stood, a mercenary cut down an unarmed guild mariner begging for mercy.

From the bow of the ship, Amos roared at the mercenary, "Fight's over if he gives up, you stupid fuck! We're here to take cargo, not lives!"

"Says you," the mercenary shot back. "You paid me to fight, and my blade's not red enough yet."

Amos stomped across the deck to the mercenary, and without breaking stride, grabbed him by the belt and jerked him towards the railing. Before the mercenary knew what was happening, Amos picked him up and threw him overboard.

"Anyone else feel like not following orders?" he bellowed. After scanning the deck for any challengers, Amos pointed his mace up at Vechas. "Double share of the profits for retrieval of the white sash to you Vechas!" Turning towards the *Formica*, the corsair captain called out, "Move the cargo to our hold, and be gentle mates! It is glass, after all."

As the *Formica* crew followed Amos' order, Thorne relaxed and moved back onto the corsair ship. He was near the forecastle when Dirty Dreebs approached him.

"You seem none the worse for wear," the thin Venhadar said. He grunted and then added, "Guess I lost that bet."

"Where's Essen?"

"He's fine too. Didn't fight much. Knocked a couple men down, but seemed reluctant to do it. As soon as Amos got things under control he went to go find his wife," Dirty Dreebs said.

The mage bobbed his head.

"You alright?" Dirty Dreebs asked after studying the mage.

"I killed a guild mariner," Thorne answered. "I thought it would be a big deal, killing my first man. But it was so easy."

"You've got a killer instinct," Dirty Dreebs mused. "Guess it shouldn't be a surprise. There's no reason why a few mages wouldn't have it."

"What do you mean?"

Dirty Dreebs shrugged and replied, "Some people are just better mentally equipped to handle violence, to take a life. That's not good or bad by itself, but it might be why those people seek out danger."

"I suppose," Thorne said absently.

"Don't feel bad because you think you're supposed to feel bad," Dirty Dreebs said. "No use wasting time on what's already done. Just keep moving forward. Those you're trying to help will thank you for it." The Venhadar grasped Thorne's elbow briefly before walking away to join the other *Formica* crew in unloading the guild ship.

Thorne watched the chaplain leave and wondered if it could be that simple.

· · ·

The aftermath of the raid was considerably more civil than Thorne was expecting. He watched from the *Formica's* deck as the surviving guild ship crew were gathered on the quarterdeck and made to sit under the watchful eye of several mercenaries. Dirty Dreebs performed last rites to the each of the slain, guild or *Formica* crew alike, before the dead were wrapped in cut sections of replacement sail. After being weighed down with a length of spare chain, the dead were cast into the sea.

While the corsair chaplain performed his somber work, the *Formica's* crew transferred the cargo. Amos' corsairs worked with a practiced efficiency. Everyone knew their role and there was little banter. For the crew, fighting was the means to an end and what they were doing now was the real work.

While the large wooden crates were being moved to the *Formica's* hold, Esen crossed back onto the *Formica* from the guild ship. The foreigner looked visibly agitated, his hands curling into fists and then opening again. His nostrils were flared and his mouth pressed into a thin flat line. Esen's skin had the oily sheen of someone who had been in the sun and salty ocean air for some time.

Esen saw the mage and stomped up to him. "Claire's not here," the foreigner said through clenched teeth.

"Not here," Thorne echoed, preoccupied with what Dirty Dreebs had said to him. He was still processing the idea that he was a natural killer and not really paying attention.

"No one knows anything about her," Esen said with increased volume. He swept his arm out to indicate the entire guild ship. When Thorne didn't immediately answer, the foreigner slammed his fist onto the railing. "Where is she?" he shouted.

"What?" Thorne mumbled. He couldn't shake the feeling that he was missing some meaning in the chaplain's words.

Esen pressed his face close to Thorne's and barked, "Help

me!"

Thorne realized that he must appear callous to the foreigner. He saw the desperation in Esen's eyes. The foreigner was lost now that his plan of finding Claire on the guild ship was a failure. Thorne took a step back from Esen and said, "Our best bet is to find Claire's father in Haywood. I'll go talk to Amos and find out how long it will take to sail to Banks now that the raid is complete."

Esen took a moment to digest what the mage had said. The worry in his eyes lessened, but the features of his face were still drawn tight. "Fine," he answered shortly.

Thorne pushed off from the railing, walked around the *Formica* crew, and made his way to Amos' cabin at the stern of the ship. As he approached, Thorne heard Vechas' raised voice through the closed door. The mage drew near the wall and leaned close to listen.

"This is exactly the type of ship I want, Amos," the Sehenryu said irately. "Let me have it. A quarter of my plunder would be yours when we hunt the same waters."

"I know your ambitions well, Vechas," Amos answered. "But my deal with the guild was to relieve the ship of its cargo, not the guild of its ship. Something will float your way if you've the patience for it."

"I'm done waiting!" Vechas snapped. Thorne heard the impact of a powerful fist hitting wood. The Sehenryu continued, "How many years have I served you? Have I not proven myself capable? You've given me my fill of adventure, captain, and for that I'm thankful. However, now I want more. I want to command."

"My answer is no, Vechas," Amos said, an edge now in his voice. "And if you feel it's time for you to go off on your own, then you are free to do so once we reach Banks."

It was quiet for a moment before Vechas called out,

"Whoever is skulking at the captain's door, you best announce yourself now or there'll be hell to pay!"

Thorne opened the door and stepped inside. It had taken Vechas far longer than Thorne was expecting to sense his presence. The Sehenryu must have been considerably agitated for his empathy to be so impaired.

Vechas glared at the mage until it registered that Thorne was not a *Formica* mariner. With a final pointed look at Amos, the Sehenryu pushed past the mage and slammed the cabin door on his way out.

Thorne turned back to Amos just in time to see the corsair take his hand off of an ornate dagger that was on his desk. Amos didn't look particularly perturbed by the previous conversation or Thorne's interruption. He crossed his arms over his chest and rocked back on his heels, his gaze somewhere over the mage's shoulder. Still looking at something in his mind's eye, Amos said, "It won't be too much longer that we're tethered to the guild ship, and then we'll be on our way to Banks. I'm assuming that's what you're here to check on."

"Yes," Thorne answered. "Esen's wife wasn't on that ship, so we need to make haste to Haywood."

"Glassblower guild, eh?" Amos said absently as she smoothed the front of his linen shirt. He blinked a few times before his eyes refocused on Thorne. "Once we're under sail again, it'll be a day and a bit more before we'll be ashore. Now you understand that given our adventure here we won't be sailing into Banks proper. There's a little cove a few hours hike away where we'll drop anchor. I'm sure you'll be able to make it the rest of the way on your own."

"That's fine," the mage answered. "I'll go let Esen know." Thorne took a step towards the door and then paused. Looking over his shoulder he said, "I'm sure the guild ship crew will be relieved to be freed. You've shown a remarkable amount of restraint for a corsair. I wonder if Vechas would have done the same."

Amos grunted and replied, "He has these little tantrums every now and again. Once he gets his double share he'll be happy. It would do him well to remember that there's a lot more to being a captain than just running up on unsuspecting guild ships and bashing heads. It takes patience, which Vechas doesn't have yet."

"Bashing heads," Thorne repeated, looking down at his feet. "How do you do it, Amos? How do you live with yourself, with the ghosts of those you've killed?"

"I remind myself about all the ones that I didn't kill," Amos replied. "I have to kill when I need to, but I'm a mariner, not a killer." After being silent for a short while, he asked "You take your first life today?"

Thorne nodded.

"It's the way of the sea," Amos said. "The strong kill the weak until they're not strong anymore. There's no morality in it, just survival."

Both Dirty Dreebs and Amos seemed to have pragmatic views on killing, and Thorne somehow found that comforting. Feeling a little less burdened than before, he left Amos' cabin and went to find Esen. While it was surprising to discover that he had a killer instinct, he wasn't going to let it overpower his existing sense of identity. He was an Archive mage. He was a Paragon.

CHAPTER FOURTEEN

"I suppose this is where we part ways," Dirty Dreebs said after stopping in front of Banks' sole carillon tower. "It's best if I contact our fence alone, and I would wager that you're eager to continue your search."

The carillon tower began to toll fourteen high bells, and Thorne glanced up. The blue of the cloudless sky was steadily darkening, another clear indicator that there was only an hour until dusk. Looking back at Dirty Dreebs, the mage said, "I suppose you want to get back to your ship. I can't imagine that sitting in that small bay with stolen cargo would be good for Amos' nerves."

Dirty Dreebs brushed the comment away and replied, "Amos is made of sterner stuff, as is the rest of the crew. Besides, once arrangements are made, we'll have no trouble bringing the cargo here."

"Oh?" Thorne prompted, curious to hear more about the on-land aspects of smuggling.

"You saw how easy it was to walk into Banks. This far south there's little fear from B'nisct so the cities often don't have walls. Haywood is a rare exception, so that's why I've prepared these for you." Dirty Dreebs handed Thorne a folded, but unsealed, document.

"What's this?" the mage asked with a frown.

"A letter of introduction that'll allow you entry into Haywood," Dirty Dreebs replied.

Thorne opened the document and scanned it. His eyes lingered at the name at the bottom. "Now I see why Amos values you as part of the crew," he asked. "Your name and stamp can get the *Formica* into any port along the coast, am I right, chaplain?"

Dirty Dreebs smiled, but remained silent.

"How long to Haywood?" Esen asked, ready to be on his way.

"About a full day's walk from here," answered Dirty Dreebs. "You'll be there by this time tomorrow if you get an early start."

"Or we could be there by dawn tomorrow if we leave now," Esen said.

"I wouldn't advise it," Dirty Dreebs cautioned. "While Haywood is on the prince's highway, you'll have to follow the rapid transport route to get there from here. It's mostly farmland in between, but it has a reputation for not being the safest."

"Why?" Thorne asked.

"This far south of the capital means there's not much military presence," Dirty Dreebs answered. "Highwaymen are not uncommon, and there are rumors that a couple of the smarter gangs are consolidating their power and trying to extort escort fees from the guilds."

"Then it won't be long until there is a military presence here since the guilds won't tolerate being bullied," Thorne said. "But that doesn't help us now. I agree that walking during the day is best." Before Esen could protest, the mage added, "Esen, getting a decent night's rest here is going to make the travel to Haywood less strenuous and likely faster."

"And you'll probably want to get some provisions as well, which you'll be able to get today with an hour of daylight left," Dirty Dreebs said. "That reminds me, I have this for you." The Venhadar reached into his pocket and pulled out a small pouch, which clinked as he handed it over to Thorne.

The mage opened the bag and saw it was full of Sovereignty currency. Examining one coin, he asked, "Why are you giving us money? We hardly did any work on the ship. To be honest, I'm still unsure why Amos agreed to take us on."

"Charity is one of my religious duties," Dirty Dreebs said. "As for the captain, he makes his own mind up about things. Maybe he decided that he likes you. In any event, this should be enough to get you decent room and board here. If you haggle with the innkeeper, you might even have enough left over to buy some supplies for the trip to Haywood."

"Thank you, chaplain," Esen said. "Blessings of the Small House on you."

Dirty Dreebs held a fist up, then slowly opened his hand and spread his fingers out wide. "May your ancestors guide and protect you," he replied. The Venhadar parted with a nod and disappeared around a corner.

Thorne looked at Esen and said, "We need to find the blacksmith and the glassmaker shop before we settle down for the night."

"Why?" Esen asked. "The glassmaker shop isn't going to know where Claire is anymore than the mariners on the guild ship we raided."

"True, but they sometimes also sell resins crafted by Archive alchemy," Thorne returned. "Those would be for me, but the blacksmith is for you. You're unarmed, and we need a way to make fire once we leave town."

"You can't make fire?" Esen asked as they started walking down the street. "I thought that was something all wizards could do."

Thorne shook his head and started walking in the direction of the merchant district. After Esen caught up to him, the mage answered, "Make fire, no. Manipulate it, yes. There's a difference."

• • •

Later that night, Thorne and Esen sat on the floor of a tiny unfurnished room that the mage imagined had once been a closet. The one saving grace of the cramped space was a window that faced the harbor and let the warm ocean breeze freshen the stagnant air inside. The only inn that would take the small amount of money they had left after shopping was close to the wharf. Their meal had been just as meager as their accommodations, and while Thorne did not mind, Esen grumbled a few times that they had spent too much money buying supplies.

Sitting underneath the window, Thorne glanced at the brightly glowing ball in his hand. Slightly smaller than a hen's egg, the resin glow sphere had been charged with his mana and was the only source of illumination in the room. He would have liked to purchase a second, but after buying Esen a small knife and short rod of flint from the blacksmith there weren't many coins to spare. As it was, they had just enough to pay for decent accommodations once they arrived in Haywood.

From the open window the mage heard someone start singing. The voice was feminine and sad. Thorne listened for a moment and recognized the song. He closed his eyes and leaned back to rest his head on the wall.

"I know this," Esen said across from Thorne. "Claire would sing it when she got homesick."

"Just wait it out," Thorne said, his eyes still closed. "She'll give up after a while."

Thorne waited for Esen to ask what he meant. Instead he heard the creak of the door opening. The mage opened his eyes just in time to see the foreigner leave the tiny apartment. "Esen, wait!" Thorne called out. "You damn fool," he muttered as he rose and closed his hand over the glow sphere, abruptly putting the room into darkness.

By the time Thorne stepped onto the sparsely lit street Esen was already standing several paces out on one of the short piers. The foreigner looked about for the source of the singing, which seemed to be coming from under the landing. Thorne was about to go grab him, but decided it was better for Esen to learn this lesson first hand. The mage quietly made his way to a broken cart that was close to the pier and watched.

After the song ended, Esen turned a full circle, looking intently in the waters around the pier and finally up towards the clear moonlit sky. The air was still and there was no one in sight all along this section of the harbor. A few large ships limited the view of the surrounding area, but aside from the mysterious singer, Esen appeared to be alone.

"Where are you?" the foreigner called out.

"You heard my song?" a gentle voice replied. "Can you help me?"

"Yes, where are you?" Esen repeated.

"I'll come up to you," came a reply from under the pier. "Please wait there."

From his vantage point, Thorne watched as an Ishwos female gracefully pulled herself up onto the pier. Standing dripping wet near Esen, the nude Ishwos appeared human except for her blue skin and short hair so pale that it bordered on whiteness. With her back to Thorne, he could see three pairs of gills along her ribs. Like most of her race, this Ishwos was very lean.

Esen was clearly taken aback by the appearance of the Ishwos. He retreated a step and held up his hands as if to ward her off.

She leaned forward and asked again, "Can you help me?"

Dropping his hands to his sides, Esen replied, "What do you need?"

The Ishwos clasped her hands together and brought them to her bare chest. "My partner, he's missing. We came here looking to trade, but he's been gone for over a day. He should have returned by now."

"What's your name?" Esen asked. His initial surprise faded, as his voice was no longer tentative.

"I am Kalina."

Esen turned and pointed towards the city and said, "Wait here. I can go find some City Watch to help you."

"No!" She reached out and grabbed his hand. Stepping close to him she pleaded, "I can't wait any longer. I need to find him now. Please, will you help me?"

The foreigner stiffened when Kalina touched him but relaxed after looking at her closely. "Alright Kalina, where'd he go?"

Gently turning Esen towards the city she answered, "I saw him follow some sailors over there."

Esen took a few steps and paused, "Wait, why didn't you go after him when he didn't return?"

Kalina gave him a gentle push that started him walking again. "I'm afraid. I don't like being on land. Or alone," she answered.

The pair stepped off the pier and onto the broad stone platform that transitioned into a wide street that had several narrow alleys leading between the harbor warehouses. Kalina kept her hand on Esen's back as she guided him towards one particular alleyway. She looked behind her, and in that instant Thorne saw the deception. Her innocent and vulnerable expression had vanished and was replaced with the look of a predator.

The mage pushed more mana than he needed into the glow sphere and stepped out from behind the cart. "Stop!" he commanded. Holding up the glow sphere, the bright white light illuminated the area and threw long shadows along the wharf.

Kalina let go of Esen and took a step back towards the pier.

"Where are the others?" the mage demanded as he

approached Esen.

She pointed towards the dark alleyway. In the light of Thorne's glow sphere Kalina's eyes were completely black, giving her an otherworldly appearance.

"Tell them not to prey on the sailors of Banks again or they'll answer to Thorne, Paragon of the Archive."

"What is a Paragon?" the Ishwos said, fear creeping into her voice.

Thorne pushed a burst of mana into the glow sphere and it flared brightly.

Kalina shrank back and covered her eyes.

"I am," the mage said in a chilling voice.

"Oy, what's going on here?" called out a stern voice from the street.

Thorne and Esen turned to see a pair of City Watchmen walking towards them. Both were carrying lanterns and one had his short sword drawn. The mage heard a quiet splash behind him and glanced at the pier to find that Kalina was gone. Concentric circles rippled in the water where she dove in to escape. The mage closed his hand around the glow sphere and extinguished the light.

"Mages don't normally skulk around the docks at night," one of the sentries said. "State your business here."

Thorne gestured toward the water and said, "An Ishwos female tried to lure him down that alley."

The guard holding the sword grunted in frustration. "That bitch is back again? I thought the beating we gave her accomplice would have been enough for them to leave." Looking at the other sentry he commanded, "Go get another patrol. We need to run a more thorough sweep of the alleys here." Looking at Thorne he added, "You best get back to wherever you're lodging. Don't want you getting mixed up in our little hunt."

As they walked back towards the inn, Esen kept looking

back towards the wharf. "Why was she singing? Who was she?" he asked the mage.

"Part of something bad. Maybe thieves. Maybe slavers. Maybe cultists. All of them prey on the unwary here along the docks. It was a trap."

"How do you know?"

Thorne was silent for a few steps and then finally let out a deep breath. "I learned the hard way during my traveling education," he replied.

• • •

The sun filtered down through the forest and spotted the well-traveled road that connected Banks to Haywood. Once they had entered the woods after leaving the harbor town, the air became still and heavy, which coupled with the midmorning heat made Thorne sweaty and thirsty. It didn't help that Esen was pushing the pace hard, his long strides continually lengthening the distance between him and the mage. Several times Thorne had to call for him to stop. Esen did, albeit reluctantly, but had taken the lead again as they now ascended a shallow, but long, incline.

Both men were in foul moods. Esen had made it clear that no more time could be wasted getting to Claire's father and that he would lead on this final leg of the journey. His sense of urgency was palpable. Thorne suspected that the foreigner was also agitated about what had happened the previous night. Despite being saved, Esen probably didn't like that he had been deceived and was moments away from being the victim of some evil plot.

As for the mage, he brooded for different reasons. He was still no closer to understanding why an Archive mage would try to kill Esen. The black robed assassin in the Archive infirmary troubled him because there was sureness in their actions that suggested they had done that work before. Who were they? Was it someone he knew, someone living a double life at the Archive?

As he obsessed over the evil lurking in the shadows of the Archive, he began to question the wisdom of his quest with Esen. What did he think he was going to accomplish on this self-made Paragon assignment? Things were not going as expected, and the mage doubted they would find answers in Haywood. Deciding to engage Esen on his dilemma, Thorne quickened his pace and asked, "What if Claire's father doesn't know anything about Karnoff?"

"Then we go search for her directly, like I wanted to in the first place," Esen replied between heavy breaths. The brawny foreigner was finally starting to fatigue, but he appeared intent on pushing the pace until they reached Haywood.

"Where would we even start?" Thorne pressed. "It might be better to have the guild get involved. They certainly have the resources to help the search. If Claire's father has enough influence, he could even get aid from the prince. I'm sure that if Sovereignty agents were dispatched, they'd find her faster than the two of us working alone."

"What about the Archive?" Esen replied. "Maybe we should have asked about Karnoff before we went to Port."

"Archive mages don't kidnap people," Thorne insisted. "Are you sure of what you saw that night?"

"Don't question me about what I saw," Esen growled. "If we don't get answers from Claire's father, then I'm going to the Granick Archive and not leaving until I find him and learn why he and those soldiers took Claire."

"You have no proof of wrong-doing," Thorne reasoned. "They could say that she left on her own and you made up the story, maybe even got robbed on your way to Yaboon."

"You could vouch for me," Esen said.

"Why would they listen to me?" Thorne asked.

"Because you're an Archive mage! Surely, you must be a person of note." Esen's expression became cruel as he added, "Unless the most impressive thing you've done is help a corsair steal from the guilds."

Thorne felt his face flush hot at both the insult and his own shame. Without knowing it, Esen had hit his ego in a very tender spot. He wanted to have a clever retort, but could think of nothing so remained silent.

When it was clear that no response was coming, Esen gave him a hard look and commanded, "Walk faster."

The mage let Esen get a few steps ahead of him again and watched the foreigner stomp his way up the gently rising hill. As they crested a small rise, they saw a rapid transport pulled off to the side of the road.

Four caribou pawed at the ground and snorted while two Sehenryu and a human woman stood near the back of the carriage. The Sehenryu were dressed for the road in durable canvas pants and sturdy boots. With matching green vests and similar grey fur, the pair might have been indistinguishable from each other save that one looked less weather-beaten and wore a long knife while the other's attire was covered with dust from the road. The woman wore dark red alchemist robes that were beginning to fray at the bottom hem. On the ground nearby was a large leather pack.

"What's going on here?" Thorne muttered as he watched the woman point at one of the rear wheels. The mage scowled when Esen strode past the carriage without stopping or even looking in that direction. "Esen, wait a minute!" Thorne called out as he approached the robed woman. "Where is your home Archive?" he asked her while taking stock of her travel-worn attire.

"Savamont," the woman replied. "I've been on my traveling education for a few months."

"If that's the case, then why are you going by rapid transport?" the mage asked.

"I'm not," she replied. "I happened upon them just today. I came from Haywood and am on my way to Banks."

"We just came from there," the mage replied. He pulled out the Archive guilder around his neck and said, "I am Thorne, from the Yaboon Archive."

The woman smiled, seemingly relieved to have found a fellow mage. "Sera," she said, placing a hand on her chest.

One of the Sehenryu gave a small cough, and Thorne turned to see both the coach driver and his companion watching them.

Standing several paces down the road, Esen glared at everyone with an impatient expression. "We don't have time for this," the foreigner said.

"Please," the coach driver spoke up. "While we greatly appreciate Sera's arrival, we would be most grateful if someone perhaps more experienced could render us some aid. I am Pelental, and my security detail here is Andon, and we are terribly embarrassed about our damaged rapid transport. We do not wish to test the patience of our current passenger. We must get to Haywood most expeditiously."

"Who's inside?" Thorne asked, shifting his head in an attempt to peek between the curtains of the two small widows of the carriage.

"It doesn't matter," Esen said forcefully. "We have our own business and must make haste."

"Now wait a minute," Thorne said giving Esen a disapproving look. "Archive custom is to render aid to mages who need it when on the road, especially for an apprentice on their traveling education. This won't take long."

"We need to find Claire now!" Esen said angrily.

"Maybe you should go," Sera said quietly. "I don't want you to get into an argument because of me."

The mage gave her a kind look, but his expression soured when he locked eyes with Esen. "They need our help, Esen. This will go a lot faster if you work with me."

"I'm done with you," the foreigner seethed. "This is it. We're parting ways here for good."

Thorne slid his hands into his pants pockets and realized that he had the advantage in this situation. "You won't get very far without me," the mage said, intentionally being cryptic.

"So you say," Esen said, and then stormed away from the carriage and down the hill.

"Will he be alright alone?" Sera asked as she watched Esen retreat.

Thorne shook his head in disappointment and said dismissively, "He'll be fine." Looking back at the broken carriage he asked her, "What's wrong here?"

"They said the carriage hit a rut and snapped the rear axle. I thought I could mend it, but the wood won't respond to my mana."

"You can't regenerate dead wood," the mage replied. "That would only have worked if the tree was still alive, and it would have been too slow. You can only move in the direction of entropy now."

"So we can't fix it?" Sera asked, the disappointment obvious in her voice.

"Let me take a look," Thorne said. He went to the back of the carriage and knelt down. One rear wheel was tilted inward and clearly out of alignment. The mage lay down on his back, wriggled underneath the carriage, and looked up at the axle. A thick crack with jagged edges grew out from where it originated at the hub of the askew wheel. Getting out from under the carriage, Thorne examined the wheel and found that the weight of the coach had tilted the wheel such that the top was now pressed tightly against the body.

"The break is near the hub. It's hard to see, but it might go all the way through the bushing," Thorne said, looking at Andon and Pelental. "You carry no replacement parts?"

Pelental shook his head and replied, "It would add too much weight and slow us down."

"All it would take is a replacement axel and you could be on your way," the mage replied. Struck by a thought, he added, "I think I have an idea. Wait here."

"What are you doing?" Sera asked, following Thorne as he turned to leave road and enter into the woods.

Looking back at the apprentice, Thorne said, "No, I need you to wait here too." He fumbled to come up with an excuse why and eventually said, "You have to make sure it doesn't get any worse."

"How?" Sera asked with a confused expression.

The mage didn't answer, but instead quickly left the road and scanned the surrounding trees. It did not take long before he found a young poplar whose trunk was slightly thicker than the width of his hand. He turned back towards the road and was relieved to see that the surrounding foliage mostly obscured the carriage and those standing near it. Putting his back tot the road, Thorne materialized a mana knife with serrated edges. Using the arcane blade like a saw, he quickly felled the tree and stripped off the branches until he had a log nearly as long as he was tall. After dissolving his mana knife, Thorne dragged the log back to the road.

"Those edges are so clean," Sera said as the mage dropped the log by the back of the carriage. "How did you cut that down?"

"Advanced techniques," Thorne said. "That's not important now. Here is where I need your help, Sera." He knelt next to the log and gestured for the apprentice to follow suit. Once she was next to him, Thorne said, "We need to compress all the fibers in this entire log so that it assumes the form of an axle. We'll have to compensate for the natural taper of the tree and any knots."

"Alright," Sera said tentatively. "I don't have much experience with such a precise application of mana."

"No better time than now to practice," Thorne said putting both hands on the log. After Sera did the same, he pushed some mana into the wood. He felt his arcane energy absorb into the bark and seep into the wood, first the tissues, then single cells. Once the log was saturated and his effort stabilized, he glanced over at the apprentice and asked, "Can you feel the individual fibers?"

"Yes," breathed Sera, focusing on her hands as they rested on the log.

"Can you feel the individual cells?"

Sera gave the smallest shake of her head.

"That's fine," Thorne said, looking down at the log. "The fibers should be enough. Now, using that web of mana you've woven, I want you to squeeze the fibers tightly together."

Thorne used his mana to feel the wood shift and compress under Sera's control. The log shrank as the wood became denser. The bark began to separate from the wood, cracking and flaking off, revealing a smooth, pale cylinder with a few protuberances running along the length where there were once branches.

"I'm squeezing as hard as I can," Sera grunted. "But I can't get those knots down."

"Don't worry," Thorne said, reassuringly. "I can apply a bit more force."

The mage focused on the areas where Sera's control of the wood was weak and compressed the fibers down. When a final squeeze reduced the size of the log to a degree where it resembled a lathed axle, Thorne said, "Now, this is the tricky part, Sera. I'm going to withdraw my mana, so you'll have to keep everything compressed yourself."

"What, why?" she said, alarmed.

"Because you need the practice to build up your endurance," Thorne answered. "Also, because I have to generate the blocks that the carriage will rest upon so we can replace the axle."

Sera took a moment to process what the mage had said, and then replied, "You're doing the hard work, aren't you?"

"It's all hard work," Thorne replied. "Are you ready?"

"Do it."

Thorne slowly withdrew his mana from the log.

Sera strained through grit teeth, but the log maintained its compressed form.

The mage felt a jolt as his arcane energy returned to him, and he felt the familiar elation that resulted in manipulating the elements.

"Now the tricky part for you," the mage said. "Take your hands off of the log, but keep control of your mana. You'll have to maintain the form at a distance."

"I wasn't very good at that back at the Archive," Sera said, still keeping her hands on the log.

"It has to be done."

Sera gave Thorne one last unsure look before turning her attention back to the log. With a deep breath, she removed her hands from the log. The form held.

"I did it!" Sera said with a crooked smile.

"Well done," Thorne said. "Now it's time to do my part."

The mage moved to the rear of the carriage and got on his knees again. Pressing both palms on the ground he pushed mana into the soil and waited for it to yield to his command. "Go," he murmured as a small sinkhole formed underneath his hands as the earth compacted and shifted. Keeping his palms on the interior wall of the hole, the mage formed two square blocks, which rose from the ground at the rear corners of the carriage. With a series of creaks and groans, the coach raised a few inches, supported by the earthen blocks.

"Andon, Pelental, if you would be so kind as to remove the wheels and axle from the carriage, we have the replacement ready," the mage said, still maintaining focus on the earth blocks supporting the coach.

The two Sehenryu did as they were instructed, Andon, using his knife to knock out the pin holding the wheel to the axle. Once all the hardware was removed, they took the new axle and shoved it into place, followed by the wheels.

With a heavy sigh, Pelental pointed to the bit of axle protruding out from the wheel and exclaimed, "There are no holes for the pin to keep the wheel from falling off."

"Not a problem," Thorne said with labored breath as he lowered the blocks so the carriage rested on its wheels once more. Not wanting to expend any more mana than necessary, Thorne left the sinkhole only partially refilled. As he stood the mage felt lightheaded and grabbed the coach for support. Trying to pass everything off as a test of the axle, he gave the carriage a hard shove and said, "Appears to hold well. Sera get close to this wheel."

After the apprentice did as she was bade, Thorne instructed, "Now, decompress the wood here at the end of the axle. The wheel will rub, but it should be more than enough to get them back to Haywood for a proper repair."

"Oh, that's clever," Sera said with widening eyes. Smiling, she grabbed the end of the axle as it expanded in her grip, showing a clear edge near the wheel. After performing the same feat on the other side of the carriage, she joined everyone at the front of the coach.

"How can we thank you?" Pelental said with his hands clasped in front of his chest.

"Sera will need to ride with you to Haywood," Thorne answered, gesturing towards the apprentice. "If she gets too distant from the axle her mana will disperse and it will decompress again and probably shatter your wheels."

"It would be an honor to have you sit at my side," Pelental said, looking at Sera. Turning to Thorne he added, "There is a step at the back where you could stand."

The mage nodded in agreement. "I'll do that up until we pass my companion. Then I would ask that we collect him as well."

"I'm most sorry, but there simply isn't room to accommodate another person," Pelental said with genuine disappointment.

Thorne waved the lament away and replied, "Then just slow down enough so that I can jump off. I'll walk the rest of the way with him."

"We are in your debt," Andon said to Thorne, the first time he had spoken since meeting.

As Sera and Pelental climbed up on the coach's bench, Thorne and Andon walked to the back. The Sehenryu guard nimbly hopped onto the narrow rail at the bottom of the carriage and gripped a wooden handle that was attached three quarters of the way up.

As Thorne tried to follow suit, his sense of equilibrium inverted. He lost his balance and awkwardly flopped to the ground.

"Are you alright?" Andon asked, looking down from her perch.

The mage carefully stood and fought off a wave of dizziness that threatened to topple him again. "I'm fine," he lied. It wasn't the worst mana crash he'd ever experienced, but Thorne knew he'd need to eat soon or risk becoming ill. Hopefully

Esen's anger helped drive him swiftly along toward Haywood, that way he'd be able to ride on the rapid transport longer.

Pelental skillfully handled the caribou and in short order the carriage was racing once more down the road. As the ground zipped past, Thorne stuck his head out to the side and closed his eyes. The wind rushing through his hair and over his face felt good, and he tried to take long slow breaths while keeping a firm grip on the coach. Once he began to feel better, Thorne opened his eyes and watched the trees speed by. Looking past the caribou, he saw that they would soon emerge from the forest and enter into the farmland that surrounded Haywood.

Spying Esen before Thorne did, Pelental slowed the carriage just enough for the mage to hop off before accelerating again. The mage raised a hand in parting at the retreating coach and said, "Be safe, Sera."

Esen appeared surprised when the mage approached him, walking through a billowing cloud of dust. "Why'd you get off?" the foreigner asked.

"Thought you'd like the company," Thorne answered.

"That's a lie."

"Then you might like having these," the mage said, reaching into his pocket and pulling out the signed documents Dirty Dreebs gave them. "Without these, there was no way you were getting inside Haywood."

Esen grunted and resumed walking toward Haywood. "You could have just gone back to Yaboon," he said after Thorne caught up to him. "Why are you still here?"

The mage frowned at Esen and then looked away. While he still had questions about the foreigner's story, the assassin in the infirmary was enough of a confirmation that some larger plot was at play than just an abduction. "Maybe I do believe that an Archive mage took Claire," he finally said. "I want to find out why and until then, we need to work together. Can I get your word that you won't run off again?"

Esen gave him a hard look, but after a tense moment answered, "Fine." The foreigner then looked up the road where the walled city of Haywood waited for them in the distance.

CHAPTER FIFTEEN

"I'm sorry, sir," the guild agent said with forced politeness, "but Geridan is not in the city."

"What?" Esen yelped loudly.

Thorne exhaled a deep breath, helpless to stop the quickly deteriorating conversation. With Dirty Dreebs' letter of introduction, entry into Haywood was a painless affair but Thorne had trouble keeping up with Esen's frantic pace once inside the city. Thankfully, Esen needed to ask for directions to the glassmaker guildhall so the mage had a chance to buy a small loaf of bread with their already meager funds. He didn't like being so low on cash and cut off from an Archive, but he needed to eat or suffer another bad mana crash. Still chewing the last mouthful, Thorne trotted to catch up to Esen once the foreigner had gotten his bearings. They walked hurriedly so Thorne did not have much time to take in his surroundings.

Esen had thrown open the guildhall door once they arrived, stormed past the short line of customers, and then demanded to see the guild master.

"Please, sir," the agent replied. "You need to wait behind these other patrons."

"I'm done waiting!" Esen roared. "Where is he?"

Visibly shaken by the foreigner's aggressiveness, the agent took a step back from the counter to put more space between them. "I'll go check," he said. "Please wait here."

The agent disappeared up a set of stairs to the left of the

counter.

Esen stared intently at his retreat, ignoring the sour looks of the people behind him.

Thorne stood off to the side and tried to appear neutral in the whole exchange. Outside, twelve high bells began to toll, so everyone here was trying to get their final business done for the day.

Abruptly, two large figures stomped down the stairs with the agent trailing meekly behind. One was a Sehenryu male, and the other a rough-looking human man. Both were dressed like mercenaries, but each had a large gold glassmaker crest pinned on their left shoulder. They walked up to the Esen, and Sehenryu said to him, "You're causing problems here, so you need leave."

"Not until you tell me where to find Geridan," Esen replied, not backing down.

"You don't understand," the Sehenryu replied threateningly. "You're not wanted here, outlander." He used his short fingers to pantomime a walking motion towards the door.

"Why are you –"

Without warning the Sehenryu's companion threw a haymaker that connected near Esen's temple.

The foreigner's legs buckled and he crashed to his knees.

The other patrons in the guildhall gasped as the guild security grabbed Esen by the arms and dragged him out of the guildhall.

The guild agent stepped up to Thorne and warned, "They'll be coming for you next if you don't leave on your own."

Thorne gave him a hard look before walking out of the guildhall. He gave the guild security a wide berth as they dumped Esen into the street and went back inside. The mage approached Esen and saw that he was still regaining his wits. Kneeling down, Thorne said, "That could have gone better."

Esen rolled up into a sitting position. His eyes had a glazed look to them when he replied, "I have to go back inside. They have to know."

Thorne helped Esen to his feet and led him across the street. They both looked at the glassmaker guildhall for a short while. "We can't do anything right now," Thorne said. "Everyone inside is on their guard, and if they're smart they'll get the City Watch involved."

"So what now?" Esen said with a pained expression.

Thorne thought a moment, then answered, "If Geridan left the city on guild business, there's likely correspondence or records inside about where he went. The guild secretary would have those documents in their office."

"How are we going to get back inside?" the foreigner asked. "We'd need a dragon's luck for that to happen now."

"We might be able to make our own luck," Thorne said. He looked up at the second story of the guildhall and continued, "We'll just have to wait until eight or nine low bells tonight."

"Why so late?" Esen asked with a confused expression. "He'll be long gone from the guildhall."

The mage gave his companion a conspiratorial smile and replied, "That's the point."

• • •

As expected, the streets were mostly abandoned in the hours after midnight, save for patrols of the City Watch. Thorne and Esen moved cautiously through the shadows and down dark alleyways until they were finally pressed up against the backside of the glassmaker guildhall. Above them, a second story balcony running the width of the building obscured their view of the overcast night sky.

After being thrown out of the guildhall, they found meager

but clean accommodations nearby. Finishing a bland meal of fish stew and hard bread in the large common room adjacent to the kitchen, they had rested. After the tolling of eight low bells Thorne and Esen snuck out and took a circuitous route back to where they were earlier in the day.

"Now for the tricky part," Thorne whispered as he looked at a large window that was at eye level. "Any guess where this opens up into?"

"The first floor hallway maybe," Esen whispered. "Could be an office, but how will we know if it belongs to the guild secretary?"

"We'll do some searching once inside," Thorne answered. "First, I need a boost to open this window."

Esen crouched and let the mage step onto his shoulders. With little effort, the foreigner stood while Thorne kept his hand on the wall to maintain his balance. Once Esen planted his feet and steadied himself, Thorne gripped the lower edge of the double paned window and looked for a seam. Slowly and with care he summoned his mana knife, making blade wafer thin and narrow. He then slid the arcane blade between the upper and lower panes of glass where the latch kept the window locked. With a sharp flick of his wrist, the latch flipped open. After dissolving the blade, Thorne carefully lifted the lower pane and slide it upwards.

"I'll climb in and then help you up," Thorne said, looking down at Esen. Grabbing the sill, the mage hoisted himself halfway through the open window. He then wiggled forward, sliding into an empty hallway. After standing, Thorne leaned back out of the window and reached down for Esen to grasp his hands. The mage had to strain to get the big man up. Fortunately, Esen was able to grasp the bottom of the windowsill and pull himself inside.

"What are we looking for?" Esen whispered as he looked

down the dark hallway.

"In the guild secretary's office there should be recent correspondence, things from the past month or so before they get archived by the guild historian," Thorne said. "Any of those documents might have information about scheduled meetings for high ranking guild members and their travel arrangements. It's our best chance to find a clue where Geridan is right now."

Thorne took the glow sphere from his pocket and charged it with a small amount of mana. The orb glowed with a pale bluish light, which he partially shaded by closing his fist. "Which room is it?" he asked, opening his hand slightly to let more light escape and illuminate one of the doors along the hall.

Esen shrugged his shoulders and pointed to a different door farther down the hall that was closer to the receiving room of the guildhall. The pair crept along and quietly opened the unlocked door.

Once inside, Thorne looked to Esen and asked, "Can you read?"

The foreigner gave him a sharp look and snapped, "I might not be a scholar like you, but I know the letters and numbers of this continent." He added, more gently, "I can read well enough, thanks to that missionary. And to Claire."

The two men searched the large, but sparsely furnished office. Opposite the door they entered was a large desk with a series of cabinets on the wall to the right and a large buffet table on the left. A small shuttered window was behind the desk.

"Look in the desk drawers, and I'll try the cabinets," Thorne instructed.

Turning to the bank of cabinets, the mage pulled one drawer out and found several leather-bound ledgers. Picking one up, he flipped though the pages and found it was a dated account of the glassmaker guild's dealing with the prince's household staff for fine drinking goblets. The other ledgers were similar but for wealthy city governors in the Granick province.

"Any luck?" Thorne asked, looking over his shoulder at Esen.

The foreigner shook his head and replied, "I've found notes for guild council meetings and recent travel arrangements for the guild treasurer but nothing for the guild master."

Thorne closed the drawer and joined Esen at the desk. "Where'd you find the travel records?"

Esen stepped back and pointed at the open and empty desk drawer. "There's nothing else in there, but the one next to it is locked."

The mage jiggled the handle and verified Esen's assertion. "Let's see what's so important," he murmured. He summoned his mana knife and wedged it between the drawer and the frame. The wood creaked as he attempted to pry the drawer open, but it held fast. Pulling his arcane blade free, Thorne looked at Esen and said, "That's a good lock. I might have to manipulate the wood directly to –"

Bright lantern light streamed though the open doorway.

Esen and Thorne looked up and saw two large figures step into the room, each holding a short sword.

The one holding the lantern pointed his sword at Esen and called out, "Hey! What are you two doing here again?"

Thorne recognized the guards as the Sehenryu male and his human partner from earlier in the day.

"Make this easy on yourself, chaps," the man said taking a step towards Esen while the Sehenryu advanced in Thorne's direction. "Come with us outside so we can turn you over to the City Watch, real peaceful this time. You might only end up with a crippled hand or a month in prison for this if you give up now."

"Drop your sword," the Sehenryu commanded to the mage. "I don't want to get blood everywhere in the secretary's room."

Thorne glanced at Esen out of the corner of his eye. The foreigner clutched a glass inkwell and had it posed for a throw. "Go back the way we came!" the mage shouted as he assumed a defensive stance and focused his attention on the approaching guard.

The Sehenryu snarled, "There is no escape!" With two quick thrusts, he advanced on Thorne and lashed out with a powerful strike meant to cleave the mage from shoulder to hip.

Blocking the blow with his mana knife, Thorne took a step forward and pushed the Sehenryu's sword aside. Still clutching the glow sphere with his other hand, Thorne lifted it up and pushed a burst of mana into it. The resin greedily absorbed the arcane energy and flared a brilliant white light.

The Sehenryu cried out and covered his eyes with his free hand.

Thorne heard the sound of something heavy shatter as he plunged his mana knife into the Sehenryu's chest. The arcane blade met little resistance and the mage stabbed his adversary twice more before retreating back and lessening the light from his glow sphere.

As the Sehenryu collapsed to the ground his short sword clattered next to him.

Thorne kicked it away and then looked over at Esen. The foreigner held his wrist and grimaced in pain, but the other guild security was gone.

"Where'd he go?" Thorne asked as he glanced down the hallway.

Esen shook his head and answered, "Don't know. He cut me when I threw the inkwell, but your light scared him away."

"We need to go," Thorne said, grabbing Esen by the shoulder and pushing him into the hallway.

"What about the locked drawer?" Esen asked, holding his wrist close to his chest.

"Too late for that now. We have to make ourselves scarce."

As they approached the open window, Thorne heard a frantic voice outside shout, "Help! Murder in the glassmaker guildhall! Murder!"

The mage dissolved his mana knife and helped Esen climb onto the window ledge. He noticed the foreigner's left hand was slick with blood. After they were clear of the building, Thorne said, "Stay low and in the shadows."

Neither man stopped running until the shouts from the guild security were distant and the lantern light from the inn where they were lodging was in sight.

• • •

"It's too tight," Esen grunted as Thorne pulled on the knot at the foreigner's wrist.

After returning to the boarding house, the mage grabbed a pitcher of water from one of the communal tables where meals were served. Once Esen's hand was washed clean, Thorne was relieved to find the wound was not deep, but with no linen to wrap the cut, he was forced to use a strip of Esen's tunic to bind it. With a little luck they wouldn't have to worry about an infection.

"If you want to stop the bleeding, this is how tight it needs to be," Thorne replied, adjusting the knot over the cut one final time. "At least until the morning, leave it alone."

"Don't you have magic that can heal me?" Esen asked.

Thorne scoffed and answered, "Mages can bend the laws of nature, but we don't work miracles." He paused at the thought for a moment, and then added, "Besides, those techniques are beyond me."

"What does that mean?"

The mage frowned. "It means I might have been able to do

more about your wound if I had learned how to apply mana for bodily repair."

"So there is healing magic," Esen's voice was more accusatory than Thorne liked.

Shaking his head, Thorne answered, "No, not in the sense that you're thinking. A precise application of mana to your wound could constrict your veins to slow the bleeding and clot faster, but it wouldn't close the cut. Likewise, mana could deaden nerves to stop the pain, but your reflexes would also be affected. Your body still has to do the majority of the work, but an Archive physician could help the process along."

"Then why can't you do any of that?"

Thorne narrowed his eyes and spat, "I just told you." He took a deep breath to calm down and continued, "I never learned those techniques and trying to do it without training is dangerous. I could cripple you if I made a mistake." He pointed at the dressing and said, "At least with this you have a fair chance of recovering fully in time. You're lucky that he got only a glancing blow in before he ran." The mage scoffed, "So much for loyalty to the guild. Coward."

Esen's expression darkened to match Thorne's. After gingerly rotating his injured wrist, he said, "Better a coward than a corpse. You seem rather comfortable with murder."

The foreigner's words hit a soft spot and Thorne found himself grinding his teeth at the comment. He didn't want to admit it to himself, but Esen was right. Killing the Sehenryu was easy, and this time it just felt like something that needed to be done. Now that Esen brought it up, that callousness distressed him. He wanted to feel worse for killing, but he didn't.

"And what would you have done?" Thorne asked rhetorically after a long pause. "Whether you lost your hand, which you still might, or ended up in a prison cell to languish for a month, either one wouldn't help you find Claire."

Esen's eyes flashed with anger when his wife's name was invoked. His fierce expression faded after a few breaths and he replied, "Given the circumstances and our need for haste, I do admit that there was probably no better alternative."

"Good. You keep that in mind since I doubt Claire's kidnappers will just relinquish her without a fight." The mage paused before adding, "We'll have to be more careful in the city now. They'll be searching for us."

"So what do we do?"

The mage looked at the ceiling and thought back to the last Paragon meeting where Reihana asked about their spy networks across the continent. While he didn't have any contacts in Banks, now that they were more inland things were different. "I know someone who might help us here, now that we've exhausted all other options," he said.

"Who?"

Thorne's gaze dropped down to Esen before returning to the ceiling. "An old acquaintance of my family's," he answered reluctantly.

CHAPTER SIXTEEN

Reihana looked out the small carriage window, but she wasn't watching the countryside race past or the wispy silver clouds lazily drifting across the sky. Instead she alternated between wondering how Thorne had evaded her at Port and cursing the caribou pulling the carriage for not moving faster.

After her violent encounter with three would-be assailants, she had spent the next day scouring Port trying to find Thorne and the foreigner with no success. Somehow they had gotten help and snuck onto a ship. As she watched several vessels leave Port, Reihana knew she could stay there no longer. She had already deduced they wouldn't go straight after Geridan's daughter because that would be like searching for a particular grain of sand on a beach. Instead they'd travel with all due speed to Haywood where Geridan administered the glassblower guild. With that course of action, there was a very real risk Thorne would learn the truth behind Claire's abduction and her role in it.

She had to reach Geridan before them or her plans would be in jeopardy, given she wasn't sure of Karnoff's current whereabouts. After making the decision to leave, Reihana secured a rapid transport to take her directly to Haywood from Port. As far as inland routes went, the prince's road was typically easy travel if the weather cooperated and took two or three days to complete. If Thorne and the foreigner traveled via a ship, they'd have to travel down the coast and then back towards the center of the continent, so unless unexpectedly delayed, Reihana would get to Geridan well before them.

Without warning, the carriage slowed. Reihana's eyes snapped into focus as she looked out the window, crooking her neck to see towards the front of the carriage. The bottom of the driver's bench obstructed her view, so she banged on the roof of the coach to get his attention.

"Why are we stopping?" she called out.

"We're at the River Curven checkpoint," the driver shouted.

Reihana threw herself back into the bench in annoyance. The River Curven was the natural border between the Yaboon and Granick provinces on the southern half of the continent. Here the river was not so wide but had deceptively fast moving water, so it was the perfect place to set up a well-fortified border crossing. Though not all roads had checkpoints, especially those closer to the frontier, the prince's highway and other major travel routes were littered with them. While the guilds were vocal in their complaints about the tolls required to pass through, they were paid so travelers could benefit from Sovereignty soldiers patrolling the road and keeping them free of bandits or B'nisct swarms.

After what seemed like a long time, Reihana banged on the carriage roof again and called out, "What is taking so long?"

"They're reviewing my transport guild documents," the driver yelled back. "Took my guilder too for inspection."

"This is asinine," Reihana muttered angrily. Not tolerating being in a stopped carriage any longer, she threw the door open and stepped out to glare at the border crossing. The bridge that spanned the river was built from timbers anchored by huge pillars that looked to be whole tree trunks planed smooth. There were thick sidewalls that rose to slightly over shoulder height to prevent anything from tumbling off the edge. Facing the carriage was a closed double-door gate, with a platform hidden behind a short wall above it. Standing on the platform were two bowmen, both dressed in the colors of the Granick Sovereignty. On the ground was a third soldier, a pikeman, who stood out in front of the gate reading a set of yellowed documents. It was unclear how many more were positioned on the other side.

The pikeman ambled over to the front of the carriage. His black hair was greasy and the early start of a beard suggested he had not seen his barracks for a few days. However, his eyes were bright and his expression alert as he handed the documents and a guild medallion back up to the driver and said, "Papers all appear to be in order. The toll to cross over into Granick province is three ducats."

Reihana dug her thumbs into the opening of a pouch cinched at her belt and pulled it open. She retrieved three hexagonal discs made from translucent red resin. Devised as a way to prevent mages from being constantly robbed when traveling, the tokens did not have any value themselves but when taken to an Archive were exchanged for Sovereignty standard currency. She took a few steps towards the pikeman before she thrust out her hand.

"Here," she said. "Now open the gate."

Looking down at the tokens, the guard's eyebrows bounced up in surprise. "Archive money!" he exclaimed, glancing up at Reihana. "Are you a wizard?"

"I am an Archive mage, yes," Reihana replied coolly. Most arcane practitioners and alchemists much preferred being called something other than a name historically associated with demons.

The pikeman made no move to take the offered tokens and instead replied, "Keep your strange coins. You can pay for crossing another way."

"Is that so?" Reihana replied as she dropped the tokens back into her pouch.

Using his pike to gesture at the river, he said, "The grain mill that is a bit up the river is broken. Go fix it and we'll let you through."

Reihana scowled and shook her head. "No, I'm in a hurry. I'll double the toll if you let me through now. You can split the extra with your mates if you're feeling generous. Keep it all if you're not."

The sentry took his pike in both hands and gave her a serious look. "And I said, go fix the grain mill and I'll let you through, wizard."

"Why do you care what happens to the mill?" Reihana snapped. "You're a soldier fed by military stores. What's one rural mill to you?"

The pikeman nodded toward the countryside, but kept his eyes locked on her. "My brother's a farmer out here," he said simply. "Mill's important to his livelihood."

Reihana blew out a deep breath. There was no way the sentry would be bribed if he had a personal stake in getting the mill fixed. For the briefest moments she thought of forcing her way past the checkpoint. It wouldn't be hard to overpower the three soldiers here, but glancing back at the carriage she discarded the idea. She would also have to kill the rapid transport driver if he saw her use secret Paragon techniques. That would never work because the trained caribou wouldn't respond to her commands as an unfamiliar driver.

"Is there a place to cross elsewhere?" Reihana called up to the driver.

"For individual caribou, maybe, but not a team pulling a carriage," he replied. "Rapid transports are meant to stay on the roads. We'd crack an axle or injure a caribou trying to ford the river." He shrugged and added with genuine feeling, "I'm sorry, but it'd be faster just to help him than going somewhere else. I could take you there, we'd just have to go slowly."

"Fine, I'll do it," Reihana replied. She stomped to the carriage, jerked the door open, and climbed inside. She heard driver say something to the pikeman, probably an estimate of distance to the mill, before the carriage turned off the road to carefully travel parallel to the river.

． ． ．

The grain mill was situated along a gentle bend of the river where the banks were uncommonly high. Built on a solid foundation of stones and mortar, it was a large building constructed from roughly cut planks that had been left unstained and were now weathered gray. It would have been a fine subject for a pastoral painting save for the giant wheel that lay half submerged at the edge of the river.

Reihana stood on the opposite bank where the mill was built and scanned the river. The water level was quite low, with broad stretches of mud and rocks exposed on either side. Even so, the river was at least three times as wide as she was tall and rolling along quickly. The rapid transport driver was right, trying to ford the river would have been disastrous, but that realization didn't alleviate her ire.

She glanced back at the carriage and watched the driver untether the caribou so they could rest and graze. The well-trained animals wouldn't take flight once free, but would stay close to the carriage and the protection that they associated with it. The driver had told her he would stay with the carriage while she worked. Reihana assured him that she'd send along food to him once she had appraised the situation.

Turning back towards the mill, Reihana decided it was time to stop being angry at the situation and get to work. She charged both of her hands with a substantial quantity of mana before squatting. The long prairie grass pushed up around her and brushed her face as she pressed both hands firmly onto the ground. Her command of the earth radiated out around her until she focused it forward, feeling the muddy banks and the sand underneath the river. Manipulating the mud with her arcane energy, Reihana summoned a series of earthen pillars that spanned the river. As the blocks broke the surface of the river, the sand quickly dried, leaving a rough yet stable surface that would provide sure footing.

Maintaining her focus on the conjured footbridge, Reihana took measured steps and crossed the river. Near the middle, she noticed a Venhadar female had come around the mill towards the riverbank. She wore a dusty green shirt with long sleeves tucked into brown pants. Her blonde hair was pulled up in a loose coil on the top of her head. An impassive expression was on her face as Reihana approached.

"Another wizard," the Venhadar said, clearly unimpressed. "I hope you can do better than the last one."

Reihana was taken slightly aback by the cool greeting before remembering she was out in the country where folk still clung to old superstitions about arcane practitioners. She gave a close-lipped smile before replying, "I am Master Iris, from the Yaboon Archive. It appears you have a problem with your mill." She gestured towards the wheel embedded in the river.

The Venhadar grunted and jerked a thumb at her chest. "Gilly. I run the mill here. Been in the family for three generations." She looked at the wheel and added, "Yup, got a problem. A few days ago a wizard, young lass, a Sehenryu, tried to help, but just ended up dropping my wheel into the muck."

"Was she an apprentice on her traveling education?"

The miller gave Reihana a strange look and then pointed back to the wheel, "She tried some crazy type of floating magicks. Tore the wheel clean from the axle, but then she dropped it. She must've been sick or something because she puked everywhere for a couple hours. Didn't think a body that small could hold so much liquid." Gilly chuckled and then finished, "She left that same day. Said she couldn't help now that the wheel had sunk so low into the riverbed. We've been trying to dig it out, but not making much headway. It's just me here today, but I've got a couple of lads who help when the grain comes in."

Reihana listened to Gilly's story, but the words "floating magicks" stuck in her head. Could that apprentice have been foolish enough to try a gravity manipulation? Reihana shook her head in disappointment. No wonder that Sehenryu had such a bad mana crash. Manipulating gravity was an advanced technique and needed years of training and practice to accomplish even at a basic level. The hubris of the apprentice to think she could do it was aggravating, especially since it was unnecessary.

"A sequence of earth manipulations should push the wheel up and back into place," she mused aloud, studying the wheel as the river flowed around it.

"Huh?"

"I can help you," Reihana said shortly.

"We'll see," the miller grunted. "Can't do much worse than that last one."

Reihana looked at the wide stretches of sand along both banks and asked Gilly, "Was the wheel not turning because the water was too low?"

"Yup. Been a dry few months. Wheel starting moving slower and slower until one day it just stopped. If it just would rain, the water'd go back up, and we'd be fine again. That other wizard wanted to lower the wheel."

Reihana shook her head and said, "That never would have worked. How would she have transferred the force upward? You'd need to forge a vertical crank with a toothed cone on each end."

"I dunno. She seemed pretty confident, so I just let her try. I thought it was better than doing nothing. Learned my lesson on that one."

Reihana felt her face grow hot at the oblique insult to mages in general. She gave Gilly a look that was not quite scornful, but kept silent any biting words. Instead, she nodded and turned to face the river while pushing mana into both hands. She knelt and pressed her palms into the ground, reaching out with her mana to the area underneath the wheel. Her brow knitted together in concentration as conjured clamps of sand fastened themselves to three points on the waterwheel. Adding more mud to the base of the clamps, Reihana slowly raised the wheel and rotated it into an upright position. She had to re-energize the earth she was manipulating several times as the wheel moved with agonizing slowness towards the mill. Once the wheel was correctly in place, she locked the earthen supports keeping it stable with a final surge of her mana.

As she stood up, Reihana's vision tunneled and a single high-pitched tone deafened her. She took a wobbly step forward and fought back a frightening dizziness. Sweat ran down her neck and her shirt clung to her back. Gulping air, she tried to focus on the wheel and use it to get her bearings. After what seemed like an agonizingly long time, the screech that only she could hear was replaced by the thumping of her heart. Much more slowly, her vision improved. She hadn't exerted herself this much in some time, and the lack of training almost resulted in a mana crash. Standing up a bit straighter, Reihana made sure she felt composed before turning to Gilly.

"Well, now that's something else," the miller said amazed, still staring at the wheel. Looking over at Reihana with newfound admiration she added, "Much obliged. Guess you're a better wizard than I gave ya credit for."

Still feeling wobbly, Reihana wasn't in the mood for faint

praise. "I'll need to stay here for the duration of the repair," she explained. "I'd appreciate it if you work with some haste to secure that wheel."

"You're not done? Can't you just magic the sand blocks to stay there and be on your way?"

Reihana shook her head, which she instantly regretted as her balance upset again. After a sharp intake of breath, she answered, "No, my arcane energy is keeping the sand blocks in contact with the wheel. Once I get too far away, it would dissipate and the sand would collapse and the wheel would fall before it's attached to the building."

"But what about the materials wizards make? Resins and such. I got some. Aren't those permanent?"

"Yes, but those are made with alchemy."

"Whatcha mean?"

Reihana gave a patient smile and replied, "You can think of magic as energy, and alchemy as physical things, but sometimes they can be interchanged, or be the same thing. There's beauty in it, don't you think?"

"You're a strange lot, you wizards," Gilly said, shaking her head.

Reihana considered Gilly's comment and then nodded. Now was the perfect time to sow an idea. "Maybe so," she said, "but despite our strangeness, we want to help people. That's the purpose of magic, or at least that's what I think. If mages were more accepted across the continent, then they might become more common. If that happens, then magic could be used for everyone's benefit." She gestured towards the mill, "You might have been already up and running again if that were the case."

The miller drew her head back as if encountering a bad smell. "The idea of more wizards running around might make some people nervous. Best to keep you in your towers, in the big cities, and call you out only when we need you."

"You sound like the council," Reihana grumbled under her breath. "I want something more."

"Come again?"

"It's nothing, just thinking about home," Reihana answered more clearly.

"Huh. Well anyway, shouldn't take too long to fix now that the wheel's in place. I'll go fetch the lads."

• • •

Three days later the rapid transport passed through the main gate of Haywood. It had taken two days for the miller and her workers to fix the wheel. Once the job was done Gilly got a free ride on the rapid transport to the bridge checkpoint to confirm that the repair was complete. After crossing into Granick province, with the caribou rested and now urged on by the driver, it had taken another full day to arrive at their destination. The prince's road from the River Curven checkpoint wound south and paralleled the mountains until it reached Haywood, and was sparsely occupied. Reihana noticed a pilgrim caravan plodding along near the farms just outside of Haywood, but only because they caused the rapid transport to slow slightly until they cleared the road. Otherwise, Reihana had spent the journey either obsessing about where Thorne and the foreigner were or cursing the fool apprentice who pulled the wheel free from the mill. If she ever found out who they were, she'd make sure they never attained Master rank.

At Haywood, Reihana exited the carriage the instant it stopped at the transport guild stables and rushed down the street toward the guildhalls. She was familiar with the city, having traveled there several times to meet with Geridan. She had worked hard to bolster her spy network here, ensuring that she would be well appraised about current events with Yaboon's provincial neighbor to the west. If Thorne was in the city, she would learn about it very soon.

At the glassmaker guildhall, Reihana flung open the door and walked up to the counter, bypassing several people waiting in line and ignoring the critical looks they gave her. Looking at the slender clerk who was assisting a pair of well-dressed Venhadar males, she demanded, "Tell Geridan that Master Reihana of the Yaboon Archive is here to see him. It is urgent."

"Oh," the woman uttered, taken aback by Reihana's forceful entry and request. She stammered, "I-I'm sorry, but the guild master isn't here today."

"Where is he?" Reihana demanded.

Before the shaken woman could reply a Sehenryu male, broad-shouldered with black fur and bright yellow eyes, emerged from one of the rooms behind the counter. Making eye contact with Reihana and recognizing her, he replied, "I'll step in here, Larali. Master Reihana, please come with me."

Reihana stepped around the counter and followed the Sehenryu she knew as guild secretary Kyrine back to the office he came from a moment ago.

After he closed the door, Kyrine walked around his desk and sat down. "I could tell this was serious the second you walked into the guildhall," he said while cocking his head. "Your sense of urgency is nearly palpable and overpowered all of the other emotions I felt outside my office."

"I must talk to Geridan immediately," she said impatiently.

"Larali was being truthful. He's not here, but in Haven, and I must admit that I am glad for it."

"What?" Reihana asked. In all of her dealings with Geridan, he had always reiterated that Claire was to be returned to Haywood. Those were the instructions she had given Karnoff, and neither of them had been informed of any change in plans. Why was the guild master not here?

Kyrine gestured to a spot behind Reihana and replied, "Last night a pair of would-be thieves broke into the guildhall and ransacked this very office. One of our people was unfortunately killed near where you stand. The strange thing is that they took nothing, so I can only guess what they were after. With Geridan being so engrossed in his current negotiations, this is an unwelcome problem."

Reihana glanced down and noticed the bloodstains on the floor. Kyrine was made of sterner stuff than most guild officers if he could work alone in a room where someone was murdered the night prior. "They haven't caught whoever did this?" she asked.

"Not yet, however I doubt the culprit was foolish enough to stay in the city."

Both of Reihana's hands clenched into fists as all the pieces fell into place. Thorne and the foreigner had indeed beaten her here, but were also stymied when learning Geridan wasn't in the city. If he was a stranger to the glassblower guild, then Thorne had no agents here. In that case he was not going to be told where Geridan was currently. He and the foreigner must have been the ones to break in last night.

"They would be that foolish if they didn't find what they were looking for here," Reihana said decisively. "I will catch them for you. Consider it a personal favor from the Yaboon Archive to the glassblower guild."

"What about your urgent matter with Geridan?"

Reihana looked out the window behind Kyrine, already mentally roaming the streets in pursuit of Thorne. "How long will he be in Haven?" she asked.

"Despite his abrupt departure, he said it would be a prolonged stay," the Sehenryu answered while rubbing his hands. "If you must speak with him, then traveling there will likely be the most expeditious way. He will be one of the governor's guests."

"Thank you, Kyrine," Reihana said, looking from the window back to him. "You have been very helpful. It will be remembered."

"Good hunting," he replied. The Sehenryu rose from his seat and asked, "Can you see yourself out?"

Reihana nodded and left the guildhall as urgently as before. She finally had Thorne and the foreigner within reach. It was time to deploy her network. It would take much of the remaining day to talk to the necessary people, but by the first low bell tonight, the city of Haywood would no longer be a safe place for those two.

Kyrine said Geridan was in Haven, which was a neighboring city in the Granick province. She'd be able to deal with Thorne here and then take a rapid transport to the guild master. If Karnoff wasn't there already then she would reassure Geridan personally that Claire's return was imminent. Feeling more confident, she rested a hand on her belt and felt the scabbard of the knife she had obtained from her agents in Port. The resin blade might not be as satisfying to use as her mana knife, but Reihana was certain she'd nonetheless enjoy watching the life fade from Thorne's eyes with it in her hand.

CHAPTER SEVENTEEN

"Why are we here again?" Esen asked the next morning as he and Thorne entered the tanner guildhall. Neither had slept well and having skipped breakfast to get an early start on the day put them in no better spirits. The mage tried to move them quickly, but without arousing too much notice, back toward the cluster of guildhalls where they had been the night before. After finding the drab one-story building, they looked over their shoulders one last time to see if they were being watched before going inside.

"This is the proxy for the mercer guild in this region," Thorne replied. "There's not enough business going through Haywood to maintain a presence, so the mercers pay a fee to allow their business to be conducted here."

"And there's someone here who can help us?"

The mage shrugged and muttered noncommittally, "I haven't spoken to him in a long time. Last I heard, he had moved to this area after amassing a small amount of wealth and was attracted by the promise of land ownership."

"Land ownership this close to the coast?" Esen said, with raised eyebrows. "He must have a personal connection with the prince to get that type of offering."

"Perhaps," Thorne said, his expression darkening slightly. "For a number of years he was a shrewd agent for the mercer guild. No doubt he had made connections elsewhere."

Thorne observed that this particular tanner guildhall was

modestly decorated and furnished. Along one long wall were complete hides of various large animals stretched on decorative wooden frames. The opposite wall had portraits of past guild masters and other notable members. In the center of the hall rested a large sturdy table, with leather upholstered chairs encircling it.

They walked to the back of the hall where three doors presumably led to offices given the lack of a second floor. This early in the morning the main hall was empty. Thorne gave two loud knocks on the center door.

"That leads to the hallway," came a voice from the door to his left. "Enter here instead."

Opening the left door, Thorne and Esen stepped into an office that looked similar to the one they were in last night. Behind a large desk, a portly human male with ruddy skin stood up. His eyes crinkled at the corners and his smile was genuine when he asked, "Eagerness to get business underway early in the morning is something I admire in anyone coming through our doors. Welcome to the tanner guildhall. I am Remmie, guild secretary. How can I assist you?"

Thorne was about to speak, but then paused. He had thought of a number of ways to ask where to find his acquaintance, but now none of them seemed appropriate. Old feelings that made him uncomfortable had filtered through the normally impermeable barrier he had erected to block out his past.

After a moment of awkward silence, Esen said, "We're looking for a family friend of his."

Remmie's expression became a mixture of confusion and annoyance. "Does that person have an association with the guild?"

The mage nodded and said, "Um, yes, through the mercer guild. A Venhadar named Burtrim."

The guild secretary's eyes jumped in surprise. "Not many

people know he's in this region. He's been trying to keep a low profile after his land title had been granted." Remmie tapped his chin and added, "He's afraid that long lost relatives are going to come and try to impose themselves on him."

"Yes, well, you can see that we are not some distant relation," Esen said, giving Thorne a sidelong glance. "Can you direct us to him?"

Remmie looked critically at both of them for a moment and continued to tap a finger on his chin. Finally he said, "Well, I'm not comfortable sharing the details of his estate, but it so happens that you'll likely find him at the Venhadar fane right now. He took a nasty fall off the roof of his house and has been receiving care there for the past week."

"Fell off his roof? How is he not dead?" Esen asked.

Before Remmie could answer, Thorne interjected, "At the temple. Very good, thank you, Remmie."

The mage left the room and was nearly to the guildhall door before Esen caught up to him.

"What was that all about?" the foreigner asked, grabbing Thorne's arm to stop him. "Why are you acting so strange?"

Thorne pulled himself free of Esen's grasp and took a step away from him. "I'm fine. Let's just go find the fane."

"Do you know where it is?" Esen asked. When Thorne shook his head, the foreigner said, "Well, thankfully I made a more polite exit than you. Remmie told me where to go."

With Esen doing an impressive job of navigating the city, they found themselves in front of the fane a quarter of an hour later. The imposing stone temple could easily have been mistaken for a castle keep, albeit constructed from polished marble. Thick pillars supported an overhang covered with ornate carvings that depicted scenes of feasting and song. A short set of stairs led up to a broad platform where a series of small braziers were burning with flames colored red, blue, or green.

"The oblates coat the charcoal with minerals so it burns with different colors," Thorne said as they ascended the stairs.

"It smells bad. Acrid, like a blacksmith's forge," Esen commented with a scrunched face. Glancing at the mage he added, "Or an alchemist's laboratory."

"Alchemy and religion can coexist just fine," Thorne replied, not hiding his agitation.

"If the price is reasonable," Esen countered.

"Let's focus on finding Burtrim," the mage snapped as they walked across the threshold.

The fane interior was not as dark as Thorne expected due to the numerous domed skylights in the ceiling that allowed a generous amount of sunlight into the small atrium.

"Are you looking to talk to someone?"

Both Thorne and Esen turned to see a Venhadar female approach them. She had tan skin, shoulder-length black hair, and wore plain clothes dyed in hues of grey and green. What seemed out of place was the bloodstained leather apron she wore.

"They sacrifice animals here?" Esen said, aghast.

"What? No!" the Venhadar said. "I just came from work. I'm a butcher, but I'm having trouble with one of the farms where I get my livestock, so I came here to ask my great uncle for advice."

Before Esen could continue the conversation, Thorne interjected, "We're looking for where they treat the sick and injured."

The butcher pointed down a small hallway to their left. "Infirmary's that way," she said. "One of you hurt?"

"No, thank you for the help," Thorne said before he headed in the indicated direction.

Once again Esen was left in Thorne's wake. When he caught up with the mage, he said, "Why do you keep doing that to me? You're not very good with people are you?"

"That's what I've been told," the mage replied tersely.

The temple infirmary was not as well stocked, equipped, or staffed as the Yaboon Archive, but Thorne appreciated that it did have the same calm and quiet atmosphere. The greeting area only had furniture fit for Venhadar, so both men stood and waited to see if Burtrim was receiving care. After a short wait they were led down a hallway lined with large alcoves that were furnished with cots and small tables. Some of these treatment bays were occupied, though most were empty.

"Burtrim, you have visitors," the nurse said before leaving. Thorne and Esen stood partly in the alcove, partly in the hallway and looked down at an elderly Venhadar lying on a cot. A thin black blanket was pulled up to his chin. His face was wrinkled, and coupled with a short beard and hair of silver-white, Burtrim looked to be of considerable age. His eyes were closed and breathing regular, so the mage assumed he was asleep.

Standing over him, Thorne felt his jaw tighten as he thought about the last time he saw the elderly Venhadar. At the time he was a young man preparing to leave his family estate and travel to the Archive to begin his training as a mage. It was not a happy parting, and he had done his best to hide his anguish until the rapid transport was on the open road.

"Can we wake him?" Esen whispered, rousing Thorne from his unpleasant recollections.

"The nurse did speak to him," Thorne replied quietly. "But typically at the Archive we're supposed to leave those under care to rest."

"So we just stand here and wait? Time is not a luxury we have right now."

The mage shrugged and gave Esen a sidelong glance. If he was being honest, Thorne was in no hurry to rouse Burtrim. After so long, he was afraid of what the old Venhadar would say.

Opening his eyes, Burtrim spoke, "You look tired, Thorne. Maybe you'd like to switch places with me?"

The mage's surprised expression elicited a chuckle from the old Venhadar. "Pretending to be asleep allows me a chance to see who is creeping down this hallway," Burtrim said. "The prince might have granted me land and title, but he also has been quick to send his tax collectors. And they doggedly follow me everywhere, even here."

As Burtrim sat up, the blanket slid down his chest to reveal he was wearing a white sleeveless shirt. If his sinewy arms were any indication, despite being quite old, Burtrim was in good physical shape. Wrapped around his right wrist and hand was a thick bandage. He shook the club-like limb and said, "To think they'd try to accost a loyal and elderly servant of the Sovereignty here in a fane seems quite rude, don't you think?" The broad smile he gave Esen and Thorne suggested that they should also find humor in the joke. Instead, Esen looked confused and Thorne scowled.

"We're short on time, Burtrim," Thorne said. "I know you keep on top of current guild dealings, even in your retirement. Do you know if Geridan left the city? Where is he?"

Burtrim's smile faded. "I've heard some things," he replied evasively. "Don't have any spies in Haywood, do you?"

The mage shook his head and replied, "I'm only here because we've run out of all other options."

Burtrim scoffed and said, "This must be a bitter medicine, to swallow your pride and come find me for information. If I remember correctly, on the day you left your home you swore that you'd live your life free from your family's influence. How has that worked out for you at the Archive?"

The old Venhadar's words cut Thorne deeper than he wanted to admit, but he kept up a stoic façade and stared down Burtrim. "If you're only going to chide me, then we'll go and leave you to your convalescence," he said.

Shoving the blanket off of him, Burtrim swung his legs over the edge of the cot and let them dangle before he stood up. "I'm done resting. Come with me," he said.

Hushing the quiet protestations from the nurse, Burtrim led Thorne and Esen out of the infirmary. As they left the fane, the mage told the old Venhadar a shortened version of Esen's plight and why they needed to find Geridan. Saying nothing, Burtrim nodded as he took them inside the tanner guildhall.

Remmie was quick to greet them happily. "Burtrim!" he exclaimed "What are you doing up and about so soon?"

"Helping an old family friend," Burtrim said with a sidelong glance at Thorne. "Do you have the records from the last major guild master meeting?"

"I do, but why?"

"We're looking for Geridan. Need to find him quick." With a whisper, Burtrim added, "It's family business. Urgent."

Remmie stroked his chin and leaned back on his heels. "Well, I don't need to look at the records to tell you that Geridan left rather abruptly for Haven not too long ago. The way they were packing his rapid transport, it looked like he would be gone for some time. If you need to find him, then I'd go there."

"You're a pearl, Remmie," the old Venhadar laughed. "Can you write these lads up a letter of introduction so they aren't harassed getting into Haven? Then we'll be out of your hair."

"Sure thing, but you better put in a good word with the prince for me!" the secretary said with a grin. "Us old timers are what keep the guilds running, so we need to stick together."

After Remmie returned to his office to begin drafting the letter, Esen turned to face Thorne. The foreigner looked confused and frustrated. "What is going on here? You got the information we needed in less than an hour for something we've been struggling to do for over a day. Why didn't we go to him first?"

He jerked a thumb at Burtrim.

"Oh, so you don't know?" Burtrim said with a contemplative expression. Gesturing with his bandaged hand he continued, "Your companion is the reluctant scion of a high-ranking guildsman for the noble order of mercers and tailors. His father helped raise the guild to prominence amongst the major guilds." Giving a reproachful look at Thorne, he added, "You could have inherited it all."

Esen scowled and said, "Thorne's father is a guild member?"

"A name borne of tragedy," the old Venhadar said sadly with the shake of his head. "And not the name he was born with, mind you."

"Enough!" Thorne spat.

From inside his office, Remmie looked up from the letter, only returning to it when Burtrim gave him a calming gesture.

The mage lowered his voice when he said, "I am Thorne now. That old name, I have cast it aside."

"Your father hasn't," Burtrim returned.

"I wouldn't know," Thorne said, suddenly unable to look the Venhadar in the eye. He turned his gaze back to Remmie and watched him finish writing the letter of introduction to Haven. The guild secretary folded the note, sealed it with a wax stamp, and then returned to the group.

Esen snatched the paper before anyone else could take it. "Much appreciated," he said before flashing an irritated look at the mage.

"Yes, well, you two best be on your way," Burtrim said awkwardly. "I think I'll stay here and catch up with Remmie a bit."

Esen stormed out of the guildhall while Thorne made a slower exit. The mage grasped the handle of the door and held it open a moment before looking back at Burtrim and Remmie. "Thank you," he said, locking eyes with the old Venhadar. "It was good to see you again."

Burtrim placed his uninjured hand over his heart and then raised it in a parting gesture.

When it was clear that he was not going to speak, Thorne left the guildhall and gently closed the door. He found Esen a short distance down the street, where the foreigner was pacing back and forth with his hands balled into fists and his expression fierce.

"Are we ready to go?" Thorne asked after joining him.

Esen's nostrils flared as he stabbed a finger at Thorne. "You!" he seethed, making the word sound like an accusation. "You could have gotten us on a guild ship at Port. Your family contacts are obviously powerful. Why keep them secret? If you had used them before, then we wouldn't have spent days on a corsair ship!"

"Keep your voice down," Thorne hissed as he looked over his shoulder. A few passersby gave them curious looks, and the mage did not like the extra attention. "It is much more complicated than what you think."

"No, it's not!" Esen was shouting now. "I came to the Archive looking for the mage who took Claire, and since partnering with you we've been waylaid at every turn. Are you helping me, or the abductors? Is your family involved in this whole affair?"

The mage's face flushed with anger. Discretion suddenly gone, he snapped back, "Now wait a minute. You would have been assassinated if I hadn't intervened in the infirmary, or likely died attacking the guild ship if I hadn't alleviated your dehydration."

Thorne jabbed his thumb into his chest and continued, "I'm your best chance of finding Claire and learning why the Archive is involved, but if you think you can do better on your own, then go!"

Digging the last two coins from the small purse that Dirty

Dreebs gave him, Thorne flicked one of them onto the ground at Esen's feet. "There," he said, pointing at the coin. "That's half of what money we have left. See what help you can buy. I was working for free, but now I'm done!"

Esen stared daggers at the mage as he bent down to retrieve the money. Standing with a rigid back and his chin jut out, the foreigner scowled at Thorne. "Fine," he said and turned away. Esen paused a moment before hurriedly walking down the street.

Watching Esen leave, Thorne mistook the cramping in his stomach as protestations from a stressed body, but when he forced himself to relax, he felt the familiar gurgle of hunger. Skipping breakfast had been a mistake. Looking at the last of his money, Thorne sighed and decided he might have a clearer head after eating. Trying to blend back in with the rest of the people on the street, the mage made his way to the open-air market.

• • •

Acting as the hub of the city, the market in Haywood was a boisterous and chaotic mixture of customers and vendors, with each shouting and haggling over all manner of goods that ranged from food to jewelry. Livestock in pens added to the cacophony of voices, as did the hammering of ores being fashioned into knives and other tools. For as unpleasant as it all sounded, the stench was what bothered Thorne the most as he walked through a thick layer of grime attempting to navigate the narrow aisles and jostling crowds.

The mage learned long ago that in a busy market a long line meant something good was being sold, so he joined several people waiting for a chance to buy some type of meat-filled pastry. As he gently fought for position amongst the other eager customers, Thorne wondered what Esen had decided to do with his solitary coin. The foreigner wasn't completely empty handed, he also had the letter of introduction, but even so, the trek to Haven could be perilous for an unprepared traveler and thieves would likely be unkind when they found he had no money. The mage wasn't enthusiastic about his own solo journey back to Yaboon, but at least he would be able to adequately defend himself if accosted on the road.

Thorne made it to the front of the stall and pushed down his money on the counter, careful to keep his index finger on it so some pickpocket wouldn't get an easy chance to swipe the coin. "Give me whatever is selling the fastest here," he said to a chubby woman with a stained apron and blonde hair tied up in a messy bun.

She pried the coin out from under his fingers and inspected it a moment before retrieving a short wooden paddle. Shoving the paddle into a clay oven at the back of the stall, she pulled out a golden brown pie. "Don't drop it. It's hot," she said playfully, offering up the pastry.

The mage carefully scooped up the pie and gently shuffled it between his hands so he wouldn't burn them. As the rich smell of minced meat and spices wafted into Thorne's nose, his mouth watered. Closing his eyes, the mage raised the pastry to his mouth for a small bite.

Pain shot through Thorne's wrists as a piece of wood slapped across them, sending the pastry flying. Before he could react, the wood coiled around his wrists like a snake, binding them together. Looking up, the mage saw Reihana's cold expression bearing down on him. She drew close to him and he felt the pointed tip of something hard against his ribs.

"No quick movements," Reihana hissed in his ear. "This resin dagger is very sharp. Come with me."

She grabbed the arcane fetters and jerked the mage away

from the stall before those around them could figure out what was happening. Staying close to his side, Reihana led Thorne out of the market and down a short dead end alley. Once they were out of sight, Reihana pushed him so his back was pressed up against the wall of a house. Holding his bound hands off to the side, she positioned the dagger so the slightest movement would drive it into his gut.

Trying to remain calm, the mage met her intense gaze. "How did you find me?" he asked with a dry mouth.

"You left a trail that even Torstein could have followed," Reihana said contemptuously. "Though I doubt he has the connections with rapid transport operators necessary to get anywhere with speed."

"Given the situation at the Archive when I left, you should be accompanied by at least one constable," Thorne said, stalling for time. "Or picked up a mercenary or two."

The coldness in Reihana's eyes was replaced by a predatory gleam. "I'm going to save the council the trouble of binding your magic, and I don't need any help to do it."

"What does that mean?"

"I'm here to purge the program of disappointment," Reihana said, pushing the dagger forward. With a hard expression she added, "Anything you want me to convey to Mirtans?"

Thorne's eyes flicked over Reihana's shoulders, then back to her and replied, "For someone so big, you really are light on your feet, Esen."

Reihana looked over her shoulder and was met with a splash of scalding hot soup. Screaming, she let go of Thorne and brought both hands to her face, trying to scrape the steaming liquid off of her.

Thorne quickly sidestepped around her and dropped to one knee while Reihana reeled from the unexpected attack. The mage slapped both of his still bound palms to the ground and shoved mana into it, forcing the stone street to become soft.

One of Reihana's legs sank shin-deep into the road as she toppled over and landed hard on her shoulder.

Thorne solidified the ground once more and trapped Reihana's leg in stone. Looking up at Esen, Thorne called out, "Run!"

The foreigner dropped the wooden bowl he held and dashed out of the alleyway, Thorne following right on his heels. The two men pushed their way through the crowds of the market while Esen picked out a path at random. "We need to find a place to hide," he said over his shoulder to Thorne.

"There won't be any place hide from her agents," Thorne replied. "With the City Watch and glassmaker guild also looking for us, it's too dangerous to stay. We need to leave the city right now."

"We won't get very far on foot," Esen protested.

The mage's eyebrows shot up. Taking the lead, he said, "Follow me, I have an idea."

They slowed their pace just enough to keep people on the street from giving them a second glance as Thorne navigated to the eastern city wall. When the mage saw the stables and a familiar rapid transport carriage near the gate he lengthened his stride and began scanning for the area for anyone with a uniform. The caribou housed in the stable snorted loudly as Thorne and Esen passed them and a few stamped their hooves impatiently.

"Easy there," someone called from inside the stable. A moment later Pelental stepped out.

Relief washed over the mage. "I know we just parted not too long ago, but I am greatly in need of your help, Pelental," Thorne said, the words tumbling out in a rush.

Surprised by the sudden arrival of Thorne and Esen, Pelental jerked back. "Oh! What's the problem?"

"We must travel to Haven as fast as possible," Thorne said. He held out his hands to show the Sehenryu his wooden restraints. "We've run into a bit of arcane trouble here and need to leave immediately." When Pelental's face compacted into an expression of confusion and wariness, Thorne added, "I can assure you that the Archive will compensate you for the cost of this trip, but we don't have the time to explain further. Can you help us?"

Pelental's face relaxed as he looked in turn at Esen and Thorne. "These caribou are still fatigued from their last trip," he said.

"You have no fresh caribou?" Thorne asked. He looked over his shoulder, expecting Reihana to pounce on them at any moment.

"Unfortunately not," Pelental replied. "We had a team very late yesterday, but it was taken out by another unexpected request. You Archive mages are very persuasive, I must admit."

"Wait," Esen said. "An Archive mage took a rapid transport?"

The Sehenryu nodded and answered, "Yes with a trio of Sovereignty soldiers and a young lady. They were escorting her somewhere."

"Claire!" Esen exclaimed. He reached out and grabbed Pelental's shoulder. "We must catch them!"

The rapid transport driver freed himself from Esen's hold and put his hands up in a warding gesture. "One moment please," he said. "Using this team of caribou again so soon is going to be detrimental to their health. With no others in reserve, I'm going to have to charge you double the normal fee."

Thorne exhaled loudly in disbelief. Not a day ago, the Sehenryu had been in his debt, and here he was preying on their desperation. With an agitated grunt, the mage replied, "Fine, just get us out of here."

Crossing his arms across his chest, Pelental said, "I'll need some sort of collateral, unless you can pay me now."

"We don't have time for this," Esen said as he looked towards the gate. "Claire is less than a day's travel from me."

"Here," Thorne said to Pelental as he reached under his shirt. Retrieving the Archive guilder, Thorne pushed it into the Sehenryu's hand. "Take this. It's all we have left."

Pelental looked at the medallion with a critical eye, and Thorne thought the Sehenryu was going to refuse it. Then with an approving grunt, Pelental pocketed the guilder and looked toward the stable "Alright," he said. "It will take a few minutes to harness the caribou. Until then, go wait in the carriage."

Thorne and Esen followed the Sehenryu's instructions and waited quietly in the coach as they listened to the sounds of Pelental preparing for their departure. From their limited vantage point, Thorne pulled back the carriage's curtains and scanned the area for signs of Reihana. Only after Pelental had guided the rapid transport out of the city did Thorne notice the pain in his chest from his shallow breathing. But as the farmland surrounding the city came into view, the mage allowed himself to slump into his seat and take a deep breath. They had escaped, for now.

CHAPTER EIGHTEEN

It was nearly a quarter hour after leaving Haywood before the wooden fetters around Thorne's wrists relaxed. The slat didn't straighten completely, but opened enough for the mage to wriggle his hands free. Holding up the curved slat to inspect it, Thorne sighed and shook his head. Reihana's power really was in a tier above his own, being able to hold control over an object for such a distance. Setting the slat down next to him, the mage looked across to the opposite bench where Esen sat. The foreigner looked cramped in the small coach, and he hadn't moved since pushing the curtain aside to look out the narrow window at the farm fields racing past.

"Why'd you come back for me?" Thorne asked. It was the first time that either of them had spoken since leaving the city.

Esen pulled his finger away from the curtain and let it drop back over the window. He turned and looked at the mage with a thoughtful expression. "Once I had calmed down, I realized that you were still the best hope I have for stopping whatever Geridan has planned for Claire," he said. More reluctantly, he added, "And that I shouldn't be so quick to make judgments about your family. It could be argued that I came to the continent because I wanted to distance myself from my own family."

"I wasn't trying to hide it from you," Thorne said, defensively. "Look, we've already come this far, and with what happened in the alleyway, I hope you understand that I'm risking life and limb to help you. Something isn't right here, and I want to discover what is going on at the Archive and how Claire and the glassmaker guild are involved."

"I'll," the foreigner paused searching for the right words, "I'll try harder to keep my emotions in check."

Thorne thought back to his outburst when he threw money at Esen's feet. Feeling ashamed, he replied, "I'll do the same."

Esen sniffed sharply and looked to the side. Trying to change the subject, he said, "I didn't get a good look. Who was that in the alleyway?"

In his mind's eye, Thorne replayed the altercation. "Reihana," he said. "She's an Archive mage. In a way, you might say I answer to her."

"Why did she attack you? Did she track you down for desertion?"

"Unclear," Thorne answered with a shake of his head. He thought back to his last conversation with Reihana at the Archive. The mage figured she would be angry that he had taken the initiative to help Esen but never would have guessed she'd have such a deadly plan. Even tracking him down and bringing him back to the Archive seemed like overkill. However, her words in the alley about purging the Paragon program of disappointment suggested that she had some hidden malice towards him. Maybe she wanted to get rid of the only made mage in the Paragon program.

"Well, it was easier than I thought it would be to sneak up on her," Esen said, leaning back on his bench.

"Her peripheral vision is quite poor," Thorne replied.

"How do you know that?" Esen asked, looking at the mage.

"It's one of the strictly followed rules at the Archive," Thorne explained. "The arcane energy in our bodies slowly destroys our nerves, so a mage's senses erode with time. This can be dangerous, not only to the mage, but also to anyone working with them in an alchemy lab, so we get regular examinations at the infirmary that are documented and shared with relevant colleagues. It's a way to keep everyone safe at the Archive."

"So you work closely with her?" Esen asked.

Thorne looked toward the curtained window and scowled. "Not closely enough it seems," he answered. "If she came all this way for me, then she's not going to stop now. We need to find Claire and learn why Karnoff took her."

"Could Reihana be involved?"

"Perhaps," Thorne answered, a troubled expression on his face. "I might not know her as well as I think."

Esen waved a dismissive hand and said, "Well, she certainly caught you unaware in the market, but next time you can use your magic sword like at the guild office and fight back."

The mage scoffed, "If only it were that easy. She can summon a mana knife like I can, but truth be told, she's much more powerful than I am." Thorne leaned forward and said, "Things have gotten complicated. We can't let her catch us again, and I fear that she'll be right on our heels very soon."

Esen pulled back the small curtain again and looked outside.

Thorne did the same and looked back where they had come from. To his relief, there was nothing behind them but billowing dust clouds.

"I really was looking forward to that soup," Esen lamented after a time. "I'm hungry."

The mage thought about the meat pie he dropped when Reihana found him and his stomach tightened up in protest. "Me too," he agreed. "But we're out of money and things to barter, so we'll have to get creative once we're in Haven."

• • •

The twilight sky turned violet, giving just enough contrast to see the brightest stars. Thorne and Esen had sat for several hours in relative silence, each content to be left with their own thoughts. Reihana's appearance and lethal designs weighed heavily on Thorne. The Paragon principal agent certainly ruled over the program with little tolerance for dissent or unauthorized initiative, but for her to want to kill him for helping Esen seemed extreme. Did she have some secret resentment toward him that she decided to act upon now that an opportunity had arisen? Arguing with himself in circles, Thorne felt much wearier than he should, given the relative ease in which they made their way to Haven.

Unexpectedly, they started to slow, and the wooden joints of carriage groaned in protest. Both Esen and Thorne were shaken from their respective reveries and looked at each other quizzically.

"Why are we stopping so early?" the foreigner asked as he pulled back a curtain and looked up at the sky.

The mage thought for a moment and replied, "We left unprepared for night travel. Pelental doesn't have a lantern, so it might be getting hard to see the road."

Letting go of the curtain, Esen pounded his fist on the front wall and shouted, "How is the road?"

After the carriage stopped, Pelental yelled a reply, "There's another rapid transport blocking us."

Thorne leaned over far in his seat and opened the door to peek outside. He saw that the rapid transport Pelental spoke of was positioned diagonally across the road. Two soldiers wearing Granick colors were bent over the thick central trace, each holding leather straps from separate caribou harnesses. A single lantern hung from a metal hook above the carriage roof, casting a flickering light on the empty driver's bench below it. A short distance away off the road a third person kept watch over the four caribou that were lazily grazing on the tall grass. In the increasing darkness it was hard to make out any details other than the great size of the person. All three looked up in Pelental's direction, but failed to offer any greeting before returning to their tasks.

Scrutinizing the carriage, the mage saw that the coach's curtains were drawn across the windows, but a blue-white light escaped around the edges. The coloring was instantly recognizable to Thorne as coming from a weakly charged glow sphere. There was a mage in the coach, though why they weren't outside helping with the repair, Thorne could not guess.

"Stay here," Thorne instructed Esen as he got out of his seat. "I'll go take a look." The mage retrieved his lone glow sphere and charged it with a white light before exiting the carriage. After hopping to the ground, he walked up to where Pelental sat high up on the carriage driver's bench. "What do you make of this?" he asked the Sehenryu.

"Looks like some of the straps snapped, or they lost a couple buckles," Pelental replied. "Either way, they'll have a hard time resuming travel again tonight, especially when their caribou are fatigued. They look quite content just to graze and rest here."

"I'll go see what I can do," Thorne said. He held up his glow sphere to illuminate a path and cautiously approached the other carriage. The mage saw one of the curtains pull back slightly, though he couldn't make out any details of who was watching him. A few steps before Thorne reached the carriage, the door opened. The mage drew back in shock when a man he recognized exited the coach and closed the door.

"Karnoff," Thorne said slowly, his features becoming hard.

The man pressed his lips in a chilling smile while he pushed his hand against the seam between the door and wall of the carriage. His hand pulsed with a dark amber color that faded when he removed his hand. That small area was now a singular section of wood, the seam between door and wall having been fused together.

"This is certainly a surprise," Karnoff said as he took a step toward Thorne. "I never expected to cross paths with another Yaboon mage out here, let alone someone I know. Isn't that funny?"

Thorne never liked the snide way Karnoff spoke. With a pointed look at where Karnoff sealed the door, Thorne replied, "That's extra cautious of you."

Karnoff gave a dismissive wave and motioned for Thorne to join him at the front of the carriage. "Simple protection measures. I'm sure you've done the same on your own assignments." Stopping near the empty harness, he added, "As you can see, I've got extra Sovereignty support, though soldiers are not the best equipped to handle a problem such as this. Might you be able to lend them a hand?"

The two soldiers stood stone-faced in the tangled mess of leather straps and wood blocking. More than anything, they looked unsure of what to do now that Thorne was there. The mage extinguished his glow sphere and put it in his pocket. He was about to reply when he heard Esen cry out.

"That's him! That's the Archive mage that took Claire!"

The foreigner had left the door open to Pelental's carriage and was half the distance to Thorne and Karnoff. Esen stood rigidly and pointed an accusing finger at Karnoff, his mouth agape and eyes wide.

From inside the carriage, a woman began shouting, "Esen! Esen, I'm here! Esen!"

"Irik!" Karnoff barked loudly, not taking his eyes off of Esen.

Thorne took a few steps back from Karnoff and watched as the large man left the caribou and stomped to place himself between Esen and the carriage. He was also wearing a Sovereignty soldier uniform. Clasping the hilt of a sheathed sword, the man blocked the path to the carriage.

Moving to stand next to Esen, Thorne gave him a quick sidelong look and said quietly, "Were these the soldiers that came to your farm?"

The two soldiers holding the caribou harnesses dropped them to the ground and joined Karnoff at the front of the carriage. They also rested their hands on their weapons.

"Those two yes," Esen said pointing, "and this big one must have been the person who attacked me from behind and knocked me out. I never saw his face, but Karnoff did call him that name."

Claire's shouts from inside the carriage became more frantic until Karnoff slammed a fist onto the wall near a window. "Quiet!" he roared.

After Claire went silent, Karnoff addressed Thorne and Esen with a condescending tone. "You are the culmination of terrible luck on this damned assignment. First there was the storm after leaving Port that took us further out to sea. Then Geridan decided on a whim to work in Haven for a month. This whole thing would have been done if he'd just stay put! So now, here we are, with an exhausted caribou team and a broken harness just on the outskirts of Haven when fate has one last nasty surprise for me. A trinity of bad luck, wouldn't you agree, Thorne?"

"Let her out," Esen demanded.

"Why? I doubt the deal has changed," Karnoff said.

"What deal? Why did you kidnap her?" Thorne asked, confused.

"So you don't know," Karnoff answered. With a furrowed brow he looked over to Esen, who was still being blocked by Irik. After a moment of thought he said, "I don't know what Reihana is playing at, but this was my deal from the start. Mine. I brought it to her, and I'm not going to have one of her parallel-running schemes stop me. I have ambitions too!"

"What does Reihana have to do with all of this?" Thorne asked, stunned by Karnoff's rambling.

"I'm not giving you the chance to find out," Karnoff replied, his features suddenly hard. His hand whipped over the opposite arm and summoned a mana knife. Pointing the arcane blade at Thorne, he called out to the soldiers, "Kill them both!"

The soldier called Irik jerked his sword free and rushed Esen.

Thorne glanced over in the foreigner's direction and watched him scoop up a handful of dirt with one hand while holding his small dagger in the other. Before the mage could move to help, Karnoff dashed at him and lunged forward, seeking to drive his mana knife through Thorne's torso. Thorne leapt back and summoned a mana shield. The diameter of the arcane film was slightly larger than his forearm and protected him from clenched fist to elbow.

At the sight of the conjured shield, Karnoff snorted in derision. "So typical of you, Thorne, always being on the defensive. I suppose it's only appropriate, being the weakest Paragon."

The two soldiers that flanked Karnoff drew their weapons and tried to circle around Thorne and cut off any escape. Suddenly, the soldier to Thorne's left darted forward and brought down his sword in a diagonal slash. The mage snapped his shield around and deflected the strike. As he flung the sword aside, Thorne drew back his shield-bearing arm and smashed the edge of his shield into the soldier's unprotected throat.

Lacking a pithy retort to Karnoff's insult, Thorne leveled a cold stare at him while stepping over the body of the soldier he'd just killed.

"Cut him down!" Karnoff shouted at the other soldier.

It was barely perceptible, but Thorne heard the waver in Karnoff's voice. Despite his appearance of power, Thorne realized that his fellow Paragon didn't want to put himself in harm's way.

The second soldier approached Thorne more warily than the first, giving the mage time to morph his mana shield into a blade and assume an attack posture. Not wanting to draw the fight out long enough for Karnoff to find an opening to attack, Thorne lunged forward, driving his adversary back with a series of stabs.

The soldier dodged the first few thrusts, and then parried with his sword.

As his mana knife was turned aside, Thorne crouched and chopped at the soldier's unprotected knees. The arcane blade sliced through sinew and across bone.

With a cry the solder collapsed.

Wasting no time, Thorne fell upon the soldier, plunging his mana knife into the man's chest. Standing back up, the mage pointed his arcane blade to the slain soldier and shouted, "No one to hide behind now, Karnoff!"

Thorne could see that that the Paragon's stance betrayed a hesitation to act. It looked like Karnoff was going to speak, when a shout from the carriage drew both men's attention.

"You'll pay for what you did to my eye, you bastard!"

Thorne and Karnoff turned and saw Irik standing atop the carriage, holding the driver's lantern out in front of him. The soldier's other hand covered half of his face.

Esen was climbing up to the soldier, but froze when he saw Irik lower his hand, pull the small hatch open on the lantern, and slosh the fish oil fuel onto the roof of the coach.

"No!" Esen shouted, heaving himself upward.

Irik threw the lantern down, igniting the oil seconds before Esen tackled him. Both men tumbled to the ground as the carriage erupted in flames.

Oily black smoke billowed up from the carriage roof and flames wrapped around the edges and spread down the walls.

Claire began screaming inside.

Thorne locked eyes with Karnoff and saw fear. Before he could engage him, Karnoff sprinted off into the night. Thorne had a split second to choose whether to pursue the Paragon or try to stop the fire.

A shrill scream from the coach sent Thorne to action. The mage careened around the coach and saw that both Esen and Irik were lying in the road. Neither were moving, but the latter was certainly dead, given the foreigner's dagger had been driven to the hilt into Irik's chest.

Focusing his attention back to the carriage, Thorne tried to figure out a way to stop the fire. The air was too dry to pull moisture out of it, so a focused rain shower wasn't possible. With his mind racing, his next thought was to conjure a wind strong enough to blow out the fire, but worried that would just end up fanning the flames.

The glass from one of the small carriage windows shattered and Claire's arm reached out. With a pained cry she drew it back inside and wailed as fire consumed the coach.

With his jaw set, Thorne planted his feet and tensed his body for a very risky elemental manipulation. Holding his hands out as if he could grasp the air around him, the mage pushed mana into his fingers. Feeling the weight of the air, he pulled it away from the carriage. Straining under the effort to manipulate so much gas, Thorne saw starbursts in his vision, but still he pulled. The air around the carriage slowly compacted and drew away from the coach, but the effort was too much. Too late, Thorne realized he didn't have the strength or stamina to maintain his grip on such a volume of air. He continued to struggle and pushed himself to the limits of his power, but as his vision tunneled down to a point the last thing he heard before losing consciousness was Claire's desperate scream.

CHAPTER NINETEEN

Dawn had already broken when Thorne awoke. The mage opened his eyes and blinked several times to clear the film that made his vision opaque and blurry. He had a terrible headache and his joints hurt, but as he pushed himself into a sitting position Thorne realized that feeling pain meant he was still alive.

Slowly scanning his surroundings, Thorne saw that he was wasn't on the road where he collapsed but a short distance away in the grass. His gaze stopped at the carriage, or what remained of it. The iron bands that held the wheels together were the only recognizable structures in the burned remnants. In a few spots the morning sunlight scintillated where fragments of broken glass pushed through the mounds of ash and debris.

"Karnoff is gone. So is Pelental."

Thorne jerked his head around at the sound of the voice behind him and instantly regretted it. The world kept spinning even after he stopped moving and his stomach lurched violently. The mage flopped over onto his side and his stomach heaved, though was nothing to retch up. He lay there for a moment trying to gather the strength to sit again, as he came to the painful realization he was suffering from a mana crash exacerbated by dehydration and hunger.

Giving up on sitting and instead rolling onto his back, Thorne looked up and saw Esen standing beside him. Covered in dried blood, dirt, and ash, the foreigner looked terrible.

Esen sat down next to Thorne, crossed his legs, and put his hands in his lap. Looking over at the burned wreckage, he said, "When I regained consciousness, it was still burning, but there wasn't much left. I found the other soldiers and pulled them all off the road in a pile together. I was going to add you to the heap, but you groaned when I picked you up."

The mage's expression drooped as he shook his head. "I'm sorry, Esen," he began. After a pause, Thorne continued, "I tried to stop the fire, but it was too big. Too big." He murmured the last words looking down at the ground.

Despite feeling the effects of a severe mana crash, what was more painful was the anguish that Thorne felt from Karnoff's actions. It was devastating to think that the Paragon program was being used in such a way. Claire was dead, burned alive, and for what? What could be so important that a Paragon had to go to the frontier and kidnap her? Karnoff's words about Reihana were cryptic at best, but it hinted she was involved in some way too. Did the Archive council approve all of this, or were Karnoff and Reihana acting alone? Trying to make sense of it made Thorne's headache worse.

The mage looked up at Esen and saw a man completely alone. He was crushed and discarded, a husk of his former self, and who could blame him? He had witnessed his wife's murder in the most horrible of ways. He had chased her halfway across the continent only to lose her when she was within arm's reach.

For a long time both men were silent, absorbed in their own inner struggles. Finally, Thorne said, "This isn't right. Karnoff has to be brought to justice. I can't believe that the Archive would sanction such an act. He had to have been working alone, gone rogue."

"How can you be so sure?" Esen asked hoarsely. "Just how well do you know your guild?"

"Well, I," Thorne began, but his voice trailed off. Having

never engaged in gossip mongering or many social functions, he couldn't truthfully say he had his finger on the pulse of the Archive. Thinking back to his last conversation with Donier, Thorne realized that his friend would be in a much better position to know about any goings on that would run counter to established Archive protocols. Regardless, the mage now had even more misgivings about how Reihana operated the Paragon program. "I don't know, not for certain," he said finally, resignation heavy in his voice. "And it's still unclear how the Sovereignty military is involved."

"You could ask them," Esen said as he pointed at the bodies. "But I don't think they're in the mood for conversation right now."

Taking extra care to maintain his balance, the mage gingerly stood up and looked over at the three slain soldiers. "Who knows," the mage said thoughtfully. "They might have something to tell us after all."

Leaving Esen, Thorne walked to the bodies and knelt down next to the large man called Irik. Looking at the bloodstained blue and cream vest, the mage noticed that it fit very snug, while those of his companions were much looser. In fact, none of the uniforms seemed to fit the soldiers well, and while tailored clothes could only be afforded by the wealthy, the military typically did a better job of outfitting their soldiers. Ill-fitting clothes could be a liability on the battlefield, and no Sovereignty prince wanted to give the impression of a sloppy army.

The mage had never handled a dead body before, but didn't find it as unpleasant as he expected when he began shifting Irik's limp arms and legs to get access to his pockets. All were empty, however when Thorne pulled down on the neck of the soldier's tunic, he saw a silver chain. Grabbing Irik's hair to lift his head, the mage pulled the chain free and found that it was a guild medallion. Cupping the guilder in the palm of his hand,

Thorne saw the iconography of the glassblower guild.

Moving over to the other two dead soldiers, Thorne retrieved matching guilders around their necks. Finding a guild medallion on one solider was an oddity, on two a coincidence, but on three was a pattern. Being Sovereignty military was a profession, and no true soldier would also have membership with a guild. Taking Irik's guilder back to Esen, Thorne showed the medallion to him and said, "I don't think they were actually Sovereignty soldiers."

Esen took the guilder and examined it closely. "Geridan, you bastard," he said through gritted teeth. Then with a roar, the foreigner hurled the medallion down the road.

After watching the guilder toss up a small plume of dust where it landed, Thorne looked further down the road and saw several carts flanked by a few dozen people walking at an unhurried pace. After watching them for a few moments, he could hear the long droning song of a religious hymn.

"It's the pilgrimage," he said to Esen after recognizing some faces. "It actually caught up to us. Didn't the shepherd say they were ultimately going to Haven?"

Esen nodded and then said, "I have to talk to him so he can give Claire last rites." He looked back at the ashes and blackened fragments of the carriage, then added softly, "Also to ask for help burying what's left of her."

• • •

The reunion with the pilgrim caravan was not a happy one, and only the mercenary escort seemed unfazed by the dead Sovereignty soldiers. Finding the road blocked by the wreckage left from the burned carriage, the caravan stopped. With a single mercenary as an escort, the shepherd came to Thorne and Esen to hear what had happened. Thorne stood back as Esen tried to recount the past night, but it only came out in halting, fragmented sentences with frequent, long pauses. Finally, piecing enough together, the shepherd wrapped an arm around Esen's shoulders and led him into the camp being set.

With Esen and the shepherd gone, and working to set up a camp for the evening, the pilgrims mostly ignored Thorne, save for the occasional sidelong glance in his direction. Once alone, the mage's physical and mental resilience began to quickly ebb away. He found a barrel next to a cart and rolled it back to where he was standing before and sat down. Once he was sure that he wasn't going to topple over from fatigue, Thorne rested his forearms on his knees and exhaled deeply.

"Do you ever tire of being an outsider, Master mage?"

Thorne looked over his shoulder and saw the flagellant walking towards him. Holding two cups, he handed one to Thorne. The mage took it and lifted it in a salute of thanks before taking a sip. It was a weak broth that tasted like chicken fat, but his stomach did not revolt when he swallowed, so the mage slowly drank until the cup was empty.

"Thank you," he said, handing the cup back to the flagellant.

The man nodded, then gestured back to the caravan and said, "You could have sat on that barrel next to the cart, even leaned against it for support and no one would have stopped you. Why did you feel the need to move away?"

The mage looked up at the flagellant and thought for a moment. Deciding that he had nothing to lose by being honest, Thorne answered, "It's just a force of habit, I suppose. I'm not very social at the Archive and keep mostly to myself."

"That sounds lonely," the flagellant replied. "But maybe that's why you get along well with Esen. It's a friendship distant from your everyday life."

Despite feeling terrible, Thorne couldn't help but huff a little laugh. "I wouldn't call us friends," the mage said. "I'm helping him. He's in over his head."

"All the more reason to make yourself available to connect with people. You might not share our faith, Thorne, but you could find what you're looking for with a pilgrimage of your own."

Something that Thorne couldn't quite put his finger on about the flagellant's words made him angry. Perhaps it was this stranger presumed to know him better than himself. Or worse, maybe he was right. Not wanting to give the flagellant a victory, Thorne said caustically, "What enlightenment am I seeking then? Or what am I trying to atone for?"

"You tell me."

Thorne scowled and looked away. His eye caught the dead soldiers. "At the moment, I'm trying to find answers," he replied.

"Aren't we all?"

"Perhaps, but mine can be obtained if I just get ahold of the right person." Turning back to the flagellant Thorne said, "Tell me, why would a member of the glassblower guild masquerade as a Sovereignty soldier?"

The flagellant started, surprised by they question. "What do you mean?"

"If you've the stomach for it, go see for yourself. The two smaller soldiers are still wearing guilders around their necks. That's something you wouldn't see on a true provincial soldier."

The flagellant slowly walked to the slain soldiers and knelt down. After examining both for some time, he stood and continued to look down at them. When it became clear that he wasn't going to return, Thorne got up off of the barrel and joined him. The flagellant had a troubled look on his face that went far beyond the stress of seeing a bloody corpse.

"Tell me again what type of journey you and Esen are on," the flagellant said.

As Thorne recounted his meeting and travel with Esen thus

far, the mage observed the flagellant's face. Though he could not be certain, Thorne got the impression the flagellant recognized the men on the ground. Looking at the flagellant's waist, Thorne noticed a few links of silver chain. "Are you part of a guild?" the mage asked.

The flagellant composed himself, though his expressionless face seemed fake to Thorne, like a mask donned to hide his true nature. "As I told you when we last spoke, for the duration of this pilgrimage I am only the flagellant." Abruptly, he walked away and left Thorne to contemplate the conversation and his situation, alone.

The wind began to pick up and Thorne watched the tall grass at the side of the road bend double over. A series of wispy clouds crossed the sun and the mage felt chilled after a few minutes. "What am I doing out here?" he murmured to himself.

Thorne knew he wasn't thinking clearly, but the guilt and doubt seeping into his thoughts were unshakable. If he had done as he was told back at the Archive, would Claire still be alive? But were it not for his actions in the infirmary, Esen would surely have been murdered. And if he hadn't helped the foreigner, then he never would have stumbled upon Karnoff's duplicity. However, that was problematic itself, as it suggested that the Paragon program, or at least Reihana, knew what he was doing. Up until a few days ago, he thought he knew his direction in life, but now Thorne felt that nothing was certain anymore.

Thorne wondered where Esen was within the camp. He looked back at the closest cart and was surprised to see the pilgrimage's shepherd walking towards him.

"We will hold last rites for the deceased at dusk tonight," the shepherd said as he stopped in front of the mage. "I would ask of you a small favor, if you are willing."

Regarding the shepherd warily, Thorne replied, "What do

you want me to do?"

"Don't worry," the shepherd replied. "It has nothing to do with the service, and you may stay uninvolved with it if you choose. I need your help with a practical matter beforehand, and our mercenary escort is not quite equipped for the job."

Thorne drew in a deep breath. He still didn't feel good, so he said, "I'll do what I can, but I need to eat first. Do you have any food to spare?"

"Of course. Let's go find you some nourishment and then you can work tonight."

• • •

Grave digging was not something Thorne thought the pilgrims would need help with given their number, but according to the shepherd his flock did not bring any hand tools, and the mercenaries were reluctant to use their swords to dig holes deep enough for the slain soldiers to be buried. The shepherd passed Thorne off to a young family to rest and recover, none of whom were interested in conversing with an Archive mage. Consequently, Thorne spent most of the day resting and eating bland but filling food. It was a mixed blessing, but the fatigue from his mana crash made it easy not to dwell on what happened the day prior or wonder where Esen was amongst the pilgrims. It was just too exhausting, so the mage spent the day mindlessly watching the mundane activity around the camp.

As the sun traveled low in the sky, Thorne felt less dazed and ill. He quietly thanked the family for looking after him and could see relief on their faces with his parting. He walked a short distance from the camp to the place where the shepherd had asked him to dig three holes. The shepherd had insisted that the soldiers be given the dignity of a proper burial regardless of their crimes and refused Thorne's suggestion of one large mass grave.

The mage knelt down and pressed his palms into the grass until he felt the firm ground underneath. Taking a deep breath, he pushed mana into his hands and held it there a moment before forcing it into the ground. The mage felt the sensation of arcane energy flowing out into the soil, and he shaped it into an ellipsoid the length of a human. With a grunt of exertion, Thorne compressed his mana, and with it the soil, to form a deep hole.

Thorne repeated the process twice more, and after making the final hole he felt dizzy and weak again. Not nearly enough time had passed for him to recover from the mana crash. He would need to be very careful for the next few days, lest he become seriously ill. With the Granick Archive infirmary far away, he didn't like his chances for recuperating quickly.

Thorne looked back towards the camp and saw two mercenaries were watching him. The mage waved his arm until they each picked up a slain soldier by the legs and dragged them to the graves. They callously rolled the bodies into the holes and then returned to the edge of the camp. One mercenary stood over the remaining body while the other disappeared into the heart of the camp. He returned a short time later with the shepherd and the flagellant. With each mercenary taking a leg, they dragged the final soldier to the last pit and rolled him into it. The mercenaries then returned to the camp, leaving Thorne, the shepherd, and the flagellant looking down into the holes that contained the dead men.

The rites for the soldiers were simple and short. Once the shepherd was done with his prayers, he returned to the camp without looking in Thorne's direction. The flagellant stayed a few moments longer, but when Thorne took a step in his direction, he left the graves as well. The mage watched the flagellant's retreat, fresh wounds on his back bleeding through the thick layer of salve applied to the cuts. In the quickly darkening twilight, Thorne soon lost sight of him.

With a look down at the graves, Thorne dissipated his mana and released his hold on the earth. The holes collapsed inward, entombing the dead soldiers. Given the displacement of earth from the bodies, the three dirt mounds looked out of place amongst the tall grass, but the mage knew the wilderness would quickly reclaim the land.

Returning to the camp, Thorne saw that all of the pilgrims had congregated near where Claire's carriage had burned in the road. Several of them held lanterns, the yellow light casting flowing shadows on the grass as the daylight waned. When the crowd noticed the mage, they parted and allowed him to move up to where the shepherd and Esen waited. It was the first time Thorne had seen the foreigner all day. Esen looked exhausted as he stood hunched over with an ash-filled serving bowl in his hands.

With a nod from the shepherd, the mage knelt and created a circular hole that had similar dimensions as the bowl. He then stepped off to the side, away from the gathered pilgrims but close enough that he could see and hear the service. The quiet murmurs from the congregation died off when the shepherd raised both of his hands over his head.

"The Small House welcomes all who seek comfort in times of sorrow," he called out in a clear voice. "The Father, the Mother, and the Child are no strangers to the despair felt when confronted with death. Let us remember how they struggled, how they grieved, and how they healed. Let us sing the story of the Small House's first loss, that of their sole oxen."

The shepherd led the pilgrims in a solemn hymn. As the assembled group sang earnestly, Esen could have been mistaken for a statue. The foreigner remained in his stooped position, staring at the contents of the bowl as tears streamed down his face. As the final words were sung, the last rays of daylight vanished, leaving only the glow of lanterns to push back the darkness.

"On this pilgrimage, we are blessed with the protection of the Small House," the shepherd called out. "However, all families will know loss at some time. It is inevitable, but we can learn much from the Child. Let me recount the story of when the Child learns about death."

Though it was told with passion and clarity, Thorne didn't hear a word of the shepherd's story. The man's voice faded into the background as Thorne watched the anguish on Esen's face grow. Searching the crowd, Thorne saw similar expressions from some of those gathered, no doubt remembering lost loved ones. When he saw one small girl weeping, her father's hand gently on her shoulder, Thorne's chest tightened. A memory of crippling loss from his own past flashed before his eyes, but with a quiet growl he pushed it down to the black place where he put all his grief. He stood with a clenched jaw and rigid neck for the remainder of the service, staring at Esen and looking for any signs of life from the foreigner.

During the final droning hymn, the pilgrims lit candles that they had been holding. In the warm candlelight, the shepherd touched Esen's arm, rousing him from his grief-stricken trance. Esen raised his head and locked eyes with Thorne.

The mage held his gaze for a moment, and then compelled by something he couldn't explain, reached into a pocket and pulled out his glow sphere. Charging the resin, Thorne produced a warm yellow light over the gathering.

Esen looked to the shepherd. After getting a nod from him, the foreigner knelt near the hole and gingerly placed the ash-filled bowl in it. The song ended and the crowd quietly returned to the camp to tend to their own cooking fires in preparation for the evening meal. Thorne watched them all go, including the shepherd, until Esen was alone. The foreigner still knelt next to the hole, starting down at the remains of his wife. Thorne approached with his glow sphere and noticed Esen was shuddering. He placed a hand on Esen's shoulder and felt his quiet sobs.

After a short while, Esen looked up at Thorne with bleary, red-tinged eyes. "I'm glad you're here," he said in a halting, thick voice. "I want someone to witness this, but I don't think the shepherd would have understood."

Thinking that the foreigner meant the burial, Thorne asked, "Wouldn't he be the best one to ensure that all of the rites of the Small House were followed properly?"

Esen shook his head and said, "This has nothing to do with laying Claire to rest."

The foreigner stripped off his shirt and placed it behind him. He drew his dagger and held it out in front of his bare chest, blade horizontal. His features hardened as he spoke in a language Thorne guessed to be Esen's native tongue from the southern continent. Making shallow incisions on the left side of his chest, Esen proceeded to carve an X over his heart. When he was done cutting himself, he held the knife over the hole and let a few drops of blood fall onto the ashes.

"What did you say?" Thorne asked as Esen wiped the blood from his knife and returned it to his belt.

The foreigner looked up at him and answered, "I swore a blood oath to find the Archive mage, the one called Karnoff, and kill him."

Shocked by this declaration given Esen's previous reluctance for violence, Thorne said, "Do you think that is what Claire would have wanted? This doesn't sound like anything that would be found in the Small House's teachings."

Esen shook his head. "No, this is an old custom from my homeland. Claire would have not understood. Will you try to stop me? Was this man not of your guild?"

Thorne crossed his arms over his chest, the movement erratically shifting the light from the glow sphere. "He tried to kill me too. No, I won't stop you, but I would ask you to spare him the breath to explain why he took Claire. I still can't believe that the Archive would sanction such an act. I'm duty-bound to report back about any rogue mage."

Standing, Esen said, "If you help me find him, I will grant him that much extra time, but no more."

"Understood," Thorne said. He looked down at the ground and added, "Should I close the hole now?"

"No," Esen answered. His face tightened with emotion before he said, "I will do it with my bare hands. Please leave me alone so I can have a few final minutes with my wife."

Thorne nodded and turned away. He resisted the urge to look back as he walked into the camp. He found the crude tent assigned to him was cold and dark and empty.

CHAPTER TWENTY

Reihana paused, uncharacteristically hesitant, in front of the glassblower guildhall in Haven. The rage she felt when leaving Haywood the day prior was gone. Furious that Thorne had escaped her resin knife, she had spent far too long searching for him, convinced that he and the foreigner would be traveling on foot, so her surprise was complete when one of her agents informed her that two people matching Thorne and Esen's descriptions had been at the rapid transport stable. It was unclear if they learned that Geridan was in Haven, but the rapid transport driver had only a few roads to choose from and Haven was the closest town. Regardless, when Thorne and the foreigner discovered Geridan's whereabouts they would eventually have gone to Haven.

Taking her own rapid transport, Reihana was informed by the driver the only thing of note on the road had been a pilgrim caravan they passed in the night. She spent the next two hours wandering the markets while waiting for the guildhalls to officially open at four high bells. As that hour came and went, her ire was replaced with concern for how Geridan would react to her unannounced arrival. Now at the threshold of the glassblower guildhall, she thought of a few pretenses to see the guild master, but all of them rung hollow to her, especially given that she didn't know where Karnoff and Claire were. Perhaps he was already here and she was worrying for no reason. Rubbing the nervous sweat from her hands and setting her jaw, she opened the guildhall door and stepped inside.

The interior of the glassmaker guildhall was much brighter and well lit than most buildings of similar size due to the numerous large windows present. A few of them were beautifully fashioned ornate stained glass panels depicting fantastic battles, rose gardens, or abstract geometric designs. In the center of the room rested an oblong desk. An old woman sat behind it examining small glass tiles of varying thicknesses. She looked up as Reihana approached her.

"My name is Master Reihana, Archive mage from Yaboon, and I'm here to see Geridan."

The corners of the old woman's mouth puckered as if she found the request distasteful. She set down the glass pieces on the table before replying, "The guild master's schedule is full for today. What's this all about?"

"His daughter, Claire."

The woman's eyes grew wide. Pushing herself to her feet, she instructed, "Stay here."

As Reihana watched the woman ascend a staircase set against the back wall, her hands began to sweat again. Geridan wasn't the most powerful guild master, far from it in fact, but he nonetheless commanded a vast merchant network, had considerable wealth, and traded in influential circles that included the regional governors and on occasion the Granick prince. That combination, and perhaps a natural aggressiveness in his personality, made him an intimidating individual to negotiate with. Reihana was typically the dominant person in most interactions, but with Geridan she knew that the guild master was in control.

In a much shorter time than Reihana was expecting, the old woman returned downstairs. Her previous sour expression was gone, replaced with a furrowed brow. "He'll see you immediately," she said quietly. "All the way in the back, right side door."

Reihana watched the old woman busy herself with the glass tiles and do her best not to look up. With a tentative gait, Reihana walked to the staircase and ascended to the second floor. At the top landing she looked down a long hallway. The only windows present were at the end the hall, giving the entire upper level a dark, claustrophobic feeling.

All of the doors in the hallway were closed save the last one on the right, which was slightly ajar. Taking a moment to steel herself for what was to come, Reihana flexed all of her fingers and shifted her lips around until she felt the stiffness alleviate somewhat. With effort to show a relaxed confidence that she did not feel, Reihana went down the hall and pushed open the door.

The first thing Reihana saw was Karnoff sitting on the floor in the corner of the room, two rough-looking men looming over him. Geridan glowered at her behind a wide desk. The guild master wore a linen shirt with a tailored silk coat. His silver hair and beard contrasted sharply against his dark eyes. Expensive jeweled rings were on his hands, which rested on top of a stack of papers. Geridan might not have been a governor, but the way he dressed and how he carried himself projected the same aura of authority. Reihana suddenly felt small and penned in.

"You've saved me the trouble of finishing this missive to you, Reihana," Geridan said, not using her Archive rank in a clear show of disdain. His face grew red and contorted as he yelled, "Have you come here to answer for this atrocity?"

Reihana took a step back and raised her hands up as if to ward off a physical blow. "G-Geridan, what are you talking about?" Reihana stammered. "Why is Karnoff on the floor under guard? Where's Claire?"

Geridan sprang from his seat at the mention of his daughter. "You don't know?" he seethed. His hands balled into fists as he leaned over his desk and screamed, "She's dead!" He whipped his hand out and pointed a finger at Karnoff. In a quieter, but no less intense voice he continued, "This one, he came to me last night with his tail between his legs, whimpering a story about how she was burned alive in a rapid transport carriage. He said it was Claire's abductor and another Archive mage that killed her."

"It's true," Karnoff pleaded from the floor. Looking at Reihana he added, "It was Thorne! He found me somehow and attacked. There was nothing I could do!"

"Be silent or I'll cuff you again harder," Geridan bellowed.

Reihana noticed that the left side of Karnoff's face had the characteristic black veins under his skin that were the result of an iron burn. "Let me talk to him," Reihana said with a gesture towards Karnoff. "If what he says is true, then Thorne has to be stopped, and we're the best ones to do it. If we can capture him alive, you can find out why he attacked Claire and extract whatever vengeance you see fit."

Geridan stared at Reihana without answering, and for a tense moment she worried that his response would be to exact his revenge on her. Here in the heart of the glassblower guildhall, she now understood just how little negotiating power she had. If it came down to violence she and Karnoff were more than capable of cutting their way out, but an attack on Geridan would not go unnoticed, or unpunished.

Composing himself, the guild master returned to his seat. "Move them next door," he said with a glance to his men. "Only Reihana may leave."

One of the men pulled Karnoff to his feet and shoved him towards he door, nearly knocking into Reihana in the process.

Turning, she opened the door and followed Karnoff and his escort into a sparsely furnished room. A plain desk sat in the back near a pair of large windows, while empty bookshelves lined the interior walls. The wooden floorboards creaked as Reihana and Karnoff were marched inside.

After Geridan's men slammed the door shut Reihana gave Karnoff a venomous glare. "You absolute fool!" she hissed. "Why did you come running here? After Claire was dead you should've returned to me. Now everything we're trying to accomplish is in jeopardy."

"How was I going to do that?" Karnoff replied, no longer cowed with Geridan's men gone. "My rapid transport was destroyed, and I wasn't going to get another one. Haven was the closest city that I could get to on foot. Claire's husband and Thorne were chasing after me, and I'd rather take my chances here than on the open road."

"Even so, with his daughter dead, Geridan is in no way going to honor the deal I made with him."

"Fuck your deal!" Karnoff barked. "You're already the principal agent for a secret program at the Archive. Do you know what most mages would give for that opportunity? Your high-minded goals for having mages better integrated into society aren't going to be achieved in your lifetime."

"I'm tired of waiting," Reihana said with a dangerous look in her eye. "As the council governs now, the Archive will only ever be content to develop knowledge, materials, and contraptions for the guilds, which leaves us merely subservient to them. We should stand on our own and be respected for what we can do. Getting guild support for the Paragon program was only the initial phase. I want to see a time when every mage is a Paragon."

"The Sovereignties would never allow it. At best, they'd force us to weaponize our existing research, and at worse would conscript us as soldiers whenever it suited them for some damn border squabble."

"If each Archive was full of Paragons, do you really think

they could force us to do anything?"

Karnoff considered Reihana's words. Nodding slowly, he replied, "We live in a world where you have to be either smart or strong to survive. For those of us who command the arcane elements, why not be both?"

"Then you do understand."

"So what do we do now?" Karnoff asked.

Reihana grasped at the open air in front of her and answered, "We capture Thorne and offer him up to Geridan. It won't compensate for losing Claire, but it will redirect his anger away from us."

"What's to stop Geridan from complaining to the council afterwards?"

"He doesn't want knowledge of why Claire was retrieved from the frontier to get back to the prince since it involved a scheme to escape taxes. He knows the Paragon program is secret, so any indiscretions on his part would be revisited in kind."

Karnoff gave her a skeptical look and said, "Do you really think that money is going to stop him from talking about the death of his daughter? Can a father be that cold?"

"Yes, and possibly much worse," Reihana replied. Putting her hands on her hips, she continued, "Let me deal with Geridan. For now, stay here and be a docile prisoner."

"Where are you going?"

"To cast a city-wide net for Thorne," she answered. "With Geridan's influence as guild master, the City Watch will be involved. I'll make a public bounty for Thorne on behalf of the Archive at the mercenary guild. There won't be anywhere safe for him after that is done. I will talk to Geridan again and make sure you aren't maltreated."

Karnoff reached up and touched the side of his head. "That would be appreciated," he said with a grimace.

CHAPTER TWENTYONE

Approaching Haven a day after the funerals, Thorne got the sense that something was wrong. With an overcast sky shading the afternoon sun, the mage could see a large crowd of people at the main gate of the city and a larger than normal City Watch presence. He and Esen were near the front of the pilgrimage, walking ahead of the carts and most of the congregation, but slowed their pace when they saw the blue and cream livery of Granick Sovereignty military pikemen also working with the City Watch. It appeared that people were being searched before they were admitted to the city. With a multitude of archers manning the battlements above the gate, the crowd was understandably passive.

"I don't understand," Esen said as he and Thorne stepped off to the side of the road to allow the caravan to proceed. "Pilgrimages aren't normally stopped at the gate, especially those ending the journey in their home city."

Watching the Sovereignty soldiers accost people gathered at the gate before allowing them to pass into the city, Thorne realized what they were doing. "They're searching for someone," he said with raised eyebrows. "They're searching for me."

Esen glanced at him and then back towards the city. "How can you be so sure?" he asked.

"Karnoff," Thorne answered. "He must have fled here during the night. He knows that I'd be coming after him."

The foreigner looked both surprised and impressed. "Are

Archive mages really so influential?" he muttered to himself. Turning to Thorne, he asked, "Are those soldiers just glassblower guild security in disguise, like the men who traveled with him?

Thorne shook his head and replied, "No, something tells me those are genuine."

"We'll need to hide our faces," Esen said after some thought. "Wait here."

The foreigner waded into the slow procession of people and disappeared.

While Thorne waited, he alternated between watching the pilgrimage approach the gate, and the soldiers searching through the already gathered crowd. The City Watch didn't seem to be working particularly hard, but the soldiers were much more aggressive in their task.

"Here," Esen said, reappearing at Thorne's side and shoving something against his chest.

The mage looked down and collected a dusty blanket. Following the foreigner's lead, Thorne wrapped the blanket around himself and pulled an edge over his head. Hunching over to appear smaller, the two men drifted into the middle of the plodding pilgrims and worked their way to the rear of the group.

As the lead pilgrims joined the crowd at the gate, an imposing soldier stomped out to meet them. In a commanding voice, he shouted, "What is this?"

Someone at the front must have replied, but it was not to the soldier's liking.

"Get back, you gutter rats!" Looking back to several of his men, he bellowed, "Find the fugitives! You there! Go check those carts!"

The Sovereignty pikemen were brutally efficient in their work. Thorne watched a soldier rip a woman's hood from her head. He grabbed a handful of hair as she whimpered, looking up at him with terrified eyes. With a grunt, the soldier pushed her towards the gate and continued his search. The lead cart was ransacked as a pair of soldiers climbed inside and heaved anything small out despite the pleas from nearby pilgrims.

Thorne felt his stomach drop as he watched the soldiers assault people at random. Despite the growing murmur of agitation from the crowd, no one did anything to provoke the soldiers or City Watchmen for fear of being denied admittance to the city or imprisoned.

Esen leaned in close to the mage as they drew closer to the gate. "We're not going to make it," he said in Thorne's ear. "We're going to have to fight."

The mage glanced at his companion in surprise. This was not the same man he met at the Archive infirmary. After swearing the blood oath, Esen's demeanor had changed. While Thorne didn't disagree that they might have to resort to violence, now was not the time for being reckless with so many innocent people around them.

"Wait," Thorne said. "I have an idea. I need your knife."

"Doesn't steel burn you?" Esen asked as he retrieved his weapon.

The mage used his blanket as a hand covering and carefully took the knife from Esen. He held it tightly through the thick fabric and sighed while looking at the blade. "It will," he said. "Try to catch me if I collapse."

Acting quickly so he didn't lose his nerve, Thorne cut into his scalp. The pain from the cut was brief and quickly eclipsed by an intense burning sensation. The mage drew in a hissing breath as a scorching heat washed over his face and down his neck. A slick, greasy sweat began to bead up on his skin as the poisonous effects of the Iron Bane manifested.

The jostling from the crowd made the mage stagger, but

Esen's sure hand on his shoulder kept Thorne upright. He felt a wetness running down his forehead and instinctively reached up to touch it. Blood stained his fingertips.

"What are you doing?" Esen asked as he snatched back his knife.

Thorne smeared the blood all over his face. "Scalp wounds bleed a lot, so I'm making a disguise," he replied.

"You look sick and injured, but is that really a disguise?" the foreigner asked.

"Watch."

The mage felt queasy and faint. He knew he'd have one chance to get past the sentries before he'd need to treat his wound or it would quickly become worse from the toxic effects of the steel that touched his skin. The mage fought back the urge to retch as he pushed himself through the crowd and suddenly called out, "Home from traveling the land! We are of one blood! Blessed be the Father, the Mother, and the Child!"

A nearby soldier jerked his head in Thorne's direction. "Come here!" he commanded as he grabbed Thorne's blanket.

With wide eyes and a leering smile, the mage cried out, "Blessings of the Small House upon you!" He dragged his fingers across his forehead and then quickly smeared his blood onto the soldier's cheek.

"Get away from me, you zealot!" the soldier shouted after touching his face and seeing his fingers slick and crimson.

"The Small House welcomes all of you!" Thorne called out in what he thought would look like religious rapture as he looked up towards the sky. "We are of one blood!"

The soldier shoved him towards the open gate.

The mage continued ranting until he was inside and past all of the soldiers. As the pilgrimage slowly reformed inside the city, Thorne used the blanket to cover his head and tried not to be too obvious in his search for Esen. He hoped the foreigner was able to deceive the sentries in a similar manner and gain entrance.

As the temporary burst of energy and resilience brought on by his risky gambit passed, Thorne felt sick once more. The cut on his head burned, but now he had a headache that throbbed in time with his heartbeat. He fought to keep his balance steady, but turning his head to look for Esen made the whole city spin.

"Are you alright, Master mage?"

Thorne turned quickly, which he instantly regretted. His vision grew bleary, and he momentarily saw two shepherds standing next to him. The mage closed his eyes and took a deep breath in an attempt to steady himself. To his relief he found that when he opened his eyes again there was only one shepherd looking at him with a concerned expression.

"I'll be fine," the mage croaked. "I need to eat and get the cut on my head mended."

"Come with me to the sanctuary," the shepherd said, offering Thorne an arm for support.

Thorne reached out and grasped the shepherd's shoulder. "Have you seen Esen?" he asked as they walked further into the city.

"I think so," the shepherd replied. "Some of us have already moved on, but I stayed behind to make sure all of our carts made it through the gate. There's still one more outside, but it doesn't look like you can wait."

•••

The shepherd took the mage directly to the sanctuary infirmary and put him in the care of a pair of parishioners. The elderly couple gently stripped him to the waist and washed the blood from his face and hair before giving him a bowl of thin broth. They told him the salts they added would help ease the weariness in his muscles, but as Thorne swallowed the tasteless liquid, he figured he'd just have to take their word for it. The burning ache in his head did lessen after a few hours rest, but the tolling of fourteen high bells, heralding the last hour of daylight, seemed painfully loud.

Ignoring the couple's pleas for him to stay and rest more, Thorne slid into his dirty shirt and went to find Esen. He was relieved to find the foreigner sitting in one of the sparsely populated pews in the cavernous worship hall. As the mage approached, Esen looked up and the corners of his mouth crept up in the barest semblance of a smile.

"I'm glad to see you up and about so quickly," he said. "The shepherd told me he took you to the infirmary."

Thorne sidled past him and sat down in the pew. Not in the mood to discuss his recovery, the mage asked quietly, "How'd you avoid the guards?"

Esen looked down at his feet with a vacant expression. "I picked up a small child who was about to be trampled," he explained. "Since she was crying and making such a fuss one of the City Watch just ushered me though." He touched his chest where his holy symbol hung underneath his shirt and added, "It was the Child that guided me past danger. I'm sure of it. I stayed with her until she was reunited with her family here. That wasn't too long ago. In fact, I was just about to come check on you."

"I'll be in much better shape after I get something substantial to eat," Thorne said. "The broth I was fed kept me hydrated, but not nourished. Whether manipulating the arcane elements or suffering from the Iron Bane, mages need to keep their food intake fairly regular to maintain their mana."

"Then you're in luck," Esen replied. "We've been offered a place at the communal table here. It's simple fare, but better than nothing."

"I've a better idea," the mage answered. "Let's go see if we can make some discreet inquires at a few taverns. Someone has to know if Geridan or Karnoff is in the city. Going directly to the guildhall is too risky, especially if the Sovereignty military is genuinely involved now. We can get something more filling to eat out there while we ask our questions." He gestured vaguely to indicate outside the sanctuary.

"The food is free here," Esen reminded him. "We don't have any money."

Thorne looked up at the alter and replied, "I think the Small House can provide." He got out of the pew and approached the altar. Next to three small wooden statues that represented the Father, the Mother, and the Child, was a shallow bowl that had a collection of coins in it. It was a paltry offering plate, but Thorne wasn't in a position to be particular. Scooping up a few coins, he returned to sit next to Esen. The foreigner had a shocked expression on his face.

"You're stealing!" he hissed. "That money is for the poor!"

"We are the poor," the mage replied. "We've been living hand to mouth since leaving Yaboon."

Esen grunted in disapproval, but followed Thorne out of the worship hall. No one stopped them, or even seemed to notice, when they left the sanctuary.

Outside, the city was darkening as night began to fall. Thorne looked up at the sky and saw a few of the brightest stars already shimmering. The last business of the day was ending and pairs of City Watchmen were lighting oil lamps at street corners.

"Do you know Haven?" Esen asked as Thorne led them down the street.

The mage shook his head and replied, "We'll just walk until we find a tavern. In a city this big, it shouldn't take too long."

Thorne's intuition proved right as just two streets over they found what they were looking for.

"The *Wet Whistle*," Thorne said reading the sign that hung over the tavern door. "Sounds busy inside. Usually means the food is good."

"Or cheap," Esen countered, looking over his shoulder at the mage as he pulled open the door.

They had to fight for space as the large central eating area was overcrowded with a mix of humans, Sehenryu, and Venhadar in the midst of loud conversations and drinking. Shouts to the barman were frequent, as was the banging of mugs onto the bar and the few tables that were pushed along the walls.

"Who do you want to ask first?" Esen said, putting his face next to Thorne's ear.

"Maybe we can get some help from her," Thorne said, pointing to a woman dressed in a traditional alchemist robe who was sitting near the end of the bar. Flanked by two dour-looking men in leather armor, Thorne recognized her as a mage on her traveling education, the sabbatical all arcane practitioners take to get real world experience before attempting to attain the rank of Master.

They shouldered their way to her as Thorne reached for his borrowed Archive guilder, only to remember that Pelental still had it as collateral. The woman turned and watched them approach with a critical eye, already on her guard. Thorne didn't think her expression was a good sign, but tried his best to look friendly as he said, "While you're not a familiar face, it's nice to see another mage."

"Uh-huh," she replied, clearly unsure what to make of him.

Thorne put a hand over his chest and said, "I'm Thorne, from the Yaboon Archive. This is Esen. Which Archive are you from?"

The woman frowned at them but then answered, "Granick. I'm Wendolan."

Thorne placed two coins on the bar, which caught the attention of the barman. The burly Venhadar was surprised when the mage only asked for one beer and one mug of water. Taking the money, the barman left two full mugs on the counter next to where one of the stern, silent mercenaries was leaning.

"How long have you been here?" the mage asked Wendolan after retrieving his mug of beer.

"The day before yesterday," she answered. "I've been here long enough to resupply and recruit Jannes and Michem here from the mercenary guild as an escort. We're heading north to the frontier tomorrow morning."

"Have you met any other Archive mages here in the city?" Thorne asked, trying to sound casual.

"Did your resupply take you over to the glassblowers shop?" Esen interjected before Wendolan could answer.

"No," she replied, giving them a sidelong glance. "Are you two looking for someone?"

Thorne noticed that Jannes and Michem were starting at him with an uncomfortable intensity. He recognized the look of a predator fixating on its prey. The mage felt a strong urge to escape that was amplified from being in the crowded tavern with little room to maneuver. "No one in particular," he said, trying to disengage from Wendolan. "Sorry to bother you."

"Your name is Thorne," Jannes said, his tone making it sound like an accusation. His body tensed like he was going to pounce on the mage. Michem looked ready to do the same.

Stalling for time, Thorne took a long drink from his mug and set it back on the bar. There were too many people for him to consider summoning his mana knife, especially with Wendolan being a mage. Scanning the bar, he saw Esen's full mug of water. Grabbing it, he took a sip before holding it close to his chest with both hands as if considering Jannes' comment.

"That's right," the mage said with a nod. He looked Jannes

in the eye and knew it was only a matter of time before the mercenary's veneer of civility melted and his true nature emerged.

A scuffle broke out across the tavern, and the conversation in the room paused as most patrons turned to watch a pair of rough-looking men wrestle each other to the ground. Taking advantage of the situation, Thorne elbowed Esen in the ribs and nodded towards the door. Esen silently followed as they pushed their way to the exit. They were in such a rush to leave, it was not until they were outside that the mage realized he still held the mug of water.

Thorne and Esen had only just made it around the corner of the tavern when they heard a shout behind them, "Oy! Wait there you two!"

The yellow light from the street corner lamppost didn't do much to illuminate the alleyway, but Thorne could see easily enough that Jannes and Michem had found them. The latter had a long knife in his thick hand. The mercenaries stood shoulder-to-shoulder, blocking easy access to the street and the front of the tavern. Backlit by the lamplight, both men's shadowy faces were all the more menacing.

"Where's Wendolan?" Thorne asked, his eyes darting from the mercenaries to the street behind them.

"Still in the tavern," Michem said. "Forgot about you the instant you were out of sight. Good thing too, since we don't want her here for this little meeting."

"There's a bounty on you, mage," Jannes said, shaking a finger at Thorne.

"I don't think so," Thorne said. "I just arrived in Haven." Thinking quickly, he pushed mana into the cup of water, gradually heating it. Keeping his eyes focused on Michem's knife, the mage struggled to insure just the right amount of arcane energy was used to make the water boil, but not spill over.

"Even so, an open contract was posted this morning,"

Michem replied, taking a step forward that put him within striking range with his knife. "The whole guild knows of it. But if you don't believe me, then why don't you come back to the guild with us and we'll show it to you. It'll make collecting the bounty that much easier for us."

Thorne flung the boiling water in Michem's face.

The mercenary cried out and covered his scalded eyes, dropping his knife in the process.

Esen took advantage of Jannes' hesitation and rushed forward, grabbing the mercenary and shoving him against the side of the tavern. The foreigner followed up with a brutal blow to Jannes' head. Before the unconscious mercenary fell to the ground Esen grabbed his collar and held him up.

"Don't kill him," Thorne said, seeing that Esen now held his knife. "We've left too many dead bodies in our wake."

"With more to come when I find Karnoff," Esen said letting go of the mercenary's armor and watching as he thumped to the ground. Esen turned to Michem, who was sitting and clutching his face in agony. Grabbing one of his hands, Esen pulled the mercenary's arm up over his head.

"Did Karnoff do this?" the foreigner demanded. "Did he convince the governor to post the bounty?"

"Fuck off," Michem spat. "I'm not saying anything –" The mercenary's reply was cut off by the sound of bone crunching, immediately followed by his sharp cry.

"You have four more fingers to break," Esen said through clenched teeth. "Start talking."

Without waiting, Esen bent another finger back until it snapped. The mercenary howled.

"That'll bring the City Watch," Thorne said looking towards the street. "We need to go now."

Esen dropped Michem's arm and followed the mage's quick escape down the alleyway. They stopped running before they emerged on the next street over from the tavern. Trying to act casually, they slowed their pace as they returned to a well-lit street.

"Maybe we should take the pilgrimage up on their offer for dinner," Thorne suggested. "I've had my fill of taverns for tonight."

Esen nodded and then said, "After returning what money you have left to the alms bowl."

The mage wasn't in the mood to argue and gestured for Esen to lead the way back to the sanctuary. This second narrow escape of the day was a hard lesson learned that it was not just the City Watch and military looking for him in Haven. However he did it, Karnoff had made the city very dangerous.

• • •

When Thorne and Esen returned to the sanctuary it was not long after the first low bell of the night had rung throughout the city. The mage was expecting the dining hall to be much the same as the one found at the Yaboon Archive, and while it was in terms of form and function, the atmosphere was markedly different. There was little conversation at the long communal tables, and what did pass between the pilgrims was uttered quietly and with downward cast eyes. There was a tension amongst the congregation that suggested something worrying had happened.

Esen and Thorne sat down next to a young woman whose companions were two older men. The men looked to Esen, and then to Thorne. They gave both unwelcome expressions but kept eating in silence. Ignoring the men, Esen's face softened, and he asked the woman in a gentle voice, "Is there trouble?"

The woman seemed hesitant to speak, but then said quietly, "The flagellant is missing. He's not in the sanctuary, and only a few people can even recall that he entered the city. The final prayer service of the pilgrimage is tomorrow and an important part of it is the reclaiming of his true identity. His disappearance is a bad omen."

"He has to be here somewhere in the city," Esen said.

Thorne jerked upright as he had a flash of insight. Abruptly standing, he looked down at Esen and commanded, "Come with me a minute."

Once they were alone in the antechamber before the worship hall, the mage stopped and leaned up against the wall.

"What is this all about?" Esen asked, his tone a mixture of confusion and irritation. "That was rather rude to just leave the cafeteria in the middle of a conversation."

"I didn't want the pilgrims to hear this," Thorne said. "I know where the flagellant is right now."

Esen rocked back on his heels in surprise. "Where?"

The mage leaned in close and said with a quiet intensity, "He's at the glassblower guildhall with Geridan and Karnoff."

"That's absurd," Esen said with a frown.

"It's not absurd, Esen," the mage said looking the foreigner directly in the eye. "When I took him to see Karnoff's dead soldiers, he reacted very strangely. He recognized those men, I'm sure of it. He also had a silver chain hidden in his waistband. I could never see the medallion on it, but I've no doubt now that it's from the glassblower guild."

"Then why didn't he do something before when we told him who we were?" Esen asked.

"So he wouldn't give himself away," Thorne said. "Karnoff had a head start, so all he had to do is keep playing his part in the pilgrimage."

"Then whatever plot he was part of died with Claire," Esen said.

"All the more reason to get that bounty posted and send the mercenary guild after us," Thorne reasoned. "I fear that the sanctuary won't be safe for much longer. He knows we have precious few places to rest here in the city."

"This is all conjecture," the foreigner said with agitation in his voice. "Don't you have any spies here? Someone who could help us?"

"I don't," Thorne admitted. In the following silence the mage thought back to the last Paragon meeting and Reihana's insistence on expanding their networks. It was a prescient warning, and somewhat ironic given that she was chasing them now. He wondered how long it would take before she was in Haven looking for him as well. "Let's go back and eat something," he said. "It's been long day."

"I'm not hungry," Esen replied as he turned away from the mage. Quickly walking down a narrow hallway that led to the sanctuary's sleeping quarters, the foreigner left Thorne alone to consider their worsening fortunes.

CHAPTER TWENTYTWO

After the tolling of three high bells the next morning, Thorne and Esen joined the pilgrims once again in the dining hall. The events of the past day had drained them and both slept poorly. Waking with the pilgrims at fourteen low bells, they watched the sunrise though the high windows of the worship hall. Esen participated in the service while Thorne stood silently as far back from the worshipers as possible. Now they sat amongst the faithful, eating a breakfast of porridge and milk. The mood was better than yesterday, the conversation a bit louder and laughter more frequent.

They were sitting at the end of a communal table eating when the shepherd entered the dining hall with a troubled expression. Scanning the tables quickly, he walked purposefully towards Thorne and Esen. Without preamble he said in a hushed but urgent voice, "Members of the mercenary guild are searching the worship hall and sleeping quarters for you. You don't have much time to hide. Come with me, quickly."

Leaving their breakfast half-eaten, Thorne and Esen followed the shepherd out of the dining hall and away from the main areas of the sanctuary. They were led down a quiet hallway and into a small room with several shelves and large cabinets. Resting along the walls were tall candelabras, rugs, and small tapestries, all suggesting a storage area for the worship hall. The shepherd pulled open one wardrobe and commanded, "Inside, quickly."

Esen stepped toward the open door, but then pulled back, his hand covering his nose. "It reeks of incense," he said.

Thorne peered inside and found nothing out of the ordinary. Several religious robes and capes were hung from a dowel. At the bottom were pairs of ornately decorated shoes resting on top of several threadbare wayfarer cloaks. Even with all of the clothes, he surmised that he and Esen should be able to fit relatively comfortably inside.

"There's a false panel in the back," the shepherd said, gently pushing Thorne into the large cabinet. "The catch is near the bottom right corner. It opens into the hidden chamber. Wait for me to retrieve you and stay silent."

The mage took a step into the wardrobe and ran his fingers along the seam between the back wall and the bottom until he found a gap. Digging his fingers under the panel, he pulled a small section of the back wall upwards. Getting down on his hands and knees, Thorne crawled into darkness. The small amount of light that bled into the hidden chamber provided just enough visibility for him to avoid bumping into the wall or low ceiling.

Thorne turned around in time to see Esen enter the hidden room and shift to the side to look back through the wardrobe at the shepherd.

"Stay silent!" he commanded one last time before moving the panel back into place. With a wooden thump, Thorne and Esen were left in darkness. The mage heard the shepherd rearrange the clothes and robes that hung along the pole before closing the door. There was a metallic click of a key in a lock, and then silence.

It took a few minutes for Thorne to realize the blackness of the room was not absolute. Two horizontal slits the length of his forearm were on one wall to his left very close to the ceiling. Through these narrow openings the scantest of light entered the room. Thorne was disorientated, so he didn't know if the light was coming from outside, or an interior hallway. Since the light wasn't flickering at all, the mage surmised it must be the former.

Letting his eyes grow further accustomed to the dark, he saw Esen hunched over near the false wall. His head was pressed against the panel and he appeared to be listening for any sounds from outside. On his hands and knees, Thorne crawled next to him and did the same. At first all the mage could hear was his heartbeat in his ears, but then from outside came the stomp of heavy boots.

Through the thin false wall and the thick wardrobe door, Thorne heard an angry voice demand, "Open this one as well."

"But this is where we keep our religious vestments," the shepherd replied.

"And it is also large enough to hide a fugitive," the voice answered. "I told you before, the governor has issued a bounty for the Archive mage that killed the glassblower guild master's daughter. The contract stated that no safe harbor was to be granted, and therefore searching sanctuaries are permitted. Now unlock the door unless you want to watch me smash it open."

Thorne heard the wardrobe door being unlocked, then a series of thumps as clothes were shoved against the sides. Soon after, the door was slammed shut and a different voice barked, "Go to the kitchen next!"

In the silence that followed, Thorne heard Esen sigh in his ear. The mage was afraid Esen was going to give them away, but instead he shifted away from the false panel and sat against the wall, settling down for a long wait. Unsure whether the danger has passed, Thorne stayed where he was and listened. As they waited the small space became uncomfortably warm, and the mage started to feel claustrophobic. After hearing five high bells from somewhere outside, Thorne was about to move near the narrow vents when the wardrobe secret panel swung open and blinding light poured into the small chamber.

"The danger has past for now, my friends," the shepherd said, backlit and looking much larger than normal as he reached down to help Thorne and Esen out of the wardrobe. Once they were all standing in the storage room, the shepherd said to them, "The mercenaries are gone, but they threatened to return without notice. I fear you might find yourself in there again."

"Why do you have this?" Thorne asked, gesturing to the wardrobe. "I've never heard of a sanctuary having such hiding places."

"Do you really think that the Archive is the only place where secrets are kept and traded?" the shepherd asked with mock disbelief. He gestured towards the wardrobe and continued, "We use this in emergencies, especially to hide people who have unjustly run afoul of local governors. Only sanctuary shepherds, a mason loyal to us, and those hidden away know about their existence." Giving Thorne a serious look he finished, "I would appreciate your discretion."

Thorne inclined his head and replied, "Of course."

The shepherd looked at Esen and said, "If you would be willing to help me, those mercenaries knocked over one of the bookshelves in my study. I'd appreciate your help righting it." Turning to Thorne he said, "Master mage, just so I can keep track of you, would you please return to your quarters? I'll send Esen to collect you for the midday meal. While I think the safest place for the time being is here in the sanctuary, they might return unexpectedly. I can't protect you if you leave, so please consider staying here until we can write a petition for clemency. It will likely go unheeded by the governor, but it is important to try."

Esen followed the shepherd while Thorne walked alone

back to the quarters he shared with the foreigner. Once in his room, the mage sat on the edge of the raised platform that served as his bed. It was hard and uncomfortable, but better than sleeping on the cold stone floor. He was considering his next moves when there came a tap on the door.

"Come," the mage commanded.

The door opened slowly. In the entryway an adolescent boy stood, his face painted with worry.

With a relaxed expression, Thorne asked, "What brings you here, Orin?"

"Why were those mercenaries looking for you?" the boy asked, finding his voice.

Thorne studied him before replying, "They think I did something bad, killed someone," he replied.

"Did you?"

"No," Thorne answered, though it felt like he was lying. He wasn't directly responsible for Claire's death, but the mage still felt guilty for not being strong enough to save her.

"I'm here because I have something for you," Orin said. "Not like last time. It won't hurt you, but will still help keep you safe." He held out his hand and showed Thorne a symbol of the Small House carved from wood.

Thorne took the small sculpture and rotated it in his fingers. "Thank you," he said absently as he studied where a knife had whittled away the sharp edges around the three posts that represented the Father, the Mother, and the Child.

"What do you think? Do you like it?" Orin asked with the hope of someone looking for approval.

Thorne looked over at the boy. "Thank you," he said again. Struck by a thought he added, "This is a gift that represents something you believe deeply in, correct? I'd like to do the same."

The mage reached into his pocket and pulled out his glow

sphere. He pulsed a bit of mana into the resin and it began to radiate a soft yellow light. The mage's smile was genuine when he saw Orin's eyes grow wide at the sight of such a minor arcane manipulation. "This is a glow sphere," he said. "Mages at the Archive use it to make light at night and in dark places." Extending his hand he said, "I'd like you to have it."

Orin reached out, but hesitated before taking the sphere. "It's not hot," he said. Turning over the sphere and examining it carefully he asked, "How long will it glow like this?"

"As long as I am here in the sanctuary," Thorne replied. "You'll know I've gone when the light goes out."

"Oh," Orin said, sounding let down.

"I wouldn't let it bother you," Thorne said. "Someday you will meet another mage, and they could charge it again."

"Thank you," Orin said. After marveling at the glow sphere a bit longer, the boy looked at Thorne and said, "You're the first wizard I've ever met. I thought you were scary before, but now I think that maybe you're not so bad."

As Orin got up to leave, Thorne noticed that Esen stood in the doorway. The foreigner stepped aside as Orin left.

After the boy disappeared down the hall, Esen said, "I appreciate your change of heart. You didn't have to reconcile with him."

"It's not a change of heart," Thorne replied, "My misgivings about the Small House, about all religions in general, are still the same." He looked past Esen to the small section of hallway visible and said, "It's about self-preservation. I want that boy to have a good opinion about the Archive."

"Why?"

"In the end, what the Small House is trying to achieve and the Archive's goals have some overlap, and we should try to work together within that space." He looked back at Esen. "And though I am reluctant to do so, I must admit that I am thankful for the shepherd's help. He's been able to do things that I couldn't."

"It must be humbling to make that admission, especially given the power that the Archive wields," Esen said. He walked over and rested a hand on the mage's shoulder. "You represent your fellow mages well, Thorne."

Thorne bobbed his head, but said nothing. Esen's words should have been gratifying, but if he was being honest, the mage wasn't sure he agreed.

• • •

Unable to calm his nerves amongst the pilgrims as they performed their daily devotions, and tired of being isolated in his sleeping quarters while hoping the shepherd could get his bounty annulled, Thorne snuck away that evening to the sanctuary's crypt. The subterranean chamber had the same feeling of heaviness as Masters Hall at the Archive, with its stone ceiling seemingly compacting the air and slowing the movements of anyone who walked inside.

After Thorne descended the switchback stairs into the crypt, he walked around the perimeter to get a feeling for the space. Having given his only glow sphere to Orin, Thorne used a lit candle to survey his surroundings. A long hall stretched before him adorned with small ornate doors stacked three high on both sides. Each door had a bronze plaque affixed to it engraved with a family name and some had guild crests as well. The mage walked down the hall reading some of the family names as he approached a small stone alter flanked by empty sconces.

Thorne attempted to place the candle on the alter, but found its wax bottom was not cut even. Frustrated, the mage removed his shirt and wadded it into a small nest. After putting the candle in the cloth, he managed to rest it on the alter.

The mage stood still with his feet firmly planted and closed his eyes. He imagined himself in the woods just outside Yaboon at the training area he frequented with Mirtans. Recalling his last training session against the Sehenryu, he took in a deep breath and summoned his mana knife. Thorne looked down at the arcane blade, the blue film looking ethereal in the weak candlelight. While he could alter the prismatic properties of his arcane energy, and often made his mana blade amber, in this place Thorne felt that a somber color was more appropriate.

Pushing out his breath with a hiss, he began a series of striking drills. It was impossible to gauge the passage of time, but as Thorne worked through his training routine he guessed an hour had gone by. He was finishing a complex sequence of attacks when he noticed out of the corner of his eye a flicker of light descending the stairs.

Thorne dissolved his mana knife, fearful of being discovered by one of the pilgrims, but even without his arcane blade visible, he looked strange standing sweaty and bare-chested alone in the crypt. He was relieved to see Esen's face illuminated in the candlelight.

"I've looked everywhere for you," the foreigner said. "I wanted to make sure you hadn't snuck out of the sanctuary without me. What are you doing alone down here?"

"Just trying to keep some combat movements fresh in my muscles," Thorne replied. "I was taught by an old Sovereignty soldier, and he said to train like your life depended on it, because it does. Given our current situation, this seemed like the only place where I could practice and not be seen. I imagine that the shepherd wouldn't approve of such activity."

"No, I suppose not," Esen said. He paused a moment before saying, "I wasn't really paying attention when you did the same on the *Formica*. Will you show me?"

"What for?" Thorne said, surprised. "You seemed to handle

yourself just fine at the guildhall in Haywood. And you killed Irik as well. He was a trained fighter from the glassblower guild. What could I teach you?"

"Those were luck," Esen said. "Just being a little bit faster than them, a little bit stronger." He tapped the hilt of the dagger at his side and continued, "Against someone like you," he shook his head and corrected himself, "like Karnoff, I'm not so sure."

"You won't be fighting Karnoff alone," Thorne said. He studied the foreigner and noticed a doubt that was not there before. Esen knew what he had to do, but appeared afraid that he would fail. Without really thinking, the mage said, "I'm not much of a teacher, but let's give it a try. Put your candle on the altar and stand here next to me."

Doing his best to recall the earliest lessons Garret taught him about footwork, advancing and retreating against an opponent, and striking distance, Thorne guided Esen though the fundamentals of Sovereignty military combat techniques. Next, he introduced a few basic attack and defense sequences. Esen was able to mimic the movements well enough, but not with speed or precision.

"You make it look so fluid," Esen commented at one point. "So effortless."

Thorne shook his head and replied, "Not effortless in the least. I've been training like this for a long time and haven't even come close to the natural grace of others." With downcast expression added, "Like Mirtans."

"The Sehenryu at the Archive infirmary? She's a fighter?"

"One of the best I've ever seen," the mage said, recalling their last duel. "I hope she's doing alright."

"You're a good friend, to be thinking of her now given our current circumstances."

"We're more like rivals than friends," Thorne replied. "We

train together but we don't really socialize."

"Why not?"

"Believe it or not, I have a hard time letting people get close to me," Thorne said.

"I don't know the politics or alliances of where you come from," Esen said with a shrug. "But you've proven yourself to be steadfast and trustworthy. I am all the more certain that it was the providence of the Small House that led me to you." He put his knife away, retrieved his candle, and started to walk towards the crypt's exit. Looking over his shoulder as his foot touched the first step, Esen said, "And I consider you a friend."

It was well after Esen's candle had stopped throwing wavering shadows on the stairwell that Thorne realized he had been standing rigidly. Trying to relax, he shook loose his arms and rolled his head a few times. Despite being tired, he felt the nervous energy of the past day had not been released. He summoned his mana knife again and ran through a few cycles of transmuting it to a shield and then back into a blade, each time trying to make the transition faster. Once he was back to wielding a knife again, he held it out in front of him and raised up his opposite hand in a mirrored gesture. It was time for the real test.

Thorne tried to pull mana from his other arm and summon a second mana knife. He could feel the arcane energy manifest, but he didn't have the control to pull it out of himself in a form that was stable. Instead of a blade fashioned from arcane energy, he only succeeded in pulsing small bursts of mana that dissipated the instant they were outside of his body. The mage growled in frustration and shoved his hand into the wall just as a pulse ejected. The force of the expelled mana jerked the mage backwards and left his arm momentarily numb.

Thorne dissolved his mana knife to rub his aching palm, but stopped when he noticed where he hit the wall. The area had a glassy appearance, and the mage realized that his uncontrolled mana burst had melted the stone's surface. Looking down at his palm, he said quietly, "Not a second knife, but maybe useful all the same."

CHAPTER TWENTYTHREE

Thorne set a steaming bowl of soup down on the long communal table in the sanctuary dining hall before sitting down next to Esen. Another day had come and gone, and the mage grew increasingly restless and frustrated. With the City Watch, the military, and now probably Reihana hunting for them in the streets, along with the mercenary guild poised to search the sanctuary at any time, Thorne felt like a caged animal.

He had spent most of the day in the room he shared with Esen alternating between dozing, trying to think of a way to search the city for Karnoff without being detected, and writing a few notes on some paper that was loaned to him by the shepherd. It was an unproductive way to spend his time, which also contributed to his agitation. The flagellant was still missing, which troubled the pilgrims greatly, but made the mage even surer that he was part of Reihana's scheme.

Esen seemed to be handling his captivity a little better with his involvement in daily sanctuary activities. He helped with some of the pilgrims' tasks for maintaining the sanctuary as they readied themselves for the end of the pilgrimage. Throughout the day he checked on the mage, but Thorne suspected it was to make sure he hadn't left the sanctuary rather than to see if he needed anything. It was well after the first low bell of the night had rung out when the two of them walked to the cafeteria to eat dinner.

"What have we got tonight?" the mage asked with little

enthusiasm as he sat down at the table. When Esen didn't answer right away, Thorne looked over to his companion and noticed he was staring at his meal with a blank expression.

"The dregs of barley soup," Esen eventually said with resignation. "If we had arrived sooner, we might have gotten some bread. They're already starting to clean dishes, you know. That's how late we are to eat."

"You could have come without me."

Esen waved his hand dismissively and scooped up some broth. He had brought it halfway to his mouth when he paused and asked, "What were you writing? Was it a letter?"

"It was nothing important," Thorne answered.

Esen ate some soup and was about to say something when a small Sehenryu male approached them.

"You need to go to the worship hall. There's a messenger there for you," he said nervously.

"Trouble?" Esen asked, his face darkening.

He shook his head quickly and answered, "I don't know, but he asked for both of you by name."

Thorne set his still clean spoon back down on the table. "You can stay and eat if you like. I'll go."

Esen stood up with the mage. "No, I should go as well. No one will disturb our meal for the few minutes we're gone."

Leaving the Sehenryu in the cafeteria, they walked to the entrance of the worship hall where they found a dour-faced Venhadar woman absently looking around. When they approached, her posture stiffed and her eyes locked with Thorne's, her expression unkind.

"Are you Thorne, a Yaboon mage?" she asked in a gruff voice.

Thorne inclined his head and replied, "I am."

Turning to the foreigner she said, "And you are Esen?"

"What is this about?" he asked instead of answering.

The Venhadar reached into her vest and pulled out a letter. "I was given instructions to deliver this to you."

She held out the letter to Thorne, who took it tentatively. The instant the paper left her hand, the Venhadar walked away.

"Wait," called out Esen. "Who sent this?"

The Venhadar ignored him and picked up speed as she barreled out the sanctuary.

When she was gone, Thorne examined the letter. Written on thick, well-crafted paper, it was folded tightly but had no seal. Carefully pulling the note open, Thorne read aloud for Esen's benefit, "Go to the glassblower guild warehouse tonight at ten low bells and seek revenge on the one who was responsible for Claire's death. You may even have the opportunity to set things right for the guild, as well as the Archive."

Thorne looked up with a perplexed expression and found Esen shared it.

"That doesn't make any sense," the foreigner said. "Why would we want to help the guild?" With his brow furrowing deeper he asked, "Who sent this?"

The mage shook his head and answered, "It's signed, *From a friend*. This has to be a trap. It feels like something Karnoff would scheme."

"So what do we do?"

"We should eat," Thorne replied. When he got a blank expression from Esen, he added, "We're can't afford to go into this weak. It's several hours before ten low bells, so let's go have dinner and rest as best we can."

Esen opened his mouth, appearing to have some rebuttal, but ultimately pressed his lips into a thin line and then gestured for Thorne to lead them back to the cafeteria.

The dining hall was all but deserted when they returned. Back in the kitchen, the clinking of mugs could occasionally be heard along with indistinct conversations of the pilgrims doing the washing. They found that their soup bowls and utensils were undisturbed where they had left them, and quietly returned to their seats.

Esen picked up his spoon and then looked over at Thorne. "You decided to go the instant you read the note, didn't you?" he said.

Thorne stared down into his now cold meal. "We can't stay here," he replied. "It puts the sanctuary at risk and doesn't bring us any closer to finding Karnoff. Or Geridan." He turned and looked at Esen with a weary expression. "I'm tired of continually coming up empty handed, being one step behind. This might be a trap, yes, but it's also the opportunity we need to get some answers."

Esen put down his spoon and picked up his bowl. Bringing it to his lips, the foreigner took a deep drink of the broth. He grunted softly and said, "This reminds me of Claire's cooking. Simple, but you can taste the work that went into it."

Thorne followed Esen's lead, picking up his bowl and drinking the soup with large gulps. Setting the empty bowl down he said, "Food gives me the nourishment I need to power my magic, but it brings me no joy."

"Cooking for Claire made me happy," Esen replied. "It was something special we shared out on the frontier, a respite from struggling to coax vegetables from the earth, a quiet moment to enjoy each other's company."

The foreigner sniffed loudly and cleared his throat. "Things can never be the same again," he said. "Karnoff took everything from me. It almost doesn't matter what happens in the guild warehouse. Either I'll die or he will."

Thorne was shaken to hear such talk from Esen. "While I agree that our predicament is rather bleak, what happens at the guild warehouse absolutely matters," he said. "Whether you like it or not, this is bigger than you and Claire. Our mystery writer said as much. I need to make sure your newfound fatalistic outlook doesn't get me killed too. I want Karnoff held accountable for what he's done, and I refuse to believe that he was sanctioned to take Claire."

"You're still concerned about protecting the Archive's reputation?" Esen scoffed.

"I'm protecting my home!" Thorne said fiercely. After pausing to calm himself, he said, "When I was younger, I lost someone close to me too. I took it very hard and the strain broke my family apart. The Archive became a place where I could channel my fear, my anger, into something productive. Everything that I've achieved is because of the opportunities afforded me there."

"Anger I can understand," Esen said with a nod. "But not fear. With all of your power, what can you possibly fear?"

"Being a disappointment. Being forgotten."

Both men sat until they heard the tolling of two low bells from the carillon outside. They left the table and returned to their shared room in silence, opting to find what rest they could until later that night.

• • •

As the last of nine low bells rang out, Thorne and Esen snuck out of the sanctuary.

After leaving their quarters, they took a short detour to the room that contained the wardrobe they had hidden in and retrieved two hooded cloaks. Now, outwardly appearing as sanctuary pilgrims to any casual observer, they exited via a seldom-used door that opened into a narrow alleyway. An overcast sky made the middle of night that much darker, and a stillness that bordered on eerie had settled in.

Thorne was thankful for the extra warmth that the sanctuary

cloak provided as the outside air chilled him. He had forgotten how cold the nights could be this far south on the continent. Careful to make sure they weren't being followed, they made their way up the alley and to the front corner of the sanctuary where a broad street was illuminated by periodic lampposts.

"How far away is the warehouse again?" Thorne whispered over his shoulder to Esen as he scanned the street. An occasional person walked by, hurrying to or from something, but otherwise the street was empty. The mage knew it was only a matter of time before a pair City Watchmen showed up as part of their regular rounds. They would have to keep a low profile as the Sovereignty military and guild mercenaries would be supplementing such nightly patrols.

"I was told it would take about half an hour if we walked on main streets," Esen whispered. "But that's a bad idea if we don't want to get caught. We can't fight our way out of encounters with the City Watch, right?"

The mage nodded and said, "I'm not too keen on skulking like a thief through the alleys either. We already did that once, and I didn't like the outcome." He paused as lantern light shone around the corner up the street. Two armed and armored City Watchmen, a human and a Venhadar, slowly walked in their direction. Thorne and Esen shrank back into the alleyway and pressed themselves into the sanctuary doorway until the patrol had passed. Once the lantern light shifted away, Thorne took a tentative step back out in the street.

"We should be clear for at least a quarter hour," he said. "I think I have an idea for how we can stay in the shadows and also travel on the major streets."

Without waiting to see if Esen was following, the mage walked briskly down the empty avenue. As they approached an intersection, their pace slowed. A large lantern hung on a tall post at each corner, and flickering yellow light blanketed the ground and crept up the walls of the surrounding buildings.

"Anyone watching here will see us for certain," Esen said. "There's no way we can skirt around, and the buildings are too tight here, no alleys or gaps to squeeze through. Do we go back?"

"Just wait," Thorne said. He reached out towards the nearest lantern and charged his fingertips with mana. Instantly he could feel the moisture and the previously imperceptible currents in the air. Drawing back his fingers and manipulating the air, he fashioned a small bubble around the lantern. Once formed, he pulled the air away until the bubble was a vacuum. The lantern dimmed as the flame shrank, and then went dark. Thorne released the bubble and dissipated the mana charge in his hand. Now there was a dark area at the intersection where they could pass.

"Go, quickly," the mage commanded. He scurried through the intersection and turned down the next street, not stopping until he found a small gap between buildings where he could press in. Only a few steps behind Thorne, Esen followed him into the small hiding place.

"That worked well," Esen said as he peered back the way they came. "It might even delay the next patrol that comes by if they stop to relight the lantern."

"I suppose," Thorne said absently, looking down at his hand. The arcane manipulation had been effortless, and he had done it almost without thinking. Even though Esen wasn't looking at him, Thorne turned his face away in shame. If only he was stronger, then he could have saved Claire with the same technique. Remembering the overpowering flames that engulfed the carriage, Thorne balled his hands into fists and shut his eyes.

Thorne tried to block it out, but was assaulted by the mental image of Claire's coach burning. In his mind, the burning carriage changed to that of Karnoff backlit by a great bonfire. His eyes were mocking and cruel. Thick smoke cloaked the rogue mage for a moment, and when it cleared Karnoff was replaced by Reihana. The Paragon principal agent had a look of scorn, her hands resting on her wide hips. She flicked one of her hands in a dismissive gesture at him, one corner of her mouth curling up in a sneer. She then turned her back to him and faced the bonfire only to turn back around a second later. In that blur of movement, Reihana was replaced with Mirtans. The Sehenryu's expression wasn't one of derision, but rather sadness. She spread her arms out wide and summoned a mana knife to each forearm. Dropping her arms to her sides, she shrugged, seeming to ask why he couldn't perform such a simple feat.

"I'm sorry," Thorne mouthed the words, but did not speak them aloud. Taking a halting breath, he opened his eyes and saw that Esen was about to sneak out from their hiding spot.

"We should get moving again," Esen said over his shoulder as he stepped into the street, completely unaware of Thorne's silent internal struggle.

The mage composed himself as he followed Esen to the next intersection.

Staying well out of the light, the foreigner looked up at a lantern and asked, "Can you do the same thing again?"

Thorne glanced up to the lanterns hung over the intersection, and then down the street ahead of them. "We've got another problem," he said while pointing.

Two buildings down from them was a bustling tavern. Warm light from the windows spilled onto the street and revealed three cloaked figures huddled nearby. The door opened and a pair of Venhadar left the tavern, thankfully walking away from the intersection. One of the cloaked figures shut the door, and as he turned, Thorne saw a sword hanging from his belt.

"Mercenaries," the mage said to Esen. "Can't go that way. We'll have to find an alleyway around."

"That'll take longer," Esen protested.

"Can't be helped," Thorne replied as they turned and trotted down a side street.

Trying to balance speed with stealth, they moved obliquely across the town using alleyways and squeezing between buildings. They found that most of the major streets were being patrolled by the City Watch or had posted sentries from the mercenary guild. Thorne and Esen considered themselves lucky that they didn't cross any ne'er-do-wells in those dark hidden places who might have given them away.

They had just arrived at the street where the city's guildhalls were located when ten low bells rang out. Out of the dozen guildhalls, there were two that had windows alight, which made their outside signs readable. Thorne saw that one of them was the glassblower guild, but thankfully there were no posted guards at the door. In fact, the street was suspiciously vacant.

From the second floor window, a backlit figure looked down on the street. From where Thorne and Esen were hiding, it was unlikely the person could see them, but all the same Thorne found himself holding his breath. After a few moments, the figure stepped back from the window and disappeared.

"Someone's working late," Esen commented as they approached a warehouse on the next street over.

They found the street with the warehouses conspicuously empty as well. Lining both sides of the street were towering box-shaped buildings that all had large twin doors on the front for carts, and smaller entryways for foot traffic. What was strange was that there were no patrols, no sentries, and no guild workers. Given the importance of commerce throughout the continent, Thorne found it odd there were no workers or security personnel in sight.

Using the information that Esen had obtained from the pilgrims, they cautiously approached the large unmarked building belonging to the glassblower guild. Esen reached out and jiggled the door handle and was surprised to find it unlocked. He slowly pulled it open.

"Are you ready?" Esen asked.

The mage's expression grew serious. The time for doubt and self-pity was over. Karnoff knew they were coming for him and Thorne needed to focus on what needed to be done. Esen wasn't equipped to take on a Paragon alone. Thorne was confident this was a trap, but they had come too far to back out now. He was going to keep his word to the foreigner. He nodded and replied, "As ready as I am going to be."

CHAPTER TWENTYFOUR

Reihana read the note once more, studying both the penmanship and word choice.

"What do you think?" Karnoff asked eagerly.

They were in the room adjacent to Geridan's office, though the guild master was not there presently. While Reihana had found more comfortable lodging after signing the contract for Thorne's bounty at the mercenary guild, Karnoff had been kept here. Geridan was still a hurricane of emotions from Claire's death, and until Reihana produced another culprit, Karnoff was going to take the blame. She had convinced the guild master to give her some time to capture Thorne, but in exchange Karnoff was to remain under guard at the glassblower guildhall.

Reihana looked away from Karnoff and read the entire message out loud, "At ten low bells tonight go to the glassblower guild warehouse. Those you are seeking will be found there." She lowered the note while giving Karnoff an accusatory look. "Who sent this message?" she demanded.

Karnoff gestured at the thick paper in Reihana's hand and replied, "There wasn't a signature or a seal." Growing more excited he added, "But it means they're here, Thorne and the foreigner. They're not running anymore."

"They've got no place left to go. Geridan is here," she answered. With a scowl Reihana waved the note before she dropped it on the bare desktop, and then said, "This is some sort of ruse to get you out in the open. I suspect those two aim to force a confession from you about Claire's abduction. I clearly underestimated Thorne's network here if he's been able to move about without me knowing."

"All the more reason to go," Karnoff replied.

"No," Reihana said decisively. "This is obviously a trap, and I have no intention of walking into it, for no other reason than I don't want to further aggravate Geridan by potentially damaging his warehouse or whatever is inside. I'll not further imperil our already strained relationship."

"What's to stop Thorne from burning it down to the ground if we don't confront him?"

Reihana sniffed derisively and replied, "Despite his unsociable tendencies, that's not in his nature."

"What makes you so sure?"

She walked to the window and looked out at the darkened sky. Most of the windows in the neighboring buildings were dark, save for a handful where the flicker of lamplight could be detected. There were a smattering of people visible in the street, but they were indistinct bodies likely walking from the guildhalls to either their favorite taverns or homes. "He's the sole heir of a wealthy mercer guild family," she said finally.

Karnoff seemed unimpressed. "So I've heard from Torstein's mocking. What of it?" he said tersely.

She walked to the desk where her glow sphere illuminated the room with stark white light. Reihana picked up the sphere, which tilted the shadows in the room at severe angles, and began to pace between the window and the closed door.

"I was the one who suggested to Olaf his inclusion in the Paragon program," she explained.

"Really?" Karnoff said, genuinely surprised. "I figured he was forced upon you. With your general popularity at the Archive, most ignore the open secret that you hate made mages."

"Hate is too strong a word," she said, trying to keep her voice from betraying her annoyance at Karnoff's indiscretion. "I begrudge their privilege at having a choice to unlock their minds to the arcane. I can't comprehend them. How were their lives constructed that living with the Iron Bane is better than whatever they had before becoming a mage? In any event, they'll never be as powerful as a born mage, so I'm normally fine to leave them to their second tier existence at the Archive, but with Thorne I thought I could use his family connections." She scoffed, "Only too late did I find out he's a pariah."

"Then let me get rid of him," Karnoff argued.

Reihana's brow furrowed as she pursed her lips. She had been thinking about how to salvage the situation and already had the makings of a new plan, but she'd need to carefully gauge Geridan's current mental state. "Let me go talk to Geridan," she said finally. "He's likely eating at this hour, and afterwards might be more amenable. Stay here for now."

Karnoff opened his mouth as his eyes narrowed, but then he paused. His face relaxed and he replied, "I understand. There's still time, so I'll wait."

She waited to see if there would be any delayed protestations, but Karnoff looked satisfied for the moment. With a final nod to him, Reihana turned and walked to the door. She pounded her fist on it twice and called, "Let me out."

The door opened and Reihana saw two unfamiliar men, both aggressive-looking and armed, standing outside. She stepped into the hallway and descended the stairs. Reihana imagined she was already talking to Geridan, thinking of possible outcomes of the conversations, and paid no notice to the curious looks she got from those still in the guildhall as she left.

• • •

Geridan was eating a simple meal, a shallow bowl of onion broth with no accouterments, which surprised Reihana. They were in a small parlor adjacent to the guild master's guest room in the governor's mansion. The city's administrator was currently entertaining other wealthy visitors, but had extended an invitation for Geridan to stay at his house while in Haven on business. She had been delivered to him by a maid in a plain uniform but offered no food, so she stood near the lit fireplace and watched him slowly drink his meal in silence.

With a final quiet slurp, Geridan set the bowl on the table and looked over at Reihana. "Have you come to tell me you found your quarry?" he asked, sounding drained. Before Reihana could reply he continued, "It had all seemed so simple. Go to the frontier and get Claire to come home. Home to her family, home to her awaiting marriage."

Without warning the guild master picked up the bowl and hurled it at the hearth. Reihana flinched at the sound of the bowl shattering while bits of pottery bounced off her legs. Geridan rested his elbows on the table and buried his face in his hands. She watched him quietly cry and made no attempt to comfort him, afraid that such a gesture would turn the mercurial man's grief into rage. After his shoulder's stopped shuddering, Reihana took a tentative step towards the table, keeping a close eye on Geridan's hands.

"You still may be able to salvage your deal with the shipwright guild," she said. "Start by introducing me as the Paragon who brought Claire's murderer to justice. Then offer my services to them as a personal favor."

"What? Why?" Geridan asked, looking up at her with watery eyes. "Claire's marriage was going to strengthen the connections between our guilds and forge a new a family bond. Its value can't be measured, so what can you possibly offer as recompense?"

Reihana chose her next words carefully. "Paragons can operate outside of guild charters and Archive oversight. Its secrecy from the Sovereignty is an invaluable asset. Tell the shipwright guild you used Paragons to track down Claire's murderer. They would be interested in having shadow agents to help them in their dealings with the prince, yes?"

She was taking a gamble here. Paragons were never intended to be assassins or clandestine enforcers, but Reihana had learned long ago that being tactical, rather than strategic, was the best way to achieve a long-term goal. What she was describing to Geridan now was the very definition of a rogue mage, and in the past those who had tried anything remotely similar were met with swift retribution from the Archive council. There were many cautionary tales told to apprentices about the consequences of not following the tenets of the Archive, and a mage that participated in violence or overt aggression was not to be tolerated.

"Your agent still needs to be punished," Geridan said.

"What do you want done?"

"I want to take something he will miss dearly."

Reihana was unsure about the vagueness of his statement. If both Karnoff and Thorne were killed, then Olaf would ask some hard questions, that is if he ever found out the truth about what happened to them. "I understand, and that is fine," she said, raising up her chin and looking down her nose at Geridan.

Remembering Karnoff's mysterious note, she lowered her head and said, "Karnoff received a note that told him to go to the guild warehouse. Thorne is supposedly waiting for him there."

"What?" Geridan said sharply. He stood up and added, "How was a letter sent to him inside the guildhall, and who delivered it? No one knows he's there, and only ranking guild members have authorized access to the upper level of the guildhall."

"I don't know," Reihana replied truthfully.

Geridan shoved himself back from the table and stood up. The firelight reflected threateningly in his eyes when he told Reihana, "I want to see that letter. Now."

• • •

When the guards in front of Karnoff's room saw Geridan they quickly stepped aside as the guild master marched up to the door and threw it open.

Karnoff was gone.

"Where is he?" Geridan bellowed as he stormed into the room.

Following closely behind the guild master, Reihana's eyes immediately went to the back wall and the open window. As Geridan raged about, shoving the desk and knocking over bookcases, she walked around to the window and looked down. A drop from this height would no doubt result in a broken bone and the inability to walk away unaided, for a normal person.

Karnoff had simply floated down to the ground. Gravity manipulations were tricky when working with inanimate objects, but doing it to yourself was considerably more perilous. Reihana didn't know when Karnoff had perfected the skill, but of course that was what he had done. He had grown impatient after listening to the carillon tower ring out ten low bells and decided to go after Thorne himself.

"He went out the window," Reihana said as she turned back to Geridan. The guild master's chest was heaving with effort, the room's lone chair smashed at his feet.

With a forced calm that was betrayed by the wild look in his eyes, Geridan replied, "We are going to the guild warehouse, and you are going to kill him and anyone else skulking around there."

CHAPTER TWENTYFIVE

With no lantern or glow sphere, Thorne conjured his mana knife to light the way as he closed the warehouse door. The arcane blade's weak luminescence was quickly swallowed up by the huge cavernous space, but occasionally dust motes gently floated through the mage's conjured light. Wooden crates nearly as tall as a human were stacked three or four high in widely spaced rows in the center of the room and along the walls. Near the wide double doors to the mage's right were two weathered carts, their wheels covered in dust from the compacted dirt floor. He and Esen stood in an open area that was roughly half the size of the sanctuary's dining hall.

A wide balcony protruded inward from the second floor of the warehouse, but Thorne could not see well through the tightly spaced pillars of the short balustrade, so it was unclear what was stored on the upper level. The only thing he could discern were the large windows that presumably ventilated the warehouse and helped light the interior during the day, however they now did little to help them. From where the mage was standing he didn't see the stairs that led to the walkway, but surmised it must be in the rear of the warehouse. Craning his neck upwards, he could barely make out the rafters and a set of rails from which hung several pulleys and ropes to offload and move heavy cargo.

"He could be hiding anywhere in here," Esen said, his knife

gripped tightly and at the ready.

"Karnoff isn't one to hide," Thorne replied. "I know that much about him. He's a coward that will run when the odds are against him, but now he has the advantage. He'll show up when he wants to be seen."

"All the same, we should make sure there aren't any nasty surprises for us before he graces us with his presence," Esen said.

Thorne joined the foreigner as he slowly walked through the mazelike rows of crates. The crates were assembled from thick boards and branded with the glassblower guild crest, the contents, and a date. Careful to shine his weak light in the dark corners and gaps between crates, they searched the area near the front of the warehouse without finding anything amiss.

Next they walked along the wall at the back of the warehouse in search of the stairs to the walkway above them. Thorne's light had reached the first step when he heard a door slam from the front of the warehouse.

"Are you hiding in here, Thorne?" a jeering voice called out. "What would the others think of such tactics? Rather beneath a Paragon don't you think, to be skulking in the dark like a cutthroat, no?"

"Karnoff," Thorne hissed, as he spun around to face the front of the warehouse.

A white light burst into existence near one of the carts at the entrance to the warehouse. Thorne and Esen ducked behind a stack of crates. Peeking around the corner of the crate, Thorne saw Karnoff standing in an open area near the warehouse entrance. His attention was focused on the second story walkway. He held his glow sphere up high in one hand, while his other was resting at his side wreathed in a slight golden glow. He had charged his arm with mana in preparation for a quick response should he be attacked.

"Don't make me search for you, Thorne," Karnoff called out again. "I want things sorted by the time Reihana gets here."

At the mention of the Paragon principal agent, Thorne straightened. With a clenched jaw and narrowed eyes, Thorne stepped out from behind the crates.

"So you are here," Karnoff said, his tone surprised as he watched Thorne approach. "That letter I received turned out to be true. I'll have to thank my mystery friend if he ever reveals himself."

"What are you talking about?" Esen asked as he stepped out from his hiding spot and followed Thorne. The foreigner held his knife poised to leap towards Karnoff at the least provocation.

"I received a note that said you were going to be here tonight for some poorly thought-out sabotage as an act of revenge against Geridan," Karnoff answered. "I'm sure one of Reihana's spies found you out. I'll be sure to ask her shortly."

Thorne and Esen stopped once they entered the open area at the front of the warehouse. The mage glared at Karnoff and demanded, "Why would she help you?"

Karnoff looked momentarily confused before he replied, "Because she wants this assignment to succeed. She's got a lot invested in establishing a strong connection with the glassblower guild. They are going to be our entry point into the guild masters' council meeting."

"Assignment?" Thorne said in disbelief.

Karnoff laughed. "Of course you wouldn't know!" he said. "But yes, she's the one who assigned me the task of collecting Geridan's daughter from the frontier."

"What? No!" Thorne shouted, as if the conviction in his voice could make what Karnoff said untrue.

Karnoff's expression became serious. He waved his mana charged hand in a dismissive gesture and said, "It doesn't matter, anymore. Your short and unremarkable time as a Paragon ends tonight!"

Karnoff dropped to one knee and slapped his hand on the ground. The impact pulsed with a golden light as his mana was instantly absorbed into the dirt floor. Without warning a tower of crates groaned and toppled over right above Thorne.

"Watch out!" shouted Esen. He shoved the mage safely out of the way, but the topmost crate clipped the foreigner's shoulder and threw him to the earth. Esen's head bounced off of the hard dirt floor and he collapsed as the crate exploded open, spraying glass shards everywhere. The light from Karnoff's glow sphere made the ground sparkle.

Karnoff looked at Esen's motionless body and callously remarked, "Maybe not dead yet, but once I've killed you, Thorne, I can correct the mistake I made out on his frontier farmstead." Crossing his wrists in front of him and then snapping them downward, Karnoff summoned a mana knife to each arm. He dropped his illuminated glow sphere on the ground and then stalked towards Thorne, a predatory smile on his face.

Thorne's eyes flicked to Esen and then back to Karnoff. The mage got an idea and darted around a toppled crate and out of Karnoff's line of sight.

"Don't make me chase you," Karnoff called out. "I have little patience for cat and mouse games."

Thorne ran down the lane created by rows of crates until he came to a stretch of the wall was only one crate in height. He jumped, grabbed the crate, and hoisted himself up into a crouch. From his elevated position, the mage watched Karnoff enter the row where he had just been.

Looking around, Thorne found a coil of rope with a heavy pulley at the end resting not far from him. The rope was attached to one of the rafters. Picking up the pulley, he flung it down towards Karnoff. The pulley swung down and looked like it was going to crash into Karnoff, but he dodged aside and sliced through the rope, sending the pulley clattering to the ground.

Looking up to where Thorne stood, Karnoff scoffed, "Disappointing."

Bending his knees, Karnoff jumped and rose unnaturally high into the air. Karnoff landed on top of the crate wall and glared at Thorne. Shifting into an attack stance with both mana knives pointing at Thorne, Karnoff said, "You need to do better."

With a set jaw, Thorne dashed towards the rogue mage.

Karnoff tensed and then knelt on the crate. He slammed a fist into the wood, his mana knife penetrating the boards. Thorne was about to take a step on the crate adjacent to Karnoff's when it exploded. Fragments of wood and shards of glass blasted upwards, cutting Thorne's exposed skin. He covered his face with his mana knife and closed his eyes, but his momentum kept him moving forward onto the destroyed crate.

Thorne toppled over, bounced hard on the crate's edge, and then tumbled down to the warehouse floor. The impact left starbursts in the mage's vision as he struggled to get on his hands and knees. A short distance from him, Thorne heard Karnoff land on the ground. Thorne used his mana knife like a shovel, scooping up dirt and glass shards from the ground. With a flick of his wrist he flung the debris at Karnoff.

The rogue mage swept his arm across his body and generated a burst of wind that sent the airborne glass speeding into nearby crates, the tiny projectiles making small popping sounds as they impacted.

With Karnoff momentarily distracted by the cloud of dirt and glass, Thorne sprang to his feet and leapt forward. With an upward slash, the mage knocked Karnoff's left arm up above his head. Finding his opening, Thorne cut into Karnoff's unshielded inner arm.

The rogue mage cried out in pain and the mana knife on his injured arm winked out of existence. Karnoff backpedaled a few steps and raised his remaining arcane blade in a defensive position. "Perhaps Mirtans wasn't merely boasting when she said you were improving," he hissed. "She was so protective of you, after all. But then again, I suppose those of you at the bottom need to stick together to survive. Reihana certainly thinks so."

Thorne's face flushed hot at the insult. He knew Karnoff was trying to goad him into acting rashly and making a mistake, but he didn't care. Snarling, he lunged at Karnoff. Thorne's strike was sloppy, but his momentum was enough to push Karnoff back a step when their mana knives locked.

Karnoff used his injured arm to brace his mana knife as Thorne continued to shove his arcane blade forward. Through gritted teeth, the rogue mage said, "What is it you hope to achieve, Thorne? You're not strong enough to slay me, and you're certainly not clever enough to stop Reihana."

"I'm here to make sure those with the title of Paragon are worthy of it," Thorne answered. With a movement that took the rogue mage by surprise, Thorne used his off hand to release a mana burst into Karnoff's chest. The technique Thorne learned from Vechas and modified in the sanctuary's crypt sent Karnoff staggering backwards.

Karnoff clutched his burned chest with his injured arm, the mana knife in his other hanging limply at his side. The rogue mage's breathing was ragged and there was hatred in his eyes as he stared at Thorne. Karnoff sidestepped towards one of the crate walls and stabbed his mana knife into the wood. A buzzing sound raced down the line of stacked containers past Thorne, immediately followed by the sound of the crates exploding.

Thorne had only an instant to transform his mana knife into a shield, and he didn't have enough time to move his defenses completely into position before the crate he was standing near detonated. The force of the blast slammed the mage into the opposite wall of boxes and shredded his unprotected skin with fragments of wood and glass.

With the air knocked out of his lungs, Thorne crumpled to the ground and landed on his back. He stared up at the indistinct blackness of the warehouse ceiling, his hearing deafened by a high-pitched ringing in his ears. The pain of dozens of cuts made his skin feel like it was on fire, but he was too dazed to move his limbs. His mana shield was gone.

As he laid on the ground gasping for breath, Karnoff approached him and stomped a heavy boot onto Thorne's chest. "I'm sure Mirtans will mourn you," the rogue mage said, drawing back his mana knife for a fatal strike. Suddenly, his eyes went wide, his mouth agape.

Looking battered, but with an expression of unnerving resolve, Esen drew close to Karnoff from out of the shadows, his knife buried deep in the rogue mage's side. The foreigner used his free hand to grab Karnoff's hair and yanked it back, exposing his throat. "A quick death is more than you deserve," Esen whispered in his ear. "Consider this a mercy from the Small House, and from Claire."

Esen pulled his blade free and then viciously stabbed it into Karnoff's neck. The foreigner's steel knife turned Karnoff's blood black from the toxic effects of the Iron Bane, and it ran freely over Esen's hand. In Esen's powerful grasp, Karnoff's body sagged, both arms now hanging limp. Esen held on to Karnoff until the rogue mage's eyes became dull and lifeless before letting go, making sure the body didn't land on top of Thorne.

Reaching down, Esen pulled the mage to his feet and helped steady him by resting a hand on each shoulder. "Are you alright?" he asked.

"I'll live," Thorne rasped. Looking down at Karnoff's body, he shook his head. "I should be dead. Karnoff might have been a coward, but there is no question he was the better fighter."

"Perhaps so," Esen began, letting go of the mage. "But you were a match for him long enough for me to get my revenge. For that I am indebted to you. Now I think that Claire can truly be at peace."

"And you?" the mage asked. "What does your future hold now?"

Esen was silent for a moment, then answered, "Now that my blood oath to Claire is complete, it is something that I will have to consider."

"We can do that back at the sanctuary," Thorne said. "We've tempted fate much too long here. Let's go."

They left the destroyed corridor of crates and had turned the corner to the open area at the front of the warehouse when they both stopped. Standing near the carts were two humans, a man and a woman. The man held a lantern above his head that cast a yellow light on him and his companion. With greying hair and stern dark eyes, he was dressed in fine tailored clothes and had an aristocratic look to him. Next to him stood Reihana.

"Geridan, you fiend!" Esen seethed. "I came here for the Archive mage that took Claire, but it was you that no doubt issued the order. I lost her because of you!"

Esen drew his knife and took a menacing step towards Geridan when Reihana held both arms out in front of her.

"Stay where you are!" she commanded.

Esen lurched to a halt and grunted as he crashed to his knees.

At the same time, Thorne felt unnaturally heavy. Standing became a struggle and the mage fell to his knees. Thorne realized that Reihana was performing a gravity manipulation on them both. The technique was a difficult one that only the most powerful of mages could master. To execute it on two targets simultaneously was a feat far beyond Thorne's ability. He watched as Esen slumped to the ground. His breathing became labored and his muscles strained against their own increased weight.

Thorne charged both hands with mana and attempted to lessen the gravity pulling on him, but he only succeeded in keeping himself upright. He was locked into place on his knees, and it was only a matter of time before his strength ran out and he ended up on the ground like Esen. He was weakened from fighting Karnoff, but more to the point, Reihana was simply more powerful than he was when it came to manipulating her mana. For the moment he could only stare as Reihana and Geridan approached him.

"You should have left well enough alone, Thorne," she said.

"So this is your wayward agent," Geridan said with contempt. He swept his lantern in front of Thorne, which bent long shadows amongst the walls of crates. "I can only assume that the two of you somehow managed to murder Karnoff. Where is his body?"

With great effort, Esen lifted his head off the ground and glared at the glassblower guild master with hateful eyes. "It's not murder. It's revenge," he grunted.

"Then you understand what's in store for you," Geridan said. "You kidnapped Claire and absconded to the frontier to live a squalid existence as a sharecropper. Did you not think that I would use all of the resources at my disposal to bring her home?"

"Lies!" Esen barked. "She came willingly to escape your schemes! Did you really think she wanted that arranged marriage?"

"A foreigner isn't going to understand the intricacies of it," Geridan scoffed. "Claire might have thought of it as a cage, but it would have been one constructed with the finest windows from which she could admire manicured gardens. She would have wanted for nothing and fulfilled her duty to her family. As the daughter of the glassblower guild master, she knew her place was to strengthen our legacy, and what better way than to have a alliance with the shipwright guild?"

"Enough!" Reihana commanded. "Stop wasting your breath on him. He cares nothing of your scheme to broaden your guild empire." She shifted her glare from Esen to Thorne and continued, "You have made quite a mess of things, Thorne. Not only have you fouled up what would have been a very advantageous agreement for the Archive and the glassblower guild, but you killed a fellow Paragon." She smiled cruelly and added, "With your death you will finally have made yourself useful as a scapegoat."

"Olaf will no doubt question the death of two Paragons," Thorne replied, still not believing that the Archive counsel would be part of whatever Reihana had arranged.

"Only if I was foolish to report them both at the same time," Reihana said. "As far as anyone else knows, you snuck off into the night to find the assassin that tried to kill him," she nodded at Esen. "As a concerned principal agent I attempted to find you, but came up empty. Your disappearance will remain a mystery. Karnoff met an unfortunate end here in Haven trying to expand his spy network. And I can finally finish the job I attempted at the Archive infirmary," looking down at Esen. She shook her head and said, "All my loose ends will be tied up. The old man will never know of this debacle."

Thorne was still processing Reihana's admission of guilt when something whistled through the air and pierced one of her outstretched hands.

With a scream, Reihana clutched her bloody wrist and hunched over in pain. On the ground just behind her, an arrow lay.

As Thorne's body became lighter, he recirculated his mana

to end Reihana's grip over him. Looking towards the raised walkway, he saw no fewer than ten lanterns flare into existence. The lantern carriers were flanked by a pair of bowmen, each with an arrow nocked and drawn on them.

"Stay where you are if you value your life!" came a shout from the walkway.

While half of the lantern bearers and archers remained on the interior balcony, the remainder made a quick procession to the back of the warehouse and down the steps. They entered the open area at the front of the warehouse and fanned out in a flanking position so no one could escape. As Esen and Thorne got to their feet, they saw someone familiar step into the semi-circle of archers. Dressed in fine clothes and wearing a glassblower guild medallion prominently around his neck, the flagellant appraised Geridan and Reihana with a disapproving expression.

"What is the meaning of this, Wallace?" Geridan demanded, his expression defiant.

"Your machination is finally revealed," the flagellant replied. "How long did you think you could keep this hidden from the guild?"

"Had it been successful, our increased profits would have been more than fair compensation for working outside of the bylaws," Geridan answered, glancing up to the walkway. "You always did have most of our security outfit in your back pocket. It appears that your scheming has paid off. Your ascent to guild master will be as swift as your transition from common member to officer."

"Perhaps," Wallace said. "If the guild wills it so. Until then, I am assuming interim governing duties and calling an emergency meeting to inform all guild members of your secret plans. While most might have approved of an alliance with the shipwright guild, and even some might have turned a blind eye to attempts at skirting the Sovereignty's taxes, none would have condoned trading Claire's free will for such gains. It is unconscionable, and her death is ultimately on your hands."

"Your righteousness will be your undoing!" Geridan spat. "The sanctimonious always hide the most profane sins! The pilgrimage you undertook, the flagellation you suffered, the religion you so prominently flaunt, all are ultimately meaningless. Enjoy your victory now, Wallace. It will be short lived."

"Matyew, Omar, Pieter," Wallace commanded. "Escort the guild master to our agreed upon location. Take the side streets and keep him secured until I call for you."

Two archers flanked Geridan as a lantern bearer motioned for the former guild master to follow him.

After giving his escorts an icy glare, Geridan stiffened his chin and followed them out of the warehouse.

Watching them leave, Thorne wondered what fate had in store for Geridan. He was both wealthy and well connected, so chances were his failed plot would end in a punishment far more lenient than what he deserved for the crimes perpetrated against his own daughter. The mage could not fathom why such a man would do something so cold and calculating to his own kin.

Wallace turned his attention to Reihana, who stood slightly hunched over, occasionally glancing at the archers with hooded eyes. She looked sick from the effects of the Iron Bane. The flagellant took a step towards Reihana and said, "And now we must decide what is to be done with you and the Yaboon Archive's involvement in this foul business."

Without thinking, Thorne spoke up, "Reihana was working outside of the Archive council's oversight, just like Geridan was for your guild. Let me return her to Yaboon so that we can deal with her duplicity in our own way."

"And what is that?" the flagellant asked.

With baleful eyes, Thorne looked at Reihana and said, "We will bind her power to manipulate the arcane elements, take her magic away." He paused and then added, "And also revoke other privileges she has enjoyed within the Archive."

"I will have a letter drafted to your council tomorrow," Wallace said. "You have proven yourself trustworthy, Thorne. I will leave this matter with the Archive as long as I can get your assurance that no other such schemes are being pursued."

The mage shook his head and replied hesitantly, "The best I can do is say that Reihana will be held accountable for what she has done here. I will ascertain if suspect arrangements have been made with the other major guilds and try to stop them." He scanned the area around him and added, "Hopefully in a less destructive manner."

"Indeed," the flagellant said. "Can I assume that you have no objections to a guild security detail accompanying you to Yaboon?"

"I would welcome the assistance," Thorne said. His body suddenly felt heavy as the room tilted to one side. He grunted and grabbed Wallace's shoulder for support.

"What's wrong?" the flagellant asked.

"Mana crash," Thorne croaked as sweat beaded up on his face. Taking a few deep breaths, Thorne watched as the warehouse leveled back off. He looked at Wallace and said, "I need to eat soon to regenerate my mana."

"You need to have your wounds tended as well," Wallace answered. "Both can be obtained at the sanctuary. We should leave now."

"Wait," Thorne said. "There's one more thing we need to do here."

Letting go of Wallace, the mage stooped to the ground and retrieved a broken plank from a nearby crate. Pushing his mana into the board, he felt it become pliant. The exertion made him lightheaded, but he did his best to ignore it. He approached Reihana and said, "Hands out, principal agent."

Reihana opened her mouth to speak but hesitated. Thinking the better of it, she clenched her jaw and bent her arms at the elbow to expose her wrists.

Thorne noted that her injured hand was still bleeding and the skin around the wound was an ashen hue. Reihana's veins had also turned black, the toxic result of her contact with iron. He took the board and wrapped it tightly around her wrists, making sure to angle its edges such that she would not be able to slip free.

Wallace stepped close to Thorne and said, "You might think me cruel, but given what I've seen of her power, I must insist we replace those with iron manacles once we return to the guild hall."

Thorne was about to protest, but the flagellant raised his hand and said, "We will put them over her sleeves so she is not tortured for the entire journey back to Yaboon. It is merely to incentivize her compliance. Surely you see the wisdom in this, no?"

The mage glanced at Reihana, who continued to scowl back at him, and then nodded his agreement.

"Very good," Wallace said. "I also suggest that we hold her at the guild hall until I can prepare a rapid transport for you to Banks. We will tend to the wound on her hand so it does not fester. Once you have recovered your strength, I will arrange for your passage on a guild ship bound for Port."

"I am grateful for such expediency," Thorne said. "However, there is still the matter of the mercenary guild, the City Watch, and even the Granick military hunting for me under the assumption that I am responsible for Claire's death."

The flagellant gestured towards the door and replied, "These too will be remedied in short order. Geridan is not the only one who currently has the governor's favor. Now if we can be on our way, I still have a very difficult task ahead of me tonight that I must complete."

"After all of this, what could you possibly consider a challenge?" Thorne said in disbelief.

"Asking forgiveness from the shepherd and the pilgrimage for leaving the sanctuary unannounced."

CHAPTER TWENTYSIX

"It's your roll, Thorne," Esen said, but his companion wasn't listening.

Both men were sitting on the floor inside the forecastle of a glassblower guild ship. Arranged as the crew's sleeping quarters, it was currently abandoned with the exception of Thorne and Esen. To escape the midday heat they had retreated there, and while dimly lit, it provided slightly more interesting surroundings than the vast emptiness of the open ocean. The captain had taken them far out from the coast in an attempt to find better winds. They had left Banks a few days ago, and fair conditions had steadily sent them towards Port.

Thorne glanced at the pair of octahedral dice in his hand, still thinking about the prisoner held in the bowels of the guild ship. Somewhere down in the hold, under the vigilant eye of no less than a half dozen armed sailors, Reihana was locked in chains. She had been an obedient prisoner as they rode a rapid transport to the coast before boarding the guild ship, not that she had much choice. Wallace had assigned a small team of guild security to ensure the Paragon principal agent had no fewer than three drawn swords inches from her at all times with orders to kill her if she made any aggressive movements. They were the only reason Thorne was not personally watching her, though he still worried they may not be enough to contain her should she try to escape. His worry had grown with each passing day and was taking a toll on him.

Before they boarded the ship, Wallace, the flagellant no more and dressed in the rich clothes of a wealthy and successful merchant guild member, showed Thorne a letter sealed with the emblem of the glassblower guild. He told Thorne that it contained a full account of the illicit agreement between the guild, Reihana, and Karnoff as recounted by Geridan himself. The guild master had accepted a deal, the details of which weren't shared with Thorne, for his cooperation. Wallace also said the letter assured the Archive of the glassblower guild's assistance and discretion regarding the matter, provided that they would return a formal declaration that no other similar deals with any other of the major guilds would take place.

The final provision of Wallace's letter was what concerned Thorne. How many other surreptitious assignments had Reihana sanctioned, and for what purpose? While the mage could imagine Skevald or Torstein having no compunction about such things, would Mirtans? The thought of her taking Karnoff's place turned Thorne's stomach. Would he have been able to fight her in earnest if she had been the one in the glassblower guild warehouse?

"Thorne!"

The mage jerked his head back at the sound of Esen barking his name. "Sorry," he mumbled as he tossed the dice onto the deck, not even bothering to look at the numbers.

"If you didn't want to play you should have just said so," Esen grumbled while scooping up the dice.

"Sorry," Thorne repeated in a faraway voice. "My heart isn't in it right now."

"You were losing anyway," Esen replied, setting the dice on the deck.

"I've had a lot of time to think about my return to the Archive," the mage said, attempting to explain his distant mood. "Things didn't end the way I expected, much worse in fact.

Learning what Reihana has been doing behind the Archive's back has eroded my faith in what the Paragon program was designed to do. And Claire died because of it."

Thorne stood up and shifted his weight from foot to foot, nervous energy compelled him to move but the forecastle was too cramped to pace. "Karnoff is dead," he continued, "and Reihana is in chains on her way to the Archive for reprimand, but somehow it doesn't feel finished. There's something gnawing at me, and I can't put a finger on it."

"It's understandable," Esen said, also standing. "You're returning home to uncertain circumstances. Your trust has been betrayed. That's more than enough cause for someone to be uneasy about their future."

The mage stopped swaying and rested his hands on his hips. "And what about you?" he said. "Will you go back to the frontier, back to your farm?"

"No. I'll stay in Port. Try to find Amos."

"The corsair?" Thorne said, surprised. "Why?"

"I like the idea of stealing from the guilds."

Thorne stared in surprise and replied, "How can a devout follower of the Small House say such a thing?"

Esen looked Thorne in the eye and answered, "My faith died with Claire." He paused and then continued, "I'm hoping that on the open ocean I'll find some measure of peace. The frontier is harsh, and by now my farm is either destroyed by a B'nisct raid or a pack of coyotes have eaten all my chickens. With no one to tend my crops, those too will be gone." He touched his chest and said, "It's time for me to move on. Who knows, I might even learn to swim."

Thorne nodded as he studied Esen. Before him was a man who had suffered much but remained unbroken. While he did not agree with the idea of Esen joining Amos' crew, Thorne could not fault him for wanting to find a community where he could belong.

A chorus of yells from outside cut through the silence, "Yaboon coast on the horizon!"

"We'll be in Port before the day is out," Esen said, looking toward the door. "Should we go to the deck and watch?"

Thorne bobbed his head once. While he was happy that the sea leg of the journey was over, he was reluctant to leave the ship. He realized that Esen was right. He didn't know what his return to the Archive would bring. "I'll join you in a few minutes," the mage said. "You go on ahead."

As Esen went up on deck, Thorne headed towards the captain's cabin to ask for some paper, ink, and a stylus.

・・・

Standing on the pier and attempting to stay out of the crew's way, Thorne and Esen watched for the rapid transport. On their approach to the harbor, the ship's captain told them to disembark last, as it would take time for a mariner to get to the Port branch of the glassblower guild, who would then dispatch a carriage for their travel to Yaboon. Reihana remained in the ship's hold, still under armed guard, and would only be brought up once the rapid transport was at the pier. While they waited, Thorne took two letters out of his pocket. He offered them both to Esen.

"What's this?" Esen asked, taking the folded papers.

"One is a note to the owner of a pub here, *The Harp*. It's located a few buildings away from the gate on the main road that leads out of Port. He'll help get you into contact with Merhai. The second is a message to Merhai herself asking that she help you find Amos."

"I was planning on going back to *Shorty's*," Esen replied looking in the general direction of the Venhadar tavern.

"You might get a warmer welcome than we did before, but if he's not in Port you'll need Merhai's help. Wallace has given us a remarkable amount of assistance, and all at glassblower guild expense. However, we don't have any funds ourselves, and you're going to need some before you join Amos' crew. Merhai will make sure you get what you need."

"I," Esen began before pausing. Gazing down at the letters in his hand, he grinned. "Thank you," he said looking back at Thorne. "Not just for this, but for all that came before it. You saved my life when Reihana tried to kill me, you left your Archive without a second thought to track down Karnoff, and you helped me get my revenge. You risked so much and all for a stranger, a foreigner."

"A foreigner, perhaps, but no longer a stranger," Thorne said, offering a hand. "A friend."

Esen shook it firmly and replied, "May the blessings of the Small House be upon you, Thorne. I hope that we meet again under better circumstances."

At a loss for words, Thorne simply smiled. He watched as Esen turned up the nearest street that led away from the harbor and vanished into the crowd.

He took a deep breath, thankful for Esen's short good-bye, and was about to look for a place to sit when a rapid transport appeared from a side avenue, the wheels clacking loudly on the harbor's uneven stone landing. In addition to the driver, Thorne recognized one of Wallace's handpicked guild security sitting on the bench at the front of the carriage next to the driver. The four caribou harnessed to the transport didn't seem to mind the smooth stone pavers or the close proximity to so many people. They stopped with a call from the driver and stared forward, waiting for the command to pull the coach once more.

The guildsman jumped down from the driver's bench and approached Thorne. "Are you ready to depart for the Yaboon

Archive?" he asked brusquely. "I'm assuming we'll get instructions for delivering your prisoner once we arrive."

"The major domo must be notified immediately," Thorne said. "It's highly irregular to deliver a mage to the Archive in chains. We're not looking for a scandal."

"We'll drive to a side entrance," the guildsman said, the annoyance in his voice making it clear that he didn't like being questioned. "If you operate at all like a guild, then discretion will be of upmost importance when we arrive."

"Very well," Thorne replied, not quite satisfied. "But it will just be me and Reihana. Esen has decided to remain in Port."

The man shrugged as if it mattered little to him one way or the other. He strode down the pier and up the gangway to the ship. He disappeared for a short while before reappearing with his fellow guild members and Reihana. The Paragon principal agent squinted, her eyes unaccustomed to daylight after being in the bowls of the ship for days. She looked grimy and fatigued but still carried herself proudly as she was escorted from the ship to the rapid transport. Thorne watched carefully for any signs that she might try to escape, but there were none.

One member of the guild security contingent entered the coach first. Once he was seated inside, Reihana was guided by sword point into the rapid transport.

Thorne took a step towards the door, but another of the guildsman said, "I'm sorry, Master mage, but our instructions from the treasurer were to have only guild security with weapons at the ready in the coach. He wanted to make absolutely sure that we arrived as expected at the Archive. You'll have to ride with the driver."

"Of course," Thorne said, bowing his head in acquiescence. Though embarrassed to admit it, he was relieved he would not be sitting in the tension-filled carriage. It would have been incredibly uncomfortable to endure Reihana staring at him the entire journey.

Climbing up to the driver's seat, Thorne had barely gotten into place before the driver had the caribou moving again. The animals trotted through the city streets, pausing only briefly to be cleared at the city gate. Once outside on the prince's highway, the driver let the animals run at full speed and the rapid transport hurtled towards Yaboon.

• • •

Once at the Archive, the carriage stopped at one of the lesser-used side entrances. Thorne felt relieved that they would not be parading Reihana in chains through the front atrium. After a brief wait where a guildsman went inside the Archive to notify the major domo, a pair of Archive constables, one Sehenryu male and one Venhadar female came outside. The white sashes at their waists moved slightly in the late afternoon breeze, and both were holding short iron rods that would immediately communicate to Reihana they were not to be tested.

As the Venhadar constable pulled open the carriage door and guided Reihana out of the coach, her face was a mask of neutrality. It was obvious her calm was forced, but Thorne couldn't imagine her acting any differently given the circumstances. As the constables grabbed her by the shoulder and escorted her inside, she turned and looked at him. Her eyes burned with hatred.

"This is only a temporary setback, Thorne," she said coldly.

The constables wasted no time taking her inside, a pair of glassblower security in tow to deliver the letter Wallace had readied for the Archive council.

Thorne followed them, but distanced himself from the group as they marched down to the lower levels of the Archive where locked cells for holding rogue mages were located far from normal daily operations.

Although new apprentices juvenilely called it the Archive's dungeon, the reality of it was more curious than severe. While the walls and floor were solid stone, the rooms were warm and well lit from glow spheres embedded in the ceiling. The most striking aspect of the cells were their lack of doors. In their place stood wide open arched frames constructed from amber resin blocks.

As the group entered a cell, Thorne noticed the only furniture present was a bench made of the same pearlescent orange resin that was used to fabricate the chrysalises in Masters Hall. Turning around, the mage saw a third Archive constable join them. The human female carried a large wooden chest in her arms. She set the chest on the bench, opened it, and retrieved two halves of a resin ring with a diameter of about a hand's length.

Approaching Reihana from behind, the constable assembled the ring around her neck and locked it tight with a pair of resin bolts taken from the chest. She repeated the process with two anklets. Finally, she took out a resin cylinder and two half rings. With these three items the constable put one of Reihana's hands in the cylinder and then locked it in place with the ring parts around her wrist. Repeating the process with the other hand, Reihana looked like she was wearing a rigid, uncomfortable muff.

The constable looked at Thorne and said, "Master Thorne, before we remove the iron manacles from Master Reihana, would you please charge the doorframe? The pad is in the hallway."

Thorne nodded quickly and exited the room, and as he did the mage noticed that each resin block of the doorframe interior had an alchemic symbol etched that roughly translated to *push*. In the hallway he saw there were additional resin blocks embedded into the wall that ran up to and across the ceiling and then down the opposite wall. Stopping about at chest height, there was a round protrusion about a hand's width in size.

He pressed his hand on the knob and pushed mana into it. As the resin greedily absorbed his arcane energy, Thorne heard a hum from behind him. Turning around he saw the resin archway vibrating. The faces of the resin blocks facing the hallway all had the alchemic symbol for *pull* etched on them. Wearing a collar and hand restraints made of the same type of energy-absorbing resin that comprised the archway, Reihana had no way to manipulate her mana. While the resin blocks remained charged, she would be unable to escape, her restraints being tethered to the archway to keep her in the cell.

Thorne returned to the cell and watched a guildsman remove her iron manacles. After casting their malice-filled eyes on the Paragon principal agent for the last time, the guild security detail left the room. Thorne assumed they would proceed to the Archive atrium to find the major domo, who would assist them in delivering Wallace's letter to councilor Tarbeck.

The female Venhadar constable methodically checked Reihana's garments and person to ensure no contraband would be left with her in the cell. After the inspection was complete, the constable turned to Thorne and said, "Master Thorne, you may go. Thank you for your assistance."

It was a polite, but unequivocal, statement that he should leave. Thorne gave Reihana one final glare before turning and leaving the lower levels of the Archive. As he ascended the stairs that would return him to the atrium, he felt very tired. It was not the sickening fatigue of a mana crash or the tiredness that came from working all night in his alchemy lab, but an emotional weariness from the past week that finally caught up to him. He had intended to check on Mirtans as soon as Reihana was in Archive custody, but the mage decided that would have to wait.

Not really paying attention to his surroundings, and ignoring the questioning glances and brief greetings he received, Thorne made his way to the dormitories to find a cake of soap, a change of clothes, and a quiet place to collect his thoughts.

•••

Thorne felt better once he was clean and dressed in navy blue alchemist robes, but his desire for quiet was now replaced with an intense hunger that was starting to given him a headache. Leaving the dormitories for the cafeteria, the mage wondered what would be on offer when a scribe rushed down the hall towards him with a concerned expression.

"Master Thorne," he blurted. "Councilor Olaf wants to speak with you immediately about Master Reihana. Please come with me."

"Olaf?" the mage asked confused. "What is here doing here?"

"He was scheduled to return to the Granick Archive several days ago," the scribe said, rubbing his hands together in a nervous manner. "But after the assault in the infirmary, he felt compelled to stay and help with the investigation."

"I see," Thorne said with forced calm. As he was led through the atrium and up the large staircase to the second floor, Thorne's mind raced over a number of worrisome scenarios. Was Wallace's account of Reihana's involvement in Claire's kidnapping going to be ignored and she to be released? Did Olaf suspect that he was also involved in the Paragon principal agent's plot? Was he to be punished for his role in Karnoff's death?

The scribe escorted Thorne down the hallway leading to the Archive council room at a frenzied pace. Along one wall were display cases full of successful alchemic syntheses that included the production of simple metal alloys, multifaceted prisms and gemstones, and various types of resins. Along the opposite wall were regularly spaced doors that opened into the alchemy labs. As he walked by Thorne detected a peculiar odor that was the commingling of smoke, ozone, and chlorine.

At the ornate door that led into the council meeting room, the scribe rapped his knuckles hard on the darkly varnished wood. "I've brought Master Thorne as requested," he shouted into the door.

"Come," answered a voice that Thorne recognized as belonging to Olaf.

His task complete, the scribe retreated back down the hallway and left Thorne alone. The mage took a moment to compose himself before he opened the door. Stepping inside, Thorne noted that the large windows on the far side of the room were covered by thick drapes. Glow spheres regularly spaced along the walls lit the room. Crossing the threshold, Thorne saw the only person in the room, sitting at the table and facing the door, was councilor Olaf.

"Thank you for coming on such short notice," Olaf said with a practiced smile that held no warmth. He picked up an open letter from the table and waved it gently in a circle. "This message from the glassblower guild is quite shocking, as is the fact that Reihana is now locked in a cell. While the former gives context to the latter, I'm afraid that more than a few here, not the least of which is councilor Tarbeck, know she is under confinement." He paused and set the letter back down on the table. Leaning forward, he said, "I am most keen to hear your version of these events."

Thorne pulled out a chair and sat down at the table across from the councilor. For nearly half an hour he described what he thought were the most relevant points. He recounted how he saved Esen from Reihana's assassination attempt in the infirmary, Claire's horrific death and burial, how Reihana had tried to kill him in Haywood, and the confrontation with Karnoff in Haven. He was more vague concerning his dealings with Amos and the voyage from Port to Banks, as well as much of the events in Haywood, feeling that it was better to keep the focus on Reihana's trespasses and less on what he had done to survive the past week.

Olaf kept an impassive expression until Thorne had stopped talking. Then the councilor raised his bushy white eyebrows and said, "Which leads us to turning our attention to this untidy aftermath." Relaxing his face, Olaf leaned back in his chair and continued, "It's impossible now to keep the Paragon program secret, which is unfortunate since it was just beginning to bear fruit."

"In what way?" Thorne asked.

Olaf didn't answer but instead looked up and stared vacantly at the ceiling, his brow creased in thought. The councilor hummed and then smacked his lips. He lowered his gaze to Thorne and said, "In addition to the services you Paragons have performed, there was also a small research and development part of the program."

Thorne gave Olaf a confused look and replied, "It was for the development of resins suitable for weapons or armor. What of it? It was never of much interest to any of us and didn't progress very far. Reihana and Ghent did some experiments in their laboratories, but for the rest of us it was largely a theoretical exercise."

Olaf tapped the table as he said, "If the provincial princes found out we were training combat mages, there would be unpleasant consequences. However, if we reveal to them that the program was instead focused on the development of new materials and that Reihana and Karnoff were attempting to negotiate a smuggling arrangement with the glassblower guild, then that would soften the blow to all parties involved."

The councilor stood up and paced the length of the back wall, his fingers gently brushing the curtains as he passed. "All current Paragon assignments will be nullified," he said, speaking more like he was thinking out loud then talking directly to Thorne. "The worst of it is that we'll have to dissolve the program."

"I see," Thorne said, not knowing how else to respond.

The mage's noncommittal reply did not appear to surprise Olaf. "The Paragon program was an experiment, and a risky one," the councilor said. "It took considerable persuasion for the others on the council to agree, and it was on a probationary basis. There'll be no support for it now. As you might expect, Tarbeck is furious." He huffed and then spat with uncharacteristic anger, "Damn you Reihana for your selfishness! What could possibly be so important that you'd take such a risk?"

"What is to become of her?" Thorne asked. He stood up, stepped to the side of his chair, and locked eyes with Olaf. "You can't keep her in a cell indefinitely."

"She's going to be made an example," the councilor answered. Studying Thorne, he said, "You are now the acting Paragon principal agent, Master Thorne. Your first, last, and only official duty is to inform the others that the Paragon program is over. Assignments to new research, commerce, or scholarly units will be distributed to the others in short order. You will also communicate to them that they are to be witnesses to Reihana's binding."

Thorne nodded. "This is sure to cause quite a uproar," he said. "She's popular here and such a punishment is going to raise quite a few questions. Are you prepared to reveal the program to the larger Archive as the reason for her binding?"

"There's no stopping that now," Olaf replied. "My new goal is to keep any utterance of Paragons to the prince as something unlikely to be believed. My spies are already spreading conflicting rumors in the city. It goes without saying that you and your fellow Paragons are going to be under active surveilence for the foreseeable future. Freedom of movement outside the Archive will be restricted."

Outside, the tolling of four low bells rang out. Olaf walked around the table and approached the door. He pulled it open and looked back at Thorne. "Take this advice as you will, but I recommend you keep a low profile for a while. Reihana commanded the loyalty of many here, as you said before, and your involvement in her fall from grace will not go unnoticed."

After the councilor was gone, Thorne stepped up to the table and rested both his hands it. Leaning forward, he blew out a deep breath. He tried to process what had just happened, but couldn't focus. Feeling completely overwhelmed, he remained in the council meeting room until his headache intensified to the point where he needed to lie down. As he left the council meeting room, he knew that food from the cafeteria would fill his belly and help with the headache, but nothing was going to ease the knot in his guts.

CHAPTER TWENTYSEVEN

Thorne and Mirtans sat on a bench outside the Archive herb garden adjacent to the kitchen. The Sehenryu wanted to soak up some of the midday sunshine and Thorne had obliged. As she raised her face to the sky, Thorne studied her carefully. He was happy to see that she looked healthy, the daylight making her short fur appear luminous. She told him that the infirmary physician had released her the day after he left the Archive with Esen. It was a severe, but acute, paralysis of her hands, so the physician told her to reduce her mana expenditure for the next few weeks. She would make a full recovery in the short term, but the Iron Bane would continue to slowly erode her nerves so it was only a matter of time before the damage would be permanent.

Sitting in the herb garden, Thorne tried to sympathize. He knew in time he would only vaguely remember what basil or cilantro smelled like after his sense of smell and taste eroded away. It was a sacrifice he'd willingly make all over again, but the chronic disease that accompanied magic use was severe and unforgiving.

It had been three days since his return to the Archive and just yesterday he had assembled the remaining Paragons to tell them of Olaf's mandate. It had gone about as well as expected. Torstein and Skevald stormed out the second that he was done speaking, while Mirtans and Ghent sat in stunned silence. Thorne told them to ask any questions they had to one of Olaf's scribes who had accompanied him. He then retreated to his alchemy lab, the only place where he could get any privacy, and spent the rest of the day reviewing his research notebooks.

The next morning Mirtans sought him out and asked for some company. It was an unusual request, so the mage quickly agreed.

Now that they sat outside, Thorne thought he would be able to relax, but he found the opposite happening. His body tensed as he worked up the courage to ask the question weighing heavily on his mind. "Did you know?" he asked quietly. "About what Reihana was doing?"

Mirtans looked at him with her vibrant cat-like eyes. "No, but I knew she was hiding something."

"Why didn't you tell me?"

Mirtans shook her head. "There was nothing you could have done."

They were silent for a long time before she said, "Reihana's fatal mistake was that she went after you. If she had just stayed here, she would have been able to deny any involvement in trying to kill that foreigner or working with the glassblower guild. Everything could have been blamed on Karnoff. You didn't experience it because she never gave you anything important to do, but she had to be directly involved in every Paragon assignment. She couldn't just delegate and relinquish control, and that's what led to her downfall."

Thorne nodded as he absorbed what Mirtans told him. "And what of the others? Now that we're done, what have they said?" he asked.

"Torstein and Skevald despise you. They blame you for taking away their means for feeling important. They say you've brought shame down upon them." Mirtans chuckled and added, "They don't know the meaning of the word, but the resentment they feel towards you is genuine."

"Ghent?"

"He doesn't care. His ennui is palpable."

The mage looked at Mirtans, searching for some hint as to her feelings. Finding nothing, he asked, "And what about you? You've been rather reticent in expressing your opinion on the whole matter."

The Sehenryu replied, "You've always wanted distinction, Thorne, and now you have it. How did it feel to be the final Paragon principal agent? The one to unintentionally expose the program to the Archive?"

"It didn't feel good."

"I would imagine not," she replied.

"You didn't answer my question."

Mirtans stood and looked down at the mage. "You shouldn't be seeking my approval," she said. Turning her face up to the sky, she closed her eyes and soaked up more of the sunshine before glancing back at the Archive. "It's about time," she said casually. "We should go."

The mage stood and arched his back to stretch out a little. "Alright," he said. Thorne knew that Mirtans could feel his apprehension, but it wasn't in her nature to try and reassure him. He realized that by asking to keep her company, she had already communicated her support. They walked at an unhurried pace back inside the Archive, neither eager for what was waiting for them.

• • •

The room was small and empty of furniture save for a chair constructed from thick wooden beams with the back set at a fixed recline and a small table. On the chair's headrest, armrests, and front legs were leather straps with buckles made from strong resin. Sound was dampened by thick cream-colored drapes that ran from the ceiling to floor, though the room had no windows. Instead, glow spheres embedded in the ceiling radiated a sterile white light, which left the room feeling static and disorientating. It was different from the rest of the Archive, as if this place was dissociated from normal space and time.

When Thorne and Mirtans entered they saw that Olaf, the councilor's personal scribe, one of his apprentices, and Ghent were already there. The councilor gave Thorne and Mirtans a tight lipped smile that was mere courtesy, and Ghent ignored them completely.

They moved to the left side of the room, opposite Ghent and Olaf, and waited for the others to arrive. As they waited Thorne appraised the Paragon he knew the least about. Tall, pale skinned, with silver hair and a matching beard, there were some in the Archive who had unflatteringly dubbed him The Ghost. A born mage, Ghent's aptitude for magic was impressive. He reached the rank of Master at a very young age, but the Iron Bane had quickly robbed him of that youth. Ghent was about the same age as Thorne, but looked more than twice as old.

"You're staring, Thorne," Mirtans murmured.

The mage looked away from Ghent to the small table. On it was a bowl half-full of water, a resin knife with a thin blade, a glob of grey paste on a small slab of slate, a short section of thick rope, and several folded linen handkerchiefs. Thorne had only read accounts of binding a mage's mana but had never seen it. Being such a rare event, he could only imagine what Reihana was feeling at the moment.

"She's here," Mirtans said as her eyes grew wide. The Sehenryu looked at the door an instant before it was pulled open.

Torstein and Skevald stomped into the room with matching scowls. Looking like they had just come back from training, they were dressed in heavy boots, canvas trousers, and leather cuirasses. The skin on their faces had the greasy sheen of dried sweat, and both of their hands were dirty. The twins took up flanking positions near the door as four Archive constables escorted Reihana into the room.

The former Paragon principal agent was dressed in the same clothes as when she had arrived. While free of the neck and leg circlets that had kept her confined, she still wore the heavy resin hand covering. Reihana's face was blank as she surveyed all of those who were in the room. Her arms hung limply in front of her as she walked in, and her body posture was far more relaxed than it should have been given the circumstances.

"Be on your guard," Mirtans whispered. "You can't tell from looking at her, but she's radiating hatred. Skevald and Torstein are both agitated."

The constables removed the resin hand covering and helped Reihana into the chair, then buckled the straps around her arms, legs, and neck. Three of them drew their knives, one took a position between Torstein and Skevald to block the door, while the other two positioned themselves at the back and side of the chair. The final constable approached Olaf and received a document produced from the councilor's pocket.

The constable opened the document and read in an authoritative voice, "Master Reihana, here are your trespasses of Archive law."

"This is a farce!" Torstein interrupted.

"Be silent!" Olaf warned. "Your purpose here is to witness, but you should also take it as a warning. The Paragon program is finished and if I ever discover that you are using your martial techniques or attempting another one of Reihana's illicit schemes, it will be you next time in this chair."

Torstein took a menacing step towards Olaf. "Do not threaten me, old man," he said jabbing a thick finger at the councilor.

Olaf's expression went slack. He stood a bit straighter before he replied, "I think you and your brother need to stay put for the remainder of this meeting."

The councilor raised his right hand, which pulsed with an amber light before he pulled his arm close to his chest. Both Skevald and Torstein jerked slightly and they grunted as an unseen force pulled on them.

Futilely straining against the immensely strong gravity manipulation holding him in place, Torstein struggled to speak but managed to get out, "You're stronger than you look, old man."

"You'll stay there until you learn to follow protocol," Olaf said before turning his back to the brothers. Olaf wielded his mana so seldom, preferring instead to use his spy network or powers of oration, but he was arguably the most powerful human mage at the Archive. What Olaf had done to Skevald and Torstein was a pointed reminder. He looked at the constable and commanded, "Continue."

The constable read on, "You acted outside of your authority as an Archive mage and as a member of a privileged research group to further your own ambitions that ran counter to established Archive tenets. Punishment today is meted out for the following transgressions. One, you made an unsanctioned deal that would have enabled the glassblower guild to undermine Sovereignty tax law via the shipwright guild. This egregious abuse of power as the Paragon principal agent is a betrayal of trust granted to you by the Archive council. Two, you dispatched Master Karnoff to kidnap Claire, the daughter of glassblower guild master, Geridan. Claire would not have been killed if she had remained on her frontier farm. Three, you attempted to kill Master Thorne and Claire's husband, Esen, to cover the previously mentioned acts. Each of these offenses would be cause to censure you and strip you of Archive privileges, however the martial techniques you possess as a Paragon make you an imminent physical danger to the Archive, and for this reason, Master Reihana, your mana will now be bound."

The constable set the paper on the table and drew the knife from his belt. With a single stroke, he deftly cut Reihana's shirt, starting at the neckline and ending at her navel. Grasping fabric in each hand, he pulled it away to lay bare Reihana's sternum but stopped short of exposing her breasts. He put his knife away and picked up the rope from the table. "I'm told you'll want to bite down on this, Master Reihana," he said gently, but firmly.

Reihana opened her mouth and bit down on the offered rope.

After the constable had taken a position next to Skevald near the door, Olaf picked up the thin resin knife and held it over Reihana's exposed chest.

Reihana's cool façade melted away at the sight of the knife. Her nostrils flared as her teeth clenched on the rope and braced for the inevitable. Her eyes grew wide as the councilor sliced into her.

Thorne watched as Olaf made a series of shallow cuts in Reihana's chest. Impressed with the councilor's steady hand and somewhat surprised by the lack of blood, Thorne struggled to make out what Olaf was marking into her flesh. When the work was done and the councilor stepped back, Thorne saw a five-pointed star carved on Reihana's body with alchemic symbols in the center that translated to *cease power*.

Setting down the knife, Olaf took a linen handkerchief and mopped up Reihana's blood from her wounds. Working quickly, he applied the grey paste, rubbing it into the cuts. When it touched her skin, Reihana breathed in deeply and jerked violently. She made an inhuman sound as her face turned bright red, the muscles in her neck straining. The grey paste quickly drained of color and became a brilliant white. As the paste blanched it dried and became flaky, specks of it tumbling off of Reihana's body as she bucked against her restraints.

Olaf pushed down firmly on Reihana's chest and a shimmer of blue light emitted from the councilor's hand. Reihana's body slumped into the chair, as she lost consciousness. Olaf took a clean handkerchief and dipped it in the water bowl, then wiped away the paste. When he was done, in the center of Reihana's chest was the binding tattoo, no longer blood red incisions but a pitch-black series of scars.

"If you would, constables," Olaf said, sounding tired. "Please remove the restraints from Master Reihana and fetch a stretcher from the infirmary. She should not have to suffer the added indignity of such hardware while she recovers there. She is no longer a danger to us. Her magic is bound."

CHAPTER TWENTYEIGHT

Reihana opened her eyes and before the ceiling of the Archive infirmary came into focus she knew that something was very wrong. It wasn't the ache in her chest or the heaviness of her limbs, but instead something she could no longer feel. The arcane energy in her body was imperceptible. She knew her mana wasn't gone, once tapped it flowed through a body until death, but now she was cut off and couldn't sense it anymore. Her body felt foreign, hollow, like something vital had been taken away.

It was as if she had woken from a nightmare, and a terrified feeling raced from the back of her neck to the pit of her stomach, and through the ache in her chest she felt her heart pound. She suddenly began to sweat heavily and felt much too hot. With clumsy fingers she pulled the thin sky blue blanket down to her waist. Every movement felt off, imprecise and awkward, so she tried to remain still and concentrate on her breathing. With her eroded vision, she couldn't see down to her chest well, but she could feel the edges of her cut shirt and the cool air against her bare skin.

A short time later, she heard someone walking along the corridor of treatment bays towards her. Rolling her head slightly on the blanket that propped up her head, Reihana saw a Venhadar female with the yellow sash of an infirmary medic.

Stepping up to Reihana's cot and looking down at her with an expression of professional concern, she said, "Tell me how you're feeling, love."

"Different," Reihana croaked with a dry mouth.

"That's to be expected. You've been through quite an ordeal."

"How would you know?" Reihana groaned, the effort to speak more taxing then she expected. "Have you ever treated someone who had their magic bound?"

The medic took a step back, startled at the blunt question. Quickly regaining her composure, she answered curtly, "No, but I've read about it."

"And what have you read?"

Looking at the ceiling for a moment, the medic then gave Reihana a serious look and replied, "That there will be an adjustment period. All of your body's systems are acclimated to having mana flow through them, and the disruption caused by a binding is going to make you feel different. On the bright side, the effects of the Iron Bane will be slowed since you won't be accessing your mana anymore, so that's something."

Ignoring her response, Reihana turned her head and closed her eyes.

When it became clear to the medic that the conversation was over, she said, "Well, all the same, I'm glad you are awake and alert. Now I can tell councilor Olaf he can come to see you."

"Olaf to see me?" Reihana asked, opening her eyes. She hadn't expected that the old man would want anything to do with her now.

"Yes," the Venhadar answered. "He requested that he be brought to you as soon as you were conscious."

"I see."

Reihana closed her eyes again and took a deep breath. She felt the medic's hand on her shoulder. It was meant to be a reassuring gesture, but she was alarmed at how the touch made her skin crawl. It was an unnatural reaction, and she was frightened at the thought of having to perceive the world without the presence of her mana.

Pressing her eyes shut more tightly, Reihana kept them closed until the she couldn't hear the medic's footsteps in the corridor any longer as the Venhadar left her treatment bay. Once alone, Reihana opened her eyes and tilted her head down to look at the binding tattoo on her chest. She watched the large sigil widen slightly as she breathed in, and hated it with all of her being. She didn't feel the shame she thought would accompany such a mark. She felt the opposite. If this was the cost for her conviction, for believing that mages should be freed from Archive shackles to help the populace directly, then so be it. If she couldn't do the arcane work herself, she would act through her allies.

Quiet footfalls amongst the treatment bays announced Olaf's arrival. The councilor was alone and appeared contemplative once he stopped next to her cot. "The infirmary staff tell me that you're recovering well," he said. "I would speak with you about your future here at the Archive."

"Can't this wait?" Reihana said before a thought struck her. "How long have I been here?"

"It's been a day since your mana was bound," Olaf replied. "To be awake and conversational is uncommon this soon after such an ordeal. I attribute that to your considerable natural resiliency."

"Olaf, why are you here?" Reihana said with tired irritation. "You had ample time for whatever this is about when I was in confinement."

"What I want to discuss requires a certain amount of discretion, as it concerns the Paragon program in general, and Torstein and Skevald in particular," Olaf said. "Torstein is rather thick-skulled, but I believe he got the message that I won't tolerate any acts of retribution on Thorne. All Paragons are going to be under surveillance until a time comes when I am satisfied that the fallout from this ordeal has been managed. So, I'm here now to ask that you reinforce my previous sentiment with those two. I believe that they are much more likely to follow your instructions over mine."

"You've taken everything from me," Reihana said. "Why would I do that for you? In fact, what's going to stop me from marching to the prince as soon as I can walk? Would you kill me here in an infirmary bed, much as I tried to do to that foreigner?"

"Reihana, you know I haven't taken everything from you, and that there are worse things than death," Olaf said, his pleasant tone at odds with his words. "No, I think that you, Torstein, and Skevald are going to keep quiet and enjoy the comfort and safety that the Archive affords. It's a dangerous world out there for mages, wouldn't you agree? And we also wouldn't want any of your associates, family, or friends hurt, would we now?"

"So I'm a warning?"

"A reminder that Archive tenants are in place for the protection of all mages, and it is the duty of all mages to uphold them, lest we be crushed by the whims of some prince who wants to write his legacy in blood."

"I thought that was the whole point of the Paragon program, to be able to take care of ourselves."

"No, to defend ourselves when necessary."

"I don't see a difference."

"And that is why you were a poor choice for Paragon principal agent. A shame that I only see it now." Olaf turned and looked down the length of treatment bays and watched the end of the hall. Without looking at Reihana he said, "Take care, Master Reihana. Be assured that I am always close at hand if needed."

Reihana disliked the double meaning to Olaf's parting

words. She suddenly felt very tired. She closed her eyes with the intent to rest and think but instead quickly fell asleep.

● ● ●

A few days later Torstein and Skevald came to see her, an Archive constable discretely following behind. The twins could be heard long before they were seen given their preference for wearing heavy mining boots. Both had dour expressions, but at least Skevald seemed happy to see her, giving her a brief smile as they approached. The constable tailing the two Venhadar stopped a few treatment bays away to give them some privacy, but continued to watch carefully.

"We've got a babysitter thanks to Olaf," Torstein said derisively while glancing at the constable. "Not sure when we'll be able to give him the slip."

Reihana had regained enough strength and coordination to prop herself up into a sitting position and was happy not to be straining her neck to see who was nearby. She had asked for a new shirt yesterday and with some help from the infirmary staff been able to dress more comfortably and cover the binding mark on her chest. She was glad that Torstein and Skevald weren't able to stare at it.

She gave them both a small smile. "No one else to come and see me?" she asked.

"Mirtans still might," Skevald said, though he didn't sound very hopeful.

"Ghent?"

Torstein scoffed. "Not unless Olaf orders him to come here. I don't think he does anything unless he's forced. Who knows where he is now? Probably holed up in some library fruitlessly searching for a way to reverse the sands of time."

An awkward silence ensued as the twins struggled for words befitting Reihana's situation. Finally, Torstein blurted,

"Karnoff sure fucked this one up." He glanced over his shoulder at the constable and mumbled, "Sorry," as he turned back to Reihana.

She lifted her bandaged hand off her lap and waved the apology away. It was a miracle that the archer's arrow hadn't severed any tendons, but still a major injury nonetheless. Under the layers of thin fabric, she could wiggle her fingers slightly, but they were stiff and certain movements of her wrist still hurt. She had been told such wounds were slow to heal.

Swallowing with some difficulty, Reihana said, "This is hard for me to ask, but I need you both to keep your heads down for a while."

Skevald nodded, but his twin furrowed his brow.

"How long?" Torstein asked.

"Until I learn to function without my mana. That could be a while."

"Does it hurt?" Skevald asked with a kindness that Reihana hadn't heard in the Venhadar before.

She shook her head and replied, "Not like you think. It's like after having your arm chopped off. You know it's supposed to be there, but it's gone and you can't quite figure out how to get your life back to the way it was when you were whole. Right now I feel strange, weak."

Her words had an impact on the twins, though in different ways. Skevald appeared concerned and a little sad as he looked at her. Torstein was tougher to read, but Reihana saw apprehensiveness in the Venhadar's posture and expression, which was rare given his normal confidence.

A silence settled amongst them before being broken by the sudden movement of the constable standing alert as someone new entered into the treatment bay corridor. A female Sehenryu, dressed in a cream vest and trousers, walked casually past the constable. She raised her hand in greeting, the thick stylus in her hand almost completely hidden by her short tan fur. When she stopped next to Reihana's cot, she assessed everyone with alert yellow eyes.

"Good morning," she said in a high-pitched voice. "I'm a third-year scribe assigned to councilor Tarbeck's staff."

Reihana watched the twins shift uncomfortably at he mention of Tarbeck. She wasn't sure what Olaf had said to the Yaboon Archive administrator, but she was sure it wasn't the truth, at least not all of it. "Do you need something?" she asked with forced politeness.

"Oh, that's what I'm supposed to be asking you," the scribe said with soft chuckle. Seeing everyone else's dark expressions stopped her abruptly. "Um, I'm here to introduce myself as your escort while you adapt to Archive life without your mana," she paused and shifted the ledger in her hands before adding, "and some of your privileges as Master."

"Thank you, but there's nothing I need at the moment."

"I understand. Before I go, I need to ask what personal belongings you want moved to the senior dormitories so they are waiting for you once released from the infirmary."

Reihana nodded mindlessly. Communal living would ensure there would be many eyes watching her. Olaf was no fool. With a Sehenryu scribe shadowing her every move, she'd have to be careful and keep her emotions in check, lest they betray her. "Can I have a bit of time?" she asked.

Growing uncomfortable with Torstein glaring at her, the scribe took a step back from the cot and replied, "I'll be back later today. Please take care."

As the Sehenryu left the treatment bay, the constable moved in to take her place at Reihana's bedside. "We should let Master Reihana rest," he said, his posture making clear that it wasn't a suggestion.

She flinched when Skevald reached out and touched her

hand. "Sorry," she said. "My skin is overly sensitive. It must be my body reacting to being without mana." She looked past the twins to the constable and said, "You two go on. I'll be fine. I need some time to think anyway."

Reihana watched the constable lead the twins away. Skevald looked back at her once before he turned the corner. Touching her chest, she felt the scars that were part of her binding mark. Losing her ability to manipulate the arcane elements, being cut off from her mana, was the worst punishment the Archive council could give out. It was meant to humble her, make her regret her past choices, and have her fall in line with Archive tenets in the hopes of one day regaining access to her mana.

If only Olaf knew the binding mark did just the opposite. For now, she'd bide her time, play the penitent, but all the while plot her next moves carefully. She wasn't going to stop just because her magic was gone. The future of the Archive, her home, was at stake.

CHAPTER TWENTYNINE

The earthenware plate was piled high with a hearty dinner. There were slabs of beef covered in thick gravy with carrots, potatoes, and onions surrounding the meat. The rye roll sitting on the table next to the plate looked soft and chewy. Though Thorne hadn't ordered beer, one apparently came with the meal. Thorne looked over from his food and noticed his companion was also studying his plate, but his expression was more wistful than critical.

"Thinking about your farm?" the mage asked.

His companion nodded and answered, "I made a meal like this for Claire the last night I was there. Chicken instead of beef, but this," he pointed at his plate, "smells like home."

From behind him, a lanky young woman wearing a dirty apron approached the table and smiled. "Meal to your liking, Trinity? And what about your mate here?"

"It's fine," Thorne said quickly.

The woman scowled at the mage before leaving in a huff to check on her other customers.

"Still quick to make friends, I see, Thorne."

Ignoring the remark, the mage said, "It's going to take me some time to remember you're calling yourself Trinity now. A lot has changed for you in half a year, no? You must come here quite a bit if you're on a first name basis with the staff."

"You don't approve?"

"It's fine," Thorne said with a smirk, intentionally repeating his response from before.

"My new name is a symbol," Trinity explained. "The person who was Esen is no more, but I wanted to retain what was best about him, and that was Claire. She was the one who converted me to the Small House, so it seemed an appropriate name to take."

"I understand completely," the mage replied.

"Do you?"

Not wanting to pursue the matter further, Thorne grinned and said, "Amos must be doing well for himself if you're here in Port for an extended shore leave."

"Things have been good," Trinity said, relaxing and leaning back in his chair, a crooked smile on his face. "Amos is an exceptional mariner who treats his crew fairly. We're mostly smuggling these days. With the provincial princes incrementally raising taxes, there's been no shortage of work. Amos actually turns down more runs than he accepts."

"Why doesn't he expand his enterprise? Wasn't Vechas looking to captain a ship? Is that still the case?"

Trinity's expression soured. "Vechas is an accomplished fighter and able mariner, but he's not fit to lead. Everyone on the *Formica* knows it, especially Amos. He doesn't trust Vechas, and I don't blame him."

Before Thorne could ask more, Trinity said, "I didn't pay good money sending a message to the Archive just so I can talk about what I've been up to at sea. I'm much more interested in hearing how you're doing at the Archive. What happened to Reihana?"

"Things are stable, at least on the surface," Thorne answered, not hiding his disappointment. "Reihana's ouster from the Paragon program wasn't without consequences. Her magic might have been bound, but she is far from powerless. She was, and still is, a popular mage at the Archive. What I did was make enemies, and I find myself looking over my shoulder often."

"You're more than capable of defending yourself, right?"

"It's not physical harm that worries me," Thorne said shaking his head.

"Then what is it?"

"Protecting my reputation, my sense of self worth," the mage replied. "When I first began my studies at the Archive, my goal was to become a Master. I thought that achievement would make me feel respected, but once I attained that rank I only felt let down. It was one rung on a much taller ladder. There were research groups doing amazing work in alchemy, energy transmutations, and elemental manipulations that I couldn't seem to infiltrate. When I was approached to be part of the Paragon program, I thought I'd finally found an opportunity for the distinction that I desired."

"But Reihana corrupted it," Trinity said.

Thorne nodded and added, "Compared to the Paragon program, the work I'm doing now feels less important, less urgent. To make it worse, I feel that somehow I've lost social capital at the Archive. Things could be much worse, but it feels like all I do is struggle."

"I might not understand the subtleties of it," Trinity replied, "but I do know that at times like these there is only one thing that you have to do."

"What's that?" Thorne asked.

"Keep fighting."

Acknowledgements

Thank you to Claire Marino, Dr. Kevin Atticks, and all of the Apprentice House Press staff. I'm grateful for your creativity, hard work, and support throughout the publishing process.

Thank you to Mom, Dad, and Kevin for your continued encouragement. I'm happy to say that this time nobody fell into a hole!

Thank you to Laura, Evie, and Lexi for your excitement about my second novel. Laura once again was my harshest critic, biggest cheerleader, and cartographer.

Thank you to Mike Gray for being a very astute beta-reader and critiquing the manuscript like an academic. Your developmental edits were a great help for making the story come alive.

Thank to you Mark Reefe for going way beyond a beta-reader to a full-on editor. The novel reads much more smoothly because of your attention to detail and knowing just the right word to add (or take away).

Thank you to Mark Drake for being a champion of my first novel. You were able to get it stocked in several libraries, which pushed me to work harder and get my stories out into the world.

Thank you to Brandon Ying Kit Boey and Ryan O'Neill for reading an advance copy of the novel and offering endorsements. Authors are often too busy to read and recommend a newcomer's book, so I appreciate that you took the time to support my second novel.

Author Biography

J.G. Gardner has a Ph.D. in Microbiology and is a scientist researching new ways to treat fungal infections. While having published many technical papers on genetics and biochemistry, he has always wanted to write novels about magic, wizards, and dragons. His debut high fantasy novel, *The Path From Regret*, was published in 2023 by Apprentice House Press. To learn more, go to his website, jgardnerauthor.com.

Apprentice House Press
Loyola University Maryland

Apprentice House is the country's only campus-based, student-staffed book publishing company. Directed by professors and industry professionals, it is a nonprofit activity of the Communication Department at Loyola University Maryland.

Using state-of-the-art technology and an experiential learning model of education, Apprentice House publishes books in untraditional ways. This dual responsibility as publishers and educators creates an unprecedented collaborative environment among faculty and students, while teaching tomorrow's editors, designers, and marketers.

Eclectic and provocative, Apprentice House titles intend to entertain as well as spark dialogue on a variety of topics. Financial contributions to sustain the press's work are welcomed. Contributions are tax deductible to the fullest extent allowed by the IRS.

To learn more about Apprentice House books or to obtain submission guidelines, please visit www.apprenticehouse.com.

Apprentice House
Communication Department
Loyola University Maryland
4501 N. Charles Street
Baltimore, MD 21210
410-617-5265
info@apprenticehouse.com
www.apprenticehouse.com

Printed in the USA
CPSIA information can be obtained
at www.ICGtesting.com
CBHW071248180724
11781CB00010B/450

9 781627 205412